THE WATERS

ALSO BY BONNIE JO CAMPBELL

Mothers, Tell Your Daughters
Once Upon a River
American Salvage
Q Road
Women & Other Animals

THE WATERS

A Novel

BONNIE JO CAMPBELL

W. W. NORTON & COMPANY
Independent Publishers Since 1923

Copyright © 2024 by Bonnie Jo Campbell

For information about permission to reproduce selections from this book, write to Permissions, W. W. Norton & Company, Inc., 500 Fifth Avenue, New York, NY 10110

For information about special discounts for bulk purchases, please contact W. W. Norton Special Sales at specialsales@wwnorton.com or 800-233-4830

Manufacturing by Lake Book Manufacturing
Map: Monica Friedman
Production manager: Anna Oler

ISBN 978-0-393-24843-2

W. W. Norton & Company, Inc., 500 Fifth Avenue, New York, N.Y. 10110
www.wwnorton.com

W. W. Norton & Company Ltd., 15 Carlisle Street, London W1D 3BS

1 2 3 4 5 6 7 8 9 0

To my darling Christopher

A woman without a donkey is a donkey herself.

—AN ADAGE FROM RURAL ETHIOPIA

We are like bowls. There have always been bowls.
They're shaped the way they are for a reason. Yes
some have curlicues or paintings of angels but a
bowl is a bowl and it has always been a bowl and it
was here before you came and it will outlast you.

—DIANE SEUSS, FROM THE POEM "BOWL"

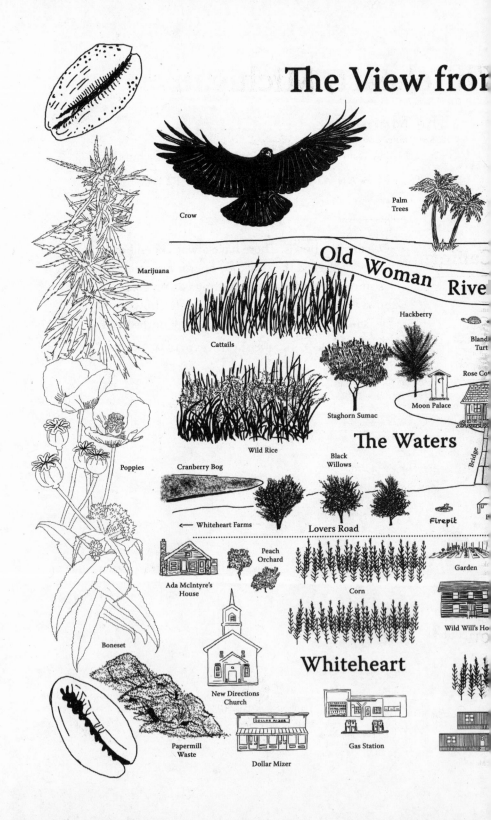

The View from

Crow

Palm Trees

Marijuana

Old Woman River

Hackberry

Cattails

Blandi
Turt

Staghorn Sumac

Rose Co

Moon Palace

The Waters

Poppies

Wild Rice

Cranberry Bog

Black
Willows

Bridge

← Whiteheart Farms

Lovers Road

Firepit

Peach
Orchard

Garden

Ada McIntyre's
House

Corn

Boneset

Wild Will's Ho

New Directions
Church

Whiteheart

Papermill
Waste

DOLLAR MIZER

Gas Station

Dollar Mizer

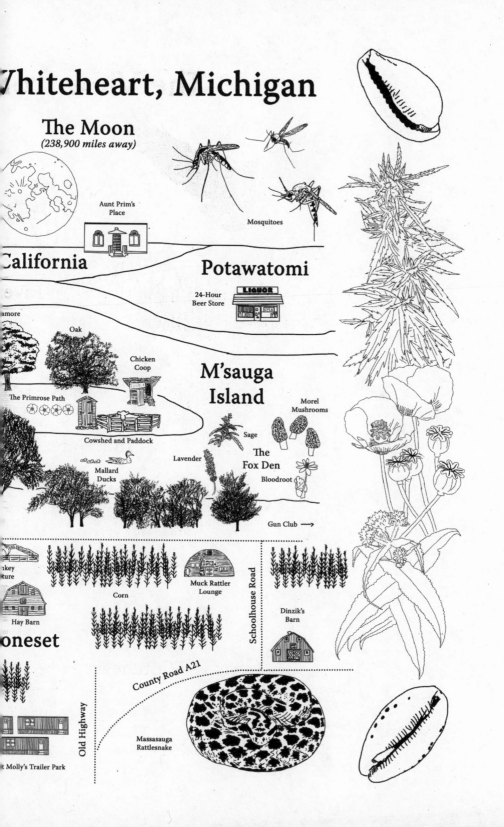

Whiteheart, Michigan

The Moon
(238,900 miles away)

Aunt Prim's Place

California

Mosquitoes

Potawatomi

24-Hour Beer Store

LIQUOR

Sycamore

Oak

Chicken Coop

M'sauga Island

The Primrose Path

Cowshed and Paddock

Sage

Morel Mushrooms

Lavender

The Fox Den

Mallard Ducks

Bloodroot

Gun Club →

Monkey Pasture

Corn

Muck Rattler Lounge

Schoolhouse Road

Dinzik's Barn

Hay Barn

Boneset

County Road A21

Old Highway

Massasauga Rattlesnake

Molly's Trailer Park

THE WATERS

CHAPTER ZERO—PROLOGUE

The town has a troubled soul.

ONCE UPON A TIME, M'sauga Island was the place where desperate mothers abandoned baby girls and where young women went seeking to prevent babies altogether. But in living memory, Rose Cottage on the island was the home of the herbalist Hermine "Herself" Zook, who raised her three daughters there. The oldest, a lawyer named Primrose, was the most accomplished; the middle daughter, Maryrose, called Molly, a nurse, was the most practical; and the youngest, Rose Thorn, was lazy and beautiful. Hermine's medicines—her tinctures, salves, and waters—are now discredited in the light of day, but at night the people of Whiteheart, Michigan, still use them if some tidy housekeeper or other busybody hasn't tossed away the unlabeled jars and bottles. Only tiny amounts of these fixes are required, as they have become more effective with time— sometimes just unstoppering a bottle is enough to release a cloud of soothing into an ailing household. The island and its women loom large in the dreams of local folks, who sometimes wake up sweating from visions of witches in black (though the island women never wore black) or of crows watchful in treetops, or of swamp streams bubbling up through the floorboards of their houses. It is said the island, where healing waters percolate to the surface, was a place where women shared one another's dreams, a place where women did what they wanted.

Anybody around here can give you directions. Head northeast off the old highway onto County Road 681 and turn left at Dinzik's barn—people will say it's red, but there's hardly a flake of rust-colored paint left on the wood—and down a potholed lane known as Schoolhouse Road, though the school burned down before anybody still living was born. Schoolhouse ends at Lovers Road. To the right is the gun club, so go left instead. Some years ago, Ada McIntyre's grandson, while drunk, kept going straight off the end of Schoolhouse Road and into the swampy waters, where he hit a tree at full speed. He's dead now, having bled to death from the hemophilia that runs in the family. Take that left, and you'll see on your left a tavern housed in a military-issue Quonset hut with the name Muck Rattler stenciled in block letters over the door.

Past the tavern, for the next mile and a half on that side of Lovers Road, there are farm fields, and on the other side (the north, the swamp side), a line of giant willows. Keep going until you come to a hay barn and a pasture on the south side of the road where two old donkeys graze, a gray jack named Triumph and a spotted jenny named Disaster, nicknamed Aster, like the flower. There is a high-ceilinged two-story house set way back from the road, with a sign at the driveway that says "Boneset." Naming a house and property was an extravagant gesture in these parts, and Wild Will was extravagant, but in fact he borrowed the name from his wife. The weathered cedar of the house and the barn—neither has ever been painted—glows silver at sunrise and sunset if you see it from certain angles.

Across Lovers Road, in a grassy area shaded by giant willow trees, sits the Boneset Table with a locked cash box bolted to the top. Through a break in the willows, if the fog isn't too heavy, you can see the edge of what everyone around here calls the Waters, where a sort of island rises up, accessible by a bridge three planks wide, strung between oil barrels floating on the watery muck. There, under the branches of sycamores, oaks, and hackberries, the green-stained Rose Cottage sinks on the two nearest corners so that it appears to be squatting above the bridge, preparing to pitch itself into the muck. Beyond the cottage, the trees give way to a mosquito-infested no-man's-land of tussocks, marshes, shallows, hummocks, pools, streams, and springs a half mile wide between solid ground and the Old Woman River. This is where Herself harvested wild rice, cattails, staghorn sumac, and a thousand other plants. Rose Cottage is boarded up now, but if you check at the county office, you can confirm that the taxes are paid up on the hundreds of acres of the Waters still owned by Hermine Zook.

The Waters occupies the northeastern quarter of the town, six thousand acres, and all of it apart from Hermine's section is under state protection for half a dozen rare wildflowers and the Blanding's turtle, as well as the endangered massasauga "m'sauga" rattlesnake. The state wetlands don't bring in any revenue, apart from a few bird-watchers stopping at the gas station. Even families in Whiteheart who have never farmed this area know how the Waters can creep into low-lying cropland and undermine what looks solid.

Half a century ago, Wild Will Zook ventured into the Waters and fell in love with Herself after she treated his rattlesnake bite and cooked and fed him the snake that had bitten him. Maybe he married her because of some spell she put on him, or maybe just because it was the most outrageous thing a man could do in this town. And it did impress everybody, made him seem even taller than he was. After they were married, he bought the Boneset land for them at a tax sale and built the big cedar house, from which vantage point he looked down upon the island, but he was never able to convince his wife to live there with him. That this high-ceilinged two-story dwelling sat empty with its windows boarded up for decades was a testament to the power and determination of Hermine Zook. People loved to decry her stubbornness, both for refusing to live there and for keeping it empty all those years, and especially for her refusal to sell any portion of her holdings, the Waters or the dry land at Boneset.

During the time she and Wild Will were together, Hermine made medicines that were pleasant, reliable, and sweet, flavored with blackberries and honey. Back then, Hermine used to let folks come to the island to bathe in the shallow mineral pools, to have their blood pressure corrected by leeches, to have their wounds debrided by maggots, even to have bones set if the fractures were simple. But after fifteen years, when she sent Wild Will away, her medicine changed. While she continued healing, she never again allowed anyone onto the island and only dispensed medicines sparingly, meeting her patients by the road, at the Boneset Table. Her cures changed; now they tasted raw, and they burned the skin upon application and the throat going down.

Similarly, the aged whiskey she had once produced for Wild Will from old stores under Rose Cottage disappeared, and she offered only the bootleg juice that took the enamel off men's teeth, and then there was no liquor for sale at all. Signs appeared at the edges of her vast swamp property, images of menacing skulls painted on trees and rocks, with no words, some with piles of bones around them.

The newly embittered potions inspired fear, and so the cures were thought to be stronger and more effective and gained Herself a new kind of respect. As more folks left their farms and began working in the paper mill, they became mistrustful of a cure that didn't include a punishment, that didn't intensify momentarily the suffering it promised to alleviate. And in more recent times, they came to her confused and angry, with slow-growing cancers of the liver and reproductive organs, disorders she could not cure. Sometimes people stood at Boneset and shouted their demands for healing across the swamp channel as though she was a dispensing pharmacy.

EVEN CONSIDERING THE PLANET'S rising temperatures, winter in Whiteheart remains long and cold, and when spring finally comes, when the ground thaws, people here begin to feel energy trickle up through the topsoil and into them through the soles of their shoes. Now, more than ever, they are hungry for beauty, and they dream about Hermine's youngest daughter, the lazy, lighthearted, golden-haired Rose Thorn, flowing back to them like a bright stream in a riverbed that has been dry, though she also might appear in the form of a sly starved animal trotting across a field. Or they dream of her enrobed in sheaves of golden wheat or rising up from the heart of the tender, pale celery stalks—even whole fields of celery rising up through the mud, though none of the few remaining farmers grow wheat or celery anymore, just corn and soybeans, as recommended by the Farm Bureau.

As a child, Rosie was so thin-skinned that she suffered from chilblains and frostbite on the short walk to the bus stop—that is, whenever she was bullied into going to school by her sister Molly. More often, she skipped school and spent her winter days in bed on the island reading Oz books and fairy tales. From the time she was a teenager, she ran away from home for part of every winter to visit

Primrose, who was practicing law in Southern California. There is more than one old photo of Rosie tucked in a Ziploc bag and hidden someplace where a man's wife or girlfriend won't think to look. None of the blurry photos do her justice, but any libation is welcome in thirsty times.

Complaining about Rose Thorn's foolishness still makes the local men and women feel cheerful, and complain they do. Recalling Rose Thorn smiling and blinking in sunlight with a beer in one hand and a Pall Mall coffin nail in the other, not bothering to swat away mosquitoes or ground bees, inspires folks to plant their gardens, to kiss their misbehaving children, and even to make love. The truth is, Rose Thorn is right here in unincorporated Whiteheart now, in the flesh, though she no longer lives on the island. She stays out of the public eye these days, and in cold weather she exists in something like the languid state of the overwintering massasauga rattlesnakes, a brumation, in which a creature still drinks to sustain itself and bites if threatened. If Rose Thorn needs something from a neighbor, it will be her daughter who comes asking for it.

In spring, the local men, before stopping in at the gun club at the other end of Lovers Road, drive past the island, sometimes idling and looking down the bank to check if the new gate leading to the island bridge is still locked. (Titus Clay, the closest neighbor, installed the gate for added security, though the more effective security is the fact that the planks in one ten-foot span of the bridge over the quickmuck have been removed.) A combination of superstition and guilt and respect and fear keeps people from trying to get across, even if it doesn't prevent men from occasionally shooting at rattlesnakes from the edge of Lovers Road.

Sometimes at two a.m., when a group of working men get kicked out of the Muck Rattler by the bachelor barkeep, Smiley Smith, they are drawn to the island, especially if there's a full moon or a remarkable crescent hanging over the mound of land like a hunting horn, or if an auspicious warm wind is blowing from the southeast. Starved for an old mystery, they head down the road to the spot where Hermine used to sit with the afflicted. They rest their cans of beer on the Boneset Table—its six legs now made of iron pipes driven deep into the earth—beneath which the little Babby Basket still hangs, lined with a fresh blanket. Where Herself once provided a rich selection of herbs and cures and medicinal eggs, something to heal wounds and ills even in bitterest winter, now there are only a few odd vegetables or berries or bark, left there by who knows whom.

Herself used to fix the rotten feet and sluggish guts of White-heart, and for every baby born here (or *babby*, as she said), she left on this table a swallow of healing donkey milk, which was said to make smarter, better-behaved children. In addition, it is said the donkey milk entered the blood to work as a prophylactic antivenom, reducing the reaction to rattlesnake bites. The milk was a way for Herself to touch every babby at least once. Though Titus Clay swears the old woman is still alive, she has not lifted a finger to help anybody for years, has not even attended a funeral to burn cedar and herbs for cleansing and for remembering the way she always used to do. Everybody knows Titus, now owner and operator of Whiteheart Farms, the acres that spread out at the end of Lovers Road, once the largest celery farm in the world, has an interest in the family that goes way beyond procuring a medicine for his disease, what Hermine Zook has always called thinblood.

Rose Cottage used to glow with the light of its inhabitants but now is dark at night and often shrouded in fog, which cloaks it from view. You can hear a frog ga-gunging or a great horned owl hooting or occasionally a goatsucker whippoorwilling. Such old, quiet sounds after hours make the men feel not only their aches and pains and patches of raw skin but also a restless worry that without Herself, the future could mean a worsening of their symptoms, along with the deterioration of the natural world that nourishes them. The cool, rich scent of swamp flowers and rot can bring to men's minds a queer longing to be touched and listened to, and since reaching out to one another is out of the question, a man will take a swig of something from his pocket. Somebody might tell a story of Wild Will, who they say stood seven feet tall and had arms like John Henry who beat the steam drill, arms scarred by barbed wire and animal bites and a tattoo on each arm, on the left the name Hermine with snakes wrapping around the letters. Wild Will was known to tell ghost stories that would shoot chills through your vertebrae and spawn a fear in you that any mysterious figure you saw in the swamp might be a water demon or a soul stealer. Though people don't recall those tales precisely, they still feel fear at any light or sound out there in the Waters whose source they can't trace.

Nobody outside the family knows the crime that made Hermine banish her husband after fifteen years of marriage. Within the family, there is some acknowledgment that what happened was not technically a crime at all—since his stepdaughter Prim was seventeen, above the age of consent, and she said it wasn't rape. Herself sending Wild Will away saved his reputation and added to his mystique by allowing him to simply disappear while still a vital and handsome man. Even if he had gone so far as to confess, many men might have made excuses for him, might have hearkened back to the Bible and refused to condemn Lot for what they saw as the crimes of his daughters.

Standing near the Boneset Table in the dark on any given Saturday night, a few men not home with their wives remember when there was life and laughter here, and sometimes they just need to express their confusion or sorrow or rage. One man pulls the revolver from his belt holster and shoots from the hip at the old green cottage, whose windows have already been shattered and covered with plywood. In response, another man takes out his 1911 target pistol from a shoulder harness and shoots a few rounds through the fog to conduct the night orchestra, establishing authority over the buzzing, whistling, murmuring creatures, who go abruptly silent. A man slides his father's twelve-gauge shotgun from the rack in the cab of his truck, aims, and fires at a remaining section of the bridge, which is already sinking on its oil barrels. However, after a few volleys, the men, who have to go to work or church in the morning, feel sick to their stomachs and decide to stop wasting ammunition on the carcass of a creature that, for all intents and purposes, appears to already be dead.

CHAPTER ONE

❦

Rose Thorn always comes home.

ONCE UPON A TIME, in the black muck floodplains of unincorporated Whiteheart, where the taxes are low, farm families used to grow the world's sweetest, tenderest celery, Whiteheart Celery. Which is to say, the town was not named for the European settlers who sought to destroy the rich Potawatomi culture that preceded them; the place was instead named for the crop that the settlers planted, the crop that supported, for half a century, the people living here.

Massasauga Island itself has a history stretching back through centuries, but the part set down on these pages only begins on May 8, fourteen years ago, when the sun shone brilliantly, though not upon the people here, since it could not penetrate the dense cloud cover. At this time, Herself still lived on the island and cured what ailed some people, though her medicines had tasted especially bitter lately, since she was bereft of her three daughters. In September, her youngest, Rosie, had run off to stay with her sister, Primrose, in California, that state being as far as Prim could get from Herself. Molly, the middle daughter, worked at the nearby hospital, but she was presently staying in Lansing, finishing an intensive nurse practitioner training program. The story of the daughters, then, begins with their absence.

On that day, a handful of men, including three sons of farmers and a hired man, drank their after-church beers and pops at the Muck Rattler Lounge, trying to ease the ache and longing they always felt after the service now. After the previous reverend's sermons, folks had left church feeling shivery, lightheaded, and overwhelmed as by a ghost story, and now they left with lists of instructions, prohibitions, and judgments. Today the Reverend Roy, nephew of the old reverend, said they should resist the temptation to ask for anything from Hermine Zook. Christ suffered, he said, and so would they. "Knowledge of God," he said, "is borne from the furnace of affliction."

As Roy had spoken these words, a lightning bolt of pain spasmed through his lower back—recent surgery had failed to provide relief—and the real pain in his voice lent gravity to his message. His own suffering was made worse while Molly was away. He didn't acknowledge her absence as the cause of the pain but saw the twin difficulties visited upon him as another test administered by the Almighty.

The men at the Muck Rattler chose to drink outside at the picnic table by the road, because it had stormed the previous night, and it would be dark inside the windowless bar until the power came back on. The five of them stood under that sky the milky color of a blind horse's eye, shouting at one another to be heard over the gas-powered generator that kept the Rattler's refrigerators running. If they had been inside, they would have missed what was coming down Lovers Road.

To the east and the west of the bar, ancient black willows, some of them eighty feet high—larger than the species ordinarily grows—stretched as far as the men could see. The ground was soft after last night's storms, and the foliage was a lush green expanse, unspoiled by the zizzing mosquitoes that would hatch in the swamp and roadside ditches once the weather warmed. This week, though their grandfathers would have said it was too early to plant, the sons of farmers were helping their fathers tune up machinery. The farmers were planting earlier and earlier as the years passed, but they didn't like to say so. Unloosening their grandfathers' and great-grandfathers' patterns unnerved them, and some had begun to indulge what felt like a curious kind of gambling spirit. A given farmer might wake at three a.m. from a nightmare of his soul slipping from his body in bed and floating away through a window cracked open, and he might then go out into his dark barn and fire up his planter or grain drill and chug along the empty road to his nearest field.

The farmers in question didn't know what drove them, but the early planting was in part a natural response to the slight warming of the planet they felt in their bones; and after one man planted his first field, the rest of the farmers sensed the rising of a new leader, and they followed suit and planted a field early as well. The men did this even though their fathers and grandfathers had taught them grain would not sprout in cold ground, even though the rash acts would trigger sleepless nights filled with worry about seeds freezing.

Most of the women waited to plant vegetable gardens, as they always had, until they saw Hermine planting hers in front of Wild Will's Bone-set House—the island itself was too shady for vegetables—but a few expressed a solidarity with the men by planting prematurely. These women, however, sprouted extra seeds for a second crop, just in case, in the egg-carton planters they kept in the little glass houses they'd built out of old single-pane wood-frame windows. All year they saved egg cartons, the way they always had, leaving their extras on the Boneset Table for Herself to fill with eggs from the herb-fed island chickens.

Titus Clay was not one of the sons of farmers at the Muck Rattler that afternoon, not yet. After the church service, he'd said he was going home with his father to check on their generators and he'd be along soon, but the men at the Muck Rattler didn't quite trust his father, Titus Clay Sr., not to start planting before the rest of them. Despite the thinblood he suffered and had passed on to Titus Jr., the great upright farmer lived in a world of certainty and was known to make a firm and binding decision at the drop of a sweat-stained feed cap. As the sunshine tried to muscle its way through the haze, they watched for Titus's truck coming from the west. Everything made more sense when Titus was with them. Though he was only twenty-four, he always had the right joke, the right Bible reference, the right comment about a man digging a hole ("Larry, looks like you're digging a pit for your worst enemy—I can see you're bound to fall in it") or about an alluring woman appearing in town ("Tie down your tarps, boys, it's a tornado in a skirt"). While they waited for him, they milled about uneasily, as though even the way they might stand or sit wasn't quite right, and readjusted their collars and belts. Mostly the men wore jeans and clean sports shirts for church, while Rick Dickmon wore a button-down, but Jamie Standish wore his usual camo pants and green T-shirt, and he was known to carry a small pistol in his pocket, even into the house of the Lord.

These men were trying to live decent, comfortable lives. They all—including Smiley, the barkeep, who would be out soon—imagined their families and friends genuinely liking and respecting them, and they pictured themselves feeling at ease when talking to anybody in town. Their bent toward humility was tempered only by their desire to be recognized as men like their fathers and grandfathers, but they didn't see themselves as particularly important in the scheme of things. Standish thought he might have been important if he'd been able to join the Marines, but at the young age of twenty-three he had an old man's feet—they were flat and bedeviled with bunions and ingrown toenails that had the tendency to get infected.

"You think it's still okay to take aspirin?" Tony Martin asked. "Reverend Roy said we should suck it up."

Nobody had an answer or even a smart-ass comment. They all hoped that wasn't what the reverend was saying. Standish shook his head in annoyance at Tony's giving voice to the conundrum. Tony, known as Two-Inch Tony, wasn't from Whiteheart, but his grandparents were from Potawatomi, on the other side of the river, and he'd married red-headed Cynthia Darling six years ago and was still trying to fit in. Cynthia had gotten drunk with Standish's wife, Prissy, in Standish's kitchen last month, and Standish, in the next room watching TV, heard them laughing about their husbands' lack of sexual prowess. The next morning he parked his truck on Lovers Road and walked over to where Hermine Zook, Herself, was sitting in a big wooden chair next to the Boneset Table, the way she often was at that time of day, her braids wrapped around her head like a crown and that damned creepy cowry shell necklace on her bosom. Now he felt like a fool. Just the memory of sitting down in the folding chair beside that witch and holding her hand where somebody might have seen him reddened him with humiliation and made his feet ache. When Herself had looked at him, her eyes had filled with tears. Who the hell was she to cry over him?

"If we're supposed to suffer," Whitey Whitby said, "then why's Reverend Roy getting back surgery?" Whitby was Titus's cousin on his mother's side, and he'd worked on Whiteheart Farms since he was ten. He was almost as tall as Titus, and though he was only nineteen, he'd managed to grow a scraggly beard. Because he didn't have the thinblood that came down the male line, Titus Clay Sr. made him do the dangerous farm jobs, such as castrating bulls and climbing into grain bins to clear clogs.

Standish looked up now and saw a crow mocking him from a branch above. He walked over to his truck on his aching feet and slid his rifle from the rack in the cab. When he slammed his truck door, the crow loped away over the Waters, showing off how free it was.

Then the wind changed direction and sent smoke from the rattling generator across the table, and Whitby erupted into a coughing fit so severe he had to put down his coffin nail next to his Mountain Dew on the edge of the picnic table. He'd been suffering from a lingering cold and sinus situation he could not shake.

"I think I'll risk damnation and ask Herself for something for this cough," Whitby said when he could speak again. He was known to be a smart-ass, a real joker, but he'd become a chain-smoker and a ruminator in these last months, and his life didn't feel fun anymore.

"My pop used to get some powerful medicine for catarrh from Herself," Dickmon said, pushing his heavy black glasses against his face. "Used to swear by it. But first she's going to tell you cut out the cancer sticks."

"Rev Roy's right. You don't need none of that witch medicine," Standish said, though his own father and grandfather had both sworn by that sweet-bitter coughing cure made with boneset, slippery elm, and honey. Standish had asked the old woman for something else, something to make his wife love him, a *philter*, he'd heard it called, and he flushed again with embarrassment at the thought of his request. In the face of the old woman's tears, he'd pulled his hand away, gotten into his truck, and left.

"What's catarrh?" asked Two-Inch Tony. He didn't look like the other men, had thick dark hair and an aquiline nose, for starters, and was shorter than the rest, strong and wiry like an acrobat, except that one of his legs hadn't grown as long as the other. But his nickname wasn't about his height or proportions. It came from people claiming his concrete flat work was thin after a woodchuck cracked the poured floor of Ralph Darling's uncle's garage. Before that, on a patio he'd poured near the Dollar-Mizer, a tree root busted through. A man can't help it, he said—his voice defensive—if the groundhogs around here are built like sumo wrestlers, if the tree roots have the strength of swamp snakes. Tony needed some paying work, but people were uneasy about the future right now, were feeling they couldn't afford to pour patios or foundations for outbuildings.

The farmers had a certain hunch in their shoulders after last year's poor yields, though you'd be hard put to get a farmer ever to admit to a good year. Some people blamed a curse by Hermine Zook, who had been in a bad mood since Rose Thorn had gone off. Rosie was a bright spot in all their lives. Even a decade ago, people would come to sit beside Herself at the roadside hoping for a chance to see the pretty, dreamy girl reading a book in the grass or walking slowly and lazily across the bridge from the island. If she talked back then, she talked about the characters in books, as though their adventures were real, or she'd say she saw a troll under the bridge.

Whitby continued, "Grandpa said Old Man McIntyre lived to be a hundred because he drank that aloe water she made. And you know he worked every day of his life until he fell over dead in his berry bog. That's the way to die."

"I'd rather die a warrior," Jamie Standish said, nodding sagely.

"Pop said McIntyre died at ninety-nine. Never made it to a hundred. Nobody in Whiteheart ever made it to a hundred," Dickmon said, puffing out his barrel chest. He was fed up with Standish and his militarism. Dickmon had a closet full of guns himself, but after he and Hannah Grace had gotten an early scare in her pregnancy, he didn't even want to talk about shooting or killing. Didn't the rest of them see how damned precious life was? Especially Standish, who had a four-year-old daughter, ought to see.

"Except Herself," Whitby said.

"How's she a hundred years old?" Dickmon asked, exasperated. "She can't even be seventy. She's got an eighteen-year-old daughter."

"She looks like she's a hundred, wrinkled old heathen," Standish spat.

"What's crawled up your ass and died?" Whitby asked. "All she does is help people. If you don't want her help, don't ask her for it."

"Yeah, so does Satan help people if he wants their souls."

"When they cut old McIntyre open after he died, they looked inside him and said he was clean as a newborn baby," Whitby said. "That's what I heard."

"Nobody's cutting me open when I die," said Ralph Darling, patting his belly affectionately. "I don't want anybody knowing what's inside me." At twenty-six he was already developing his father's round beer gut and the strange habit of patting it that way. His father drank quietly at home, but his grandfather, Old Red, had been a famous local drunk known for passing out in public. Like Old Red, Ralph felt inclined to congregate with others, and so nobody knew where his drinking would land him.

"I think Rev Roy just woke up on the wrong side of bed," Whitby shouted over the generator, which had just kicked up a notch, "without Molly."

The men paused to enjoy Whitby's irreverence as the generator rumbled on. Whitby couldn't help but question every man who thought highly of himself, as the reverend seemed to. He had recently witnessed how a certain great man might not be so great as people thought, and he wasn't sure what to do about it other than feel cynical.

"Them two've only been dating ten years," Standish said. "If he really believes in suffering, he ought to get married."

Smiley Smith opened the door of the Muck Rattler and stood on the threshold. "Hallelujah, amen, and let the women weep!" he announced. He stepped out and let the homemade screen door swing shut and rattle into place behind him. He hadn't taken the winter plastic off the wooden frame yet, and it was torn and flapping. Smiley was drying his hands on a white cotton bar apron as he approached—an apron that always seemed to have blood on it, though there was no raw meat in the Muck Rattler, just the pizzas his mother made. Smiley's hands were always clean and chapped from wiping the bar down or washing dishes. He had a receding hairline, was old enough to be the father of most of these younger men, though he'd never married or had kids himself. "Beautiful day in the Waters. The birds are a-singing."

"Bet the muck rattlers are coming out of their holes right now," Standish said. "If I could shoot me six of them this year, I could get a pair of boots made like Wild Will's."

Among the snake accessories Wild Will had collected—keychains and bottle openers and bolo tie clips—his snakeskin boots were famous. The m'sauga was a protected species, but protecting something venomous seemed plain wrong, like defending sin, and certainly no man would complain about another man shooting one.

"You can't even lace up the boots you're wearing," Dickmon said, adjusting the black plastic frames on his face and straightening his button-down shirt, which was a little tight now, maybe from Hannah Grace's rich cooking. His pop's heart disease was a cautionary tale he knew he would have to heed at some point. "You look damn sloppy."

"My feet need to breathe." Standish couldn't talk about his foot pain with these guys. The pain was from the same troubles his ma had, but it didn't stop her from chasing men.

In the ditch on the Waters side of Lovers Road, male redwing blackbirds trilled for mates from the swaying tops of cattails. Chorus frogs creaked, and green frogs twanged. M'sauga rattlesnakes buzzed, and the men's trigger fingers itched to shoot them, if they could only catch a glimpse.

"Who is that?" Darling asked, squinting easterly down Lovers Road, toward the gun club a mile away. He stood up on the picnic table to get a better look. The rest of them looked too, but the way the road curved, the figure was just then obscured by the sand willows and red osier dogwoods.

"You must be eating too many carrots. I don't see nothing." Whitby squinted.

"Why won't they open the range on Sunday?" Standish asked, because they were all looking in that direction.

"Could be a dog," Dickmon said. "At church I heard Ed Cole was looking for his yellow Lab mix."

"I seen that hound this morning before church, crossing River Street, after some bitch in heat, I'm sure," Darling said, his hand resting protectively on his belly. "What do you suppose Titus is doing? You don't think he's planting, do you?"

Darling's father refused to sell his land to Titus Clay Sr., and he wasn't the only one: Titus Sr.'s own aunt, Ada McIntyre, who owned the other half of Whiteheart Farms, its orchards and berry bogs, also refused. But Ada let Titus Sr. farm her fields so long as Titus Jr. helped with the fruit. Her own grandson Alan used to help before he bled to death in the swamp last fall. Women like Ada were carriers of the thinblood, but they had no symptoms.

"Titus didn't say nothing about planting," Whitby said.

"Man would be a damned fool if he started planting before Friday," Dickmon said and braced himself for disagreement. Saying a thing with such confidence was risky since he wasn't even farming now. Dickmon's father had sold out to Whiteheart Farms six years ago, before moving to Alabama and leaving Rick five acres and the farmhouse, which needed endless repairs.

"Definitely somebody walking," Darling said.

"They tell you when the power's coming on?" Dickmon asked Smiley, who shrugged.

"Hope soon. I don't dare leave the generator running if I'm not here."

The men were becoming curious about somebody coming toward them down the road, and it is true that if you pay attention long enough, there will usually be something worth seeing, even if it turns out to be just a trio of mallard ducks slipping out from the tall grasses, two drakes mounting the hen and the hen slipping out from under, leaving the drakes humping one another. Or a female blackbird giving in to a male's entreaties as he flashes his red shoulder patches on a comically bobbing cattail, or a couple of young lovers driving slowly along, looking earnestly for a private place. The men clustered around the picnic table and all looked in the same direction, feeling the weight of heavy-bottomed draft glasses or the chill of aluminum cans in their hands, feeling the vibration of the nearby humming generator.

Across the road, the swamp springs bubbled under the humid weight of the sky. Now, in spring, whole swaths of the Waters were brilliant with tiny wildflowers, thick with pollen, and in summer and fall they would brim with small sour fruits eaten by the critters and harvested for medicine by Herself, who navigated between the small marshy islands with a raft and pole. Despite the signs painted on rocks and tree trunks in the Waters around M'sauga Island, nobody knew for sure where her property ended and the protected county property began, and men didn't want to run into her sturdy figure out there, so they mostly stayed clear. There was another figure Whitby and Dickmon had both seen in the swamp, a man, or maybe a ghost of a man. Not somebody they wanted to mention to anybody else.

"Look!" said Darling, pointing. "You blind bats have to see him coming now."

"Could be somebody," Whitby said. He didn't trust his eyes these days, or rather he feared what he might see for looking. Before last fall, he'd liked working on Whiteheart Farms, liked it better than being at home, and he could look at himself in the mirror and feel okay. More importantly, he could look at other men and assume they were decent, assume they really were what they seemed to be. He'd learned since then that you didn't have to commit a crime to feel guilty; just seeing a crime could be enough.

"See, nobody listens to me," Darling said, taking satisfaction in not having been believed.

"Sure it's not a coyote?" Standish said and lifted his rifle to take aim through the telescopic sight he'd put on his father's Winchester.

Dickmon pushed the barrel of Standish's rifle toward the ground with a light touch. "Don't go shooting somebody, man. How many beers you have?"

"I'm just looking this way to focus. Anyhow, you said it was a coyote. Since when you going to stop me from shooting a coyote?" he said. "God gave me this rifle to use."

"You got that from your dad," Whitby said. "Is your dad God now?"

"God gave me the right to carry it."

"The Constitution gave you the right," Dickmon said.

"Well, God gave me the Constitution." He felt himself getting worked up. He dropped the rifle and let it hang over his shoulder on the leather strap.

The approaching creature, seen through the trees, was yellowish, the color of the grasses that hadn't yet greened up on the dry side of the road. It moved from one side of the pavement to the other, walking at a pace that changed from fast to slow, as though the walker's desire to head this way or to keep going at all strengthened and weakened. A vanguard of crows jumped ahead from tree to tree to keep pace. The figure was dwarfed by the great willows.

"Is that some kind of a humpback coming?" Smiley asked.

"Humpback?" Two-Inch Tony said. "I've never seen a humpback."

"You never seen Quasimodo?" Dickmon enjoyed pronouncing that strange name. "Anthony Quinn played him. Lon Chaney was in the silent movie."

"Charles Laughton. One of gram's favorite movies," Smiley said and leaned on the corner of the picnic table. "I've seen it a dozen times. You know, my dad said there was a man built a secret underground house in the swamp after the rendering works closed. Dad said he stole loads of bricks for building that house."

"My grandpa said that was Wild Will's brother by another mother," Darling said. "Or something like that. He said that man saved his life when he passed out in the swamp. Showed him a place underground, an old fox den. Was warm in there, even in winter."

"Old Red drank enough to have a Wonderland adventure every night is what I heard," Whitby said. If he acknowledged having seen somebody in the Waters, it might lead to a consensus to investigate, and Whitby didn't want to poke around out there.

"Probably the guy got a humpback from living in a house underground," Two-Inch Tony offered, glad to have been left an opening in the conversation. "Probably couldn't stand up."

"The hell you all talking about? A man can't live underground in the swamp. He'd be underwater," Dickmon said.

"Maybe he got a hump as a punishment for stealing those bricks," Smiley said, and Two-Inch Tony nodded. Punishment was a favorite topic with the men. It was a principle they felt certain of, that the wicked would eventually be punished.

Since last fall, Whitby had been getting a different idea, that everybody would get punished, guilty or not.

"I think it's a girl," Darling said. "Yup, that's a girl."

The men's breathing deepened with interest. The generator cycled down, threatened to stall out, and then revived.

"Probably your little sister, Standish," Whitby said. "She left church in a hurry. Whose car was she getting into in the parking lot?"

"Better not be my sister coming down here. She's supposed to be with my wife." He still liked saying *my wife*, still felt proud that a woman had married him, even if she treated him poorly.

"How'd an ugly bastard like you get such a pretty sister?" Whitby asked.

"My mom's not ugly," Standish said.

"That's for sure," Whitby said. "Your ma's a good-looking woman."

"She's not for you to look at." Standish could feel himself turning red. His mom had gotten pregnant with him young and was still a looker, it was true. His dad had been more than twice her age.

"The question remains, then, how come you're ugly?" Whitby said.

"I don't think it's a hump," Smiley said. "Looks like a jet pack."

"Jet pack? Who the hell has a jet pack?" Dickmon asked.

"I don't know," Smiley said. "The military's got all kinds of weapons we don't know about. Alien technology, guns that vaporize human beings."

"You got all kinds of theories," Dickmon said. "Hare-brained ones. You heard about how the earth is flat?"

The men all laughed, and the sound rang out over the Waters, where creatures slithered past one another and called out sharply, and hummed and chirped their fertility, and, in the case of muck rattlers, buzzed. One kind of local medicine made by Herself was still in cupboards in Whiteheart, small blue glass jars of an antivenom the texture of mucus that, if applied immediately at the wound site and through small incisions cut around it, was known to enter the bloodstream and travel like lightning through the body to chase down every molecule of venom. The antivenom was once made with Wild Will's blood—he'd been bitten so many times that his blood had become a cure. And after Herself sent Wild Will away, she made the antidote with donkey blood from the jenny, Aster, after injecting her with small amounts of venom over time.

"It's a blond girl, all right, I can see that," Darling said. "That's definitely a backpack."

"Hey, that's Rose Thorn. She's alive!" Whitby said, when she was closer. "Rosie is back from California! Where the hell is Titus?"

Rose Thorn was known for being lovely enough that when you saw her, you felt a reprieve from whatever had been troubling you. And she was famous for what she was to Titus, who had sworn to God and all of them to wait for her to turn eighteen so he could marry her honestly. When she had left town last September, Titus had gotten so upset he'd joined the army, infuriating his father. Farm boys were needed at home! After four months, to his father's relief—and his own—his thinblood was revealed, and he was given a medical discharge.

Standish finally let the sling on his shoulder take the full weight of his rifle. He was stricken with a sweet thought of his daughter looking up at him and asking why the sun came up every morning. The sight of Rose Thorn made him think how he ought to fix his ma's car, as he'd promised, though it pissed him off that her boyfriend couldn't fix it. The man treated Standish like he was a dumb kid, and his ma never stuck up for him, but they expected him to spend his day off, the one day a week he didn't have to drive to Grand Rapids, fixing her car. He said, "I knew she'd come back."

, "No, you didn't, asshole," Dickmon mumbled. "You didn't know any more than the rest of us."

As Dickmon watched Rose Thorn approach, he decided he would pick a bouquet of wild geraniums for his wife before he went home. He might lift his hugely pregnant Hannah Grace right up off the ground and hug her, even though his back was strained from driving T-posts yesterday. They'd decided to fence in part of the backyard, which was rocky with old landfill.

Seeing Rose Thorn, Smiley thought he'd take his ma to visit his gram in the Christian Comfort Care nursing home this evening, so they could all watch a movie together. He and his ma loved action movies, but his gram preferred the old movies with Fred Astaire and Ginger Rogers dancing. She'd move in her wheelchair as though dancing herself. The other men talked endlessly about their dads and grandpas, but Smiley had always felt more kinship with the women in his family.

Two-Inch Tony had an idea about the man-sized box kite he had started making last year and then stuck in the rafters of his garage. His whole family—Cynthia and their son and new baby daughter—could go out and fly it in the graveyard behind the church. What a pretty sight that would be, those rainbow colors flying in the wind! He'd run with it, with his son, no matter how much his hip hurt.

Darling and Standish set out to wait for Rose Thorn at the edge of the road. Whitby wanted to go along to meet her but felt afraid. At Whiteheart Farms, back in September, Whitby had been sitting on a milk crate beside the cider house, drinking his third stolen beer, and he'd seen Rose Thorn sneaking around outside Titus's old bedroom in the dark. After Titus's medical discharge from the army, he'd moved into the shop behind his great-aunt Ada's house. Ada's grandson Alan,

Titus's cousin, had lived there, may he rest in peace. In addition to working for his old man, Titus Jr. now took care of Ada's orchards and cranberry bog. Whitby didn't envy him. He had to spray and prune the apple and peach trees, and flood, sand, and drain the cranberry bog, not to mention harvest the fruit by hand. He'd mentioned to Whitby that he thought those acres of wetland might be put to better use.

That night in September, Whitby thought it was cute how Rose Thorn was tapping on Titus's window and calling out his name, calling out that she wanted to make love with him. Whitby knew Titus wasn't there, that he was out night fishing, and he should've told Rosie so right away, but he'd been enjoying watching her.

When a man appeared, it was not Titus, Rosie's love, but Titus Sr., Whitby's uncle by marriage and his boss, coming out from the carriage house where he'd been drinking. His wife, Aunt Mary, didn't approve of him drinking. Whitby avoided him at that time of the evening—they all did—in part because the great farmer was not a nice drunk, and also because he might put Whitby to work even though it was dark. Even as Rose Thorn said no and called out for Titus, even as she struggled, even as a flash of her thigh was revealed, Whitby couldn't believe it was happening. It had to be some kind of bad dream, the effect of the three beers. Whitby hurried to his bike and rode shakily away down Lovers Road.

If Titus noticed that Rose Thorn was acting strangely after that, he didn't say anything to Whitby or the other men, who didn't see her around for a while. And a few weeks later, when Titus asked her to marry him, it was meant only to be a formality—they'd planned their wedding for the day of her eighteenth birthday—but she refused. Nobody could believe it. Then there was an early freeze, and Rose Thorn ran off to stay with her sister Prim.

Even after all these months, Whitby wasn't sleeping well. What he'd seen had changed him enough that every way of lying in bed now made him ache; nothing was comfortable.

The men of Whiteheart had grown up—as the boys in Whiteheart were still growing up—sharing a certain flavor of camaraderie, that of looking away from one another's misdeeds. It seemed to them common decency not to mention when a man dumped waste oil in a ditch or shot a rare duck out of season or hauled off and slapped his wife or a kid in the passenger seat. When a man felt he could do nothing else for a companion, he could at least show his respect by staying out of that man's dark business. A man had his own soul to grapple with, so who was another man to point out the terribleness of a thing? In this world of sinfulness, who was any man to judge another man? But if something like that happened again, Whitby thought he'd step in right away, before it could start happening, and say, *This ain't right, sir.* No matter if it was a friend or his uncle or even the reverend.

The men at the picnic table waited as silently as hunters, hands in their pockets or resting on their weapons, watching Rose Thorn's fluid motion, her willowy arms a sweet song contrasting with the soundtrack of the rattling generator. The bulrushes in the ditch moved in a breeze, and the men imagined all that went unheard and unseen in the Waters—snakes and woodcocks and grouse slipping around under last year's flattened grasses. From a certain distance, Rose Thorn was as luminous as an angel, as expansive as the first warm spring day. As she approached, they felt rather than heard her cheap canvas tennis shoes shushing on the asphalt. Then they saw that the shoes were coated with mud, and that mud covered her bare shins and had splashed onto her knees. If she moved fluidly and brightly, she was not quite her usual graceful self.

She was wearing a funny kind of dress, and she swayed with each step leaning side to side as though tired out, her backpack strapped securely at her shoulders and waist. Whitby worried she might be hurt in some way that he couldn't see. For sure she was exhausted.

They already had a story to tell—she was back—and maybe it would be better, they thought, if she just walked right by. It would even be something of a relief, as when they aimed and fired at an animal and missed, relieved because they wouldn't have to decide whether to skin the critter and eat it or leave it to rot. Rose Thorn would be easy to admire walking away, with those tanned legs clenching and relaxing under the dress that had tails like a shirt. Just look at that caramel-colored suntan in May! Like somebody on TV! They admired her softly sloping shoulders and shining blond head, ignoring that her hair looked uncombed and greasy, thinking maybe that was how they were wearing it in California. At the sight of those pretty, muddy legs, Whitby feared he might puke up his Mountain Dew. He wished for

Titus to come right now, to save her from the labor of walking. Save her from all of them.

When she had almost reached them, the men saw how disheveled she looked wearing what turned out to be an oversized shirt. Was it buttoned up wrong? Yes, it was. Some of her hair flew about, and some of it hung in her face as though she was too tired to even push it away. She did not seem to notice them, as if she was too tired to turn her head toward the men standing off to the side of the road. Maybe the loud generator was distracting her from seeing them. Her face seemed a little swollen, as though from too much sleep, and the expression was grumpy. They wanted to see her smile; her frown reminded them that she wasn't all sweetness and light, that she could be cutting and mean at times, not a good trait in such a young woman. She wouldn't let a guy say a thing that wasn't true without commenting, not even Titus, though he was six years older than she was and loved her as much as he loved his life. Let Jesus or the reverend haunt them and hold them to a higher standard, not some witch's daughter! That lazy girl was the very antithesis of what they stood for: hard work and godliness. And yet, they couldn't take their eyes off her. More than ever, the men felt like dry thirsty land, and they needed to drink her in like cool water, needed to see her the way they needed the sun to rise, even if it wasn't going to shine on them.

When it looked as though she would pass them by without so much as a greeting, Ralph Darling entered the road to walk beside her, saying, "Don't do us that way, Rosie! We been waiting!"

The others were grateful that Darling had the tendency to speak without thinking. They'd been puzzling out what to say.

"Come sit with us," Darling said. He spoke out of a feeling that he'd put a great investment into watching and waiting over the last ten minutes, distinguishing her form from the background of cattails and yellow grass. And it was true that all the men had been waiting all the dreary gray winter and the cold damp spring to see her. On this spring day, they ached for an answer to the question of what they were living for and working for one season to the next, and if she had an answer, she ought to tell them and not keep it to herself.

"Stop and take a load off, Rosie," Two-Inch Tony said. "What you got in that pack? It's weighing you down."

She stopped and blinked as though she was surprised to see them. She'd broken a blood vessel in her left eye, and it blurred her vision. She honestly hadn't noticed the men.

"If it isn't a six-pack of Whiteheart's finest," she said, once she'd gathered her strength to speak loudly enough to be heard over the generator.

"Rosie, you ought to come sit down. You want a ride?" Dickmon said, feeling a little breathless. He wanted to say more, wanted to take her hand and lead her to the table, but he wasn't sure what Hannah Grace would think of his offering a ride to a beautiful young woman, just eighteen years old, while in the company of these other strutting roosters.

"It's so loud," Rose Thorn said.

"Storm knocked the power out," Two-Inch Tony said. "Whiteheart Farms is out too. So's your ma's place."

"You walking all the way from town? Come have a pop on the house," Smiley finally said. If they'd been alone, he would have offered all he had, not just a soda pop but food and money—maybe even a beer, despite her age. Each one of the men would have offered more if there'd been nobody to see him.

Rose Thorn looked longingly down the road toward M'sauga Island, a mile and a half away, and toward Titus's place farther on, though she couldn't go there. She'd left the hospital in Laguna Beach before sunrise, hitchhiked to Los Angeles, flown to Grand Rapids using the emergency credit card Prim had given to her, taken a bus from the airport, and then stood at the bus stop in Potawatomi, on the other side of the Old Woman River, feeling far from home. She found a bench near the river and sat there for more than an hour, starting to feel hopeless about getting to the other side, and then, as in a dream or a fairy tale, an old man, maybe a ghost, had motored up in a camouflage flat-bottomed boat.

"You going to the island?" he asked, and she accepted his outstretched hand and stepped into the boat, noticing he smelled boozy. He couldn't get anywhere near the island in such a boat, and instead he deposited Rose Thorn upstream, in back of the gun club, the closest he could get to dry land, but when she climbed out, she still went up to her shins in mud. He offered to walk her the rest of the way—insisted, really—but she said no. She didn't need anybody seeing her with a swamp ghost, especially not Herself.

"How come your shoes are all wet?" Standish asked. His heart ached a little at the sight of her canvas lace-ups untied and caked with mud. Her feet looked swollen in those little shoes.

Without a word, Rose Thorn walked through the shallow ditch and across the grass and sat down on top of the picnic table. Darling sat beside her, and Two-Inch Tony inched his haunch down into a sitting position at the other end of the table. The way her breasts bulged in the oversized duck-colored work shirt—the brand and size Titus usually wore—accentuated by the straps of her military-issue backpack, affected Standish so much he had to swallow tears, and he gazed off toward the swamp, thinking about how his sister really was running wild, acting like a slut, and their ma paid no attention, and his wife kept telling him to leave the girl alone. Rose Thorn reached up to her collarbone to adjust the straps of the pack, an action that called even more attention to the caramel landscape of her exposed chest.

"Nice to see you all looking the same," Rose Thorn said, mustering a voice that could compete with the generator.

"Good to see you, Rosie," Two-Inch Tony said to her breasts, which were taking a while to settle under the work shirt. "We ain't seen you for a long time. Do you want we should call Titus?" He heard birdsong arising from within the folds of the fabric of her shirt. Had she always been so free of gravity in this town where everything else had become as heavy as lead shot? Marriage was supposed to lighten a man's load, and then children were supposed to brighten his life, but Tony's kids just gave him more to worry about.

"I can call Titus," Smiley offered. There was no phone on the island, no way to call Herself. "He should be here any minute."

"Maybe you could call Molly for me," she said.

"Molly's gone for four more weeks. She'll probably almost be a doctor when she gets back."

"Well, I'm not sure Titus wants to see me," she said, her voice exhausted and musical. The men all leaned in close to hear her.

"Of course he does!" Darling said, stroking his pot belly. He'd forgotten that she'd refused to marry Titus before she left. Titus had serenaded her from Boneset with a few other men there, so it wasn't just Titus who heard her answer shouted across the swamp channel. "Leave me alone!" was not exactly no but pretty close.

"You okay, Rosie? You need something to drink?" Dickmon held out his can of beer, half full. He right away thought of Hannah Grace and retracted it.

"Your mom around, Smiley?" she asked. She would have liked to see a woman right now.

"Oh, she's home today. Still got the sciatica, but she's good." That his mother was able to handle her nerve pain when other people complained all the time was a point of pride in him. "Herself is going to be glad to see you, I'll bet."

"I hope so," she said quietly and waved away the smoke coming at her from the generator. She slipped an arm out of the strap and brought the backpack around to rest on her lap. She stroked it gently.

"You stayed away a long time," Whitby ventured. Seeing her up close like this was making him feel dizzy.

"That pack looks heavy," Darling said. He thought of offering his can of pop to her but then felt silly. He was twenty-one, could drink legally, but half the time he forgot and ordered root beer, which tasted better anyway. "What're you carrying?"

"Something that's none of your beeswax," she said and shook her hair back to reveal her slender neck. She was so young, but she also seemed timeless and unlikely to age. Like a famous person, the men thought.

When Darling reached for her pack, she stood and walked away from the table, cradling it.

"Sorry," Darling said and patted his belly. "Didn't mean nothing."

She circled around, and as she sat back down with the pack in her lap, a vehicle came into view, traveling straight down the middle of Lovers Road from the west. It gradually became a red-and-white diesel truck, raising dust behind it, looking like a toy beneath the giant willows. While the men were distracted, Rose Thorn made sure there was air getting into the pack. She couldn't hear anything from inside it, not above the generator noise. As the truck turned into the parking lot, she ducked behind Darling to hide herself from view while the men let out a collective sigh. Having Rose Thorn with them without Titus had felt thrilling but dangerous, like looking directly into the sun. Also, Titus's arrival meant he wasn't planting, so this was a victory for all of them. The men had done their job—they had kept Rosie there until he arrived.

CHAPTER TWO

❧

Titus Clay will always love Rose Thorn Zook.

WHILE THE MEN WERE watching Titus, Rose Thorn
picked up Darling's untouched glass of draft beer from
the table and drank it down in slow, luxurious swallows.
It was malty and flat and soothing. She hadn't been able to keep
a beer down for a long time, but this one hit the spot, made her
want another.

Titus parked right next to the door, where he always did. He headed
inside without looking over at the table and came back out with a
long-necked bottle from the cooler behind the bar in one hand and
something the size of a loaf of bread under his other arm. Halfway to
the table, Titus stopped, and the bottle fell from his hand and foamed
in the dirt. His other arm held a coyote-colored puppy, who slid down
his leg and landed on his scuffed work boot with a yelp.

"The glorious sun has arisen!" Titus shouted above the generator noise. His voice carried like nobody else's. Everybody said he
could have been a preacher. "Could that be an angel dropped down
from heaven?"

"Looks like *you* dropped something." Rose Thorn grinned through
her exhaustion, maybe didn't even feel that exhausted anymore.

Titus picked up the beer first and then the pup and brought them
both to the table. The girl puppy squirmed and wiggled and knocked
over Whitby's Mountain Dew. Whitby grabbed the Dew with a long

arm before too much spilled. Titus's bottle continued to foam in his hand without his noticing.

"Rose Thorn, love and light of my life," Titus said. Only he could talk in this flowery, romantic way with the sincerity of quoting a Bible verse. The whole landscape began to glow around them, a reflection of Rose Thorn's glow. "You came back to me just like in my dreams."

"You're paying for that, Titus," Smiley said, nodding at the longneck bottle. "Whether you drink it or spill it."

"Take all my money, Smiley. I'm the richest man in town. My Rosie has come back to me," Titus said.

Whitby picked up the puppy, cradled her in his arms. Still sitting at the table, Rose Thorn took the beer out of Titus's hand and drank most of what was left with slow, even gulps. The men watched her throat as it was revealed by tipping back her head, and every man except Titus took a long drink of something of his own. Titus took off his orange Allis-Chalmers hat and smoothed his thick curly hair and put the hat back on. Rose Thorn meant to set Titus's bottle on the table but mistook the edge and dropped it onto the gravel, where all but the last sip spilled out. Darling picked it up and placed it on the table. The dog squirmed away from Whitby and sat beside Rosie, put her little nose against the backpack. Sniffed.

"You know she's not old enough to drink," Smiley said to Titus, his voice straining to rise above the generator. "Honey, I'm sorry, but I got to ask you not to do that. They'll take away my license."

Titus looked up at the milky sky and grinned at his God, who had made him the way he was, with his passion for the land he would inherit and his passion for Rose Thorn, and his knowledge of right and wrong. He'd loved her since she was eight years old and he was fourteen, and he'd promised God and himself to wait for her, however long it took. He'd been dating a girl from Kalamazoo for a couple months now, had tasted that girl's fruits every night, but he'd gotten restless and broken it off a week ago, and now it all made sense. The whole world made sense. He grabbed Rose Thorn's hand, and she barely had time to put her backpack on again before he grabbed the other, which poked out of the rolled-up sleeve of the work shirt she was wearing—one of his own shirts. He pulled her right up onto her feet, and her exhaustion slipped away. The way the pack hung off her shoulders told the other men it did not contain stacks of cash from a bank heist, nor did it contain books, as Rose Thorn was known to read so many of. It contained something heavy and soft without sharp edges, like cantaloupes or honeydew, though they couldn't imagine how a girl would get melons in May.

Rose Thorn moved with Titus for a few steps, lightly, gracefully, getting caught up in his sweet energy, despite the disorienting roar of the generator. She gazed into his Sunday-shaven face, his dark melancholic eyes. She hadn't planned to fall in with him this way without negotiation, but here she was, the bedraggled witch's daughter in the fairy tale dancing with the town's prince. She pulled away and sat on top of the picnic table again, called the dog to her.

"Nice to see you smile, Rosie!" Dickmon said.

"What a beautiful little creature," Two-Inch Tony said when Rose Thorn resumed petting the dog.

"That's going to be a big dog," Smiley said. "Hey, Titus, you get her from Marshall Wallace's shepherd? Maybe her daddy is that roaming mutt of Ed Cole's."

"She's going to be a farm dog," Titus said. "She's going to chase off critters. Auntie Ada's got those little yappers she keeps in the house. But you want her, Rosie, I'll give her to you. I'll give you everything I got."

"Marshall got any more pups?" Standish asked. "I'd like to give my daughter one like this." His daughter was a gloomy child, and he would do just about anything to see her face light up.

"Where've you been, Rosie?" Titus asked. "You've been gone too long. You'll break my heart if you ever go away like that again."

It wasn't the first time she'd gone to stay with Prim, but it was the first time she had gone without a word and stayed so long.

Tony leaned across Darling and whispered into Rose Thorn's lap, where the puppy's nose rested against the backpack, "Maybe you're half coyote."

Rose Thorn smiled; she didn't have the energy to hide her pleasure. Wasn't that the problem? She loved Titus, she loved all of them, everybody here. Even this dog—she already loved this little dog. When she had first arrived at Prim's in California, she'd claimed she wasn't ever going back to Whiteheart and the Waters, because she loved it so much there at Prim's, so near the Pacific Ocean, but now the ocean seemed like a big empty place.

"Nice dress," Titus said. He'd heard men say that if you gave a woman a piece of clothing, you had a right to take it off her, but he decided to keep that joke in his pocket. He hoped she'd thought about him every time she pulled that big shirt on or off, every minute the cotton lay against her skin. He'd gone through a brutal dark time during which he'd thought he was finished with Rosie, but he'd come out the other side now.

"Is that blood on your hand, Rosie?" Smiley asked.

She spat on it and wiped it away. When she looked up at Smiley, Whitby startled to see that her right eye was half full of blood.

"Maybe that's rust," Whitby said, hoping it all wasn't evidence of some new violence perpetrated against her. "From a fence post or something."

When the puppy squirmed away from Rose Thorn's hand, Titus noticed a thin wash of reddish fluid coming from under her shirt-dress, trickling down her inner thigh. He flushed and handed her a red bandanna out of his pocket and gestured downward with his eyes. Then he pointed into the swamp to distract the men, saying there was a sandhill crane landing.

They all looked and saw nothing.

"Rib eye of the sky," Standish said, because that's what he always said about that big bird he wasn't supposed to hunt. Titus said his dad had seen a couple woodcocks doing their mating spiral last night.

Rose Thorn had thought she was done bleeding when she tossed away her pad at the airport in Grand Rapids. She took the cloth Titus offered and held it to her face to inhale his scent before dabbing her thighs with it and slipping it inside her underpants. When the men looked back, she was petting the dog again. Fortunately it was just a little blood, nothing like earlier, when she'd been on the plane.

Titus screwed up his forehead and silently asked if she was okay, but as well as concern, he was feeling shame for her, shame that she would be so careless (or was she drunk?). Even the lowest of women managed to take care of the blood coming out of them. He wanted to think only sweet, clean thoughts of her, but she made that difficult sometimes. Already he'd forgiven her for running off after he'd asked her to marry him, and now he needed her to be worthy of that forgiveness. He'd taken a great risk and gotten a tattoo for her last year—he could have bled to death—and she hadn't even been willing to see it before she refused him.

Darling meanwhile poured some beer into his cupped hand and offered it to the puppy. She stuck her nose in it and whimpered, and the men laughed. Still, her tail wagged with enough force that it knocked Tony's beer can right off the table. It was empty, so nobody picked it up.

Rose Thorn drank down the remaining swallow of Titus's beer, and Smiley pretended not to notice. She would've drunk ditch water had it been offered; she'd never been so thirsty.

"You going home, Rosie?" Darling asked. "I'll give you a ride for a kiss."

"Shut it, Ralph," Titus said, "or somebody'll shut it for you."

"What? It was a joke. You know me, Titus. I'm always joking." Darling didn't know why he'd said it, except he felt relaxed and familiar with Rose Thorn and was happy she was there.

"Rosie, I'll give you a ride home," Titus said. "I just seen your ma out in the garden."

"Hey, she just got here," Darling said. "Stay a little longer, Rosie."

"She's tired. Can't you boys see when a woman needs a rest?" Titus said.

"You're going to stay around, aren't you, Rosie?" Standish asked. He appreciated that she'd always had eyes only for Titus, even if she behaved loosely and sometimes said outrageous things.

"Of course, she'll stay," Titus said, holding up his beer bottle, surprised to find it empty. "She's home. Aren't you, Rosie?"

Rose Thorn stood, carefully pulled the backpack around in front of her again, and walked on shaking legs to Titus's truck. She paused to lean against the tailgate. Titus followed, briefly forgetting about the puppy, who jumped down from the table and followed, scrambling to keep up.

"You still got to pay for that beer, Titus," Smiley shouted after them.

Titus opened the passenger-side door and put the puppy in the middle of the bench seat. Then Rosie climbed in.

"Can I really have her?" Rose Thorn asked, petting the little dog.

"What's mine is yours," he said. His voice had a swing in it, like a gate that could be opened and then, just as easily, swung shut.

Being in his truck should have made Rosie feel ordinary and familiar, and it did. But she had forgotten how the familiar love, like the familiar landscape, was electrifying and energizing, intoxicating. She was so grateful for Titus, so grateful for the ride, that her eyes teared up.

She held her backpack in her lap with one arm around it, jiggling it by tapping her foot against the floorboards. With the other hand, she petted the dog, who nestled against her. The dog stuck her nose into the backpack, and Rose Thorn opened it a little so the dog could smell what was inside. The dog, her dog, could be trusted with a secret. When the puppy learned what was inside the pack, she gave a little whine, a little huff of breath.

Titus got in and slammed the driver's-side door with a great swooshing force.

"Hope you don't mind I'm still driving this heap. I'd like to give you a ride in a Cadillac limousine. Except then I wouldn't get to sit beside you on a bench seat."

He reached over and squeezed her hand before putting the key in the ignition.

Rose Thorn studied each of the familiar effortless motions involved in Titus's driving: the twist of thumb and finger to start the loud diesel engine—she loved his big hands—the bent elbow straightening as the long fingers took hold of the gear knob rising out of the floor at the center of the truck. He was left-handed but could use his right almost as deftly. She loved his arms. He squeezed the knob, and she wanted that hand on her, that arm around her. This truck was a home to her. Everything about it was familiar: the blub-blub of its engine, the smells of fuel oil and sweat, the cracked windshield—a crack extending most of the way across, just above where the wipers rested—the sun-bleached dashboard still dusted with last autumn's grain chaff, the empty Mountain Dew bottles and Payday wrappers on the floor.

Rose Thorn and Titus had spent countless hours in this truck, driving up and down this road, with the heater on or with the windows open, or parked and watching the Waters and swatting mosquitoes as Titus talked about his future, what he said would be theirs. When she disagreed with some point, such as when she said she didn't want to be a hardworking farm wife, he laughed, didn't even hear; and she didn't care, because all she wanted was moment after moment with him. She'd figured they'd work out the details later.

As the truck began to move, the dog sat up facing forward with her pointy coyote ears pricked.

"Are you okay?" Titus whispered.

Rose Thorn nodded. When he took her left hand in his and held it against his right thigh, she remembered how she loved his thighs, his hips, loved watching him walk. She leaned over the dog to be closer to him. This movement made blood gush out of her. Then she felt the backpack move, so she tapped her foot more vigorously, jostling and jiggling it on her knees.

"You should have told me you were coming home."

"Would you have baked me a cake?"

"If that's what you wanted. Just tell me what flavor, and I'll have my aunt whip one up. She loves you, you know." Ada's easy affection for Rose Thorn existed in contrast to how Titus's mother felt. She was as much concerned about the future of Whiteheart Farms as about Titus's happiness. And then there was Titus Sr.

Titus brought Rose Thorn's hand with him to shift the big gear lever into third. He drove slowly, lengthening the time they could be alone together. Rose Thorn watched the huge willows pass them on the right like scarred and gnarled old wise women. She felt the swirling, swollen mess of her belly.

"Your aunt is good, deep down in her bones, where Mama says the soul is," Rose Thorn offered.

"She is that. Oh, Rosie, Rosie, Queen of My Heart. You're back. We can start over. I forgive you for running away, for everything."

"You forgive me?" She yanked her hand away, jostling the backpack, which emitted a mewling cry. She bounced the pack again. With his eyes on the road, Titus couldn't see that her eyes were watering with the effort of holding back what she couldn't tell him. "Fuck you, Titus," she said quietly.

He reached to take her hand back, and she let him have it. He didn't know what she'd been through, and he loved her, and he knew she loved him.

"I said I forgive you." Titus squeezed her hand, jiggled it a little in a playful way. "By God's grace, how can that be a bad thing?"

Rose Thorn wiped her eyes with her sleeve, enjoying the dance of their hands in spite of everything. Whatever happened next would happen, and Rose Thorn would figure it out as she went.

"You don't understand," she said, "and I can't tell you, so we're stuck."

He gave her an agitated look, and the little dog yipped. Titus was agitated, and Rose Thorn was agitated, but the two-headed creature they made together was ecstatic at being whole again. She had tried to get over him while she was gone, tried not to love him. Now she tried half-heartedly to tug her hand out of his grip, but he held it on the seat between them.

"I don't know if you heard the bad news," he said. "Right after you left in September, Alan died in a car wreck. Dad said it was bound to happen, with all his partying and carousing."

Rose Thorn let herself cry now. She hadn't known Titus's cousin Alan all that well, but she'd liked him. Titus didn't have to say that he'd now inherit his great-aunt Ada's half of Whiteheart Farms as well as his father's.

"Hey, don't cry. I thought you might've heard that news, thought you might've come back for the funeral. Your ma came," Titus said, slowing and studying her again. After Reverend Roy's funeral service, at Ada's request, Herself had joined the family at the farm to burn rosemary, sage, and cedar and apple wood while the reverend grumbled to himself and then finally left in a huff. "You know my dad says I'm a fool to wait for you, but I say count me a fool."

"Drop me here," she said as they passed the donkeys on the left.

Wild Will's house was set back from the road and up on a little hill. On the right side of the road, the Boneset Table was heaped with jars of ointments, half-cartons of eggs with special markings on them, and plastic bags containing roots and leaves. Herself had made good use of her time alone in the winter and spring to process the herbs she'd collected in the Waters all summer and fall. Now the markings on the egg cartons were green, indicating that they were spring tonic eggs, as everybody knew them, to aid with digestion. As the seasons changed, there would be lavender summer eggs, autumn warming eggs.

Under the table hung the Babby Basket, as always, with its blanket dyed orange with bloodroot. Rose Thorn's eyes watered to see it.

"Sure you don't want to come back to the farm?" Titus said, turning left into the drive at the Boneset House, where the front yard was filled with Hermine's big sun garden. Titus used Rose Thorn's hand in his again to shift into neutral. "You can get cleaned up, have a hot shower. You won't have to heat water on the stove."

"I'm going to call her Ozma," Rose Thorn said, resuming her rocking of the backpack.

"Who?"

"This dog. You said I could have her."

"I was going to call her Scout," Titus said. "Do you see I repainted the Boneset sign?"

Titus cut the diesel engine and coasted up the driveway, and the mewling and crying rose in the relative quiet. When Titus realized the sound wasn't coming from Rose Thorn or the dog, he let go of Rosie's hand to grab at the opening of the pack, and she smacked him away. He lunged again and pulled the top fully open, exposing a human arm the size of a doll's.

"What the fuck?" Titus said, braking suddenly. "You got a baby in there? A baby? Is it alive?"

"Yes, I had a baby, Titus. Yes, *she* is alive."

"Oh, hell, Rosie. Well, it ain't mine, and you know it! Don't you tell anybody it is."

She slowly extracted the living, breathing, whimpering human being, letting the backpack containing the last clean diaper fall away like a shed skin. She held the girl, swaddled in a yellow hospital blanket, against her chest. The little girl opened her mouth as if to nurse. She'd nursed in fits and starts all day, at the airport, on the plane, on the bus that dropped them on the wrong side of the Old Woman River, but neither Rose Thorn nor the baby were turning out to be very good at it. Rosie's milk hadn't even soaked the pads in her bra the way the nurses said it would.

"Is that what you care about?" she asked. "What I'm going to tell somebody?"

"This is too much, Rosie." He didn't know where to look, and his eyes flitted outside and then around the truck cab.

The baby opened her blue-gray eyes, letting in the light and chaos and then closed them, and her crying calmed. Rose Thorn didn't know for sure, but she suspected the baby was far too calm, especially since she wasn't getting enough milk. The nurses had all commented upon how quiet she seemed, and though Rose Thorn could feel her breathing and crying all during her walk down Lovers Road, the baby had slept on the bus ride and the boat ride, had even slept to the hum of that loud generator at the bar.

"You always say you want to be a father."

"To my own baby. I don't want to raise some other guy's kid."

"Lucky baby, I guess. To know right away who wants her and who doesn't." Rose Thorn understood his anger; she understood everything about him.

"Oh, Jesus, Rosie, I wait for you all these years, and you go with another guy and get pregnant." He paused to count back the nine months. "You made a fool of me with somebody here in town."

"This wasn't something I did on purpose," Rose Thorn said and paused. She could tell him she had been molested without telling him who had done it. She could tell him she had improbably— miraculously?—gotten pregnant afterward. But he would never let up asking who it was. She could say she didn't know, but she wouldn't be able to maintain a lie.

"You slept with somebody by accident when I asked you to marry me? Who was it?"

If his anger was a rolling ball, then her anger became a mallet swinging to meet it.

"I guess I made the right choice then," Rosie said. "Think if I'd married you."

"You mean what if you married me and then had somebody else's baby? How would I ever go along with that?"

"I thought you might want her. She looks like you." She turned and held the child away from him, rewrapped her in the little blanket with shaking hands. Contrary to what she had said when she left the hospital, Rosie had no idea how to take care of a baby, and so far, no instincts had kicked in. The baby accessories from the hospital seemed all wrong. To do this right, she needed the cloth diapers from the island and blankets knitted by Herself. She'd felt compelled to check herself out of the hospital while Prim was at work and make her way back home.

The puppy climbed over her lap to lick the baby's arm. "Glad somebody's happy to see her," Rose Thorn said.

When Titus reached across the bench seat for her hand again, Rose Thorn let him take it, and she held his hand with the baby nestled on her lap, and for a moment it seemed the three of them might be okay. There in the driveway, the inside of the truck and the whole world seemed briefly to fill with yellow light. When Herself stood up in the garden and looked at them, her braids wrapped around her head, Titus let go of Rose Thorn's hand.

"I'm trying to be okay with it, Rosie, but I'm not okay. Start by telling me who it was."

Rose Thorn unlatched the truck door.

"Wait, Rosie! For Christ's sake, be careful, the truck's rolling!" He had forgotten to shift into gear. He braked and they jerked forward a little. The baby knocked lightly against the warm dash.

In the garden, Herself was leaning on her hoe, with a burlap sack slung across her shoulders. Seeing Rose Thorn in the truck, she dropped the hoe in the dirt and started walking toward the drive. She paused to pick up a deer's jagged broken thigh bone off the ground at the edge of the garden and put it in the pocket of her skirt. She used it to make holes and measurements for planting. With each footfall in her big work boots—she was wearing Wild Will's shoes—the ground seemed to shake a little. She was not fat, not exactly, but had expanded over her lifetime and made more of herself than other people. And holding everybody's rotten business—secret truths she'd never asked for—had filled her up, stretched her skin tight.

Titus's anger stabbed at him from the inside. "People love you, and you treat them like this," he said to Rose Thorn. "Nobody would be okay with this."

Why did they have to talk? Rose Thorn wondered. They could get along so well if they both shut up. If they just kissed. She wished he would help her figure out what to do next, but he was going to demand every detail before allowing them to move forward. She pushed the passenger door of the truck the rest of the way open with her foot, kicked the nearly empty backpack onto the ground, and slid out with the baby in her arms. All of this was terrifying to Rose Thorn. The baby, the diapers, her swollen, stretched body. Titus. Though the nurses had said a five-hour delivery was nothing—she was lucky with her first child, they said—it had felt like the world ending. She had pushed so hard to get the baby out of her that she saw blood.

The little dog launched herself from the truck, somersaulted down and landed on Rosie's feet. The puppy kept up as, with both arms around the baby, Rose Thorn walked over to the fence line where Triumph and Aster were standing with their heads hanging over the rails. Titus got out of the truck and followed silently. Rose Thorn suddenly feared she'd trip or drop the baby, and so she squeezed her so tightly that the baby gasped and went stone quiet again. Momentarily the child remained limp as a sponge, seemed to be trying to absorb her mother's intentions, listening uncertainly for the truth of the situation as Rose Thorn might reveal it and what it might mean for her future. Rose Thorn noticed with alarm the sharp prongs on the strand of barbed wire strung across the front of the pasture and squeezed the baby again and then loosened her hold. How was this holding supposed to feel natural? She leaned her forehead against the brown-and-white spotted jenny's face in a way that made the big plush ears twitch. She knew she should be sensing what the child felt, but she was more attuned to Aster and to Titus behind her. Aster sniffed the baby with interest; she was pregnant herself, looking as wide as she was tall. This was something the people of Whiteheart were glad to see, for the donkey's milk was important medicine for little children, but Rose Thorn felt only pity.

"Good luck, old girl," she whispered. Probably the birth would take place a little over a month from now, after at least a full year of gestation.

Titus took his place beside Rose Thorn, put his arm around her shoulders. To the crows above them in the black willows, they resembled a married couple with their first child, but Titus was confused. The old woman was approaching, and he needed to figure things out in a hurry.

"Rosie, let me show you something," he said. He pulled off his work shirt and stood in his white sleeveless undershirt. On his right arm was the simple outline of a cross, a tattoo he'd gotten on his eighteenth birthday. He turned slightly to reveal the new tattoo on his left biceps, the one he'd gotten before asking her to marry him last year, the one she hadn't seen yet. When Rose Thorn saw the inked image, she clutched the child too tightly again. Everybody in Whiteheart knew the tattoo—it was the same as the one Wild Will had gotten on his right arm after Maryrose—Molly—was born. A thorny rose with a m'sauga rattlesnake wrapped around the stem, with a tiny crescent moon rising behind it on one side and a drop of blood on the other.

"You idiot," Rose Thorn whispered. "You could have bled to death."

"I did it for you," he said. Because he had bled so much while getting the tattoo, the image was slightly blurry in spots. "I found a photo of it for the tattoo artist to follow."

"Don't blame that on me," Rose Thorn said.

Herself was now standing a few feet away, studying his arm violently.

Titus stepped away from them, back toward his truck. He'd expected them both to be impressed by the loyalty his tattoo showed toward their family, in the face of some other opinions. "My dad said I was wasting my time with you. He said you'll ruin me and the farm."

"Sure, listen to your great and glorious daddy," Rose Thorn said. "Maybe I screwed every son of a bitch in Whiteheart except you. Is that what you want to hear?"

"Hello, ma'am," Titus said to Herself. "I brought your daughter back to you. You can have her." He took off his orange cap and ran his hand through his tight curls, trying and failing to tamp down his anger. He didn't dare meet the eyes of the old woman, who was staring straight at him as if reading his soul. "Now I'm leaving."

"Why don't you go back and drink with the other six dwarves," Rose Thorn called after him, when what she wanted to say was *Please don't go.*

CHAPTER THREE

⮜

Herself knows how to raise a girl.

T HERE WERE HERBS IN the Waters of Massasauga Swamp that
could be rendered into medicine for just about every affliction:
yarrow and plantain for bleeding wounds, elderberries and
boneset for flu, willow bark for fever, and foxglove and dandelion for
too much pressure in the body. Mullein for eliminating mucous, slippery elm for sore throats, honey for ulcers, and turkey tail for the old
cancers, if you caught them early. And if you asked Herself to make a
potion or tonic to fix you, she would study the veins in your hand and
the whites of your eyes while considering what kinds of poison to add
in minuscule amounts. Bloodroot? Snakeroot? Rattlesnake venom, if
she had it?

Most people preferred not to know what was in the medicine she
gave them; even after they paid for one of her fixes, they might be too
afraid to take it, and sometimes just having it nearby was medicine
enough. Some of the cures weren't working now as well as they used
to before Wild Will went away, or even a decade ago. Parcel by parcel,
the county government and the farmers had filled in great swaths of
the Waters to eliminate mosquito-borne ague and to increase their
acreage, and the plants were responding to this loss, along with the
agricultural runoff and slightly warmer temperatures. Some plants
receded to ditches, hollows, or hummocks where they were guarded
by poison ivy, mosquitoes, snapping turtles, and meat-eating pitcher
plants. Others, exposed to toxins released into the groundwater and

streams by the mountains of sublimating waste from the Goliath paper mill, were losing their potency. The aggressive new cancers, especially, didn't respond to the old cures. And the m'sauga rattlesnakes were endangered, as were some turtles, mussels, and the local monkey flower, which could help clear rheumy eyes. It was getting to be that a person living in Whiteheart might as well go to the doctors at the hospital.

Herself would only give a strong medicine after coming to know the person who was asking. It might take one minute or ten minutes of holding a person's hand to get that sense, or it might take a year of ruminating and massaging her own biceps or talking to the ghost of Baba Rose, who guided Hermine's right hand in all things. It was Hermine's left hand that took in the trouble, and it was her right hand that was sometimes able to fashion a fix that would do more good than harm, and always the cure had a mind of its own. More recently, she could come up with possible remedies for only half the people who came to her agonizing about the symptoms that pained them.

A lot of the trouble was soul trouble. People confessed terrible things to her, humiliations to which they'd been subjected, cruelties they'd themselves committed. They wanted to pass their horrors onto her so she could digest them and share the burden of them, and this meant half the night she spent working through their dreams before even having her own. These consultations took their toll whether or not she created anything in response, and if she made a concoction, it would take a little more out of her, if only a tear or a drop of blood or a bit of skin or breath. Recently, she'd begun to lose her hearing to stop their confessions from entering her head. First a dimming in her left ear, and now in her right. She hadn't done it on purpose; it was more an inadvertent defense.

The brutes of Nowhere wanted magic, even though they didn't believe in magic, but all Herself had to offer were nudges toward wholeness, suggestions made by tinctures or waters or salves to surrender to whatever they'd been resisting or avoiding. An effective cure—beyond a few dozen simple remedies—was tenuous and affected by every mood in the town or on the island, and by any change of weather. Nobody understood how fallible she was, how little she knew, how everything she did was guided by a ghost, that the miracles she occasioned shouldn't be credited to her. Baba Rose had been a real healer, especially when it involved young women who needed permission to heal. She hadn't been afraid to take a girl in her arms, and that was as much the cure as the teas or salves she sent them away with. Baba Rose had allowed women and girls to come onto the island, those who were intrepid enough to make the journey by raft. And while Herself didn't fully regret marrying Wild Will Zook or letting him build a bridge to the island, she wished she'd never offered her medicines to him, since it had encouraged men as well as women to come, expecting her to fix them too. And she sometimes did long for the time when it was harder to cross to and from Nowhere.

This new gift in her daughter's arms could be a remedy and renewal for her own soul, if she could get them all back to the island, where a child could be properly cared for. Both Rosie and Titus were standing still at the fence line watching her face, looking windblown and fearful, and Triumph and Aster also seemed to be waiting for her verdict. Even the shepherd puppy was tipped back on its rump looking up at Hermine. The bone in her skirt pocket was poking her; she reached in to discover that the sharp tip had ripped through the fabric lining and was pressing against the skin of her thigh.

When she glanced up from the blanketed baby, she was alarmed to see on Titus's biceps the copy of the tattoo that her husband had gotten decades ago to celebrate the Rose women. Herself took in the flower, the thorns, the rattlesnake, and the moon, and she didn't notice she'd raised the thigh bone like a weapon until Titus straightened his back and looked into her face with alarm. He turned and walked to his truck, shaking his head. He raced the engine, tore up the dirt driveway backing onto the road. Both women watched him from a cloud of diesel exhaust as he headed east toward the Muck Rattler, spitting some loose gravel behind him. Like any medicine, a tattoo would have its secondary effect eventually—might establish who you were or might transform you. Might even poison you.

"Was that what you were hoping for?" Herself asked her daughter. She reached out and, with a fingernail, moved the yellow blanket so that the squished face materialized, a vision from her dreams. With her left hand, Herself pressed her cuntshell necklace against her chest and listened to the excited whispers of those souls still remaining. Her smile was an inward-turning expression, a response to the sensation of waking up after a long sleep and drinking cool clean water. "You're the only thing that doesn't come easy to that young man."

"So you want me to be easy, Mama?" Rose Thorn managed a laugh that threatened to tear her insides loose.

"He's probably the only man in this town worth a damn," Herself said. "He's sturdy and reliable as a mule. He could protect you from the rest."

And not just that, but a thinblood like Titus who could die from a cut or scrape wasn't as dangerous as the ordinary brute. Herself didn't let him on the island, but she got his help at Boneset with a lot of things, and he'd even replaced a couple of leaking oil barrels supporting the bridge planks. Herself had already been giving him the medicine she had made for his grandfather decades ago, something to take a sip of every day to thicken the blood. Titus's father, Titus Clay Sr., had wanted that cure, too, but she didn't give it to him, didn't like the way he sent his long-suffering wife around begging. The wife was so shy anytime she left the farm that she couldn't even muster any warmth or friendliness.

"I love him, Mama," Rose Thorn said, "more than my life. But I don't want to marry him."

"Well, I'll bet Titus is confused right now. Nobody's heard from you for a while."

"I'm dying of love, Mama." Rose Thorn collapsed to her knees, jostling the baby, who began to cry in earnest. The dog pressed her wet nose against Rose Thorn's bare leg. Aster looked on with concern.

"We're all dying, child."

"You loved Wild Will. I know you did. Prim told me you used to fall at his feet. How can you be so callous?"

"Love is a sharp hollow tooth," Herself said. She put down the bone, leaned it against the fence post where she could find it later. With this tender child arriving, all hard and sharp things had to be laid aside. Triumph nosed at the bone through the fence; the little dog licked it. Herself adjusted the burlap sack she wore over her shoulder and reached for the baby. Rose Thorn started to hand her over but then changed her mind and pulled the baby close. Herself could sense Rosie's ambivalence about the child, and it seemed dangerous. "But now you got his babby, I'm sure he'll overlook your bad behavior."

"Baby's not his." Rose Thorn kept hold of the bundle to be sure her mother would listen to her story, and she told most all of it, even that she'd been drunk. The only thing she left out was how she'd called for Titus by name to make love with her.

For a few minutes, Herself couldn't breathe. It was the weight of the revelation, added to all the other weight she carried. Her own girl's violation by Titus Sr. should have been a singular and personal horror, and it was, but it blended with the stories of all the other women—including what happened to her daughter Primrose in Wild Will's house—with the sad, angry plight of many of the men, and with the desecration of the Waters around them. Hadn't Baba Rose died from knowing too much? It wasn't just the rattlesnake bite that had killed her but the weight of too many sad tales. What didn't surprise Herself at all was the bad luck of Rosie's fertility.

"Last fall, I dreamed violence, and I asked you what happened," Herself said. "You said, 'Nothing happened.' You said it wasn't you I was dreaming."

"I'm telling you now." Already Rose Thorn regretted telling Herself the story. Her mother was becoming angry like a river dammed, and the air around them churned, making it difficult to move or breathe. Rose Thorn clung to the baby, fearing the floodgates might burst and they all would be washed away.

"Maybe you can eat this little dog, Mama," Rose Thorn said. "She's nice and plump. I only took her because Titus loves her."

"He doesn't know what his father did?" Herself asked, eyes on the baby. "No idea?"

"No. And he'd never believe me, anyway, not about his glorious father. And he'd hate me as the messenger. I don't want anybody to know."

"Not much you can do if a person wants to believe something," Herself said, thoughtfully. "But I'm sure you could find a way to torture him less if you want him to come around."

"Titus would torture me, Mama, if I let him. He wanted to marry me and turn me into one of those long-suffering Christian wives. That's what Prim says."

"What does Prim know about wives suffering?"

"Mama, I can't lie to Titus. I'm not a good liar about things that matter. All I can do is tell or not tell." She looked down at the baby, whose neediness terrified her, but she gave a similarly needy look to Herself. "I really thought Titus might want her. And me."

"Give him time," Herself said. She was already formulating the second curse she'd ever created. The first had been against her husband, the curse that he should live as a woman, that he should know what it was to be a woman. This curse for Rosie's sake would be simpler: that Titus Clay Sr. should never lay eyes on beautiful Rose Thorn again, nor this child.

"Why didn't you give Prim the medicine for me when she came all the way here for it?"

"Does she think I'm a shopkeeper?" Herself asked. "I don't see her for almost a year, and she shows up and puts in her order."

"It wasn't easy for her to ask, Mama. You know that."

"Well, she asked, but she didn't say anything about you. Or about that brute. It didn't make any sense what she was asking."

"I didn't tell her about him. I won't ever tell anybody but you."

"Prim wouldn't sit with me. She wouldn't eat with me. She just demanded something I couldn't give her." Herself had not suspected the baby she'd been dreaming of lately could be Rosie's. "Are you sure you don't want to marry Titus? Forget about what Prim says. If you want to marry him, you'll find a way to talk to him."

"I don't know what I want, and he hates me now anyway. Prim found me a way to get rid of this baby, and I thought I could do it, but I couldn't. Only your medicine can save me, Mama." Rose Thorn wanted to fall into her mother's arms, have her mother tell her she had done the right thing. "Mama, I know everything about me is all wrong, but I don't know what to do."

Herself paused to digest all this, tried to know how to help. She was not one for soft, kind words, and she tried and failed to gather some now. She felt only that Rosie's misery might be deadly for a child, and she could smell beer on her breath.

She also knew her daughter was partly right. Once a woman got labeled that way, she lost her private self. That rape, once known, would be a public thing, might be all that people saw in her, assuming they believed her. She was painfully aware that if Wild Will had been there, if the family were still under his auspices, this wouldn't've happened.

The donkeys had both been sniffing the puppy, and now Triumph nosed her, knocked her on her butt again, and Rose Thorn smiled at the dog's willingness to get right up and sniff again. Beyond the donkeys, the wood on the west side of the barn was lighting up silver. Across the road, under the willows, Rose Thorn saw a tangle of purple waterleaf, edible. The May apples had opened their umbrellas over creamy flowers, and a clump of white trillium waved flags of truce, a few of them blushing pink. The foliage between them and the island—elderberry bushes and silky dogwood—was already so thick that Rosie could barely see the cottage perched just above the bridge. She didn't understand why she'd wanted to leave this lovely, lush, watery place; at this time of year, she was always sure she'd never want to leave again. She heard the trill of a tree frog and the sound of her baby breathing.

"Why is it so hard to be a person?" Rose Thorn asked. "It was easier when you just told me what to do."

"Well, you were wise enough to bring this child home." Herself moved the blanket more to reveal a perfect tiny newborn hand. She was greatly relieved to see it was a girl. She knew how to raise a girl. Boys on the island would signal the end, with the way they broke trees and cracked eggs and stomped precious mushrooms. Herself adjusted the burlap sack over her shoulder again. In it were some morels and violets she'd collected and some overwintering carrots she'd dug up. Every item in her bag had mattered when she picked it, but not now.

Rose Thorn felt the coolness of the shadow her mother was casting over her. The old woman seemed like a deep flowing river that might carry her baby away downstream, and maybe that would be okay. Rosie felt ripe and swollen, and at the same time shriveled and diminished. She had always been the baby of the family, beloved and special to a woman who waited always for a new baby. Until now, Rose Thorn had been that overgrown child, still the one her mother wanted most.

"If this babby was a boy, we could all take a rest," Herself said to the ghost beside her.

"It's a girl, Mama, and you already know it. You can give her everything. It was too much for me to be the youngest. I don't want anything." At first, as Rose Thorn said this, it felt unnatural, like a lie, a martyring, but even before she stopped speaking, it began to feel true. She really didn't want anything except to lie down. And Titus. She still wanted Titus. It would be a long time—years—before she could rouse a real desire for anything else. Even for this child.

"More work ahead, then. No rest for us yet," Herself said. "We'll hide this one away from the brutes the way I should have hidden you. Now let her granny hold her."

Rose Thorn could no longer support the weight in her arms, and so, finally, she held the baby out to Herself.

"How old is she?" Herself breathed as she accepted the bundle.

"Three days."

"Oh, my girl," Herself said. "Ada came by after church and said Prim called looking for you. She said Prim was frantic. But she didn't say nothing about a babby."

"She'd call you if you had a phone. She might have told *you*."

"Imagine what horrors I'd have to listen to if I had a phone," Herself said to the baby in her arms. To Rose Thorn the baby had been a weight pulling her down, but for Herself, cradling the baby was like feeling her connection to the never-ending everything fused into pure, weightless light. In a voice laden with awe, she said, "I'm so glad you're both alive."

"That's what I come home for. To know my mother is glad I'm not dead." To be the youngest was to be the carrier of the hopes you always continue to frustrate. Rose Thorn was through carrying that burden.

"What is this plastic thing your mama's got you wearing?" Herself asked the baby. "And what's this blanket? Smells like the creeping chemicals."

"Mama, I still need you to love me. You still love me, don't you?"

"Of course, but you're careless with love, Rosie. How can a daughter of mine love all the brutes the way you do?"

"I hate Titus Sr.," she said, even though the word *hate* tasted wrong in her mouth. Strange and bitter, a small vial of pure poison. She held onto it, would not let it pass through her. Instead, she would save it inside her like a medicine for later use.

For a while she'd even considered hating Titus Jr., but she couldn't. She loved Titus's great-aunt Ada as well. All her hate would be contained in that single drop allotted to Titus Sr., she decided, and would not infect any other part of her life. She would still love the cranberry bogs of Whiteheart Farms, where she and Titus had kissed endlessly because Titus was sworn to stupidly wait for sex until they were married, even though marriage wasn't any idea of hers. And she would love this baby, this stranger.

Without the baby in her arms, her hand was free to find in her backpack the amber stone Titus had given her when she turned sixteen. "A warm stone," he'd called it, petrified pine sap. Herself had said amber should help her become courageous, but now she felt more afraid than ever. She held it to her chest, whispered, "My heart."

"Be careful with hate," Hermine said. "You can only sustain it at a price." What she didn't say was that she thought hate might help a girl like Rosie, that maybe a girl like Rosie needed a little bit of hate to ground her and keep her wary. "Let's take care of this babby now before we go hating people."

"The nurses said she was healthy, but they didn't understand why she was so quiet."

"Prim took you to the hospital?"

Rose Thorn nodded. "She hates hospitals, but she tricked me into going. She held my hand the whole time. It was almost as hard on her as it was on me."

"Well, don't you worry, little one. We'll figure out what you need right here at home." Herself unwrapped the blanket enough to see a navel cord tied in a knot. Of course, a hospital would cut the cord off too short. "Maybe you'll stay home for a while, Rosie."

"I need a smoke, Mama. I need one bad."

Hermine's whole big body was rousing. With all her daughters gone, she'd felt useless, felt her only purpose was serving the ungrateful brutes of Nowhere. Baba Rose's ghost sidled up to have a look at the baby. Baba Rose had raised foundling after foundling. She had hung the basket under the Boneset Table during a time when the people of Nowhere appreciated a mystery and weren't counting and accounting for every dollar and the whereabouts of every person born. In those days, people were allowed to live quietly in crevices and between known places and out of time even, without paying taxes or otherwise justifying or identifying themselves. Herself always kept a clean blanket in the basket in case anyone needed to give up a child. Though it had been thirty-six years since the last baby, Primrose, had appeared there, just a few days old, Herself still crossed the bridge every morning to have a look.

Herself whispered to the baby, "You are wanted in this world."

Now that Rose Thorn had handed the baby over, she could relax a little. She began to wake up from the stupor of so many months in California, where it was sunny without seasons. Being with Primrose all winter had been a swollen euphoric dream. She'd made Rose Thorn go to school, had taken her every morning, but it had been a different kind of school, where they let her read most of the time, and she'd managed to get her diploma right before having the baby.

It had been a confusing time, not only considering the question of whether to have this baby but also the things Prim had told her that she refused to accept. Rose Thorn had gone to Prim to be with a sister, not another mother. Prim was unfathomable half the time in her lawyer suits and expensive shoes, working hard to be the opposite of Herself; instead of a strong constant river, Prim was a series of sudden deluges. She was better at hauling Rose Thorn out of bed to face the morning than Molly ever had been, but then by evening, after a few drinks, she proclaimed, "To hell with education!" Her terrible confession of incest and subsequent insistence on talking about it had flooded Rose Thorn with revulsion. The implications were impossible to digest.

"I couldn't make sense of anything out there, Mama. I will never believe what she says. You're my mother, and I want to stay here with you forever."

"Not much you can do if a person wants to believe something," Herself said to the baby. "And we'll see what you really want to do, Rosie, when you do it."

In her granny's arms, the baby began to whimper with life. Maybe some instinct had led her to wait for this safe place before making her noise. By the time they walked across the road toward the Boneset Table, the baby was howling, waking up into the frustration of the world of women. The puppy sneezed before trotting across the road after them.

"Is she in pain?" Rose Thorn asked.

"No more than any new creature," Herself said gravely. (Her joy was always a grave business.) "Life isn't easy, especially when you're hungry. When did she last nurse?"

"Three hours ago I tried, but she wouldn't take much, or maybe I don't have much. I'm no good at this," Rose Thorn said. Without the baby in her arms, she felt as if her own life might be possible again, whatever that meant. She lifted her shirt-dress to show her mother the stretched and sagging belly skin. "Mama, she made hamburger meat out of me. My breasts ache. You never told me what it was like."

"I didn't think you'd need to know so soon," Herself said. "Why are you wearing that? Why don't you have on pants or a skirt?"

"I needed to come home, so I had to sneak out of the hospital in a hurry. Prim must've taken my pants home to wash them."

Rose Thorn followed her mother and her daughter over the mosaic of objects pressed into the ground beside the Boneset Table. This entryway to the island was made from generations of women bringing gifts to Herself or Baba Rose or somebody who was here before Baba Rose, pretty stones and fossils and marbles, jewelry, coins, even hardware or bottlecaps. And shells, of course, including those cunt-shells Herself didn't accept, which were most of them. Generations of walking feet had pressed all these objects into the yielding earth to create a kind of tiled surface. Herself removed from around the baby the yellow synthetic blanket and left it on the table. From the basket below, she snatched up the orange wool blanket she'd knitted and softened with bloodroot. Rose Thorn followed Herself down the wooden steps and onto the bridge, three planks wide. The little coyote-colored dog trotted behind, hesitating before setting paws on the weathered bridge planks. They were redwood, installed by Wild Will, and after more than thirty years of foot traffic back and forth showed no mildew or rot. The bridge, over which every bale of hay and sack of grain for their milk cow had to be carried on foot, had no handrail. The pup leaned so far over the edge to sniff the skunk cabbages below that she almost tumbled down into the quickmuck.

"I don't need a dog if it's going to kill my chickens," Herself said. Some dogs had the worst habits of men, but this was her way of saying she would indeed like a good dog, one who would keep rattlesnakes off the island and bark to sound an alarm if any brutes from Nowhere showed up.

The pup startled briefly at her own reflection in a little pool. When she sneezed again, the women stopped and waited for her to tumble off the bridge, but she reared back and then joined them on the island side. When Rose Thorn was little, her mother had kept her from the edge by telling her there was a troll that would eat her if she ever fell in, and she hadn't ever managed to dispel its presence. She'd discovered years earlier that crossing the bridge while drunk was harrowing, troll or no troll.

In the months since Rose Thorn had gone away and left Herself alone with no one to care for, she'd let weeds grow up along the island paths, especially the path of primroses leading to the barnyard, and she hadn't hammered in the nails that were pushing up out of bridge planks where they were nailed into cross members upon the oil barrels that kept the bridge floating. She'd let the top hinge get loose on the door of the Moon Palace, their outdoor toilet. Now Herself would get busy smoothing out all the sharp edges, filling in the holes, hacking away roots that would trip a child. She would try to inspire Rosie to work hard as well. Her right arm flushed and thrilled at the promise of the work.

After they all made it across safely, Herself cranked the handle that lifted away one ten-foot section of three bridge planks so nobody else could join them. The cable operated a device of wheels and pulleys built by Wild Will that required only occasional greasing. Sometimes when Herself closed off the island this way, she fondly remembered the old days of her girlhood, when women and girls from Whiteheart and even Potawatomi and beyond had come to the island by raft for water cures, to bathe in the mineral pools and even take herbal drinks if Baba Rose saw fit. The little girls there with their mothers flitted all over the island, chasing butterflies and picking berries. The girls Herself had raised never seemed so energetic or carefree, maybe because she'd kept them too busy. She vowed to give the new baby more time to play.

"Oh, Mama," Rose Thorn said, "I need to sleep. I hurt all over. I've never hurt this way."

"Sleep is medicine," Herself said. Sometimes the hardest part of Hermine's job was to refuse to listen to the pain on the surface; she couldn't trust herself in the face of it, was tempted to give a fix just to stop the noise. Instead, she knew she had to sit with a body until the mask of pain fell away to reveal what was under it. Ignoring the begging for relief and sympathy, trying not to hear the confessions foisted on her as if she were some sin eater or church sister. Especially the women with cuntshells overfilled her ears. To end a pregnancy beyond a very early stage was a grave business—one that might require Herself to carry the weight of the unborn soul the rest of her days—and most of the time she sent the women on their way with mint tea.

And so when Prim had visited in January, Herself had thought Prim was asking for the medicine for herself, and her irritation and heartsickness had stuck in her throat like a plug of mucus all winter. Finally things were making sense. Herself adjusted this new youngest girl higher onto her breast.

"I'll name her Dorothy," Rose Thorn said, "so she'll always come home. This dog will be her fairy godmother, Ozma."

"Dorothy Rose Zook, I guess," Herself said. "Was she born with a caul?"

"I don't know. It was hard, Mama, so hard. I disappeared in all the hardness. When I screamed too much, Prim said they could dope me, and I don't remember anything else. I think they gave me too much. I woke up and they handed her to me."

"Poor child. She'll be a great burden," Herself said and let the baby's head rest on her right arm. "That's what I see in her, Baba Rose. But we're not afraid of a burden."

"Maybe she'll save you from talking to a ghost."

"The ghosts around here make more sense than the people," Herself said. "You're lucky your sister Molly isn't here. She'd put you back in the hospital, hook this babby up to machines."

"Mama, Dorothy wasn't born here, but she'll be the one who stays here and saves you. I know she will, Mama."

"We'll see what she does when she does it."

The way Rose Thorn kept repeating *Mama* revealed to Herself that Prim had told her the truth, and the girl was resisting knowing it. She figured Rose Thorn's belief in her was every bit as irrational as Titus's belief in his father, but the girl wasn't so stupid that she wouldn't see the ugly truth eventually. Herself wasn't hiding anything. She considered the birthing unimportant compared to the raising. Of the three girls she'd raised so far, she'd only given birth to Molly.

In the kitchen, Rose Thorn sat in a ladder-back chair with a woven seat and drank some tea made with nettle, lemon balm, evening primrose, and wingstem. Herself didn't put merry or poppins in it for the sake of her breast milk, but after a half a cup, Rose Thorn had to lie down. Herself studied her while she slept with the baby, who was not easy in her mother's arms, though they'd removed the plastic diaper and replaced it with a soft cotton one with a wool cover. There was some kind of shadowy body between mother and baby, keeping them apart.

When Rose Thorn slept, it was easy to see how her peculiar brightness was her strange burden, would be so as long as it lasted, and then its absence might prove just as ruinous. How would such a beauty who barely touched the ground ever become a grown-up, a mother, someone old? The world was already eating her alive; better she be a storm like Primrose or a bossy bully like Molly, whom Herself sometimes called, if only to herself, Misery.

ROSE THORN HAD SOMEHOW held her parts together on her journey home, but once she got to the island, she collapsed and could not imagine how to reassemble herself. She missed Prim now as much as she'd missed Herself while in California. Her depression felt like her spirit dying, and so she tried to revive it with spirit from her mother's cupboard.

And whether the cause was physical or emotional, despite the ache in her breasts, her milk was not forthcoming. There was a time when the women of Nowhere would offer to nurse a neighbor child, but these days, there was no wet nurse to call upon. Denied her rightful mother's milk, the baby refused the creamy stuff from Hermine's milk cow. Titus's great-aunt Ada, who could be trusted to keep a secret, brought scalded goat milk—which was thinner and sweeter than cow's milk—and later store-bought baby formula, to no avail. In desperation, Herself even tried pea protein powder and soy calf starter made with boiled well water. The only milk the child would drink was donkey milk from the freezer, and there were only a few quarts there that Hermine had preserved for medicines. When it was almost gone, when all else failed with this stubborn child who threatened to starve, Herself went out at night and fetched the spotted jenny, Aster, who was due to foal in a month.

Aster, twenty years old, had been a gift from Wild Will. She was Hermine's good donkey, her companion who carried tools and even wooden posts for her when she had to fix the pasture fence, who helped pull big burdock roots out of the ground. She was the good body in which she'd made antivenom since Wild Will had gone. But Herself couldn't wait a month for the medicinal milk for the baby. If there'd been any other source of donkey milk, she wouldn't have done what she did. She was tempted to wish Wild Will home to do this awful task, but she wasn't ready to forgive him, and as a rule she was wary of the dangers of wishing.

At Boneset, she brought Aster inside the barn and locked Triumph out. She tied Aster's back legs in a hobble, tied her nose close to the post, and said, "I'm sorry, my good girl." She rigged up a bladder Wild Will had used for hauling water, filled it with salt water, and as Triumph crashed again and again into the wooden stock gate to get to his mate, Herself forced the salt water into poor Aster's uterus through a length of hose until the donkey lay panting in anguish. The next morning the unfinished foal lay dead in the straw, and Aster was beginning to swell with milk. Herself lamented the loss of that foal, who would have been sturdy and solid, as Aster's foals always were, and even more she lamented the loss of the relationship with her donkey, but she saw that her cruelty was justified when her granddaughter drank—and drank and drank—the donkey milk.

Herself could have created a medicine for Aster to do the same terrible work more gently and insidiously—she'd done it that way for more than two dozen women who'd come to her—but this would have ruined weeks of milk, without which she was certain the baby would have starved or required some kind of hospital force-feeding that still might have failed. Herself knew as well as any soldier in war how a life was often preserved at the cost of another life, but it didn't make it easy to live with what she'd done to her jenny, as it didn't make it easy when she helped women in that way. She buried the dead foal in the garden at Boneset, in front of Wild Will's house, while Aster listened from the stall in which she was imprisoned, her great ears pinned back, her ribs under her spotted coat still heaving days after her induced miscarriage. With his hooves, Triumph dug a passionate trench eighteen inches deep at the barn gate before giving up and going off to graze.

Herself fed Aster tender grasses and sprouts to apologize, but the first time she unfastened the hobble, Aster stomped Hermine's left foot hard and broke a half dozen small bones there. That was why she kept Aster tied and hobbled for five months, all during her milk letting. Rose Thorn visited the stall where Aster was imprisoned several times a week and talked to her or brushed her, and that soothed her some, but if a donkey could have held back all her milk from spite, Aster might have done it. Instead, each morning and night she let down enough to keep the baby alive. Usually, Herself froze the donkey milk and doled it out to the community two ounces at a time, but the precious stuff now all went into this hungry baby. For this reason, and because the baby had big ears, Herself called the child Donkey instead of Dorothy. By this nickname, they would remember the pain and trouble she had caused and to whom she owed her life.

Folks had long been in the habit of watching Herself for any evidence of curious behavior that might foretell troubles, and word got around that she had caused that jenny to abort her foal. A number of people got the idea that what she had done was pure meanness. Herself, in her usual reticence, and also consumed by her new distraction, did nothing to unkink their twist on the truth, which passed from house to house, flavored by the new reverend's sermons. The consensus: the old witch had beaten the donkey and aborted the foal as a way to prevent there being any healing milk for the children of Whiteheart. Others complained that she refused to help the men of the town, when the truth was that most medicines for men required m'sauga blood, which was in short supply. With their men and babies neglected, the town grew angry.

Though Aster held a grudge against Herself forever after the violence perpetrated on her, she instinctively loved the child who grew up across the road on M'sauga Island. It is true that we love best those for whom we suffer most.

CHAPTER FOUR

A child will make of her world an education.

O N T H E S E C O N D S A T U R D A Y in May, having just turned eleven years old, Donkey awoke under the waning Egg Moon, overheated, unable to breathe, caught in one of Hermine's embracing dreams, held against that granny's big body with its hard pounding heart by one of those powerful arms. Herself was gripping her too tightly, and Donkey sensed how the old woman's teeth had grown sharp as grizzly teeth, how hair had sprouted on her arms, and Donkey feared being eaten, feared being trapped inside the great belly of the tree-bear to drown along with all the sins of Whiteheart.

It took some strength to disentangle herself from those heavy slumberous arms, and when she was free, Donkey sat up on the pillow and calmed her heart, studied the body beside her, which must have instantly shed its teeth and thick fur, because now it looked more like a felled oak. In contrast to the girl's pink wiggling fingers and toes, Hermine's hands and feet at the ends of her limbs were brown, leathery, and twisted. She was wrinkled, crenelated as bark, studded with strange hairs, some fine, some wiry. Her ears were great floppy things, a pair of shelf funguses, sticking out from long titmouse-gray hair. But her teeth—which had somehow returned to normal size and lost their points—were shiny from rarely eating sweets other than pie and from rinsing her mouth after she ate fruits and berries, even bread. Herself ate bone marrow every day, but she cracked open the bones with a little hammer on a cutting board and never gnawed them. In spite of

Hermine's positive example, Donkey stubbornly refused to eat meat. She preferred talking to animals, studying them. Hermine wondered if it was her own regret for hurting Aster that somehow settled upon the girl, and she felt she had to eat twice as much to nourish this child.

Though earlier that week they'd removed the milky plastic from the bedroom windows, the fog outside—a vapor rooted firmly in the Waters—prevented Donkey from seeing much beyond the room, and she basked there on the bed in the pure light of Hermine's favor for now, listening to the phoebes in their nest just outside the window. As the youngest, she would inherit the island a quarter mile long, with its cottage and sheds and artesian wells and swamp pools and magnificent gnarled oaks and pawpaw trees and millions of living things that had habits worth observing and documenting in her notebook, which she knew was the center of her education. Everybody else had gone away, but she intended to stay—as Hermine, the youngest of her own generation, had stayed—to keep what was hers.

Donkey was supposed to wake her granny in the morning, to shake her out of dreams, but Donkey was enjoying being awake alone this morning. She listened to the chorus frogs conversing about mayflies, sulfur-scented swamp gas, and hungry hawks. Listened for news of Rose Thorn's return, which, like Persephone's, was always in spring. Whenever her mother was gone, Donkey wished for her return every morning. She did this despite Hermine's warnings about how dangerous wishing could be, how wishes could come true in ways you didn't want. If Rose Thorn couldn't come back to M'sauga Island today, then when? Donkey wanted to know this as much as she wanted to know the square root of negative one, for she had recently taken an interest in mathematics, after her terrible aunt Primrose sent a series of math books.

Aunt Molly educated her twice or three times a week, on her days off, but she only brought library books that had to be returned. Books from Prim were books Donkey could keep. Molly herself could barely do long division and said if Donkey wanted to know math, she should go to school. But Rose Thorn had iterated the dangers of school vividly: teachers tied you in your chair and stepped on your feet with their boot heels and yanked your braids if you got a wrong answer. Molly also said Donkey and Herself should move off the island altogether. It was not civilized and not hygienic, and it was dangerous besides, with no way to get there but the three-plank-wide bridge that still didn't have a railing, across which they had to carry bales of alfalfa for Delilah, the milk cow. Molly said the island was the family curse, because Herself wouldn't live anywhere else.

Now, sitting up in her granny's bed, Donkey felt the slithering of creatures moving under the island fog as though across her bare skin. She always wriggled out of her clothes in the night and woke up naked. She slid back under the covers and reached down to the floor for her T-shirt and then retrieved her underwear and jeans from under the covers at the foot of the bed. She was eleven years old and five foot eleven inches tall, old enough and big enough to sleep alone, *for crying out loud*, according to Molly, but the little bedroom off the kitchen was lonely without Rose Thorn. Every middle of the night when Donkey heard the snoring that meant Herself was done tossing and turning over other people's problems, she slipped out of her sheets, fed Baba Rose's kitchen fire, and padded down the hall to lie beside the big body, to inhale the scent of lavender and holy basil, to count those voluminous breaths and resounding heartbeats. During the day, Herself was stern and commanding, spoke little and never flattered, just mumbled her irritation over food and medicine and the brutes of Nowhere, but anybody who slept beside Hermine knew she became luxuriant in her joints, that she relaxed her muscles and released herself to colorful, tender, loving dreams that Donkey glimpsed in her own sleep. While Donkey's personal dreams were of animals, Hermine's were often of the island's trees and plants and soil, though often she shared sensual visions of her difficult daughters and even of Wild Will, whom Donkey secretly admired.

Donkey hoped Herself would stay asleep longer so she could read the latest book her terrible aunt Primrose had sent, *Garden of Logic* by Professor A. Schweiss, without being asked to dig up ramps, sniff for mushrooms, and scrape off tree sap resin. In a minute, she would sneak out onto the screened porch to read, and while she was there, she could also look for the man in camouflage who had been coming to Boneset some days, to the very edge of the swamp. He wasn't the first man to study the island that way, but he was the latest, and she enjoyed the way he sneaked and slithered. Donkey went ahead and wished he would be there again today so she could watch him watch, even though men would be the ruin of the island one day, according to Herself.

"Rose Thorn will come home from California when she's good and ready. Women do what they want," Donkey said, in imitation of Hermine's voice, and still Herself didn't wake up. If she wanted to be heard for sure, Donkey had to talk in a low throaty voice, which Aunt Molly declared was "creepy in a girl." Molly seemed not to realize that Herself didn't hear most of what she said, either because she couldn't or she didn't want to.

Donkey leaned out of the bed and looked underneath it for a bridge troll—though Molly said there was no troll under the bridge or anywhere else—or a murderous Lindworm dragon-snake before putting her feet on the floor. She paused to crouch at the end of the bed to nuzzle old Ozma's neck and ears. The dog sighed contentedly on her rug. Donkey used to assume Ozma was her twin, and she used to wish for Ozma to turn into a human sister, but if the dog became a person now, she'd probably be another old woman, which showed one way a wish could go wrong.

"Watch out Herself doesn't eat you today, Ozma."

Donkey remained on all fours into the hallway, only rising up onto her back legs when she was in the kitchen. Despite her remarkable height, Donkey could see little to be gained by growing up or behaving in a mature way. She shook up a half-full quart jar of Jersey cow milk from the refrigerator to mix in the cream and drank it down. In the bedroom off the kitchen, Rose Thorn's Room, she opened the bottom drawer of the dresser and took out the framed photograph of her grandfather Wild Will at his most magnificent: tall with muscles bulging below his short shirtsleeves, each fist wrapped around the neck of a live dangling m'sauga, his rose-and-rattlesnake tattoo like Titus's glowing on his biceps. She liked looking at the picture every day, liked especially that he had eyes like Rose Thorn's, and she often wished for his return, though Herself said she wasn't ready to forgive him yet, after only twenty-nine years. Donkey always put the photo back after a minute or so, because Herself would toss it in the swamp if she saw it, the way she'd tossed his brass rattlesnake keychain when Donkey asked what it was. She didn't toss away his clothes or tools, though, since they were useful.

From the hook inside the front door, Donkey took Titus's well-worn army field jacket with CLAY stitched above the pocket. The cuffs were starting to fray, but she loved the bigness of it, the manliness of it, the soft feel of the worn cotton, even the collar detail of two snakes wrapped around a staff in the symbol of the caduceus, which signified that Titus had been training to become a medic in the four months before his thinblood got him discharged. He had given the jacket to Rose Thorn, and she had worn it all the time, but she'd left in such a hurry last time that she'd forgotten to take it with her.

Donkey opened the door just enough to slip onto the screened porch, where she took *Garden of Logic* from the inside pocket of the jacket, where it fit exactly. The book contained 144 (12^2) short chapters of mathematical truths. Primrose was terrible because she had taken Rose Thorn away to California, but the books she'd sent were excellent and logical, especially this one. It said that a logical life was a life worth living and advised Donkey to keep her own list of true things, and so she sat down now and inked across the front of her notebook the title *True Things* #1. (From this point on, she would title all her numbered notebooks *True Things*.) She had for years recorded in her notebooks all kinds of facts that Herself didn't think were worth knowing, things she'd counted and measured. Even the recipes for medicines and food were written down, though Herself claimed there were no recipes, that every medicine and meal was new each time.

She sat at the table on the screened porch and opened the cover of the book to reread the inscription from her aunt: *Maybe you can grow up and bring some good sense into this family*. Logic wasn't just common sense, according to the book; it was a language just like English or Dog or Frog, and it was the language of mathematics, the language of deciphering truth, and it came from off the island, which made it more delicious. Donkey had begun devouring the book like an entire peach pie, but when she got to the chapter about ∞, she decided to slow down. Infinity spooked her—worse than that. She hated how ∞ carried a whiff of death, since both were forever. The author, Professor A. Schweiss, had written that ∞ was to be found even in small things: *You might expect to find infinity in the great expanses, but you're just as likely to find it in the body of a worm, my friend*. Though Donkey had only had the book a few days, the author A. Schweiss had become another man in her life, along with Wild Will, Titus, and the man in camouflage.

She read now about squares fitting inside circles and about cubes poured into bowls like chunks of breakfast cereal. As you made your cubes smaller, the empty space between the cubes in the bowl also got smaller, but there would always be some space left between any flat edge and any curved one—unless you made your cubes infinitely small, which Donkey had no intention of doing. This story of cubes in bowls was as compelling as "The Lindworm Prince," a story she often read aloud to Herself, in which a boy's twin brother was a large and murderous snake. Herself needed Donkey to do all her reading for her, since she'd never learned how.

Donkey went outside onto the landing to search for Rose Thorn on the bridge eleven steps below. Rose Thorn wasn't there, and she didn't see the man in camouflage. She hungered to spot him, to slowly distinguish his figure lying on the ground, somewhere in the foliage, pointing his gun and then putting it down. She might only see him when he moved, the mysterious body shifting like a piece of the mottled landscape through the swamp grasses and elderberry bushes, his sneaking no more noticeable than a snake's or a fox's. The man was not tall and rangy like Titus but wiry and short with narrow shoulders and big boots. This man's rifle seemed like a natural extension of his body when he aimed, a coming together of two arms into one. Hermine's hearing was so poor now that she wouldn't hear him even if he stepped on a stick and broke it. As much as Rose Thorn had warned Donkey about school with its cruelties and tortures, Herself had warned her about men and how they would trick you and take you away and make you forget who you were. And it's better you don't have a father, Herself said, when Donkey complained about that.

Every day Donkey heard gunshots around them, from the gun club to the east and from the river to the north and occasionally from Lovers Road. Last summer, she'd returned from gathering sassafras bark and wild grapes at the top of the island and found six holes in the porch screen—three on the east side and three on the west—where the bullets must have passed through. She'd said nothing to anyone, simply repaired the holes with little pieces of screen to keep the clever zizzing mosquitoes out. Bullet holes would have excited Molly, and even Herself if she thought there was a threat that Donkey might be shot. She might say Donkey had to move into Molly's tin can in the trailer park. In January, Donkey had found a bullet embedded in the living room wall. After she'd dug it out, she found two other holes in the opposite wall by the window, either one of which could have been the entry hole. Because she didn't want to make Herself toss in her sleep any more than she already did, she had merely recorded in her notebook the surprising fact: *A bullet can travel through a wall.* Likewise, when she sometimes found arrows stuck in the roots of trees, she quietly unscrewed the shafts and used them to stake plants in the poison garden, where Herself grew hemlock, tall thimbleweed, white snakeroot, swamp milkweed, poison sumac, and bloodroot. Poison ivy with its white berries was ubiquitous on the island and didn't need any special place.

This morning the island was alive with flowery and moldy fragrances, alive with the urgent trills and chips of birdsong, while more quietly, down low, sounds of scurrying and munching. The island was bursting with spring things to count and measure and eat—ramps and wild onion sprouts, three-leaved trillium and speckled trout lily, dandelions, horse tails, tender new nettles for tea, pokeweed shoots to boil, fiddlehead ferns to fry. This was the kind of day Rose Thorn would come home, a spring day on which the fog thinned—it never disappeared entirely from the low spots—and morels came up. But last year they'd harvested those mushrooms, then the asparagus, strawberries, raspberries, the summer squashes, the beans, the staghorn sumac, the wild rice, the disappointing crop of tomatoes, and the poor pumpkins, and, finally, the worm-chewed Brussels sprouts, and still Rose Thorn never came. And no wonder, since the last time she had come home, Molly had shackled her to a bed in the hospital "for her own good" after Rosie burned herself three times with a coffin nail on purpose. Donkey had smelled her mother's burning skin, but worse was visiting the hospital two days later, going into a chemical-stinking room to see Rose Thorn's arms tied to the gleaming bedrails, her feet similarly tethered. As soon as Prim, flown in from California, got them to untie her with a threat of legal action, Rose Thorn left town with her, without even coming back to the island. Donkey, who hated even the word *California*, had refused to go away with them or to even listen to why Rose Thorn had to go. She belonged here, on her island with Herself, and so did Rose Thorn.

Now, as Donkey traveled alone from the Moon Palace to the compost pile—where a possum had chewed the bones she'd thrown out last night—she enjoyed being a planet in orbit around Herself inside the cottage. Some mornings orbiting could feel like freedom, though each night she looked forward to crashing back down on the home planet.

Be careful not to fall in the quickmuck, Donkey warned herself, imitating her granny's voice. *Be careful of men. And poison ivy and rattlesnakes.*

She paused briefly in a circle of big stones she'd arranged just past the cowshed and henhouse, under pawpaws that hadn't leafed out yet, and sat listening to a male redwing blackbird's repeated *Conk-la-ree!* She studied the big old mother swamp oak trees, their galls like grisly breasts. Incredible that with all these raucous birds Herself could still be asleep, with no idea what Donkey was doing! Similarly, Donkey had recently made mathematical discoveries about fractions and conic sections in her notebook right at the supper table, while the old woman was completely unaware. Donkey climbed inside the hollow sycamore tree where Rose Thorn said a ghost had twice appeared. She called him "the old bartender" and said he was tall and gray and had a beard. As a girl, Rose Thorn used to sit inside the hollow tree and read Oz books. Now, a bottle of ginger brandy had been waiting there more than a year, like bait in a trap, its label mold-speckled and peeling. Donkey thought she'd seen the old bartender a few times in the swamp—tall and thin, slipping in and out of sight in the fog, far from the island— but she never mentioned men to Herself, not even ghost men.

Outside the hollow tree, there was no breeze, but the leaf litter crinkled. Donkey kicked aside leaves to see tangles of shiny earthworms, as slick as Titus and Rose Thorn in their knotted embraces, which Donkey had witnessed in the Boneset barn. She kicked the leaves back over the worms.

She followed the path lined with garden primroses to the cowshed and henhouse. The flowers already bloomed brilliant red, pink, and yellow with no attention whatsoever. Last year, without Rose Thorn at home, they were the only flowers to bloom with any vigor. Herself called them useless, though even she couldn't stop glancing at their bright, artificial-looking color. Wild Will had planted them as a gift forty-some years earlier, when Primrose was a girl, and they continued to grow now, even when Herself walked on them or stabbed them with her snake stick—the curved wooden stick she carried that had been specially carved for her by Wild Will to unearth, poke, and move plants and animals. She was delicate and respectful of most of the island's other growing things, including the evening primrose, an entirely different plant, tall and rangy with a pale-yellow blossom, that eased skin and breast pain.

Following last year's cold, wet spring that had rotted seeds in the ground, a summer drought ensued, and battalions of millipedes marched across the upstream half of the island, an omen of inconstant love. And it was true that dozens of women had come to ask for the philter Herself made with catnip, honey, and rosebuds—and a tiny amount of poisonous thimbleweed. During peach season last year, Titus had taken up with Lorena, who came to Whiteheart Farms to pick fruit and stayed with him in the shed. She made him a pie every Saturday and had a secret way of cutting it into seven equal pieces, one for every breakfast. She also had a trick for nursing unripe peaches along in cold storage so that even in December, she was able to make Titus a fresh peach pie. Titus had had other girlfriends while Rose Thorn was gone before, but whenever she came back, those girlfriends disappeared. The cycle had gone on since Donkey could remember, and that's what would happen again when Rose Thorn came home. Maybe this time she would finally agree to marry Titus, and then Titus could be Donkey's father. Who else was there for the job?

Donkey went to the henhouse to collect eggs from their twenty (2^2 x 5) chickens and to say hello to each one of them, including Billina, who liked to be held, and Big Scratch—black-and-white like a checkerboard—who liked to peck her shoes. Then she stopped to inspect Delilah, grazing in the far corner of her paddock. There at the paddock fence, Donkey was struck by a musky mushroom scent, something between an oyster and a morel, a scent she only gradually remembered. Even before she saw anything, she sensed the curve of life and was drawn close to a ruffle-scaled brown-beaded snake stretched into an S under the fence. At first, she figured it was a hog-nose, puffed up to look dangerous, and she put down the basket of eggs and did what she always did with any snake or turtle or rabbit or crayfish in her territory. She crawled on hands and knees toward it silently, toward the patch of diffuse sunlight across which it stretched.

From the crow's point of view—at any hour there was always at least one crow watching over the island—this was simply one curious creature approaching another, neither harboring ill intent. Because Donkey knew that ground-huggers feared what loomed above them, when she got closer, she dropped to her belly. The snake was fat all through its body, and the knotted tail reminded her of her own blond braid when she'd cut it off a few years ago, to Hermine's dismay; it was finally grown out below her shoulders again. She'd never come across a m'sauga on her own—and never on the island—had never had an opportunity to know a live rattlesnake or learn its language. Herself had told Donkey that if she ever did see a m'sauga, anywhere, she was supposed to run or paddle home and get help right away. She planned to do that now. Shortly. Experimentally, she darted her tongue out.

Donkey had heard the buzz-rattle from the swamp most every summer day of her life, a sound as natural and comforting as the water trickling around and beneath them, as familiar as frog song and chipping crickets and cicadas, and on summer evenings the nasal *beer* of a nighthawk, but she'd never gotten to listen to it up close. Herself had always sent her out of the way, where it was safe. Now Donkey studied the snake's rich swamp-mud pattern made up of thousands of colored scales, its spine saddled by dozens of chocolate-colored moth shapes. On top of those mud colors was a golden sheen like that on butterfly wings.

Herself had never allowed rattlesnakes to stay on the island, as they were a danger to little girls, and she regularly walked the island and shouted for them to be gone or else become medicine. What did it mean that a m'sauga had remained there anyway to meet a dark fate after being told to leave? The snake lifted its triangular head to study Donkey at eye level with equal measures of fear, anger, and curiosity. The snake's eyes were golden with vertical pupils, like cat eyes, and the girl's eyes were round and blue in their pools of white. As Donkey pushed herself forward, arms at her sides, the snake began to buzz more loudly. Imitation had always been Donkey's best teacher, so she buzzed in return. Then she whispered, "*Sistrurus catenatus*," the Latin name for this swamp rattlesnake, which sounded like *sister*. Its venom was stronger than that of any other rattlesnake, though it released that venom in only tiny amounts through its short fangs; bites were rarely deadly to anybody older than a baby. Old Baba Rose had died from a m'sauga bite, but she was old and frail by then, weighed down by a long life of healing and a necklace of more than a hundred cuntshells. Donkey slid closer, got within about a yard before the m'sauga retracted its head, tensing like a heron readying for flight.

Donkey froze in place. "Are you the Lindworm?" she whispered. The Lindworm, a monstrous firstborn twin unwanted by its mother, was thrown out the window shortly after its birth. It came back eventually to claim its birthright. In Donkey's family, where the youngest inherited everything, she didn't have to fear any such thing.

The snake's triangular head ventured toward her a few inches. Donkey was almost too excited to breathe. The creature studied her sullenly.

"If you're the Lindworm, then you're my twin brother," Donkey said. She could feel how the snake was feeling her wild heartbeat through the ground between them.

The forked tongue tasted the air. The body undulated, and the head came even closer.

"I won't hurt you," Donkey whispered. "But when Herself catches you, she'll cajole you out of your venom."

Herself would catch it, as she had caught so many m'saugas in the Waters, and milk it for venom, then freeze the creature alive in a gunny sack in the chest freezer so she could kill and skin it on the porch table. Parts would be used for making a stuck woman bleed and for healing wounds. Herself would put the hollow-needle fangs in a jar, mash the venom glands to capture any remaining poison and dry the eyeballs on brown paper. And most importantly, she would drain the snake blood; it usually took only the tiniest part of a diluted drop to make a medicine for a man. Then the kitchen would fill and overflow with the stink of cooking snake flesh, which Herself devoured as though she were starving, as though it were a remedy for all the terrible secrets that weighed her down.

In "The Lindworm Prince," the magical instructions were not for killing the serpent but provided a specific way to turn it into a brother: a girl had to wear layers of clothes that she could shed like snakeskins, and she had to scrub the snake with lye and a stiff brush. Donkey slowly brought her right hand out in front of her to touch the creature's shining back.

Without warning, her whole body was yanked up into the air and pulled straight backward. It felt like flying. After she landed with an *oof* on the soft ground several yards away from the m'sauga, Donkey lay on her belly under Hermine's tree-bear shadow. The basket of brown and white eggs lay on its side.

Herself pulled Donkey to her feet and retrieved her tall crooked stick with a snake ascending toward the knob at the top and a sharp prong that forked the tip. "Go get a clean bucket with a lid," Herself said. "Hurry."

By the time Donkey got back from the cowshed with the white five-gallon bucket, with Delilah mooing to be milked behind her, Herself was in the paddock gently lifting the m'sauga at its middle with the curved part of her stick, bringing the sliding body toward her, thwarting the Lindworm's efforts to flow away toward the swamp channel. With this repeated lifting, Herself slowly moved the creature out of the paddock. She motioned for Donkey to move away and then lifted and deposited the body like a flowing muddy stream into the bucket, where it coiled upon itself. Donkey only got a peek before Herself capped it.

"Is this how you're going to pull snakeroot?" Herself asked, and Donkey noticed some early shoots of the weed near her feet—something that would poison Delilah's milk if she ate it. There was also poke-weed she should have picked. Full-grown pokeweed was poisonous, but these little shoots were good when boiled three times. She'd been blind to everything but the m'sauga.

"He wasn't going to bite me," Donkey said in the loud, low voice she used to make it easier for Herself to hear her. She slumped as she spoke. She'd been taller than Herself for more than a year, but she still wasn't comfortable towering over the old woman in such moments. And there was no denying that once a rattlesnake was on the island, it was medicine.

"Now you're an authority on m'saugas?" Herself asked. "This snake is a *she*."

"How do you know?"

"Count her scales. Aren't you the one who counts everything?"

"I didn't know how to tell."

"Well, if you get bitten by a rattlesnake, you'll know something you didn't know before."

"You can cure me with antivenom."

"No matter if I cure you. Molly will know and take you away from me. Ask her what will happen if you get bitten. I can't have a girl on the island who messes with dangerous medicine."

"It's not fair that you kill every animal. It's not even logical." Donkey had never argued with Herself about a medicine before.

"She has the whole swamp to hide in, and she chooses to come here and show herself."

"You just say that because you want to eat her."

"If she bites you, *you'll* eat her."

Everybody knew that when Wild Will got bitten, Herself cooked the snake and fed it to him right there on the island, and then he married her.

"I never will eat a snake, ma'am." The word *ma'am* felt good in her mouth because she'd just read about palindromes in *Garden of Logic*. Her age, eleven, was also a palindrome. Their good neighbor, Ada, who made delicious pies, was one too.

"You want a bird to not eat a bug? You go talk to your phoebe in her nest, tell her not to feed her babbies."

"They can eat berries."

"Now you're an authority on what birds should eat. Baba Rose, when did my granddaughter decide she knows better than me and every other creature?"

Donkey always forgot Baba Rose was with them; Hermine carried her mother—the woman who had raised her—in her right hand, and at night Baba Rose was the flame in the cookstove, which was why Donkey had to be sure to feed the fire. A ghost would only stay around if people wanted it there, if they worked to keep it around.

Donkey walked beside Herself, carrying the basket, in which three brown eggs had gotten cracked. They would eat those first. The white eggs were for medicine. When Herself carried the snake bucket onto the screened porch, Ozma lost her mind barking and then bolted past them out the door like a much younger dog. Ozma was a strong swimmer, but she didn't usually run like she was doing now. The screen door banged shut, and Ozma settled under the porch. Herself sent Donkey out to check the Babby Basket and change the blanket if it was wet or dusty from the road, something Herself usually did after breakfast. This meant Hermine wasn't planning to sit out by the road today.

No surprise there was no baby; there never was.

Then they milked Delilah together. Donkey milked a little more each day to build up her hand strength but still let Herself do the final stripping. Then they strained the milk and bottled it in wide-mouth quart jars, which they put in the refrigerator in a way Donkey had devised that indicated which jars were older and which newer so they used them in the right order. Every week or so they skimmed the layer of cream off the chilled milk and made butter. Hermine made coffee with eggshells to drink and bacon and eggs for herself and oatmeal and buttered toast and eggs for Donkey, along with three morels they'd found, and they ate at the porch table. In winter, when the screened porch was full of firewood, the porch table was turned on its side out of the way. Now, in May, only a few rows of split oak remained, stacked at the far end of the porch, and they could eat their meals in the open air. A wind came through the south-facing screens, skipped over Herself and blew across Donkey's freckled skin, raising gooseflesh, lifting the scent of the snake from the bucket under the table.

Herself massaged her right biceps, which she often did when she talked to Baba Rose. She stared into the marshy expanse of widely spaced maple, ash, and cedar, mossy bog islands, wild rice marshes, cattails, and button bushes. Herself said the Waters would give them what they needed when they needed it. As naturally as the swamp contained boneset for fevers and snake grass for aching joints, it included m'saugas.

"The brutes of Nowhere are restless," Herself said, releasing her biceps. "They tear up the grass with their truck tires because they want their fixes. We need this snake's blood."

Donkey sat up straight. "Maybe you could keep her in a cage and milk her every day, and she would give you some of her blood too. And I can measure her, see if she grows."

"Did that snake tell you she wants to live in a cage?" Herself glared at Donkey until Donkey shrank back down. "Does she want to be bled and measured? When you're the keeper of this island, you can keep all your snakes in cages and feed them berries. You can sell this island to your aunt Molly's snake-handler church, and they'll put m'saugas in burlap sacks and keep them in the dark basement."

"But, ma'am, why do you have to eat every animal?" Donkey shouted. She tried to rise up from the table, but Herself held her wrist.

"You think you're not eating animals, Donkey? That milk, that butter—you're just eating Delilah a little at a time. You think you're not eating a chicken in those eggs?"

"I'm not."

"You think the grapes in that jelly and the oats in your bowl aren't made out of the bodies and bones of everything that crawls and creeps on this earth? You want to know so much, you'd better know that." Herself let go of Donkey and went back to massaging her right biceps, tried to milk from it the patience she needed for this confounding granddaughter.

Donkey put down her spoon. There was a new push and pull between them lately, but their arguments didn't last long. Soon Donkey picked her spoon back up, and while she was eating, she took comfort in the few things Herself didn't know, such as mathematics. Such as the man with the gun at the edge of Boneset, Donkey's own secret man.

When they finished eating, Herself sharpened her paring knife on a stone. The knife had been made by Wild Will and was precious to her, like the bridge and the contraption he had made a few years later for pulling up the boards to keep people from sneaking onto the island. He had also built the Moon Palace and installed a door in Hermine's bedroom leading outside. But Wild Will was also the betrayer she had sent away, whose personal objects (rattlesnake keychain, photographs) she tossed into the swamp; he was the owner of the boarded-up house Donkey was forbidden to enter. Donkey imagined Wild Will as a Wizard of Oz, pulling levers and assembling objects and devices. Maybe he wasn't what he said he was, but he was fine and strong anyway. This small bluish blade, which Herself would use to cut the snake's skin away, had been worn thin and narrow over the years. Donkey wondered where the rest of that blade had gone. Maybe every time Herself sharpened it, she inhaled the steel dust so she would have enough steel to make another knife inside her, something she could use in a pinch to get the two of them out of a wolf's belly.

"You probably want to eat Ozma too," Donkey said in the lowest register she had. Talking to Herself this way could be painful to the throat. At the sound of her name spoken this way, Ozma, outside on the landing, barked once.

"She would be tough," Herself said and hid a smile. Though she was grateful this child would not be afflicted with her mother's beauty, she wondered if a calculating mind would be just as dangerous.

The warm breeze carried the angry scent of the snake out into the swamp toward the Old Woman River in the distance.

"Does it hurt a rattlesnake to milk it?" Donkey asked after a while.

"It puts her in a mood."

"*I'm in no mood*," Donkey said aloud to herself, imitating Molly's voice and phrasing. This was the same tone Molly used to tell Donkey to stop chewing her hair, because a girl in the hospital chewed her hair so much the doctors had to cut her stomach open to take out a big hairball they then kept in a jar in the lab.

Molly had had the healing touch since she was a girl—it was what inspired her to be a nurse to begin with—but now she got mad at any mention of it. Rose Thorn said, "They educated it out of her." Donkey thought she'd call Molly "M," because she couldn't think of any better palindrome for her.

Donkey slid under the table and, bent double, scooted up to the bucket. The snake thumped against the side as Donkey touched the lid. Herself said, "Don't!"

"I know. I won't. But she says she can't breathe," Donkey said in a voice that she thought might be like the snake's low rattling voice.

"Maybe you'd know an animal better if you ate one now and again," Herself said.

Donkey liked to argue sometimes, but what she liked best was returning to Herself and being embraced as the favorite.

Donkey crawled out from under the table and followed Herself into the kitchen with her dishes. She watched Herself stretch plastic wrap over the top of a baby food jar and tighten a rubber band around the neck. The kitchen table, except for a small clear area for eating at one corner near the stove, was covered with an array of herbs in bowls; moth wings and dried crickets in paper cones; shiny money flowers in the bronze Primrose vase (precious because it was made by Prim when she was young, before she was terrible); roots and bark drying on paper bags; six pieces of spruce-sap chewing gum dusted with powdered sugar and placed on waxed paper on a moon-colored plate; plus shells and stones with interesting colors and shapes, collected by Donkey. Next time Herself went out to Boneset to sit and listen to people, Donkey would go along and press these objects strategically into the mosaic on the ground next to the table. There, what had once been a blob shape, Donkey was making a perfect rectangle. Also on the table, a lumpy bowl that Prim had made to match the vase, and in it, a few notes asking for healing medicine. Women slipped these notes into Hermine's hands even though she couldn't read. Donkey read them to her.

"The way you talk," Herself said, "when I die, you'll give this island over to rattlesnakes and men and looselife." *Looselife* was her term for purple loosestrife, an invasive swamp flower that was taking over the Waters and pushing out joe-pye weed and cardinal flowers.

"Rose Thorn said you won't ever die."

"We're all dying, child. Do you remember how to sink me in the Waters with rocks? Then you can do what you want with the island. Sell it to the snake handlers."

"You don't have to say it every day," Donkey said. Herself insisted she had to be buried this way in the quickmuck with her necklace of souls. "But if this snake is my sister, I should help her."

"When you're the boss, you can coddle all the m'saugas," Herself said. "Can you sit still and clam up while I cajole her, child? Or would you be better off outside?"

Back on the screened porch, Donkey sat on the dwindling stack of firewood with the notebook *True Things* on her lap, struggling to stay clammed, constructing a triangle of palindromes in which every two numbers beside each other added up to the one below and between, Pascal's triangle as described by Professor A. Schweiss in *Garden of Logic*. The triangle could go on forever, but it didn't have to.

1
11
121
1331
14641

Herself poked gingerly into the bucket with her stick, which sent the big snake thrashing hard enough to rock the bucket against the porch boards. Once the fork at the tip of the stick was placed securely over the snake's neck to hold it still, Herself reached in and took hold of the head, and then she let go of the stick. With her other hand near the tail, she gently lifted out the fat, angry body, releasing a musky underground scent. Donkey marveled at the muscular tension in the creature. The wrathful cat eyes rested upon Donkey, who squeezed her hands together so hard her eyes watered. Donkey knew this Lindworm was no ordinary snake.

Herself hummed and half sang a milking song as she guided the neck and head in her capable right hand and held the body just above the tail in her wise left hand. Moving the writhing body out in front of her, she appeared to be dancing with it, the way she sometimes danced Donkey around when a warm wind came upon them during a nighttime walk. Donkey's greatest pleasure on any walk, day or night, was in counting, sorting, and measuring the bits and pieces of roots or closed-up flowers or nuts they collected, or the crows in the trees, but Herself sometimes got carried away by a certain kind of breeze, or by the appearance of a wet-looking mushroom poking up through the leaf litter, pink like a dog's penis, or a songbird flying off to leave an exposed egg glowing pale green in the smudged light of the moon. Or after the first hard freeze, a fragile flower made of ice appearing at the base of a wingstem stalk would bring tears to her eyes.

As Donkey squirmed in her granny's playful grip on those nights, so this snake was curving and attempting to coil in tender, spiraling protest. Hermine's big arms and hands held the m'sauga with certainty, and her whole body glowed with concentration. At the apex of the snake's resistance, its body formed a fine powerful arc that was held momentarily in perfect tension, like a bow. Woman and snake were perfectly attuned to the moment and the task, each focused on the other. Hermine's absolute command over the creature, like her power over all the island, was as inalterable as the equality of the three sides of an equilateral triangle.

The storm-colored m'sauga gradually torqued her thick body into a flattened S in her silent, flowing resistance, matching the resistance of Hermine's right arm, and turned to reveal a smoky ribbed belly. Her mouth opened wide, as if in a yawn, and she revealed a pearly pink-white iridescence, the color of a princess dress or the inside of a river clam. Another wave of morel-mushroom musk rose as the venom-ous fangs bit the air in a staccato rhythm. As Herself positioned the snake's head over the jar, the snake snap-snapped at her like a windup toy, but Herself was leading this dance. She hummed as she put her thumb on the top of the snake's triangular head.

Donkey imagined into the future, imagined the magnificent Lind-worm with frost-dusted eyes dead on the cutting board. Though she'd seen hunks of dead animal every day on Hermine's plate, though she'd seen Herself kill river fish, rabbits, and squirrels, she'd never had a stronger sense of impending infinite death than in the body of this living snake, who could, herself, in turn, kill with a bite. That doomed, deadly creature embodied the very essence of ∞. Those nights when Donkey played at trying to escape from her granny's dance, she didn't pull hard enough to really get away, but what if she did? What if, as hard as she might pull against her granny's grip, she could not break it? This snake's very existence was at stake.

Just as Herself touched the m'sauga's mouth to the jar to begin the venom extraction, ∞ seemed to blossom all around them on the screened porch like a ghostly frost flower. Donkey felt the scream rise out of her, out of her control, spooling out for a long time, at first high and undulating, and then hoarse. Outside, Ozma began to bark like crazy. Afterward, Donkey kept her eyes closed for a long time, dreading what would happen next. Ozma's barks turned to whimpers. When Donkey finally opened her eyes, Herself was gently folding the m'sauga back into the bucket. She was shaking with anger.

"Go outside!" she said, when she got the lid on. "Now! Go! I don't want to see you until supper!"

Donkey pushed the screen door all the way open on its hinges and let it slap back against the frame with its full force, even knowing she might break it. "I hate you," she said under her breath.

When Ozma refused to come out from under the porch to accompany her, she yelled, imitating Hermine's angry voice, "Stay, then! I don't want you to follow me!" The force of her anger surprised her. She couldn't shake it off, nor could she let go of the desire to save the Lindworm's life.

Donkey was skulking around the other side of Rose Cottage, intending to sneak back around to look for the camouflage man, when she felt a straining energy nearby. She followed the vibrations to an artesian spring pool surrounded by moss, where she stretched out on her belly to study a bruise-colored devil crayfish a little longer than her fingers, writhing and twisting in the clear water. The *Cambarus diogenes* stretched and moaned and pushed as though giving birth, but she was actually struggling to get out of her own shell. Trying and failing and collapsing sideways in the water, then rousing and trying and failing again and pausing to rest under the water with her eyes on their stalks just above the surface. Donkey wanted to go get Herself to help, but she would want to eat the crayfish rather than rescue it from its torment.

"Herself should know what it's like to get killed so she'd stop killing everybody else," Donkey said to the crayfish. When Donkey reached out to touch it, the crayfish paused in her agonies to reach up and clamp onto Donkey's finger with one of her claws. "Let go!" she shouted. When she was able to pull away, she saw the incision on her fingertip beading with blood.

A gunshot blasted twice at close range, from the direction of Boneset; Donkey paused to listen to the empty silence following the blasts and then made her way around the back of the house, sucking her bleeding finger. She got around just in time to see movement in the elderberry bushes across the swamp channel. A person running away toward Lovers Road or else an animal rustling the branches in its hurry to flee the sound of a gunshot. Donkey had never heard a gunshot this close to Rose Cottage, and she was disappointed she hadn't gotten to see the man with the gun.

All day, the sun never managed to break through the fog, and as dinnertime approached, Donkey longed to be back with Herself, her anger having faded to a dim memory. She would ingratiate herself by filling the front of her T-shirt with ramps, pulling one of every ten plants, leaving the rest as she'd been taught, to make sure there were just as many next year. On the way back to the cottage, she stopped and found the delicate crayfish carapace successfully abandoned, and she picked it up and carried it into the cottage on top of her ramps.

Herself made a dinner mostly of leftovers reheated on the stove, beans with cabbage and ramps for Donkey and meaty cabbage goulash for Herself. Fresh sourdough bread—made from Jane Dough, their starter—and butter for both of them. Herself moved slowly and thoughtfully and said nothing much to Donkey, holding her right biceps in rumination, and though the weather was warm, she wore Wild Will's chore coat. She seemed to be communing with Baba Rose the way she did when she was working on a complicated cure.

"Are you mad?" Donkey asked. "I'm sorry I screamed."

Herself shook her head distractedly, but after eating, she clenched her jaw as though holding something tightly in her mouth. Donkey knew she sometimes sucked an herb or root to get a sense of what it would do.

Donkey took advantage of the silence to contemplate "Introduction to Calculus" in *Garden of Logic*, which promised that accepting tiny infinities would allow her to calculate the length of curves and the area underneath them. She decided she did not want to accept tiny infinities; she was not interested in the trade-off.

Most curious to Donkey was that the m'sauga was still in the bucket, not in the freezer. She wondered if Herself had been moved by her entreaties to spare the creature. Until now, Donkey had been a part of the natural unfolding of events initiated by Herself, and her complaining and resisting had been for her own pleasure and education, with no thought that she could ever influence the physics of the situation. But maybe she had changed Hermine's mind for once. This thought did not make her feel more powerful; it made her afraid, as if she were being propelled out of her orbit in the solar system.

That night, Herself surprised Donkey by asking her to milk Delilah all the way through. It felt like a further loosening of the ties that bound her, a further uncoiling.

CHAPTER FIVE

A girl has to make her own mistakes.

T HAT NIGHT, OZMA SLEPT outside under the corner of the porch, refusing to come into the house. When Donkey woke up in the middle of the night in the bed in Lazy's Room, she got up, fed Baba Rose's fire, and drank milk out of a quart jar as usual, but she did not go to her granny's bed. Instead, she put on Titus's big jacket with the pencils and books in the pockets and went out onto the screened porch in the dark. She got on her hands and knees under the table and pressed her ear to the plastic top of the five-gallon bucket. The snake was not sleeping, either, but was tensely waiting in the cool night, rattle-buzzing gently, probably sickened by the smell of the plastic. Ozma began to bark outside and wouldn't stop until Donkey carried the bucket into the kitchen and shut the door.

"Lindworm, can you understand me? I saved your life." Donkey pressed her ear to the plastic again and listened for a response, listened for the Lindworm to offer a wish. When the m'sauga finally spoke, the swampy buzz was hard to make out, but it seemed like *Set me free.*

"You're medicine now. I can't free you," Donkey whispered. Crows in the trees above Rose Cottage could only imagine what was going on inside, but spiders watched nervously from their webs in all the corners and under the table. "But I'll give you some fresh air."

Donkey worked the screwdriver under the lip of the lid and unsuccessfully tried to wedge it open. She moved the screwdriver around the edge, pulling up a little bit at a time, but the lid did not want to come free, even when she'd loosened it halfway around. She'd seen Herself do this dozens of times and hadn't realized how difficult it was when the lid was pushed down hard. She gripped the bucket with both knees and pushed up so hard with the screwdriver that the lid flew off and the bucket clattered sideways to the floor, and a great hissing, rattling spiral of energy burst into the room.

Freed from the bucket, the snake glided across the tiles and under the refrigerator before Donkey could even stand up. Through the wall, she could hear Herself snore, could feel the big right arm reaching for her. Even with the flashlight, Donkey could not locate the snake under the refrigerator. Herself had warned her about wishes, and Donkey saw now how right she was. Her wish to spare the snake had been careless. She searched every corner of the kitchen and then sat at the table waiting for a sound. She listened and factored a series of polynomials, wrought the solutions like digging roots out of the ground with such exertion that she fell asleep with her head on the table.

In the morning she awoke curled on the floor near the empty bucket. She saw no snake or evidence that one had been there. She studied the hole in the floor where the sink pipes went under the house. That hole didn't look big enough for a snake's escape. She looked at the wide, deep floor-to-ceiling cupboard. There was a gap at the bottom of the cupboard doors that the snake might have been able to slip through. Donkey slowly opened the tall doors. Inside, the four shelves were laden with medicines and ingredients for medicine-making and cooking. The lowest shelf was two and three-quarters feet off the floor, and at the bottom of the cupboard were two side-by-side hatches, both covered by painted wooden lids, both leading into caboodles under the house.

The caboodle on the right was bigger, with a light switch just inside. Donkey was slender enough that she could hang her head and shoulders inside the two-by-three-foot hatch and see an upside-down underground wonderland of jars of pickles, heaps of potatoes and squash, bunches of stringy root vegetables, and a variety of fruits on shelves that extended three feet below the house. She was too big now to hop down inside the caboodle and hand things up to Herself, as she'd done when she was little. At the moment, the hatch for this right-hand caboodle was shut tight.

The smaller caboodle on the left was where Herself kept strong medicines, and you could only reach an arm inside and pull things out if you knew where they were. Donkey was forbidden from messing with anything inside the left-hand caboodle. She wasn't even supposed to open that caboodle, but she sometimes did put mice down there rather than put them in the root cellar, where they would eat the winter stores, or outside, where they might freeze. However, the lid over that hatch was tricky to close tightly, and Donkey saw that it was ajar now and that the m'sauga could have easily slipped down through the gap and under the house.

The sun rose fully, but Donkey decided she had to find the Lindworm and coax it back into the bucket before waking Herself. She drank more milk and remembered, only after emptying the jar, her granny's claim she was eating Delilah *a little at a time*. She tiptoed down the hall to check on Herself, who was still snoring. Then she went outside to look for the man in camouflage but saw nobody. She even walked across the bridge, out to Boneset, but found no baby in the basket. She returned to the screened porch to read about π in *Garden of Logic*, but she couldn't concentrate. She'd learned a year ago that π = 3.14, but this book claimed that was not true. Pi equaled 3.1415926535 . . . where the decimals went on forever, out to ∞. This was no way to start the day. If Donkey could get the Lindworm back into the bucket, the snake could make herself into a circle in the bottom of the bucket, and the circumference of that circle would be 2 x π x *r*. But if π had a decimal that went out to ∞, Donkey might not be able to calculate an answer she liked.

When she heard Delilah mooing, she got the milk pail from under the sink and carried it into Hermine's bedroom, where the smell of lavender and holy basil did not comfort her. She stood beside the bed for a long time but decided Herself wasn't ready to wake up. She had seemed off last night, and sleep was medicine, after all. She walked down the steps and to the primrose path, swinging the milk pail in one hand and the egg basket in the other, aware of how light her bare footsteps were, how little impression they made on the island soil. However tall her body was, it was not weighed down by a necklace of cuntshells or a lifetime of other people's secrets. She kept her eyes on the ground, alert for movement on or around the path where the bright orange and pink and yellow flowers grew. Crows shook their heads at her. Without Herself to guide the process, it took her a long time to get Delilah into her stanchion and her head locked in the gate. Donkey started out strong with the milking, but her hands got tired. When she stood up to take a break, the cow lifted her hoof to stomp at a stable fly and put it down inside the milk pail.

Donkey returned to the cottage through the back door, into Hermine's room, and the old woman didn't wake up. She slept on while Donkey put the manure-tinged milk into a plastic jug for Molly's cats. Donkey read, made root beer tea with more sugar than Herself would have approved of, ate store-bought peanut butter on Jane Dough bread, and still, Herself didn't wake up. Donkey wondered if her granny was under a spell cast by the m'sauga. She didn't want to be sent away from the island for her misbehavior, so she delayed waking Herself up by drawing geometrical figures and calculating distances, but with nobody to tell about them, they didn't mean as much. By midafternoon, she felt lonely. The cottage felt empty without Herself moving around in it; it was as though the time and space here were too big for Donkey alone. She fed the fire, but Baba Rose didn't offer any guidance. Herself kept on breathing, her heart kept on beating, but she didn't even get up to pee.

Donkey slept alone again that night, and when the sun rose the following morning, she sat on the edge of Hermine's bed and bounced gently, wondering if Herself could be fooled into thinking the previous day hadn't happened or that there had never been a m'sauga, that it had all been a dream.

"Wake up, ma'am," Donkey said in her low, loud voice. She'd never been a liar before, but she now considered lying to Herself, since lying was filled with variety and possibility. *The Lindworm opened the bucket from inside*, or *Ozma released the Lindworm into the swamp*, or *I wished the snake was free, and it just happened. You were right about wishes, ma'am.* Then she heard a sound, a whisper of movement. The smell in the room was changing, becoming fertile and musky and mushroomy. She got down on her hands and knees and looked under the bed.

The mattress and springs stretched down under Hermine's weight, but beyond the bulge that held Herself, something moved along the floor. Donkey lit the bedside oil lamp and brought it down beside her. It shed a golden circle of light that reached a few feet under the bed, but the scent of its burning oil could not compete with the bitter citrus of the Osage oranges Herself kept under the bed to ward off insects. Donkey got down on her belly and pulled herself under, pausing, when something poked her, to pull a pencil out of the right-hand breast pocket of Titus's jacket.

On a few occasions there had been snakes inside Rose Cottage, once a blue racer that had wrapped itself around the arm of the standing lamp in the living room, next to the big leather couch, shining as silver as the Tin Woodman. When Donkey had tried to push its thumb-sized head into a jar, it bit her with its many tiny curved fangs. That bite had hurt a lot, and Herself had to dab it with rotgut.

Donkey inched toward the darker shadow under the bed until the lamp's light was blocked by her body. She wriggled over the thin wool rug and onto the bare wood floor, flattening herself until she could go no farther because she could not fit beneath Hermine's body pushing the bedsprings so close to the floor. As her eyes adjusted to the darkness, she saw a quiet liquid movement, and a figure slowly formed in her field of vision, almost as though Donkey were building it by wishing life to a clump of moist leaves, ashes, and boiled bones. This was how she made multiplication tables, starting by listing numbers up and down and across and then constructing the rest of the body from what had to be true. Was this how Herself saw the ghost of Baba Rose in the kitchen, by forming her a little at a time from smoke, flowers, and goulash? Was this how Rose Thorn saw the old bartender in the hollow sycamore when she'd had the right amount to drink?

Now there was no denying the swamp-mottled pattern, the triple-thickness of the body under the bed. Donkey glanced back toward the apple crate Herself used as a bedside table. Leaning against it stood the snake stick Donkey should have had with her instead of the pencil she gripped firmly in her left hand. And the snake bucket was in the kitchen. She stretched out a long leg, tried to hook her foot around the stick and draw it toward herself, but she only managed to knock it over and out of reach entirely.

"You have to go back in the bucket," Donkey whispered to the Lindworm. She felt very much educated since a day and a half ago. Her granny's warnings were right. There were mistakes she wouldn't make again. "You have to get eaten. I'm sorry, Lindworm. I was wrong."

She didn't realize she was reaching toward the Lindworm until the snake moved toward her outstretched hand. By the time she'd pulled back, the cat eyes in the triangular head were looking at her from right where her hand had been. She realized it might be dangerous to make any sudden motions that could startle the creature. She shrank back slowly, her eyes beginning to water. She felt the Lindworm criticizing her tears.

"I'm not crying," she whispered. "I just got something scary in my eye."

The m'sauga retracted and piled her dark coils upon herself. Donkey wanted to know this snake by imitating her movements, by settling herself on her own coils a safe distance away, but when she tried to move, she discovered that her hair was caught in the tines of the bedsprings.

"I'm sorry, *Sistrurus*, but Herself is the boss until she dies. Even if you're my sister."

Maybe the snake understood Donkey's betrayal, because what had seemed like fearful curiosity became an emanating anger. The Lindworm's tail, that stubby buzzing braid, became a blur. Donkey lifted her chin, moaned low, "Ma'am, please wake up!" and as she did so, more hairs caught on the metal ends of the sagging springs. Through the floorboards, she could feel the snake's heart beating in the same slow rhythm as her granny's above her.

The m'sauga moved toward the wall at the head of the bed in a rippling wave, gathering her coils onto herself once again, and her scent changed to become more like the soil around the roots of a spice bush used to treat loneliness, with a touch of the dusty ammonia smell of the millipedes that had marched over the island last year, foretelling trouble in love. The Lindworm's head ventured a few inches out from her coiled body and then traveled up the wall. Soon the head was out of sight, moving toward Hermine's pillow so slowly that Donkey didn't see it as movement but as a kind of lengthening of her body as the mass stayed constant.

Then the m'sauga twisted away from the wall like the terrible number ∞, reorienting herself to reveal her storm-colored belly so that she could navigate onto the mattress, rib by rib. That snake had hundreds of ribs—maybe 215 ribs, a semi-prime, 5 x 43—allowing it to flow up onto Hermine's bed with the ease of an exhalation. The back end of the creature was still planted on the floor under the bed, and Donkey was mesmerized by how the snake could stay put and venture forth at the same time. If she were a snake, an exceptionally long snake, her head could go to school to learn math, and it wouldn't matter if they tied her to a chair, because her tail would still be safe at home, picking mushrooms or stirring a pot that had to be stirred without stopping. She could venture out to visit Aunt Molly's eighteen cats in her tin can while the other end of her was out finding Rose Thorn 2,184 miles away in California. She could bring her mother home without ever losing her way, all without the very real dangers of wishing.

As Donkey watched the tail of the m'sauga lift off the floor, she woke up to what was happening.

"Don't bite her!" she whispered. She propelled herself farther under the bed, farther than she should have been able to go under Hermine's body. The last time, she'd let that creature slip away under the refrigerator, but this time, she grabbed the tail just above the rattle and yanked. Though some of the rattle was crushed in the crook of her little finger, what she felt with the rest of her hand was the impossible softness of the snake's skin—though it appeared ruffled and rough, it was velvety smooth—and she held on longer than she'd intended. The snake thudded to the floor, the whole long body landing like donkey turds dropping in quick succession. And then came the muscular seizing of the snake's body; in less than a second the creature recoiled and whipped around to strike Donkey's forearm, biting into the sleeve of Titus's jacket. Donkey stabbed at the snake with the pencil in her left hand and missed and stabbed again and felt it dig into the snake's body. The m'sauga retracted in pain and threw her coils backward against the wall. Then she retreated to the leg of the bed nearest the door leading outside and wrapped her coils around it.

Donkey's wounded wrist stung as though electrified. She tried to slide backward out from under the bed and felt the needle pain of hairs being pulled out of her head, but she was still held fast by a larger hank of hair woven tightly into the metal springs. Herself might never wake up, and Donkey would be stuck under this bed, under Hermine's huge body, unable to get to the antivenom. Sleep was medicine only until you died. Molly would come tomorrow with a new book from the library or from Aunt Prim and find them there and cry in exasperation over them. Or maybe Rose Thorn would arrive before then and see what had happened and lie down and die along with them of a broken heart.

The m'sauga was still wrapped around the bottom of the bedpost with her tail behind her head like an ∞ ouroboros. Donkey couldn't breathe. When she blinked herself alert, she tasted metal and thought it was the snake's venom already traveled from her hand to her mouth, but then she realized that her mouth was filled with blood. At some point in the struggle, she'd bitten her tongue. The m'sauga was moving again, folded double over herself and nosing along the door beside the bed, trying to find her way outside. She slowly unfolded until she was stretched out, like the rolled-up rug they put there in winter to keep out drafts.

Donkey called out from below, "Granny, ma'am," over and over but got no answer. She pitched her voice lower. Something must be very wrong with Herself that she didn't sense Donkey there under the bed, that she hadn't woken up for two days. Donkey should have tried harder to wake her, or she should have already gone to Ada's house to call Molly.

Donkey's attempts to push and jerk and wiggle backward out from under the bed continued unsuccessfully. There was no strength in her position, and she decided this was what it would be like inside a wolf, trying to kick and punch her way out; this was what it must've been like inside of Rose Thorn before being born, what it was like to be a crayfish trying to shed her skin. Herself always rescued Donkey, and she didn't like this taste of life without her.

She tried to reach up to free her hair with both her bitten and unbitten hands but couldn't maneuver anywhere near her head or face, not even to wipe her eyes, which watered from the pain of so many hairs being pulled out of her scalp. What good were arms and hands under here? When she yanked her head to the side as hard as she could, the bed springs tore away a whole hank of hair, and her vision blurred. She figured out that she couldn't go back out the way she'd come in— it was impossible with Hermine's body pushing down that side of the bed—so she shifted side to side, twisted and writhed, and inched her torso forward, toward the m'sauga, rib by rib. By grabbing the iron leg of the bed where the snake had earlier taken refuge, three feet from where the snake now lay straight as a yardstick, she was able to pull forward and free herself.

As she slid forward, something rolled painfully under her ribs: the pencil with which she had defended her life. Her scalp stung, and when she reached up, she found it raw and bleeding. She lurched to her feet. The Lindworm, still pressed along the bottom of the door, glowed rust-colored in the bloody light coming through the burlap curtains. Donkey pleaded with Herself to tell her what to do in the lowest voice she had, but she got no response.

The snake's lidless cat eyes reproached her. Now that Donkey had seen the speed with which the Lindworm could move around the room, she feared she would never get the creature into a bucket. She didn't understand how Herself had done it with only a thin stick. If Donkey wanted to stay on the island, she had no choice but to kill the snake and present it to Herself as soon as she woke up. Maybe killing it would break the spell and wake Herself up. Donkey could get the hatchet they used for splitting kindling from the screened porch. Or she could drop the great weight of Wild Will's Holy Bible on the creature and break its spine. *Garden of Logic* was too small to hurt anybody, but math gave Donkey an even easier way to commit this murder: bisection. The snake wanted to go outside, and Donkey could slam the heavy door on the creature when it was halfway through the doorway and cut her clean in two, as easily as striking a line through a drawing of her with a pencil. Then Herself could wake up and cook the Lindworm and fill the house with the horrible death stench of rattlesnake meat. She would make Donkey eat the creature that was almost certainly her sister so she would survive the bite, and then everything could return to the way it had been before Donkey had talked to the m'sauga.

She turned the brass doorknob and slowly pulled the door toward her. The movement nudged the snake's thick body into the room, and the whole arm's length of it wiggled side to side as it kept regaining its bearings on the doormat. Donkey opened the door farther, and the snake, sensing the current of air, began to pour around the corner. She moved through the narrow opening the way the women of the island went through doorways in winter to save the heat inside.

Donkey gripped the knob, pulled the door toward her a little more, preparing to slam it hard enough to separate tail end from head end. She'd accidentally done this dozens of times to worms—splitting ∞ with a shovel. If she could hand Herself the two halves of a snake, still bleeding, Herself would cure her with antivenom.

Time slowed to almost zero as the snake curved around the corner. In one piece. Disappeared down the steps, leaving a smeared trail of blood behind.

Donkey looked out the door at the lush, fertile island and compared it to Molly's tin can with its tiny mowed lawn punctuated by one bush. Her disobedience felt like a strange ill-fitting pair of shoes. She used to obey Herself without a second thought. And now she would have to pay the price for disobedience. She pulled up her jacket sleeve and saw the blood on her wrist, but there were no puncture marks there. The blood must have come instead from the other wound she discovered on the heel of her hand—a red bump with a little gray point under her skin. The m'sauga hadn't bitten her at all—she'd stabbed herself with her own pencil, and the lead had broken off inside her. She licked away the blood. When the wound was clean, she noticed there was no blood coming from it; the skin had had simply closed around the pencil point. Where, then, had the blood come from?

Two of the steps were smeared with the m'sauga's blood. The Lindworm itself was still there, lingering at the bottom of the steps, and Donkey saw the wound she had inflicted in the middle of the snake's body. How many times had she stabbed? She'd thought just once. As the Lindworm slid over the soft island soil, she paused to look back at Donkey, maybe preparing to offer Donkey a wish in exchange for sparing her life. Or to tell Donkey she'd just swallowed snake blood. Before either of those things could happen, coyote-colored Ozma came jogging stiffly around the side of Rose Cottage, barking.

"Go! Go!" Donkey shouted to the Lindworm, unsure whether she was more afraid for the dog or the snake. "Hurry!"

The m'sauga turned back toward the steps and barely avoided those jaws and claws by slipping under the stairs and disappearing into a crevice between the stones of the foundation of Rose Cottage. After a bout of raucous barking, Ozma walked back around to the cottage porch, sniffing without success for a way to get to the snake.

Donkey went back inside to her granny's room. She sat on the edge of the bed again and put the glowing lantern back on the apple crate. She looked at her hand in the light. Rattlesnake blood was usually diluted for medicines, and Herself had twice made a water with it that had helped a woman have a boy baby. Donkey didn't know what swallowing it full strength would do—turn her into a boy, maybe.

"I'm sorry, ma'am. Please wake up." When there was still no response, she pulled Hermine's blankets down and took her hands, shook them to revive her, but Herself clung to sleep. That's when Donkey saw that something had happened to Herself. Her left hand was cool and pale, but the right hand was hot, and the right wrist had a blood-soaked bandage wrapped all around it, and it was bulging above the bandage. Donkey could feel her granny's slow heartbeat, like the m'sauga's. Donkey pushed aside the nearest curtains to let more light in and saw the flesh on Hermine's right forearm had turned bluish. The m'sauga must have bitten her when Donkey screamed bloody murder. Or had it happened in the night, after Donkey had let the snake escape from the bucket? Donkey pressed her face into the beloved cheek and begged Herself to wake up. She went into the kitchen for the snakebite salve. Surely Herself would have immediately applied it under the bandage, but she hadn't used enough.

In the kitchen, Donkey opened the cupboard, got down on her knees, and took the lid off the left-hand caboodle, reached in for the snakebite salve. First she pulled up a jar with a red lid and a white bloodroot flower—resembling a daisy—painted on top, the salve of last resort, made with bloodroot paste. It was stronger than the snakebite salve, and she'd seen Herself use it only once, on a big mole on a woman's neck. She knew the salve could also help make a woman bleed if she needed to, but she didn't know what else it could do. Donkey shone a flashlight down into the caboodle but could not see around the corner and had to reach in blindly. The next thing she pulled up was a round dusty bottle with a dusty label lettered in a neat hand—Primrose's printing!—that read "WW Whiskey." She pulled out a jelly jar and found it contained a coiled-up length of rattlesnake shed meant to cover a wound. Another quart jar was full of yellowish liquid, and she startled and nearly dropped it when she saw, floating up from the bottom, a full-sized rattlesnake curled around itself—what Herself called "snake tea."

As she pulled these items from the caboodle, she noticed something for the first time, something hanging from a small bent nail just below the floorboards: a lone key, a key that might unlock a door, though there were no door locks on the island. She wondered what the key might be for as she reached down into the caboodle again, farther this time, and found what she sought: the snakebite salve in the blue jar.

She applied the salve above Hermine's bandage and waited, but nothing happened. She knew she should have removed the bandage, which was dark with old blood, but she couldn't bring herself to touch it. She intended to use the paring knife to poke holes in Hermine's arm so the salve could circulate, but she couldn't bear to do that either. When nothing happened, she applied the salve of last resort both above and below the wrist bandage, on both the forearm and hand. She applied the salve of last resort to her own hand wound, too, hoping it would force the pencil lead out, and she moved her finger in a figure eight around the point at the center. Within a few minutes she felt heat and noticed the flesh started to bubble. She felt the heat on her fingertips, which were similarly burning. Maybe it was supposed to be diluted with something else—she didn't know! She washed her hands and her wrist wound until they felt raw. By then her first two fingerprints had dissolved, and her wound had swelled and reddened. The places where she'd applied it to Hermine's skin were bright red and oily and gave the impression of melting.

Donkey ran barefoot the mile and a half along the stone-strewn shoulder of the road to Ada McIntyre's place. She went into the back porch of Ada's house and knocked on the door, knocked again. Ada, who was ninety-one, did not appear quickly enough, so she went out to the barnyard, into the barn, and picked up the receiver of the wall-mounted phone just inside the door.

Her hand seemed to grow huge as she poked her fingers into the number holes and dragged them around their designated arcs on the circle. The hand seemed like somebody else's hand altogether, a huge, blister-tipped Alice-in-Wonderland hand, the hand of a betrayer who would call Molly. She said, "Herself won't wake up. She's been asleep for two days!"

Molly made the trip from Whiteheart Village in twenty minutes and bustled across the bridge, complaining about the lack of a handrail. Inside the cottage, she touched Hermine's face, found it fevered, felt her neck and shoulders. When she picked up her right arm with the bloody bandage and melted flesh, Molly said, "Oh, no! What's this?"

In Molly's healing hands, Herself began to wake up, pale and confused. At this point, Molly sent Donkey running down the road again to call 911. Donkey's fingers burned as she dialed; her throat burned as she made the request, "Ambulance, 1597 Lovers Road, Whiteheart."

"What in the name of poor Jesus happened here, Dorothy?" Molly asked when she returned. Molly was as big around as Herself and a little taller (only six inches shorter than Donkey) but where Herself was solid, Molly had a swollen appearance, as though she'd put her weight on quickly, over a shaky foundation. She had short blond hair instead of Hermine's soft gray hair, small hands instead of rough long-fingered mitts. "Her wrist is a mess, and she's got a dangerous fever. Why didn't you call me right away?"

"We found a m'sauga in the barnyard. It bit her," Donkey said, noting that her aunt had by now exposed the entire swollen wrist. She knew better than to say something about a Lindworm to Molly, who objected even to a mention of the troll under the bridge. "I just didn't want Herself to kill it."

"What are you talking about? This is a bullet wound, Dorothy. I'm so sick of these careless men shooting all over the swamp. Something like this was bound to happen. It's not safe here," Molly said. She jiggled the old woman's shoulders as though jiggling her own self awake. "Mama, stay awake. Don't fall asleep on me again."

"I tried to wake her up all day yesterday." She thought of her camouflage man, but she hadn't seen him. Anyway, he had never fired while she was watching him.

"Her flesh is burned here. What did she put on it? I ought to toss every one of those poisons. And what's this in her shoulder, all healed over? Looks like—"

Molly asked the questions but didn't leave time for Donkey to explain that the scar on Hermine's shoulder was from the time Donkey accidentally fell against her and stabbed her with scissors. Now, with Herself lying there helpless, Molly had pulled aside her night-gown and was studying her mother's body with the excitement of a biologist who had gotten ahold of a new specimen, as though she'd waited her whole life to get her hands on Herself in such a vulnerable state. Donkey kept her own pencil lead wound hidden under the right-hand sleeve of Titus's jacket, for fear it would become a subject of Molly's attention. She was glad the snake hadn't bitten Herself, because maybe she could recover from a bullet, and Donkey's disobedience would be forgotten, and Donkey wouldn't have to leave the island.

"Dorothy, your granny's wrist is shattered. She could die from an infection after something like this. You should have called me sooner. Now go out and wait for the ambulance."

"Rose Thorn said she'll never die," Donkey said, and felt herself coming undone. Though she'd decided to be logical, though she'd decided not to wish anymore, she cried, "I wish she was here right now."

"Me too! Why doesn't she come home?" Aunt Molly's cheeks flushed, and her small blue-gray eyes watered too. A mention of Rose Thorn was sometimes all it took to make Molly tear up these days, as bad as she teared up whenever Donkey hurt herself. "Prim says she's working in a bar now. A bar! The worst place for that girl! She should be here taking care of you."

TWENTY-TWO MINUTES AFTER DONKEY returned to the island after calling 911, two male paramedics arrived at Boneset in a white station wagon with flashing lights, and when they crossed the bridge with a rescue gurney, they were the first men on the island in Donkey's lifetime. Apart from her fears about Herself, this arrival was both terrifying and marvelous. The men didn't venture onto the island to stomp mushrooms or break branches but followed her up the stairs and into the kitchen and back to the bedroom to help. Their big bodies seemed to fill the whole place, and they were focused on Herself in the bed, hardly even glancing around.

Herself revived enough to fight their ministrations, and, with Molly's permission, the shorter man shot her with a sedative to put her back into the sleep Molly had just pulled her out of. Herself was then strapped to the gurney and carried off the island like a two-hundred-pound bag of body parts. As they left Rose Cottage, one of them told Molly they should put a handrail up on the bridge. The bridge planks bowed as the EMTs hauled their load. They moved with the confidence of routine, unaware of the shock the island felt at their presence, unaware of the damage wrought by treating Herself this way, without consideration for her soul.

Molly took hold of the sleeve of Donkey's army jacket and dragged her through the screened porch. She stopped in her tracks, though, when she noticed a hole in the screen behind her mother's chair. She could find no exit hole in the screen on the opposite side of the porch and so concluded that this was where her mother had been shot.

Donkey wished she'd repaired that hole before Molly had gotten there. She was scared of what would come next and regretted leaving Delilah, now bellowing to be milked, and Ozma, who had never ventured out of the Waters since Rose Thorn had brought her there eleven years ago. Donkey was leaving everything familiar, except what she carried in her jacket pockets: a couple of pencils, *Garden of Logic*, and her notebook *True Things*.

She turned back to hug Ozma, who was whining behind them, and Aunt Molly pulled her to her feet by her short braid and marched her down the eleven stone steps to the flagstone base of the bridge.

"Finally," Molly said. "Maybe now I can save you both from this cursed place."

DONKEY'S FIRST EXTENDED SOJOURN into Nowhere consisted of six days in the hospital watching Herself and six nights sleeping in her aunt's tin can in Whiteheart Village, which was overrun with the stray cats Molly had adopted. Staying in close quarters with so many cats and their litter boxes served as another potent lesson for Donkey in misguided kindness toward animals.

On the second night, she opened a window for fresh air, and, distraught with worry over Herself and what they were doing to her at the hospital, she didn't notice that the window screen was loose. Before long, seventeen of Aunt M's eighteen cats had slid through the narrow opening and into the night. The next morning, Molly roused some neighbors to help them round them up and would not rest until they were all rescued again. When they were done, there were nineteen cats instead of eighteen.

After the first X-ray, the doctors told them that the bones in Hermine's wrist were indeed shattered by the bullet still wedged inside. The next day, the doctor explained to Aunt M that Hermine's wound was infected with salmonella, among other microbes, and, with no input from the sedated patient, they agreed it would be best to amputate halfway between the elbow and the wrist.

CHAPTER SIX

❦

Times change faster than the people in them.

ONCE UPON A TIME, in the low-lying fields and floodplains surrounding the Waters, farm families used to grow the sweet, crisp Whiteheart Celery, superior to any celery you can get today. Men tilled the rich black muck with mule-drawn plows or did the work with their own sinewy bodies and the aid of their wives or unmarried sisters or unlanded brothers or their lusty, restless teenage sons. The farm kids all worked, even the little ones, who would squat alongside the trenches and place ten-week-old celery seedlings at eight-inch intervals. To make this work possible for even the most dreamy or distracted or jumpy girls and boys, they each carried a stick or a deer's thigh bone or an antler, broken off to measure the distance between plants.

Then the women came along the rows and stood the little plants upright and heaped the swamp soil onto the stems, wrapped that rich muck around each one like a woolen scarf to protect it from the cold spring nights. Sometimes a woman had to stop her work to smile and take a deep breath as she watched her husband and children, for otherwise she would spill over with an unholy kind of joy, the joy of being in a body on this earth with other beloved bodies. The women revisited each plant each week to mound the dirt a little higher and higher still, and to bind the plants to sticks to keep them growing upward instead of sprawling. Eventually, when the plants were tall enough, they placed boards against the stalks to protect them from the sun and keep them soft, crisp, and blanched as pale as milk until harvest.

The celery was more profitable than other crops and had a longer season. The women and men tenderly laid the big cut celery heads to rest in coffin-shaped cardboard boxes, separating them with parchment so they could be carried on ice by the mail train every Friday from July through October, mostly to hotels in Chicago. The farm families themselves didn't eat the glamorous whole celeries, and certainly not the tender inner stalks favored by hotel patrons. Instead they collected wayward stalks throughout the season to chop and boil in soups. For themselves, they grew another kind of celery, celeriac, for its root that tasted a little like chestnuts and stayed firm even when cooked, best roasted with a fatty young hen or baked into a savory pie with onion and cheese.

When the muscles and joints of the men and women ached in those days, they prayed and took aspirin, and if that didn't work, there was a penetrating peppermint-and-cayenne ointment to be gotten from Baba Rose in the Waters to soothe them until the infinite hereafter could provide the ultimate soothing. Why wouldn't a Christian on this outrageous earth take advantage of what comfort nature offered—relief from the fever of ague, from the throbbing of a foot trampled by a spooked plow mule? Mortal joy's eternal companion was suffering, and wasn't the pain of this profane earth calling out for a profane cure? Weren't Christians obligated to find relief from bodily pain to free the soul to do the soul's work?

When the large-scale growing of celery and other market vegetables went west to California half a century ago, the celery farmers were ashamed, the way a sailor's wife was ashamed when her husband was lost to a storm on Lake Michigan. Their shame overtook in intensity their sadness over losing their fields of celery and lettuce and melon and squash, and many farmers could no longer bear to look at their wives or children in the evenings without some spirit in them. And as the men filled in the mucky celery rows to grow field crops like wheat and oats, their shame redoubled. They knew, all of them, that they should say good riddance to farming and rejoice, should take the opportunity to sell their fields to the bigger farms with expensive combine harvesters. For wasn't that the history of civilization? That the old many gods had combined into one great God? Titus Clay's father, Titus Clay Sr., that great man, would eventually farm almost every field on this side of unincorporated Whiteheart, harvesting corn and soybeans with specialized machinery he would never finish paying for. His cripplingly shy wife, meanwhile, spent her time worrying about her son's and husband's bleeding and keeping the house and garden immaculate; the Tituses' clothes were always very clean.

It wasn't just Whiteheart. The many crops of the upper Midwest were winnowed to two—corn and beans. Each supported the other by its action upon the soil, but the men saw the relationship differently; they saw themselves as corn farmers, and they embraced soybeans only because the plants fixed the soil nitrogen in the way a wife should support her husband. The native peoples of this region, of whom Baba Rose had been a descendent, had a third plant in their garden mounds, a third sister to corn and beans: pumpkins or squash, the big leaves of which provided shade at the base of the plant to protect the soil from drought. The new farmers, instead, used field irrigation systems to keep the soil moist.

Decades ago, husbands and wives stopped working together, and then they had only meals and sex and children in common, and that was when they stopped laughing together. Their separate stories no longer made sense to each other, and they began to forget the old songs they used to sing from one end of the row to another just to hear one another's voices. When the women used to hang the family laundry on the line to blow in the wind, the husbands and wives were inspired by those flapping garments to move closer to one another, to admire one another's strong bodies, to remember dancing together, and to see their daily work as another kind of dance, but then the husbands went to work at the paper mill, and the women purchased electric dryers that hid the soft movements of the clothes inside them.

There was a time when men and women accepted mystery, when spouses accepted they would not know everything about their partners: the women would never know what some of the men did on Saturday nights in the basement of the church when they donned their brotherhood uniforms; the men knew nothing of the nature of women's bleeding and their nighttime journeys to the Waters. But once people were forced to conform to a rigid schedule, any mysterious use of time made their spouses suspicious. The old men who belonged to the old fraternities began to die off, and the next generation of men feared that gathering in costume to share secrets would be seen as foolish. Many of the old men, upon retirement, moved away somewhere warm without having managed to pass on any wisdom, and those who tried to share what they knew found their sons had grown angry and unable to listen. The old men felt their virility waning, and they were left confused about what it meant to be men. They were terrified of their own womanish inclinations in old age, toward gardening and cooking, terrified of the way their eyes filled with tears at the sight of small children. The only thing they had known for sure was work, and because they were no longer farmers, work no longer made sense.

While celery grown in the field had been whitened by simply shielding the stalks from the sun, five decades of men who came afterward used chemicals in the paper mill to bleach and smooth the pulp of Michigan's old forests to create cereal boxes and food wrappers. When Goliath Paper closed, it left behind mountains of sludge at the edge of the river just downstream from the island, mounds as iconic as the church's white edifice. Gradually the paper-mill sludge settled and fused with the soil and brackish water, dispersing its toxins with every rain into the swamp and into underground wells, year after year sending its stink into the town. Long before the telling of this story, the poisons had entered the bloodstreams of the animals and people of Whiteheart, stealing into their cells, making the women more likely to miscarry and come down with cancers of their female parts. The men, too, had cancers and skin disorders, and were more prone to fits of depression, impotence, and violence.

About a year after Titus Clay Sr. had answered Rose Thorn's playful cries with drunken cruelty—something he remembered only vaguely—he was stricken blind by the vapors of anhydrous ammonia fertilizer, and he passed the operation of Whiteheart Farms (along with the debt) to young Titus, the town's favorite son. Titus Jr. was tall and strong, worked harder than a mule, paid his bills, attended church on Sunday, and was able to get along with anybody. The way he looked, the way he talked made him naturally destined to be a great man himself as soon as he got married and settled down to make a family in the big Clay family farmhouse. But Titus Sr., just before leaving for Florida with his wife, got drunk and knocked over a decorative kerosene lantern and burned the big house to the ground.

THE YEAR DONKEY TURNED ELEVEN, the year Herself was shot in the wrist and lost her right hand, Titus Clay and the other farmers fertilized fields with urea, phosphorus, and lime by the ton. Anhydrous ammonia by the thousand-gallon tank from the Farm Bureau. But the night frosts continued through the middle of May, so nobody was tempted to plant early. The rains and freezing rains were so heavy they washed the fertilizer off the higher fields into the lowlands, raising the level of the swamp and feeding invasive weeds that grew in tangles, choking the more delicate native plants, as well as the snakes, turtles, and frogs. Then, for the last two weeks in May, after the fields were planted, no rain came at all, and in early June, the crops burned under the summer sun and began to grow stunted and gnarled. Church attendance soared. Men sat in the pews tugging at the collars of their sports shirts and button-down shirts, feeling parched—even the men who were no longer farmers.

When Titus suggested to Reverend Roy that they pray for Herself, for her recovery, Roy suggested that rather than waste his prayers on an abortionist, Titus should help him waterproof the basement of the church, something the reverend had been meaning to do, because the mortar down there was crumbling. Plenty of women offered private prayers for Hermine Zook, that she might heal quickly so she could get back to healing their aches and pains—the ones they didn't want to mention to the men. Some prayed for the granddaughter, too, that big-eared freckled child who looked like Titus Clay, no denying that resemblance, prayed that she might learn her granny's secrets. For who else would help their daughters with the needs they couldn't discuss with their own doctors or husbands? Certainly not lazy Rose Thorn or Prim on her high horse out in California. Molly was a godsend to anybody who ended up at the hospital, they all concurred, but what about all the mysterious troubles a woman couldn't articulate under those bright lights?

Reverend Roy discounted the old folks' stories of miraculous healing, and he had little interest in what foolish women—including his own mother—said about deathly ill babes restored to vigorous health, young mothers risen from the depths of the postpartum abyss, and postmenopausal women renewed in spirit. He was Molly's age and had some youthful memories of Wild Will, who had been fast friends with his uncle, the old reverend. Wild Will had been a powerful man who liked to ask girls how many boyfriends they had, dare boys to climb the tallest tree in sight, and argue about church doctrine—but Roy didn't connect the memories of strength and good humor with the healing from the island. He didn't remember at all the terrible virus that had taken dozens of lives in surrounding towns but none in Whiteheart, where people drank an elderberry syrup made by Hermine before she was married.

Reverend Roy and Molly had been an item longer than Titus and Rose Thorn. They'd spent peaceful evenings together for decades, watching season after season of the same medical and lawyer dramas. Molly helped him negotiate his back pain, which had plagued him since his high school football injury. Neither of them felt compelled to get married or have kids or even live together, and their togetherness did not capture the imagination of anyone but themselves. Over the years Molly had let slip some of her mother's secrets, including that she sometimes ended pregnancies. Molly's touch soothed him in a way nothing else did, but in spite of this evidence, Roy could not fathom that some knowledge and skills rose not from church or school but out of the Waters and manifested in women's bodies—Molly's hands, for example—just as a man who knows only wells driven into stony earth by a mechanical rig cannot imagine artesian springs of clear, clean water that bubbles to the surface naturally and unassisted, the way it always had on the island.

THE SATURDAY AFTER HERSELF WAS SHOT, Titus Clay, Jamie Standish, Tony Martin, and Rick Dickmon gathered at the church to meet Reverend Roy. They entered through the back utility door with the tools he'd asked them to bring. They found the reverend down in the basement, a carpeted room with tables and chairs and coffee service set up for the reception after tomorrow's service. Since Roy had rechristened the old United Pentecostal the Church of New Directions—Roy felt the name was more inclusive and progressive—

he'd embarked upon many structural improvements. Just last year, these four men, at the reverend's request, had hung new drywall and painted this room. Now Reverend Roy led them past the tables to a small storage room, where he stopped in front of a bookcase containing books and games.

"Pull out this shelf unit, won't you?" he said and directed Titus and Dickmon to move it away from the cinder block wall.

The four men were shocked to see a door hidden back there. They had been coming to this church since they were children and thought they knew every inch of the place. Their fathers and grandfathers might have known about this door leading to a basement beneath the basement, but for these young men, it was a revelation. They followed Reverend Roy down the curving stone staircase, feeling as though they were traveling back through time or being inducted into a secret society, something they'd only heard about from their grandfathers.

In Whiteheart and the surrounding communities, the men who had joined secret societies like the Freemasons, the Knights of Columbus, the International Order of Odd Fellows, and the Benevolent and Protective Elks had weekly donned their stiff uniforms and affixed to them the insignia designating levels of lodge authority. Now when their grandsons occasionally found those old military-style uniforms in their grandfather's closets, with medals and badges sewn and pinned on, they were surprised at how small the jackets and pants were. The men following Reverend Roy down the stairs remembered those uniforms now and suspected they were connected to this journey.

Roy reached the bottom of the staircase and turned on the light, a strangely shaped unfrosted bulb that flickered on and off intermittently, as though unsure whether to reveal to the men the room they were entering. A hum filled the damp cavern, and the men saw it was coming from a dehumidifier at the end of an ancient cloth-sheathed extension cord over which Standish tripped and almost fell. Though he was only thirty-five years old, a year younger than Titus, his feet hurt all the time and didn't seem to work right.

Titus and Dickmon fetched the trouble lights they'd brought from home, let the cords wind down the stairs, and hung them from hooks in the dripping ceiling. Illuminated that way, the four walls came alive around them. On each was a ceramic tile mosaic version of an Italian Renaissance painting with life-sized characters, rendered by local masons, who hadn't realized they were artists as well as craftsmen. The men who had once met here had enjoyed the feminine secrecy with which they lovingly decorated the crypt, using brick-red, blue, and white tiles to depict the arabesques and sun symbols and crosses and human figures in the four magnificent mosaics. Through the camaraderie of their secret creations, these men had learned how to face complication and contradiction when they found it in the Bible or in their lives. During their candlelit ceremonies, they read scriptures from the Holy Bible and the Gospel of Thomas, also the Bhagavad Gita, the Zend-Avesta and the Quran, and they found there common and universal truths that any man could understand. In the Whiteheart church subbasement, these books were kept in a locked cupboard on the wall above the stone under which supposedly lay an old woman's bones. They had been thought, by the old men, to be the bones of Baba Rose's own mother, though in fact they were the bones of a lost vagrant woman who died in the Waters before ever reaching the island. The best passages of these books were committed to memory and never mentioned outside the meetings.

Titus used his blue bandanna to wipe clean a patch of tiles on the east wall, which then shone brilliantly against the mildewed grout, revealing an image of a modest Mother Mary holding a naked Baby Jesus. On the west wall was a fleshy and powerful Mary Magdalene. To the north, a skinny woman, unfamiliar to the men—the lettering below the scene said "St. Eulalia"—hung naked upside down from a tree in ecstatic agony with a breast visibly removed from her bloody torso. The fourth was the largest and most elaborately rendered: Paul on the island of Malta, holding the venomous viper whose bite would not kill him; flames rose around the pair.

Titus whistled at the man holding the snake.

"Will you look at that," Dickmon said, shaking his head. "A thing like this right here in our church."

"Beautiful," Two-Inch Tony said, putting both hands on the mildewy image of the Madonna and child. He stopped just short of kissing Mother Mary, remembering the other men. "Just beautiful."

Standish trembled at the sight of the women in the mosaics, so much that he almost fell to his knees. He mumbled, "God help me,

I only did it for Jesus and His innocents . . . your only Son, who you gave for poor sinners like me, to wash my sins away . . .''

Sometimes he imagined he hadn't shot her—surely he wasn't the only one who had put a bead on the old woman. Maybe somebody else had shot from another direction, like when there was a firing squad and one man was given a blank, so a man didn't know whose bullet had done the job. God had to know Standish's motives, so why was He punishing him with an ulcer on top of another ingrown toenail infection? Why should Standish regret the most righteous thing he'd ever done? He'd felt certain the old woman had given his fifteen-year-old daughter the medicine to make her lose her baby, which she obviously didn't want. Nobody had been able to convince him otherwise. His wife, Prissy, had refused to talk to him about it, other than to insist that he talk to their doctor. Dr. Hunt had assured him that his daughter had simply miscarried, which was common among teenagers.

"Forgive me," Standish whispered to Mary, the Mother, with her shining face and blue robes and graceful head covering.

When he'd learned that his daughter had lost the baby, Standish hadn't slept for weeks. Possessed by the need for revenge, he felt alive, like a hunter. Every word spoken in his presence during those weeks had fed his fury. He'd organized his weekend days so that he could get up early and watch Rose Cottage before Herself came out to check her empty basket and sit at the roadside with those braids wrapped around her head. He'd never dared cross the bridge, but he snuck around Boneset, where she was still well within range. A few times he'd seen the girl watching him, and when she spotted him, he slunk away down the road to where he'd parked his truck. He was driven to do these things, although he'd never consciously thought he would actually shoot a human being. But one morning he saw Herself lift a fat snake up in front of her with both hands. She held that monstrous muck rattler up as though speaking with the devil through it, the way only a witch would do, and something in his brain had short-circuited, and he fired.

He thanked God his aim had been poor, that he'd only shot her in the wrist so she might not make medicine anymore. She had flinched when the bullet hit her, but to Standish's surprise, she hadn't dropped the muck rattler; even with that exploded wrist, she had carefully lowered the snake, as though she existed beyond the human pain threshold. Now, he knew he should confess, but he didn't want to face what he'd done in any public way. He couldn't imagine telling anyone, and he argued with himself that it would do no good. Above all, he felt diminished, less alive, now that the drive for revenge had been satisfied.

He stared at the peaceful image of Mary on the wall. Why didn't all women dress that way, he wondered, in soft, flowing fabrics? Why couldn't all women be good like Mary? He slumped to his knees in front of her.

"Get up off the floor, man," the reverend said and began to orate. "I trust you men not to share what you've seen down here. I don't know what foolishness those old folks were up to, but this display doesn't seem Christian to me. I'd fill this room with gravel if I could figure out how to do it. For now, let's just stop the hemorrhaging before the foundation goes."

Indeed, there were cracks in the west wall where water trickled in and formed pools on the floor. The brilliant white and blue floor tile was visible through the standing water and also was revealed wherever the men displaced the mud with their boots. All four walls wept through their grout. Reverend Roy insisted they cover all the tile work, had them haul down the stairs buckets of block filler and scrapers, putty knives and rollers and brushes.

Under the trouble lights, the four men cleaned the walls to shining brilliance to prepare the surface. Then, without really knowing why, they covered them. For Titus—for all of them, but for Titus most of all—the job of covering the tile was torture, smearing that thick layer of filler cement over the women, especially Saint Eulalia, who would be trapped forever in her holy agony. Titus couldn't shake her. Later, he learned she was a saint to whom Spanish Catholics prayed to prevent drought. And even as he applied the waterproofing, he wondered what kind of solvent he might use someday to reveal the women again, to bring them back.

CHAPTER SEVEN

～

No place like home.

HERSELF WAS DISCHARGED FROM the hospital six days after being shot. Donkey, warmed by the heat of Molly's angry gaze, helped Herself up into the passenger side of Titus's old red-and-white diesel Ford near the hospital entrance by pushing on her tree-bear body from below, using all the strength in both her arms. Titus was right behind Donkey, offering to help. Donkey had wished for Titus to get there before the transport to Christian Comfort Care arrived—what else could she do but wish?—and he had.

Molly had arranged bed space at Christian Comfort for rehabilitation. "A nursing home isn't what it sounds like," she'd said. Donkey didn't know anything about nursing homes, only that Herself didn't want to go there. Molly now stood before the double doors of the hospital with one fist pushing out the pocket of her flowered nurse smock, the other hand pressing the cross pendant given to her by the reverend into her breastbone so hard it would make a mark. Her voluptuous figure was nearly petrified with the anger that came with her love.

Herself was exhausted and beleaguered, but beneath that weakness, her fury matched Molly's exactly, just as their bodies were about the same weight, although differently proportioned. When Donkey moved aside, Titus reached across Herself and fumbled to pull the seatbelt over her lap. Herself pushed him away. To keep him from trying again, Donkey got between them and slammed the door. It didn't quite close, because Hermine's body was not fully inside the cab, so Donkey pulled the door open wide and started to slam it a second time. Titus grabbed her from behind and held her, and Molly abandoned her angry vigil and ran over to protect Hermine's bandaged right arm. What was left of it.

"Be careful, Dorothy!" Molly said. She helped Hermine situate herself inside and closed the door gently. "For crying out loud, your granny is fragile."

Donkey had already damaged the wound once, right after the surgery to remove the hand and part of the forearm; she'd been braiding Hermine's hair and had fallen onto the bed and bumped the stump, which had blossomed red through its bandage like a grosbeak's breast.

While Molly berated her now, Donkey luxuriated in the feeling of being imprisoned in Titus's big arms, struggled only a little.

"And for Chrissakes, either she can't hear, or she won't listen. I don't know which is worse," Molly said.

The apparent deafness was confusing to Donkey too. Before coming to the hospital, Herself had always heard Donkey's voice somehow, but now Hermine only seemed to hear her when she spoke in an imitation of Titus, an even lower voice than the one she had used before. And she didn't acknowledge hearing anybody else at all.

Hermine's great body, clad in a lavender flannel nightgown, settled inside the cab of the truck. She'd hardly spoken during her hospitalization, and Donkey had had to beg her to eat this morning, since eating was a condition of being released to go home. Herself had finally relented and eaten what she called "prison slop"—a plate of fake eggs with no salt, strange hospital sausage, and toast spread with flavorless yellow grease.

"Taking her back there is not an option, Titus," Molly said, even as the thing was happening. "I know you think you're helping her, but you're not."

The entire time at the hospital and in Molly's tin can, Donkey had kept her self-inflicted stab wound covered by the long sleeve of Titus's jacket, which Molly had said made her look like a street urchin, which Donkey misheard as "sea urchin." Since her encounter with the Lindworm, she'd had dreams that her body became covered with snakeskin, starting at her hand. What remained on the heel of her hand was

a scar that looked like a melted figure eight—where she'd smeared
the salve of last resort—with a pencil point in the middle. Whatever
scar Herself would've had from the salve had been cut off along with
her hand.

For the first four days after coming to the hospital, Donkey had
enjoyed the freedom of running the halls with boys—real boys!—and
otherwise investigating or sitting in different places to work through
equations in her *True Things* notebook, but then Molly had told her
what was next for Herself: the rehab facility and hearing tests to get
a little machine she'd wear in her ear. Donkey imagined this terrible
future: Herself remaining shackled to a bed; Donkey translating what
everybody said all day and continuing to return at night to Molly's tin-
can trailer with all those cats that couldn't go outside. This morning,
even Donkey wasn't allowed to go outside, after a truck sprayed all the
miniature lawns with chemicals.

Yesterday afternoon, she had secretly called Titus on the phone in
Hermine's hospital room, imitating her granny's voice, saying, "Come
get me out of here and take me home, and I'll give you some thinblood medicine." Before then, Donkey had never imitated Herself to
mislead; she had just wanted to hear the sound of Herself come out of
her own mouth or to make Rose Thorn laugh. Since licking the snake
blood off her hand, Donkey had not changed physically, but she suspected it had made her deceitful.

Molly herself had called Titus the day Hermine was admitted
to the hospital to ask him to take care of the island chores, feeding Ozma, the chickens, and Delilah, and milking the cow. Titus had
been helping Herself at Boneset since before Donkey was born, and
she'd been giving him medicine for his thinblood, and the two of
them had various trades and schemes together, but he'd never come
to M'sauga Island.

Ada McIntyre, Titus's great-aunt and M'sauga Island's closest
neighbor, had been admitted into the hospital two days after Herself. After visiting his aunt, Titus came by Hermine's room to pay his
respects, and that's when he told Donkey to call him if she needed
anything. Molly said Ada had been admitted because she needed "real
medical care," but Donkey thought she was probably there because
Herself wasn't home to resupply her herbal heart medicine. And it

was because Ada was there at the hospital that Roger was also there. Titus called him a nephew because his cousin Alan had been like a brother to him before he went to his awful endless ∞ at a young age by bleeding to death in the swamp.

Roger was six months older than Donkey, had ears as big as hers and freckles like hers, and he disagreed with everything she said. He told her that they didn't tie him to a desk at school and that no teacher would dare pull his hair. He was eight inches shorter than she was, though he denied this plain fact, and she wrestled him to the ground as easily as she wrestled Ozma. He got revenge on her by making a gun out of tongue depressors and using it to shoot her with rubber bands. Worst of all was when Roger and two of his cousins dropped *Garden of Logic* down the waste chute, where they said it would be burned to ashes in the incinerator. Donkey had thrown the book at Roger's face for calling Rose Thorn a whore. She had never lost her temper quite the same way before and had to assume that this, too, was the angry action of the snake blood now in her veins.

Losing the book had felt like losing a friend. No longer could she turn to Professor A. Schweiss for logical comfort in a difficult moment. After a few fretful hours, during which Donkey appealed to every adult she could find, a custodian returned the book to her with the cover torn and the pages bent. It had gotten stuck in the chute, he told her, and so was in no danger of burning up after all.

"Do any of you have any idea how hard you are making things?" Molly said now as she stood next to Titus's truck. She planted her soft mitts on her hips. "For yourself and me? And Herself? Mama's not ready to go home. Not to that island. She's frail, Titus. She'll get an infection. You know she had salmonella in her wound? And how is she going to do for herself with one arm?"

"She has one arm plus three-quarters of an arm," Donkey said. "She has seven-eighths of what she had before." She spoke with confidence, but in truth she wasn't sure if a hand was part of an arm. If so, maybe she had only five-sixths of what arms she had before. There was no denying she had only half her hands.

"We'll all pray for her and work together to take care of her," Titus said. "You and me and String Bean here. Your ma just loves being home, and I can't see her being happy anywhere else." Titus took off his Allis-Chalmers hat and ran his hand over his thatch of curly hair and placed it back in the groove it had already made.

"Well, who do you think is going to have to carry everything across that godforsaken bridge and change her bandages every day?" Molly complained about the bridge nearly every time she came onto the island, which was at least twice a week. In Molly's smock pocket, Donkey could see the outline of the surgical scissors for cutting bandages and anything else, scissors strong enough to cut off a finger, but Molly had refused to cut the restraints the other nurses had put on Hermine after she tore off her IV line and got out of bed a third time, causing blood and saline fluid to leak everywhere.

"I'll help as much as I can," Titus said. He was wearing his other army jacket, which was shorter than the one Donkey was wearing and only had pockets on the chest. "Maybe I can build a handrail for the bridge when I get done with the planting. We'll get some treated lumber—even God can't afford redwood anymore."

"I had this child registered for summer school, and now she'll have to care for an old woman instead of getting an education," Molly said. "What life is that for a girl? Dorothy, if you don't go to school, how are you going to learn math? Don't you want to learn math?"

"Not calculus," Donkey said, though, strictly speaking, the answer was *yes, sometime*. It had been a big week for her education. She had read Roger's math book, and a nurse had given her a high school biology text from the Left Behind Box where Molly had taken her for shoes after she'd arrived at the hospital barefoot. For sure if she lived with Molly, she'd go to school just to get out of the tin-can trailer court. Now, Donkey studied the spindly yew bushes growing stunted between the parking lot and the hospital sidewalk. The dirt at their roots was so hard and poor Donkey wondered how the bushes could breathe. On top of the exposed roots were scattered a few woodchips and coffin-nail butts.

"An education that comes from caring for her family," Titus said. "That's important, too, Molly. I know I should have checked with you, but Herself was determined to come home."

"I know what you're up to, Titus Clay. You believe in her business as much as any bat-shit woman in this town. You're so desperate you'll drink snake venom and think you're cured. If you don't want to bleed to death, you should be more careful what trouble you get yourself into."

Donkey knew the recipe, knew Titus's thinblood medicine did contain venom and snake blood (from the dwindling, diluted supply) and four kinds of boiled roots, including a splash of poisonous snakeroot. The opposite medicine, the one that would start a woman bleeding if that was what she needed, contained venom and antivenom, pennyroyal, celery seed, parsley, fringed rue, and bloodroot all mixed up in a clamshell. Before Molly took Donkey into the hospital, she had warned her to never bring up the subject of her granny's medicines—and especially the one that would start the bleeding—in front of anyone.

Molly dropped her voice so Donkey wouldn't hear, complained to Titus about careless men shooting. The sheriff had come to the hospital room and talked to Herself and Donkey, and they had said as little as they could, since nobody avoided the law more than Herself; and it was true that Herself had seen nothing, occupied as she'd been with the snake, and Donkey had not seen the camouflage man or anyone other than Herself that day. Accident was the consensus, and nobody was very surprised. Sometimes somebody just got in the way of a bullet's trajectory. Last November a woman in Potawatomi, on the other side of the Waters, was shot because she was at the edge of the woods wearing white gardening gloves, and somebody mistook her for a white-tailed deer and killed her. The shooter confessed to his mistake in that case and got a punishment of community service.

Some people at Reverend Roy's church did feel uneasy when they heard of the shooting, and a few wondered if it had had anything to do with the young men who went around armed and talking about enforcing God's will.

But Herself saw the shooting not as the act of a single violent man but as the natural outcome of the anger and frustration of the men in the town, many of whom no longer knew what it was to be a man, apart from what was told in holy heroic stories. Whoever had shot her had merely been the vanguard. If he hadn't shot her, one of his kind eventually would have. She concluded that Whiteheart itself had shot her, and she doubted she could help the people here anymore; she needed to consult with Baba Rose in her own kitchen before she would know how to respond.

Donkey went around to the driver's side of Titus's truck and climbed in onto the blue vinyl bench seat—split so that foam cushioning showed through, covered with papers from the Farm Bureau and empty Pall Mall packs—and scooted to the middle, next to Herself. The smells were of burnt coffee and coffin-nail smoke and diesel fuel and, muskily, Titus himself.

Though Herself refused to be strapped down by the belt, Titus insisted Donkey dig the ends of the middle lap belt out from the seat and fasten it over her hips, and the snug hold gave Donkey the feeling that the seat was going to swallow her. As they pulled away from the hospital, Titus waved at Molly in a friendly way. Donkey imitated how Titus talked and how he strode with long legs, but she couldn't master his ability to breeze past other people's opinions that were contrary to his—usually Rose Thorn's but now Molly's.

"Maybe Rose Thorn will be waiting for us when we get there," Donkey said.

"That would be lovely, wouldn't it? Your mama would bring us a bit of sunshine!" Titus said. "But I wouldn't want you to get your hopes up. I was just there a few hours ago milking Delilah. You know, ma'am, you'll have to inseminate her again soon—I don't think it took last time. I could do it. I've done it a lot." He glanced around Donkey, tried to catch Hermine's eye. Herself grew rigid, and Donkey thought she'd heard Titus's low voice. It seemed like a cruel punishment that Herself was doomed to hear men's voices more than women's now, since she'd always said that men would be the island's ruin. For Donkey, though—she couldn't help it—Titus coming onto the island was a thrilling new thing!

"Roger said I was a bastard," Donkey said to Titus.

"Not while I'm driving, String Bean." He bumped her shoulder to push her away—she hadn't even realized she was leaning into him.

"Maybe Rose Thorn knows Lorena is living with you," Donkey said. "Maybe that's why she doesn't come back." In truth, everybody knew that Rose Thorn could turn up at any moment.

"Why, you're about as outspoken as your mama in the things you say."

"Don't you still love Rose Thorn?"

"I love your mama, yes, and I love Lorena," Titus said. "But I'm making a life with Lorena."

"Molly says Lorena is very young."

"Well, she's younger than Molly, that's true."

Molly was thirty-nine, ten years older than Rose Thorn. Prim was eight years older than Molly, so forty-seven now. Herself always said she didn't know how old she was, though she claimed to know that Baba Rose had been a hundred when she died.

"Don't you still want to marry Rose Thorn?" Donkey asked. Only a year and a half ago, after the two of them had gotten along all summer, Titus had again begged her to marry him. Their marriage would mean Titus could finally be Donkey's father. But her mother's illogical response had been to burn herself instead of saying yes or even no.

"You ask hard questions, String Bean," he said. Titus did this: instead of answering questions, he called them *hard. Out of my league. For God, not me.* "You've got to let me drive." Titus gently nudged her away again, and she realized she had been leaning on him again.

"I wish we were taking Ada home too," Donkey said. "She said she's going to make me a raisin pie. With maple syrup. It's the sweetest pie she knows."

"She's going to be there a little longer, God bless her," Titus said. "My dad's supposed to come up from Florida to visit her. Lorena's trying to clean up her house right now."

Donkey thought she felt Hermine's body stiffen slightly on the seat beside her.

"How come you always talk about God now?" It seemed to Donkey he talked about God a lot more when Rose Thorn wasn't there.

"Maybe he seems important now, as I get older. And wiser, I hope," Titus said. He glanced over at Herself, who gave no sign of having heard him.

"Did you check the basket every morning for a babby?" Donkey asked.

"I checked. No babies while you were gone. But Ozma's been waiting for you. She wouldn't go in the house without you. I had to feed her under the porch."

"She's probably guarding the island. Granny thinks somebody's been trying to dig up bones. She says the men took her hand to the church so they can have a piece of her soul and Baba Rose's." Donkey glanced over at Herself, who was looking out the window, maybe trying not to hear. Herself had dreamed those things, even mumbled them, while Donkey sat close to her or lay with her on the hospital bed. It still didn't seem right talking about her in front of her, even though that's what everybody did in the hospital.

Titus coughed out a laugh. "She must've had a fever. Don't worry, ma'am. I've kept a close eye on your place. Nobody's made any trouble. You've only been gone six days."

"Six is a perfect number," Donkey said. "Three plus two plus one equals six." The next perfect number, according to *Garden of Logic* was $28 = 14 + 7 + 4 + 2 + 1$. Then $496 = 1 + 2 + 4 + 8 + 16 + 31 + 62 + 124 + 248$. Perfect numbers didn't come around very often, so you had to pay attention to them.

The truck sped up when they got onto the old highway, which curved away from the swamp, and Donkey finally felt the naturalness, the inevitability, of Hermine's escape from the hospital, Donkey's own escape from Molly, though she would miss some of the cats. A pale three-quarters moon was visible against the daytime horizon, and it seemed to her a trip to the moon, 238,900 miles away, was more likely than Herself staying at a nursing home or anywhere besides the island. While they were in the hospital, the Egg Moon had slipped away, and the new Mother's Moon had arrived. After that, in June, would come the Rose Moon, what Ada McIntyre called the Strawberry Moon because strawberries, wild and domestic, ripened. After the strawberries came the mulberries and blackcap raspberries, then the blackberries, the blueberries, and finally, the cranberries. Donkey would stuff herself with berries all summer, and if Rose Thorn would come home, they'd press some of them to make precious juices.

"And we'll catch that muck rattler you saw and skin him out. Don't you worry," Titus said.

"But the m'sauga didn't bite her," Donkey said. "And it was a she."

"Safety first." Titus took his left hand off the wheel to reach across himself and ruffle Donkey's hair, which had been tightly braided by Molly this morning at the tin can.

Titus answered some questions Donkey asked on the drive (*What's that?* A tanker truck, an alpaca in a field with sheep, a billboard advertising a drug store), and Herself said nothing through six right turns and five left turns.

They arrived at Boneset and parked in front of the table. Where normally there would be herbs, medicines, and vegetables for sale, there were only a couple of rhubarb spears Titus had put out, some as long as what was left of Hermine's right arm. He creaked his door open, got out, and left it hanging open while he went around to help Herself. Donkey lifted the nearest corner of the driver's side floor mat and found the scuffed zipped-up freezer bag containing an old faded color photo she knew was always there. It was a photo of Rose Thorn, wearing denim cutoffs and a yellow T-shirt with a sunflower on it. Donkey let the mat fall back. And surely Rose Thorn was still carrying the amber stone Titus had given her, what she called her *warm stone,* her *heart.* After 621 days—Donkey kept track in her notebook—she needed her mother to come home!

Across the road in the pasture, Titus's six Herefords grazed in a row in the distance without looking up—Herself had recently let Titus graze them there in exchange for his help—but long-eared Triumph and spotted Aster, still shaggy in their winter coats, trotted to the fence line. They hung their heads over the woven wire as Herself emerged from the truck, clad in the flowing nightgown, looking like somebody from a Bible painting with her carved wooden stick. Titus had brought it from the island and pulled it out from behind the seat, but it was never meant to be a cane, since it was curved and forked at the end for moving snakes and flattening grass in search of snakes. Donkey checked the Babby Basket, which was indeed empty, and noted that she would have to change the dusty orange blanket. She spun the dial on the combination lock on the tin money box bolted to the Boneset Table, inhaling the smells of new rye grass and donkey dung. Twice around to the right, once to the left, with the whistle of a redtail hawk streaking above them, and back to the right as a welcoming wind rustled the willow leaves.

Nobody ever cut the flimsy lock to steal the money, and Titus always said this showed how people respected Herself. Nobody ever stole cures or garden vegetables either. Though everybody liked Titus, he still occasionally had tools stolen when he left his barn or garage doors open, not to mention bushels of peaches and apples stolen right off the trees in his family's orchard in season. Donkey herself used to sit brazenly in a tree and eat peaches until she was sticky with the juice. Last fall, though, Lorena had kept watch in the orchard and had shouted at her, "Hey, kid! Stop stealing fruit!" Titus said that was because Lorena didn't know her. When he said he would introduce them, Donkey shook her head. She didn't want to get to know someone who would just have to leave when Rose Thorn returned.

Donkey and Titus followed Herself across the rectangular mosaic of embedded stones, shells, jewelry, coins, and bits of bone toward the wooden steps down to the island. When Donkey had dug the bullet out of the kitchen wall last year, she'd pressed it into the soil, between two Cheerio-shaped crinoid stem fossils. She found it now and pressed her toe onto it. (Donkey had asked Molly for the bullet that had been lodged in Hermine's wrist, but the answer was another question: "What is the matter with this family?")

The island was welcoming them back with its symphony of buzzes and chirps. The syrupy trilling of robin-song filled Donkey's ears. A zigzagging mosquito landed on her arm, and she brushed it away before it stuck her. She felt sorry for Herself not being able to hear all the sounds—the mosquito's sting might come as a surprise if you didn't hear the zizz. The soothing humidity and musky ripeness was already healing the damage done to their nostrils by the hospital air filled with chemicals. Donkey hadn't even noticed how raw the inside of her nose was until yesterday when Herself proclaimed she would die if she went to a nursing home.

When the weather was dry, a stranger to the Waters might not immediately realize Rose Cottage was on an island. During times of low water, the little clumps of rushes and sedges gave the illusion of being solid land until you stepped on them. Donkey kicked off her hospital shoes and ran around Herself and down the wooden steps to the plank bridge and paused to dip her toes in the cool mud. Then she ran out onto the bridge, across the place where Molly said there was no troll, to the section where it crossed a little sandy place, a trickling rill carrying a wash of sand in which watercress grew. She got down on her hands and knees on the planks and said hello to water striders and minnows. According to Herself, foolishly stepping off the floating bridge would mean sinking up to your neck or deeper; under the grasses and pitcher plants and joe-pye weed, there were certain spots of especially deep quickmuck that would swallow a kid up without a trace. The section of retractable bridge planks that lay across a wide hump of vegetation had been left down during the six days they had been away at the hospital so Titus could come and go. Donkey had only recently become strong enough to work Wild Will's contraption herself by cranking the hidden handle with both hands. Would Herself ever be able to operate it again?

This hump halfway across was covered with berry brambles that grew up on either side of the bridge and through the cracks between the planks; the brambles grabbed Donkey's shoes and sometimes her pant legs or even the bottom of the army jacket when she crossed the bridge on a windy day. Herself refused to trim the new canes back because the dark swamp berries from this beard bramble were bigger and sweeter than on any other bush. The jelly Herself made by squeezing the juice off the seedy berries through cheesecloth with two strong hands was rich as liqueur. Herself often gently brushed the pricker arms off the bridge or braided them loosely, tenderly, as though they were strands of Wild Will's beard, for it was also here that he'd first fallen into the muck and gotten bitten by a rattlesnake. Their marriage ceremony itself—though a simple affair at the courthouse—had been a cause of excitement and a source of curiosity for the whole town. People over a certain age were still confounded about Herself taking the best man in town and then chasing him away—something Donkey wondered about too.

Beyond the bridge, the giant sycamores and swamp oaks hanging over the green-stained cottage were like surrogate mothers to Donkey, who would climb up onto the steel roof and then into their arms, to nestle in their branches. Molly considered the big trees a hazard, said one was going to fall through the cottage, but so far, every time a branch had fallen, it had already been so dried out that it hadn't even dented the sheet metal. In the hospital and at home in the tin can, Molly had taken the opportunity to talk a lot—to complain—about the island. She called the bridge floating on the oil barrels *harrowing*, though she'd grown up walking across it every day. If you listened to her, you'd think the whole lush island was a deathtrap that offered no pleasures, riches, or comforts.

As Donkey stood in the middle of the bridge looking up at the island cottage, she let herself try to see the place the way Molly described it, as a dangerous, primitive place of sinister, venomous creatures and festering infection and rot. As a "witch's house" as Roger and his cousins had said. Or the home of a "baby killer," as announced by the signs somebody had stuck in the ground by the Boneset Table. Before her eyes, the cottage grew dark and began to sag, and the waters began to bubble and exude methane gas. Suddenly seeing the dangers Molly saw froze Donkey there long enough that Herself caught up and poked her with the snake stick to get her moving again. She shook off the vision and ran the rest of the way across and up the steps to Ozma, who was waiting on the upper landing, her old coyote tail wagging.

Titus and Donkey inhaled and held their breath as, under Hermine's weight, the planks in a certain part of the bridge bowed. One of the barrels there had rusted enough that it was taking on water and sinking a little, near the spot where Donkey had once dropped a turnip just to see if it would sink or if the bridge troll would grab it. (In the years since, she'd been reminded by Herself regularly of wasting this turnip.) The barrel had been half-submerged like that since winter, but now it spawned a new fear in Donkey: What if it sank and Rose Thorn couldn't get across the bridge and Herself couldn't repair it with one hand? What if Donkey couldn't leave the island even to check the mailbox or visit the donkeys? What if she never got to go to school? When Herself stepped on the spot just over that sinking. barrel, it slurped and released an odor of fetid muck and sulfur but remained in place.

Herself had spent the last eleven years worrying about Donkey falling into the quickmuck and getting swallowed up, and now Donkey stood straddling Ozma in front of the screened porch door, squeezing her hands together at chest level, looking down and wishing she had tied a rope around that old woman's waist before letting her start across the bridge. Aunt Molly said that no part of the muck went to the center of the earth, four thousand miles below them, but nobody could deny that things slipped away under the surface never to be seen again. Herself would have to take this precarious journey every day if she was going to do her job of sitting in her chair at the Boneset Table and listening to complaints and devising cures.

When Titus tried to hurry Herself the last few steps across the bridge by taking her good elbow from behind, she reached around and whacked his leg with her stick in a way that made her totter. "Let me—" she began, leaning dangerously to her left. When she was, at last, steady again on the planks, she stabbed the redwood with her stick and finished her sentence shakily, but with resolve, "—be."

Before Herself had said she would die at Christian Comfort Care, Donkey had never worried about her dying, but now she marveled at how worrying could take hold of and clench a person like a terrible aunt's hug. As Herself made her laborious way up the steps toward Rose Cottage, Donkey went inside the screened porch and saw the shell of the *Cambarus diogenes* on the table, one pincher disconnected from the rest. She picked it up and was about to ask Herself to glue it for her. But when Herself finally made it onto the top step, she released an exhausted sigh, and so Donkey put the shell down and pushed the screen door open for her.

Herself was so slow to enter that a dozen mosquitoes slipped inside with her. To Donkey's surprise, Herself let Titus support her briefly as she surveyed disapprovingly the stacked firewood on the other side of the table.

"Still too green," she surmised, though they'd been burning the fallen oak all spring.

"Open that kitchen door for us, will you, String Bean?" Titus said.

Upon entering the kitchen, they smelled bleach fumes. The freckled tile floor was scrubbed clean, not a molecule of island mud or leaf debris or bark left on it. Even the wall behind the sink and under the apple clock seemed to have been scrubbed, and a brighter light bulb had been put in the ceiling fixture. Whatever life forms Molly hadn't killed with her cleaning must've been deep in the kitchen's crevices pinching their noses.

"Molly's been hard at work," Titus said. He put the bag of bandages, medicines, and hospital paperwork on the table.

Instead of making the place look fresh, as Molly had hoped—fresh enough for the church to want to buy the place—her scrubbing had given the kitchen a worn-out, unoccupied look. The condition of the cottage wouldn't really matter, since Roy and the other men of the church planned to tear it down and relocate their Prayer Center Outpost here, but Molly had wanted Roy's first impression of the place to be as pleasant as possible.

Titus was of two minds about such a takeover. He wanted to support Reverend Roy, but he didn't see the hurry, and he would prefer to let Herself live out her life here, in her own home. He appreciated the sentiment of a home place, especially after his family home had burned down. Titus hadn't felt quite easy with the reverend since he'd insisted they cover those brilliant mosaics in the church subbasement. Especially Saint Paul and the martyred Eulalia.

"It stinks in here like the hospital," Donkey said.

"There's milk in your pail in the fridge, but I didn't have time to strain it this morning. Can you do that for me?" Titus said. "Lorena made you the rhubarb pie on the counter there."

"Thank you." Donkey loved every kind of pie, even rhubarb, her least favorite. She marveled at how even opening and closing their refrigerator must have become normal for Titus. His being inside Rose Cottage at last was like the reappearance of a wonderful animal come back from extinction, like *Castoroides*, the giant two-hundred-pound beaver of the Pleistocene. Within these rooms, even the timbre of Titus's full voice seemed like an old wish come true.

As they all stood in the kitchen, Donkey sensed something more sinister than the smell of bleach: the coolness emanating from the stove, which had never gone out in her lifetime. Once she recognized it, the absence of Baba Rose's fire became deafening, like the silence in the air after a gun's blast. Donkey opened the little door of the firebox and confirmed there was no fire inside it. In fact, the box had been swept clean of ashes. She looked up in time to see her granny's face go white.

At this moment, Herself was struck by a weakness in her legs and the knowledge that she was alone, without the wisdom of Baba Rose, who, on her deathbed, had promised to stay until she was no longer needed. Hermine reached out with her right hand to try and steady herself on the chair, but both her hand and the chair were missing, and she barely caught herself with her hip and her left hand on the table. Titus hovered close, while Donkey located the missing kitchen chair in Lazy's Room and brought it out. But Herself wouldn't sit. The shell necklace was hanging off the chair's back—Donkey had taken it off her as the paramedics carried her through the kitchen—and for that Hermine was grateful. It was not for anybody outside the family to touch, especially not any men.

"We can start Baba Rose's fire again," Donkey said to Herself, "can't we?"

"That voice coming out of you always shocks me," Titus said. "You sound like a grown man."

Donkey was surprised he didn't recognize it as his own voice.

"Put that around my neck," Herself said to Donkey. "Make sure you bury me with it in the Waters."

"It's just a necklace, ma'am. Be logical." Donkey said this so only Titus would hear. She held the thing now for only the second time in her life. She felt the twenty-eight shells click together like a handful of loose teeth. She pressed it against her cheek and enjoyed the smooth coolness of the shells until Herself stabbed the top of her foot with her stick.

At first, Donkey couldn't imagine reaching up and over Hermine's head, but her own height of seventy-one inches was a fact, and she placed the necklace gingerly against her granny's shoulders and chest. With her left hand, Herself clumsily tucked the shells into her night-gown and straightened them, each cuntshell wrapped in its cradle of braided lavender or gray or black cotton thread now touching her skin. Herself had told Donkey that each shell was a woman's life saved at great cost, and she needed to keep the shells warm and safe while she lived, giving these souls their time in the world. Baba Rose had had over a hundred shells on her necklace when she'd finally been unable to get out of bed under the burden. Every time Herself told the story of how Baba Rose died, there was another cause, and Donkey had to assume that the ghost whose fire had warmed their cottage for so many years had died of all of it, of everything.

Herself made her slow lurching way down the hall, as though the hospital stay had aged her a decade. She paused to rest and said, "Donkey, make my bed so I can lie down and die in fresh sheets."

Donkey froze and looked at Titus, grateful that he was taller than she was.

"You just need a good night's sleep in your own bed," he said calmly.

"I'll wish for you to get a new hand, ma'am," Donkey said.

"Save me from your wishes," Herself said, and Donkey knew she was right. A wish like that might cause a human hand to grow out of her forehead. Or a monkey hand. Or the hands of a clock. Or her same hand on the same wrist as it had been, bloody and mangled and infected.

Titus lit the oil lamp on the apple crate. He looked out the window across the swamp channel in the direction of his truck, though he couldn't see it through the trees.

Once Donkey got the heavy horsehair mattress made up with a clean pair of lavender sheets, Herself fell into bed. She told Donkey to pin closed the rusty-red burlap curtains, even though she usually liked to look out at the swamp channel during the day. Before pulling them shut, Donkey saw the phoebe sitting on her nest of eggs. Probably full of all the worms she had eaten that morning.

As Hermine's head sank into the pillow, the ends of tiny feathers poked through the pillowcase. Though Herself had not had a fever at the hospital, her forehead and upper lip were now beaded with sweat. Her watery, bloodshot blue-gray eyes darted, taking in the room, as though not trusting it was her own with Titus in it. She reached across her belly to find her bandaged stump and squeezed it hard enough that Donkey feared the white breast of the thing turning red again with blood.

"Now somebody else can take over my work," Herself spat. "I'm done."

"No, ma'am. You *have* to make cures," Donkey said uneasily. At the hospital, Herself had wanted so powerfully to come home that Donkey hadn't considered she wouldn't want to return to their normal life. "What if somebody needs her life saved?"

"I don't know what I can do without that hand," she said.

Donkey saw how she meant it—without Baba Rose. In the golden lamplight, the rust-colored curtains made the room feel something like the inside of a wolf's belly. Donkey wanted to say so, but instead she said, "Every power of five ends in five. Like 25 and 125 and 625. I can prove it."

"Don't you worry, ma'am," Titus said. "String Bean will take care of you until you figure everything out. She'll be your new right hand. She'll start you a new fire."

"I need my hand," Donkey said. Had her wish gone awry already? Was her own hand the one Herself would get? She crossed her arms over her chest.

"That jacket's kind of big on you, isn't it?" Titus let his eyes fall on his own last name on the tag stitched over the breast pocket of the big jacket, *C-L-A-Y*.

"It's my shell to grow into like the devil crayfish, *Cambarus diogenes*."

"Okay, you keep on growing, kid." He reached out and mussed her hair. "How tall are you going to get?"

She shrugged. Smiled.

"Anyhow, it's a medic's jacket, so maybe you'll be a good nurse like your aunt."

Donkey said, "I'm a mathematician. I want to be a topologist."

"Molly's going to come by when she gets off her shift. I'm sure she'll bring you something for dinner tonight. And she'll change those bandages. Very handy to have a nurse in the family, ma'am. She's a saint, that Molly."

"She's mad at us," Donkey said. Even Hermine's not having a fever this morning had made Molly mad. She'd had one the previous night, and if it had lasted longer, it could have prevented her from going home this morning.

"Your aunt Molly's going to have to forgive us." Titus stepped out of Hermine's room into the living room and lifted Wild Will's Holy Bible off the shelf from between *The Blue Fairy Book* and a book of mixtures and medicines called *All Chemical*. Donkey stood in the doorway between the rooms watching him thumb through the gold-edged pages.

"Rose Thorn would forgive us," Donkey said, leaning into the doorframe. "She forgives everybody."

"Your mama can get the lions in this town to lie down with the lambs. But until she gets back, you're going to have to be the big capable girl and do everything yourself."

"I don't want to do everything myself," Donkey said. "I want Herself to do it."

"I can come by and milk Delilah tonight, but it might be seven o'clock before I get here," Titus said. He moved his finger down the Bible page. For the last year and a half he'd been in a formal Bible study on Wednesday nights with Reverend Roy and a half dozen other folks. It had started as a kind of therapy after Rose Thorn left, but it felt like more than that now, had become a kind of language for him, a code for interpreting the world without her. Lorena attended as well, though she'd been brought up Catholic. She kept the trappings of Catholicism—the rosary, the holy cards, little statues of saints—but never mentioned them.

"I'm in the beans today," he said to Donkey, "so if you need me before then, talk to Lorena. She's cleaning Ada's house. She said Uncle Mike's clothes are all still in the closet after all these years."

"How many years?" Donkey asked.

"Must be going on twenty years, poor old Ada."

Ada's husband, Mr. Mike, had died only nine years before Donkey was born. Herself had kept Wild Will's clothes in her closet for going on twenty-eight years, and they all used them. Rose Thorn wore his flannel bathrobe when she was there, and it covered her from head to toe and wrapped around her twice.

"*Farmers nowadays, all they do is talk,*" Donkey said, using her granny's words and voice.

"That is true, ma'am," Titus said, as though Herself had spoken from the next room, and he responded the way he always did: "I'm not half the farmer my daddy was, and he wasn't half of what his pappy was, or so he always said." He said this same old thing to himself as much as to them. His finger moved again over the Bible page and then stopped. "Matthew, chapter five, verse thirty. You remember that number, String Bean. Read that passage."

"You're not one-fourth the farmer your grandpa was," Donkey offered.

Titus laughed. "Is that so? You always get math in there, don't you?" To Herself, through the wall, he said, "You just rest up, ma'am. You've got a granddaughter here to take care of you. She's giving you her strong arm. String Bean, you're going to have to stay close to your granny for a while until she starts feeling better. You can't go running off after animals for a while."

"For how long?" Donkey asked. She watched as Hermine's eyes closed to shut them out.

"As long as it takes." Titus looked up at the living room ceiling tiles with their cracking ivory paint, maybe hoping to see Jesus up there weaving like a spider.

"But I have to feed Triumph and Aster," Donkey said. "And check the basket."

Herself started to snore as she hadn't done the whole time in the hospital, where her sleep had been fitful.

"I'll take care of all that. I've got to check on my cattle, anyhow. You just stay here on the island and keep an eye on your granny. Don't leave her side unless there's an emergency, and then you run down to my place. Molly's right that we ought to get you a phone."

"Roger said if Ada dies, it's Granny's fault because she's a witch. And Rose Thorn is a whore. And girls aren't as smart as boys."

"Did he say all that? That boy has picked up a lot of opinions," Titus said with irritation. He left the Bible open to the page he'd been reading and pushed the big book partway under the arch of the black sewing machine with its black thread. Herself had asked Molly to bring some other colors of thread three times, and she wasn't going to beg anymore. Out of Hermine's earshot, Donkey begged all the time for baked goodies from Ada McIntyre, candies from Titus. She would like to beg Aunt Primrose for another book like *Garden of Logic*, but she was angry with her for keeping Rose Thorn in California.

"Roger can't change fractions to decimals," Donkey said. "I told him it was easy."

"Okay, well. You just read your granny the passage I told you about: 'If your right hand offends you, then you cut if off.' You know you're lucky to have your granddaddy's Bible."

Titus squinted at Donkey again to confirm the resemblance to Roger (slight) and to Alan, Roger's father (the freckles, the ears), though she was already taller than Alan had been. Because Rosie had stubbornly refused to say a word on the issue in eleven years, Titus could only assume the family resemblance came from Alan being the girl's father, may he rest in peace. Her reticence in talking about it made no sense to Titus, was one of many challenges in trying to make a life with Rose Thorn. Even at this thought of Rosie, he had to close his eyes and regain his composure.

Donkey looked forward to closing the Bible, to seeing the gold-edged pages as a solid block of gold again. When 1,488 pages came together to form one thing, it was as satisfying as multiplying the factors of a number together to get back to the original number. To please Titus these last few months, she had been reading the Bible a few pages at a time, along with her other fairy tales, but what she liked best was finishing a page so she could close the book and put it away with the other books. Sometimes she'd seen a fishing spider with striped legs up there, so she always slid the book in slowly to give the creature time to move out of the way.

Titus produced a plastic pill bottle from his jacket's chest pocket and squeezed it in his big hand before bringing it to her. He didn't appear to want to let it go.

"Will these cure her?" Donkey asked when he finally handed them over.

"They'll just take away the pain. The hospital drugs will be wearing off soon."

"She doesn't care about pain." Donkey looked at the information on the label and then pushed down and twisted the lid off and back on twice, doing long division in her head to translate milligrams to ounces. Herself hadn't even complained about being shot.

"You're going to have to help your granny heal, String Bean. You might want to pray for her." Titus seemed satisfied by this advice, but the look Hermine had on her face in sleep suggested she'd gotten a whiff of something spoiled.

Titus moved to the hallway, where he stood silhouetted by the hall light. Seeing him framed that way made Donkey notice all the areas around him in the 2,607-square-inch rectangle of the doorway that he did not fill up, his *inverse*. According to Professor A. Schweiss in *Garden of Logic*, an inverse was all the parts of a whole thing that any chosen part—such as Titus—was not.

"Your granny said she had something for me," Titus said. "When she called. Yesterday."

As he moved down the hall toward the kitchen, the floorboards bellyached under his weight, and Donkey felt the distance between them grow, spooling out the line connecting them until she couldn't stand it and hurried to join him. She wanted both to be close to him and to keep her distance. She wanted him to hug her, and she wanted to escape his arms when he did. She wanted Titus to think she was a good girl but not too good, because when she finally succeeded in wishing him to become her father, she didn't want him to take her away to live with him all the time. Once Prim had left Rose Cottage to live with Wild Will at Boneset at age fifteen, she had never come back to live on the island, and all these years later her rare visits were still difficult for everybody.

Donkey found Titus waiting in the kitchen. He had opened the doors of the tall cupboard and was looking through the bottles on the top shelf. The sight of him there, a man, in Granny's cupboard, was terrible, until she remembered how much she liked Titus. She wanted him to close the doors, but she didn't want him to leave. The good news about the cupboard was that Molly hadn't touched anything—it was just as crowded with bottles and jars and packages as when they'd left.

"Do you think everybody has their dad and mom together up in heaven?" she asked.

"Of course they do. Families are together in heaven. That's the most important thing," he said, turning around to see her. "Do you know which of these bottles is my medicine?"

Titus stepped back to let her approach. He had been studying the bottles all week, but a dozen of them looked similar to bottles Herself had given to him in the past. Donkey began to close the cupboard, but Titus stopped her hand and opened it again. She looked around for a creature to help her, but Ozma was outside, and the kitchen spiders that had survived Molly had been scared off or were hiding.

"Maybe you could stay longer," Donkey said. Standing with Titus right in front of the cupboard was disorienting, the smell of Molly's bleach and Titus blending with the smell of Hermine's herbs. The combination made a strange musk.

He straightened his back, considered something, and stepped away, behind a chair. "Everything happens for a reason. I believe that. I've been thinking maybe God wants to stop your granny from doing something she does. Making medicines."

"But people left more notes in the box."

"I mean just . . . certain ones. Why don't you ask your aunt Molly to bring you to Sunday school? Lorena's going to be teaching this week."

"Does she teach math?"

"It's at the church."

"Would I have to handle snakes?" Donkey asked. She was glad to have gotten between Titus and the cupboard. She smelled muck mushrooms, oysters, and morels together.

"Goodness, you sound like your mama," he choked and turned it into a laugh.

"You mean the medicine for the cuntshells," Donkey said. Molly had said the same thing, that Herself shouldn't make the start-the-bleeding cure for women anymore.

"I wish you wouldn't call them that. They're called cowry shells. But that's right. I know your granny thinks she's helping." Titus clutched the back of the chair, and his knuckles went white. "But children have a right to be born."

Donkey agreed. Titus didn't seem to know that Herself didn't give the bleeding medicine for every cuntshell left at the Boneset Table; she only gave it to certain women she had sat with and listened to, and those were the only shells that went onto her necklace. Donkey wanted to keep the conversation going.

"You said, 'Thou shalt not kill,' but God kills people all the time. He killed Lot's wife. He turned her into salt," Donkey said.

"Lot's wife didn't obey, String Bean. He told her not to look back. You know, you don't have to read every passage in order. The Bible isn't that kind of book. You can just read what parts give you comfort. Skip ahead." He stepped back toward the door, took off his cap again and smoothed his curls. "I'm just saying everything happens for a reason. You read that passage I left open. Maybe your granny's soul can be helped somehow by this tragedy."

"Ma'am said a big part of her soul was in her hand."

"Your granny needs to rest now. She doesn't need to worry about seashells. Toss them in the Waters. Let those women go to their husbands or their fathers. Let them go to the reverend and leave your granny in peace."

"Okay," Donkey said. "Those pain pills are five hundred milligrams, and that's less than point zero one eight ounces." She was saying things to keep him there, even though she felt Herself all the way from her room saying, *Let him go.* She wanted to keep both Titus and Herself together and make them settle this business of the medicine between them. If Rose Thorn were there, they might have.

"Zero point one eight, you say?" Titus asked, glancing over at the clock.

"No. Point zero one eight."

Titus looked melancholy, sorry for her with his brown eyes, which were softer than the sharp blue-gray eyes of Herself and Molly and Prim, and Donkey too. Rose Thorn's eyes were entirely different, fox-colored and full of glittery light, like Wild Will's. All Irishmen had melancholy, Titus had told her, which was a kind of sorrow that would cause him to sing instead of cry. "I know your granny doesn't want to hear it, but Jesus will help you through this if you let him, so please don't shut him out."

"Granny won't open the door. She says to hell with that poor ghost coming around here." They'd had this conversation before. "God should make her hand grow back."

"I don't know all that goes on in that freckled head of yours," Titus said, mussing her hair. "My cousin Whitey's out there waiting on me, and I've got to pay him by the hour."

Donkey opened the cupboard again and smelled morel-mushroom swampiness. She looked down and saw what Titus had somehow not seen on the floor, at the back of the cupboard, under the lowest shelf. The left-hand caboodle lid was ajar, and next to it, a dark, entangled creature like a bony heap of leather. *Sistrurus catenatus*, who had disappeared under their house six days ago, had reconstituted herself in their kitchen. Her cat eyes looked up at Donkey, sullen and angry and hurt. Donkey swallowed her scream and took a breath as she lifted Titus's bottle from the top shelf.

"I set you free," she whispered, so quietly Titus could not hear. If she cried out, Titus would kill the Lindworm, even though the snake hadn't bitten anyone. Six days ago Donkey would have gone along with killing the m'sauga under Hermine's bed, but the more you helped something, the more attached you felt to its life. *Thou shalt not kill* might expand to include *Thou shalt not let other people kill.* She wasn't trying to be a liar, but misleading others was becoming easier for her with the snake blood in her veins.

Slowly, with a pounding heart, she closed the doors. Only as the cupboard latched tightly did she feel a shush of movement against the bottom of the left-hand door.

Titus reached into his right breast pocket and produced a bag of

M+Ms. He held it slightly above his shoulder, out of her grasp. "Promise me you'll read to your granny from the Bible. And no seashells."

She nodded yes. He put the M+Ms into her left hand while taking the bottle from her right.

"That's 385 of these candies you gave me so far. There's 55 in each bag."

Titus glanced up at the length of two-by-four stowed above the kitchen door. Donkey knew how it worked—it fit into brackets on either side of the door frame, installed by Wild Will—but they'd never employed it, since nobody came to the island who had to be kept out of Rose Cottage. There was one for the back door too, in Hermine's bedroom.

Donkey followed Titus out onto the screened porch and watched him leave. When he reached the beard bramble bush, he didn't even notice it but just trampled the tendrils growing up between the planks with his size thirteens. A prime shoe size. By staying still, Donkey was able to feel the little echo of each of his steps on the bridge and the tug of the line connecting them right before it snapped and left her end dangling. She wanted to follow him across and up the wooden steps and get into the cab of his truck again, but instead she picked up the crayfish shell and its detached pincer from the porch table and pressed them together and wished for them to magically adhere. *Another broken thing needing fixing*, Herself might say. Well, now Herself was broken. Donkey stared into the empty face of the shell of the *Cambarus diogenes*. The strain of getting out of that shell had seemed enough to rupture the pink body of that crayfish, but she'd had no choice, since staying inside a too-small bone cage would've slowly crushed her.

She took a small enameled bucket with a lid from the porch floor and dumped the clothespins out of it. She could trap the m'sauga in it and put it outside and close up the left-hand caboodle more securely. She slowly opened the tall doors again, but the m'sauga had disappeared down into the caboodle, underneath the cottage. Donkey adjusted the hatch door precisely and put a piece of firewood on top of it so the creature couldn't come back up.

She took a moment to visit the dresser drawer and look at her photo of Wild Will holding two m'saugas before returning to Herself, who lay motionless on the bed. Donkey sat beside Herself and said in Titus's voice, "Titus is going to come milk Delilah after seven."

There was a long silence before Herself said grimly, "Don't tell me I raised the kind of girl who waits for a man to milk her cow."

THE REST OF THAT DAY, Donkey watched Herself say nothing, dream nothing, watched her lie in that bloody light, sometimes with her eyes closed, sometimes with one eye open like a crow half-asleep, and then sometimes glancing around the room fully alert, searching for Baba Rose. Donkey thought her granny was in pain, but she knew that her taking the hospital medicine was about as likely as their traveling in a tin-can spaceship to the Mother's Moon, 238,900 miles away. Donkey made strong merry poppins tea and felt grateful when Herself drank it, but the old woman remained silent.

Without Herself saying something to remind Donkey who she was *not* all day, she lost track of who she was and got wrapped up in the animal language of the old woman's facial expressions. With no illogical statements to argue against, Donkey failed to be mathematical. Instead of equations, she wrote in her book of *True Things* all that Herself should have been saying: *Stop your bellyaching and pay attention. Be careful what you wish for. Stop tipping in your chair, or you'll break it. We're all dying.* Even things Herself said about the brutes of Nowhere: *The beggars are a plague on us. They take and they take until there's no more to take.* Being full of worry in Hermine's room, with its lavender and holy basil scent and oil-lamp smoke and the ghosts of her complaints, was not conducive to logical thinking, and Donkey's fear of the bridge troll and a wolf coming to the door bubbled inside her.

Before going to the hospital, Donkey had thought that Herself was always pulling her in with her words, so Donkey was always pulling away in response, as though they were pulling on two ends of a rope. But as the silence persisted, Donkey saw how their words and arguments passed back and forth had built a tall, strong wall between them so they could be their true selves on either side, Donkey free to express her love of animals and mathematics and to indulge her dreams of men, and Herself free to heal people and know better than anybody else. But now Herself wouldn't even be able to braid her own hair or wrap the braids around her head above her ears the way she had every morning. She wouldn't be able to make blackcap jelly or milk a rattlesnake or even hold it while she cut off its head.

Donkey watched her granny's chest rise and fall in a rhythm that seemed too slow. She knew she shouldn't wish her to live if she wanted to die. But she wanted Herself to live.

"Ma'am, I wish you would stay alive. You can have my arm," she said, pressing her lips to Hermine's cheek. "I'll milk Delilah every day now. I'll braid your hair—I'll learn to do a better job. I don't want to run around with boys anymore." It was a lie, but right now she wanted it to be true.

The kitchen was full of herbs and flowers, but Donkey didn't know which ones to use to wake Herself from this sort of gloom. It would take something more extreme than burning yarrow, which they used to wake Rose Thorn out of a hangover. In one of Hermine's favorite stories, "The Bronze Ring," the sultan was dying, and he only came back to health when somebody cut him up and boiled his bones and then reassembled him with the burned ashes of three different colored dogs.

Donkey reached across Hermine's big belly to take hold of her left hand with her own right one. She remembered Herself reassuring her when she was afraid, and she held Hermine's hand the way she'd held it as a little kid when crossing the road at Boneset those first times. As their fingers interlaced now, Herself gasped. She sprang awake, electrified, and sat up rigidly in bed, gripping Donkey's fingers so hard they hurt, putting her weight on Donkey's hand. Donkey tried to pull away, fearing Herself would eat her up. She was still in Hermine's grip when the old woman leaned over the side of the bed and vomited up everything she'd eaten at the hospital—the fake eggs made from powder, the strange gritty sausage, the nothing-toast with yellow grease spread over it. Donkey felt all her bones leaving her body and being rearranged, mingled with the old woman's, filling in the empty spaces.

CHAPTER EIGHT

❧

Everyone alive is dying.

ONKEY'S FIRST BATCH OF sourdough rolls—made with Jane Dough ten days after returning from the hospital—had burned bottoms, but Herself, sitting at the kitchen table, didn't even wrinkle her nose at them. They were also freckled from the coffee grounds Jane had picked up in the compost pile, where Molly had tossed her during her cleaning frenzy and where Donkey had found her. Rolls turned out to be easier than bread, and Donkey looked forward to melting butter onto them, even as she dreaded the thought of making them every day until Herself revived. After Donkey offered her right hand into service, Herself stopped talking about dying, but she still hadn't made any food or medicine, and if Donkey didn't feed her, she seemed content to go without eating. Without Baba Rose, Herself was in a holding pattern, waiting for a clear sign of what would come next. Donkey was happy eating the casseroles and cakes brought by women from Nowhere and the fast food brought by Molly, but Herself wouldn't touch any of it. Donkey lifted the hot aluminum cookie sheet out of the oven with two orange-and-white woven potholders she'd made on a little loom this week with Molly as part of her *art education.*

When she looked past Herself, out the kitchen window toward the Moon Palace, she saw how the late morning fog had rearranged itself, gathered itself into a wispy figure that could climb the three steps and open the door to the screened porch and walk inside, with Ozma at its side. Donkey hurried to the door, still carrying the rolls, and opened it to see the fog settling into the ladder-back chair at the end of the porch table. Except that it was not fog but a body forming before her eyes out of a stream reflecting golden sunlight, a yellow checkered tablecloth, and the bones of two hundred goldfinches.

Donkey forgot how to breathe. She opened the door wider and in doing so somehow flipped the contents of the hot pan onto the porch planks. Now the figure was fully conjured, tipping back in the chair, as Donkey was forbidden to do. There was Rose Thorn with her bare brown feet resting on the table, legs crossed at her slender ankles, her hands clasped behind her head, shiny hair as windblown as feathers. All around her, in the mid-morning haze, golden light fingered upward. Rosie was as perfect as a perfect number with all her factors adding up to make the sum of her, and the whole day now felt fresh and breezy. Ozma was sitting on the floor beside the chair, on the porch for the first time since the Lindworm had arrived.

"Granny!" Donkey screamed. "She's here!"

Whether Herself heard the scream or only sensed the excitement, she got up from the kitchen table. She poked Donkey with her snake stick and pointed at the spilled rolls until the girl bent down to pick them up off the planks. This was as proactive as Herself had been since returning from the hospital. The steaming freckled rolls were now dusted with shredded bark from the firewood. Donkey put the pan of them on top of the rusty chest freezer to cool. Then she reached out to touch Rose Thorn's bare tanned shoulder, to test if she was real, to see if a hand would pass through her the way it did in dreams. She stopped before she reached Rose Thorn, fearful of discovering her mother was a ghost. "I didn't see you cross the bridge," Donkey said.

"Look what the cat dragged in. Another child come home to tell me what to do," Herself said. Though her voice was harsh, her eyes were misted over with tenderness. "This one of yours wants to be the boss now."

"You talked!" Donkey said. For ten days the old woman had been disoriented and strange, hadn't done more than groan at getting out of bed and mumble over cures she was unable to make.

"Mama, it's lovely to be home with the immortals," Rose Thorn said, her voice musical despite her obvious exhaustion. She gazed at

Hermine's face for a while and then switched to study her daughter with interest and curiosity, as though the girl were a fascinating bit of wildlife. "My magnificent Dorothy, my genius Freckle Face. Sharp as a pencil. You can't imagine how I've missed you."

Rose Thorn was always overwhelmed by her daughter as much as by her mother. She wanted both of them to love her, and for her abandonment of them, she felt she deserved the love of neither.

"You were gone 631 days," Donkey said, trying to keep her voice flat after giving herself away with her initial scream. To not jump for joy.

"Is that so?"

"Laguna Beach is 2,148 miles away," Donkey said. It seemed safer to say only simple true things right now, but Rose Thorn's voice and her admiring gaze were real. So were the marks from the coffin-nail burns on her arm that had made Molly put her in the hospital *for her own damned good*, but they were white now instead of raw red. Donkey still didn't know why Titus wanting to marry Rose Thorn would make her burn herself. Donkey ran her thumb over the palm of her own opposite hand to feel the bump of the pencil lead, the little smoothed-out figure-eight scar.

"'Home is not just a place but an irrevocable condition,'" Rose Thorn said and smiled. She had disassembled herself and put herself back together in a more solid form since she had last been here, but whenever she did this, there were a few more pieces missing. "There's no place like it. Right, Dorothy?"

Before her on the table was the bottle of ginger brandy from the hollow tree with its mold-speckled label. If you ever asked her what her quotes from books meant, she'd shrug and smile, and if pressed, she'd say they meant what they said, and she didn't know why they took up residence in her head. Rose Thorn read for hours and hours of every day and believed in words deep down inside her bones, where the soul is.

"You're the only good thing I ever created," Rose Thorn said to Donkey. "You were forged in the fire, Freckle Face. Look at those burn marks on you."

"They're freckles," Donkey said. She still liked it when her mom said this, even though she wasn't a little kid anymore.

"Did you come back to break my chairs?" Herself croaked, jabbing her snake stick into the floor hard enough with her left hand to make scraps of firewood jump. At this complaint, Donkey wanted to cheer. She got Hermine's kitchen chair so she could sit straddling the threshold, half blocking the doorway, denying Rose Thorn entry for as long as she wanted. Donkey stood next to her.

Molly had the idea that Herself pampered Rose Thorn, but by Donkey's measure, Herself had equal contempt and affection for all three of her daughters. Until now, only Donkey had been spared the contempt. The truth about Rose Thorn, though, was that, unlike stagnant, dutiful Molly and unlike Prim, who always arrived on a wave of high-and-mighty, Rose Thorn was lighthearted and fun to be around.

Rose Thorn's face wore a worried look as she drank Herself in, noting her slightly crossed eyes, her drooping braids uncoiled from her head, Wild Will's work shirt wrinkled from sleep, the buttons strained over her big chest. When Rosie saw the empty sleeve where Hermine's right hand should have been, she gasped and put her hand to her mouth in a rare expression of genuine shock. The front legs of her chair clunked down hard. Reflected in Rose Thorn's fox-colored eyes, Donkey finally saw the horror of her granny's violated body. Molly and Titus kept saying she was fine, but her skin was pale, her muscles were slack, and she wasn't even symmetrical anymore.

Rose Thorn's eyes started watering, and it made Donkey's eyes water. "Titus was going to marry Lorena," Donkey said, "but now he'll want to marry you again. I look more like him than before you went away. I'm seventy-one inches tall. Granny lets him come to the island now."

"Titus on the island?" Rose Thorn said this with a little smile. She couldn't even say his name without smiling.

"Do you want me to give you back his jacket?"

"You can wear it," Rosie said, studying the way the garment fell like a tent over Donkey's tall, thin frame. She thought of how Titus's big shoulders and chest filled the jacket out, and she closed her eyes briefly to let a warm feeling move through her. "Who's Lorena?"

"She's from Texas. She bakes him pies. Granny only has one hand now," Donkey said, feeling her words go wonky. "She said the other hand is in the church basement, but Molly says they burned it in the incinerator at the hospital." As she said it out loud, she realized how it all must sound. What had happened was terrible!

"You're helping your granny. Good girl." Rose Thorn wiped her eyes.

"I gave her my right hand so she doesn't want to die. My hand and my whole arm. I have to wake her up and give it to her every morning before she'll get out of bed. Otherwise, she'll stay asleep. Maybe she can use your hand for a while."

Rose Thorn reached into her tan canvas backpack, which had what looked to Donkey like a bloodroot flower sewn on it, and pulled out a flattened pack of coffin nails. She squeezed it gently and held it in her lap, let her shock mellow into a kind of confusion.

"Mama, how did this happen?"

When Herself didn't answer, Donkey said, "Maybe she can't hear you. I'm not sure."

"Molly said you couldn't hear," Rose Thorn said. "But I figured you just didn't want to listen to Molly."

"If you talk in a low voice, she'll hear you better," Donkey said. "She says she doesn't care because she's tired of listening to people. She says she likes the peace and quiet. And she hears what she wants to hear."

Rose Thorn laughed.

"I hate cooking meat," Donkey said, surprised to feel her eyes crying more. "I hate the way it smells."

"My girls only come home when they want something," Herself said, as though to Baba Rose, but then jabbed her crooked stick at the floor again in frustration. Or maybe she jabbed to stop Donkey from crying. "What does this one want?"

"Same as ever," Rose Thorn said. "Your sweet love, Mama. I'm home to bask in it again. Whatever form it takes." She shook a coffin nail out of the pack. "Molly promised she wouldn't lock me in the crazy ward again. She didn't mention Titus having a girlfriend."

"You didn't bring me another burden to raise, did you?" Herself asked and took Donkey's hand in hers and squeezed it. Donkey knew that, whatever she might say to the contrary, Herself still wanted another baby more than anything in the world. And even though Donkey didn't want one, she kept the Babby Basket clean and dry under the Boneset Table, as Herself always had. She'd told Herself how illogical this desire for a babby was when there was a fifty percent chance of it being a boy, which would mean the ruin of the island.

"Sorry, Mama. No rattlesnake in this pot." Rose Thorn shook her head.

"Good," Donkey said.

Her mother, upon returning, always gave the impression of being solidly planted as she was now, bare feet on the ground, but the next time you tried to touch her, she'd have trickled away like a bright stream out of the Waters and on to the Muck Rattler or the state of California. This time, she wore a different kind of shirt than her usual tank top—still sleeveless but dressier, prettier, with a collar and pearly snaps up the front, its color as vivid as the little yellow roses that crept around the edge of Wild Will's Boneset house. Her fraying, faded cutoffs were so short that the bottoms of the front pockets stuck down over her thighs, which were as thin as Donkey's. Donkey wanted to go to the barn right now to retrieve her mother's books where she and Titus had put them last year. She hoped her mother would stay at least long enough to reread them.

"You're going to have to search in some other cabbage patch, Mama." Rose Thorn resumed tipping her chair, resumed studying Hermine's changed arm. She was getting used to it.

Donkey knew that if Rose Thorn *had* shown up pregnant or with a baby, it would've been Donkey's own fault for wishing her home. Same if she broke the chair. She'd wished her mother back nonstop, while dumping Hermine's slop bucket, while frying meat that stank like death and ∞, while chopping vegetables; she'd wished it whenever she wanted to visit Triumph and Aster but stayed on the island instead because Herself might need her.

"I think she doesn't hear you," Donkey said.

"Lucky her," Rose Thorn said and smiled. "At least people will stop bothering her."

"No, they won't. They keep sending notes. There are fifty-two notes already. She holds them in her hand but doesn't do anything else." Donkey hugged herself and leaned against the wall for stability. She felt as if things around her—her clothes, *Garden of Logic*—were going to free themselves from gravity and float away if she didn't hold on to them. She reached into the pocket of Titus's jacket to feel the torn cover of the book.

"She shouldn't have to do anything. She's done enough for other people. She should just be Herself," Rose Thorn said. "Those rolls smell good, don't they?"

"You want one?" Donkey asked, and Rose Thorn laughed. Since Donkey could remember, Rose Thorn had eaten very little beyond the occasional mushroom or flower, never bread or rolls; she preferred to drink her calories, taking lots of juice, broth, cream, eggnog, as well as the island spring waters, though Molly said they were polluted. Also, Donkey didn't know what Rose Thorn meant that Hermine should *be* *Herself*. If she didn't heal people, what would she be?

Rose Thorn opened the top of the tan backpack and took out something papery and translucent. She wrapped it around her shoulders. Herself used her stick to lift the fraying end of the shed skin. Donkey saw it was from a fat snake. She studied it more closely and saw, with some alarm, that it had a ragged hole in it, the diameter of a pencil.

"I found it by the sycamore, with this," Rose Thorn said and held up the ginger brandy. She unscrewed the lid and took a sip. "Either my ghost left this for me or a rattlesnake did."

Donkey said, "It was the ghost."

The ghostly shed hung on the end of Hermine's stick. A breeze through the screen made it sway.

"Where's the girl who slipped out of this dress?" Hermine said, like her old self. "She should be in my pot."

"I'm not cooking you a snake, ma'am," Donkey said. Did Herself remember the snake she had put in the bucket the day she was shot? Did she wonder how the snake had gotten free? Donkey switched to her manly voice. "Do you want me to put this shed in your caboodle?"

"That voice!" Rose Thorn said.

Hermine thought about it. Then she said, "Burn it."

Donkey looked at her quizzically. She knew Herself hadn't felt like making salves or tinctures or teas, but m'sauga sheds were useful in making wound coverings and poultices and, of course, were included in the medicines to get a woman unstuck. Herself had never wasted even part of one.

"Burn it in that cold fire of yours," Herself said.

Rose Thorn looked from her daughter to her mother, smiling in puzzlement at this strange new twist.

"But you'll need it. Later, when you make cures again. When you do your job," Donkey said in Titus's voice. Was it true that the fire was hers now, just because she had started it?

"You sound like the creature from the Black Lagoon," Rose Thorn said.

"When I had two hands and Baba Rose to guide me, healing was my job," Herself said. "Now I've got three ungrateful daughters and a girl who burns bacon. I'm resting up for my new job."

"What job, ma'am?" Donkey said.

"To hell with the brutes," Rose Thorn said, grinning. "Good for you, Mama."

"I'll let this one be the boss and fix the problems of the world," Herself said, gesturing at Donkey with her chin. She seemed to be making some resolve.

"I don't want to, ma'am. I don't want to be the boss. Not yet."

Donkey pinched the snake shed and lifted it off Hermine's stick and carried it into the kitchen. On the table, she stretched it out and measured it at thirty inches. Then she opened the iron door of the firebox, but she didn't toss the skin in. If even a gnarled turnip should never be wasted, how could Herself waste this precious thing? And if this was her fire, she should have something to say about what got burned in it; she didn't want to smell snakeskin burning any more than she wanted to smell bacon frying. She got a jelly jar and started, at the tail, to coil the crisp skin into a tight cylinder the way Herself had always done. When she reached the middle, the head end started to wrap around her wrist, and she had to repeatedly shake it off.

What she saw there in the middle of the shed were two holes close together, not just one. She'd only stabbed once, but her sharp pencil must have gone all the way through the snake. And then it must've gone into her hand. This meant that not only had she licked up m'sauga blood, she'd driven m'sauga blood right into her own hand. She had unwittingly made the Lindworm her blood sister. She opened the cupboard, was glad not to see the snake there this time. Carefully, slowly, she put the jar down into the left-hand caboodle with the other powerful ingredients. She noticed once again the little silver key hanging on the bent nail. This time, she took it out and looked at it, put it in her pocket, and then took it out and put it back.

When she returned to the porch, Rose Thorn was tipped back in her chair once again. "Don't you want to tell Rose Thorn to stop tipping in her chair?" Donkey asked in Hermine's ear.

"Women do what they want around here," Herself said. To Rose Thorn, she said, "Do you know your daughter wants to go to school?"

"Aunt M says my brain will rot if I don't," Donkey said. But she didn't want to go to school now that her mother was there. She wanted to avoid all the terrible things brutes did to you in Nowhere and make sure they never got hold of Herself again.

"Don't worry, I'm home now to save you from your wicked aunt." Rose Thorn grinned and righted the chair so slowly that Donkey almost cheered when the front legs finally met the floor, right next to Ozma's paw. Rose Thorn bent to stroke the trusting dog's head. "You know you'd be sharper than all your teachers. Not sure what a genius like you could learn from those old fossils and bits of crust."

"I want to learn topology. Professor Schweiss is a topologist." Donkey pulled *Garden of Logic* out of her pocket and held it up, and Rose Thorn smiled as she recognized it.

"I doubt anybody at Whiteheart Consolidated is going to teach you topology. Better we ask your aunt Prim to send you more books. Then you can stay safe here on the island with me and your granny and be an eccentric genius."

"You always say you'll stay, and then Prim takes you away," Donkey said.

"Is that how you see it? I love Prim, just like I love you and your granny, but Prim got me out of the hospital, probably saved my life. You should've come with us." Rose Thorn glanced guilty at Herself after she said this.

"I hate California."

"You've never been there. I think you might like seeing different things. There are lots of different kinds of people there. You could maybe even meet other mathematicians."

"You stayed away too long."

"I know, but I just couldn't come right back." Rose Thorn knew she couldn't expect her daughter, who still loved this island without reservation, to understand why an adult woman would have to get away for a while to feel okay.

"Are you going to stay now?" Donkey asked. *Forever?* she thought.

"So long as nobody shackles me again, I'll stay," Rose Thorn said.

She hadn't planned to leave last time; she'd wanted to stay in White-heart, but then Titus had given her the ultimatum, and she couldn't comply. Burning herself with a coffin nail, experiencing that physical pain, seeing the flesh wounds, had somehow made more sense than answering yes or no. But having her wrists and ankles tied to a hospital bed had sprung something loose in her, and it had taken all this time in California to recover. Molly hadn't personally shackled her, but she hadn't released her either. Rose Thorn couldn't imagine anyone keeping their sanity under those conditions. Even now, just the thought of being trapped in the West Michigan Memorial Hospital's psych ward again made her heart pound.

"It feels so good to be here." She looked into her daughter's brilliant face. It was true she looked more like Titus than before. "Your aunt Prim will come visit us if we all invite her."

"I don't want her to come."

"Maybe you'll change your mind. You like the books she sends you, right? She says you're going to be a great mathematician. She probably knows what a topologist is."

Donkey said nothing rather than acknowledge anything her terrible aunt Prim had said or done. Aunt Prim's books weren't the only ones Donkey liked. She'd also liked the biology book she'd read at the hospital, which had contained so many more Latin names than the ecosystems book Molly had brought from the library. Donkey wasn't ready to admit that she liked the math books Prim had sent more than any of the others, but Rose Thorn probably knew.

Rose Thorn tapped another coffin nail out of the pack and offered it to Donkey, who shook her head vigorously. Rose Thorn's smile revealed that the offer had been a joke. She lit a new one from the one that was burning down between her fingers. Donkey took a deep breath and thought of twenty coffin nails in a full pack, ten packs in a carton. People were confusing, Rose Thorn as much as anybody. She could say *come closer* and *go away* at the same time.

"You're as tall as your aunt Prim already," Rose Thorn said.

Donkey glanced at Herself and then back at Rose Thorn. "I hope Granny doesn't die."

"Oh, she's going to live forever," Rose Thorn said. "I'm sure of it."

Ozma was smiling and panting hard enough to make a puddle of drool on the plank floor.

"Somebody here loves me," Rose Thorn said and scratched the top of the dog's head.

"Titus still has your picture under his floor mat."

Rose Thorn took a thoughtful drag on her coffin nail. She held it close to her face, so she didn't have to move her hand much to draw on it. Her fox eyes settled softly on Donkey.

"I'm not bawling like a babbling babby," Donkey announced. "My eyes are just watering from your smoke."

"Sorry about that." Rose Thorn blew a column of smoke toward the Moon Palace. Truth was, without the sharp scents of Hermine's pennyroyal oil and garlic filling the kitchen, Donkey welcomed the smoke. The smell might cover the lingering odor of bleach that still seeped into the room off the kitchen. She'd been afraid to sleep with Herself since the hospital.

"You know, Prim told me your granny used to fall at Wild Will's feet stricken with love."

Donkey glanced at Herself, who gave no sign of having heard. Donkey considered the idea. She enjoyed any new way of thinking of Roger, and she remembered him lying at her feet after she'd easily wrestled him down. Maybe falling at his feet instead would be a way to avoid getting shot in the face with a rubber band.

"How did you get home?" Donkey asked. "Did you take a plane?"

"I had to take a bus. I wished I were Dorothy Gale, so I could have caught a tornado."

"Did you look at the bus odometer?" Donkey asked. "It can't be less than 2,148 miles, but it can be more if you took a longer way. Titus gave me a road atlas."

"Well, my girl, let's see. Somebody poured me onto a bus in Santa Ana, and from there I went to San Bernadino, and that bus stopped at every bumfuck town across the western US. What does that add up to?" She took another sip of the ginger brandy. When she tipped back in her chair again, Donkey saw that the bottoms of her mother's feet were as leathery and cracked and calloused as her own. A pair of yellow rubber flip-flops with daisies on the thongs sat on the floor beside her, their heels flattened like slices of hospital bread.

"Stop tipping that damned chair, Rosie," Herself said. "You must be drunk."

"They say God loves a drunk, Mama."

Donkey repeated the phrase so Herself could hear it.

"Then go wreck God's chairs," Herself said.

Rose Thorn laughed and brought her chair down again. She exhaled smoke that wrapped around some mosquitoes that had zigzagged out of the firewood, and a few of them got caught in the cloud.

"I hate the people at the hospital. They tied Granny to the bed, just like they tied you," Donkey said, even though she hadn't hated them; the nurses had been nice, and a custodian had returned her book from the garbage chute, but she saw how things would be clearer and simpler if she did hate them. To prevent herself from crying over her own illogical words, she scanned the Waters until she found a great blue heron fishing from a log perch, and she studied that bird's fierce posture. "They even strapped her down in the middle with a belt."

The heron stabbed into the soup and came up with a wriggling fish. It tipped its beak toward the sky so the fish slid into its throat.

"Molly tried to send Granny to Christian Comfort," she said tearfully.

Donkey did not admit that she had been guilty of neglecting Herself in the hospital. She'd gone in and out of the room where Herself was shackled as if the situation were normal. The hospital had spun an illusion, a devil way of seeing, where tying people to beds and hacking off pieces of their arms were normal events, and Donkey had gone along so she could run in the hallway with boys. Rose Thorn wouldn't have been fooled; she would have said something to save Hermine's right hand, to get her out of there right away. If she had been there to help.

Donkey would do everything right this time to keep Rose Thorn there so nothing terrible could happen again. Donkey would promise her enough comforts—drinks and coffin nails and, in the winter, hot bricks warmed on the fire for her feet—so she wouldn't want to go back to Prim.

"Do they know whose bullet hit her?" Rose Thorn asked. "Molly said it was an accident."

"Some boys at the hospital shot me," Donkey said.

"Somebody shot you?" Rose Thorn asked, one eyebrow raised.

"It was a gun that shot rubber bands." To Donkey's shame, more tears came. She pulled a blue rubber band out of her pocket and then put it back. She'd saved every rubber band Roger had shot at her. Rubber bands were handy.

Herself tapped her stick lightly, rhythmically, on the floorboards, and Rose Thorn smiled sadly into her cloud of smoke, which drifted and passed through the porch's screen and dissolved into the fog outside, leaving a couple of confused zithering mosquitoes stuck against the screen. One of them fell, intoxicated, to the porch floor.

"Well, let's see if she's really deaf," Rose Thorn said and then spoke into the air. "I have cancer, Mama. In my breast. I had a biopsy two months ago, and I was supposed to have surgery, but I don't have insurance, and I didn't want to go through with it. I didn't tell Prim."

Donkey held her breath and waited for a sign that Herself had heard, but there was only a pause. Donkey didn't see if Herself closed her eyes, because Donkey closed her own and erupted into sobs. Herself stopped tapping her stick and stabbed it hard into the porch floorboards. Maybe she'd heard, or maybe she was angry that she couldn't hear. Certainly, this would be in the category of things she didn't want to hear. Or possibly she just wanted Donkey to stop crying.

"I'm sorry," Rose Thorn said. "I shouldn't have said it in front of you, Freckle Face. Try not to cry. Oh, I really screwed up. I'm fine, honey. I am."

"You're going to die too," Donkey sobbed, "just like Herself."

Cancer was a rare line they didn't cross on the island. If a woman said she had cancer, Herself gave her some mushroom tea and told her to go back to her devil-doctor.

"Oh, I'm sorry. Please don't cry anymore. I'm okay. I'm just not ready for the hospital," Rose Thorn said brightly.

"Granny can't fix cancer."

"Look, I brought you a present." Rose Thorn rummaged in her pack, first taking out and holding up an empty half-pint vodka bottle ("I'm waiting for this to refill itself," she said), then an old soft blue bandanna from Titus. Next, she took out a pint-sized paper bag and handed it to Donkey, who extracted from it a painted wooden Matryoshka doll. It was shaped something like Herself, and it looked old, but its colors had lasted, the same bright colors as the primroses on the path. The glaze over the red and yellow paint had cracked, creating a pattern of scales.

"You have to twist it, and off with its head," Rose Thorn said, smiling. "Just like you're the Red Queen."

"I don't want to take off heads," Donkey said. "I don't play with dolls."

"It's a grown-up doll, for decoration."

Donkey didn't say so, but she was glad for any gift that would stay when Rose Thorn left.

"Here." Rose Thorn unscrewed and cracked open the doll to reveal another doll like the first, only smaller, and then a third and a fourth. "I found it at a secondhand store near the bus station. It made me think of all of us."

Inside the fourth doll was an amber stone.

"Hey! You put your heart in there!"

"You can hold it for now."

In Donkey's hand, the stone felt like plastic, but it was solid enough. She studied the swirly golden design inside it. She wished on it that she'd wished Rose Thorn home without cancer, but it wasn't that kind of stone. Now that Donkey knew again what it was like to be near her mother—to hear her laugh, to smell her breath—a little boozy now—to be buoyed by her lightness—she had to fear losing her all over again, this time forever. Donkey handed the stone to her mother, and Rose Thorn put it in the front pocket of her cutoffs.

"Nobody else knows about it, Freckle Face. For a little while, it's going to be our secret. Promise you won't tell anybody."

"Okay. You're sure Aunt Prim doesn't know?"

"Nope. Just you and me."

AFTER MILKING AND DINNER (Rose Thorn had coffee with cream and honey) and after doing dishes, and after Herself sat by Baba Rose's grave the way she did, both Herself and Rose Thorn went to bed, leaving Donkey in the kitchen, unable to concentrate on the kind of equations she usually loved.

When she heard Rose Thorn call out his name, Donkey went and stood in the doorway of the little room off the kitchen and watched her mother sleeping with *The Blue Fairy Book* open beside her to the story "Beauty and the Beast." Donkey had made the bed neatly this morning, but Rose Thorn had squirmed around in it to create a nest. She wore Wild Will's big flannel bathrobe like a wraparound blanket, and her hair was still wet after washing it in the kitchen sink with water heated on the stove. When Donkey slept alone, she moved little, always aware of her blankets lying smoothly over her. When she climbed out, she made the bed from the bottom up, finally lining up the two feather pillows with the bedframe. Rose Thorn, however, bunched pillows and blankets around her the way mice in a dresser drawer surrounded themselves with ragged cotton cloth or insulation or even (once) paper chewed from the pages of Donkey's notebooks. Parts of Rose Thorn would end up covered by a knot of blankets, and other parts would be bare.

Donkey saw her mother's eyes open. "You said 'Titus,'" Donkey said. "Maybe you want to marry him now."

"To hell with Titus." Rose Thorn smiled.

"Do you think I'm becoming a boy?" Donkey leaned into the doorframe.

"Now, why would you say that?" Rose Thorn asked. She was interested.

Donkey didn't feel like a boy, but she'd been speaking in a man's voice, and something about it worried her.

"Sit down on the bed with me," her mother said.

Donkey stayed in the doorway. "Boys are better at math, and I swallowed snake blood, and I'm a bastard if I don't have a father."

"Oh, Freckle Face, you worry so much. I've told you, all the best girls have no fathers. Dorothy of Oz, Anne of Green Gables, Cinderella, Huck Finn."

"Huck Finn's a boy." And Huck had a father, just not a good one.

"Oh, right."

"How come you won't tell me who my father is?"

"Do you want to bind your mama to a man she hates?" Rose Thorn immediately regretted saying this true thing, even before she saw the dismay on her daughter's face.

"You hate him?" Donkey asked, her heart snakebit, swelling painfully. Rose Thorn couldn't lie, but she could refuse to answer. "Do you hate me too? Is that why you go away?"

"Oh, poor Jesus, no."

"I want Titus to be my father."

"I know you do."

"You have Wild Will, even if he's gone," Donkey said. "You look like him."

"Do I have him?" Rose Thorn asked. The resemblance used to be a point of pride, but now it pointed at something unsavory that Rose Thorn still didn't want to think about after all these years. No denying she was his daughter, no more than denying Donkey looked like a Clay. DNA was a curse nobody could lift.

"I hide this from Granny." Donkey got the framed photo of Wild Will out of the dresser drawer and held it up.

Rose Thorn glanced at it and then back at her book. "Put that away and come sit with me."

Donkey sat down lightly on the edge of the bed, on the worn chenille spread, barely touching her mom. She wanted to curl up in Rose Thorn's arms, but she felt too big.

"How'd you manage to drink snake blood?" Rose Thorn asked as she lit a coffin nail.

"It was an accident," Donkey said. She'd rather Rose Thorn not know about her releasing a rattlesnake in the house. "I wish that Granny was more logical and that she would stop sleeping so much."

"Sleep is medicine," Rose Thorn said.

"And I wish she would listen better."

"Do you think she's faking it? She really didn't seem to hear what I said."

Donkey shrugged. "She says Molly sounds like a whining machine. She says Titus sounds like gravel crunching at the edge of the road."

"What does she do, sitting out there by the grave every night?"

"She waits for Baba Rose to tell her what to do. Baba Rose should tell her to cook her own bacon," Donkey said. "And when I go out there, she just says I have to bury her with her cuntshells when she dies. You said she wasn't going to die!"

"Oh, don't cry anymore, honey," Rose Thorn said, trying not to laugh at the deluge of tears, like Alice's in Wonderland. "You know, on the bus ride I was remembering when you popped the flowers off those daylilies and sucked the nectar. That was the cutest damned thing." Rose Thorn patted Donkey's back. "Just like Princess Langwidere of Oz popping off ladies' heads."

Donkey curled her shoulders away from her mother.

"Don't tell me you're tired of me already."

"I just don't like popping off anybody's heads or cutting off their arms or anything. I hate those Oz books," Donkey said. She knew her tears might drive Rose Thorn away, if not all the way back to California, then to the Muck Rattler, where Smiley let her work for her drinks.

Waitressing was also what Rose Thorn did in Laguna Beach, at the Sea Cave, where the tips were good enough that even she, a lazybones, could help pay the rent, even send a little money home. Lawyers like Prim were supposed to make money, but she mostly spent her time on hard-luck cases.

"You hate my books? Is that why they're not under the bed?"

Donkey didn't hate the books, and she didn't know why she was saying things that weren't true. She must be under the influence of the snake blood. "Dorothy of Kansas always goes away."

"She has to, Freckle Face," Rose Thorn said, smiling sadly. "If she doesn't go, she might lose her noodle. She always comes back home, though. Auntie Em is always glad to see her."

"I think Aunt Em gets mad too. She just doesn't say it."

"Maybe she does. Maybe you're right. Do you still love me?"

Donkey paused. "I already said it. Before you went away."

"You don't want to say it anymore?" The dog was lying on the floor by the bed, agitated by the distinct sickly yeast-fish smell Rose Thorn had brought with her—not even the coffin-nail smoke covered it. Donkey noticed her mother wasn't inhaling very much; she was just letting the coffin nail burn and send its smoke upward.

Rose Thorn studied the smoke. Maybe she didn't deserve her daughter's love, but she wanted it anyway. If her daughter loved her enough, Rose Thorn thought it could conquer the ambivalence she still felt about the way motherhood had been visited upon her. Her hatred of Titus Sr. was an ugly thing, but she had a right to it. She had begun to wonder, though, if that undigested knot of feeling might be the essence of what had showed up in her breast.

"Prim doesn't want to say it either," Rose Thorn said. "It's like pulling teeth to get her to say she loves me. She says the words don't mean anything."

Donkey used to say she loved Rose Thorn whenever Rose Thorn asked her to, and for her part she didn't quite understand why she was hesitating now. Maybe because whenever she said she loved her mother, the words just got sucked into a hole where they disappeared without a trace. What was the point? Tomorrow or next week Rose Thorn would just ask her to say it again. After withholding the words, Donkey felt a little puffed up, as though she was keeping something important to herself. She said, "But I don't want you to die."

"I'm glad," Rose Thorn said and jostled her shoulder. "Do you really think Titus is going to marry that girl? I'm sure she's just what he needs, you know. A good Christian woman who can take care of him."

"He still loves you. And Ozma loves you every day. Every minute," Donkey said. "Even when she doesn't say it. She always wishes for you to come home first thing every morning, even though Herself says not to."

Ozma of the Island stood at the sound of her name and turned around and lay down again on the bare floor. This was the first time she'd slept inside since they had gotten back from the hospital. Earlier that evening, she had growled at the left-hand side of the cupboard until Donkey shooed her away.

"What else does Ozma say?" Rose Thorn asked. The room was softening as the sun set outside the window. The spiders seemed more contented in their webs with Rose Thorn in the cottage; blackbirds bobbed more cheerfully on their cattails; even the crows watching over the cottage fluffed out their feathers more extravagantly.

"She can smell something's wrong with you. She says she's scared." Donkey smelled it, too, the fish-yeast.

"Tell Ozma not to be so serious. We've got a lot of time." Rose Thorn sat up and wrestled Donkey into lying down beside her. She held her daughter around the middle, rested her chin on the girl's shoulder. Donkey's body thrilled at her mother's physical attention, and she pretended to resist, pretended to be small and helpless. From the safety of this embrace, she sensed the lump in her mother's right breast. She pulled away and turned to look at it, as small as the tip of her pinky, slightly bluish and triangular, like a baby m'sauga's head pushing out against her skin. Everybody knew a baby m'sauga had as much venom as an adult. Rose Thorn covered herself and went back to reading "Beauty."

"Mom," Donkey said, and saying that palindrome made her eyes tear up again. "Maybe I was a twin when I was born, but you threw the first baby in the swamp because it was a Lindworm."

"An interesting thought," Rose Thorn said brightly.

"If you did, she would be older than me, so it would be okay."

"I would have noticed something like that," Rose Thorn said, looking at her out of the corner of her eye, "don't you think?"

CHAPTER NINE

❧

Rose Thorn always comes home.

WHEN WORD GOT AROUND that Rose Thorn was back, men and women who lived in Whiteheart and were one or two or three generations removed from their family farms felt a curious buzzing in their feet and their legs, as well as farther up than they wanted to discuss. They gathered the kids and drove out of town to set foot on what they knew or imagined to be their old family property; some had only the vaguest sense of location and perimeter, and some had to traverse parking lots that used to be woods or back fields. And every family in town felt their connection to the Waters, remembered the old stories of the bubbling marshland and its wildlife and ghosts. Whole families pulled themselves away from the television and made their way to Lovers Road, braving the mosquitoes, hoping to feel the mud in their bones and swamp water in their blood and to catch a glimpse of Rose Thorn. Many of them driving down Lovers Road had their interest sparked by the sight of Titus Clay's prized Herefords grazing in the pasture beside Wild Will's Boneset house.

Those who continued along the edge of the Waters, down the road to Whiteheart Farms and Ada McIntyre's house, saw the sturdy, hardworking Lorena, her hip-length hair gathered into a thick braid that hung over her shoulder as she tended the extravagant garden Ada was famous for, where flowers as well as vegetables grew, including a big patch of heirloom celeries. Lorena planted her feet firmly on ground fertilized for generations with cow manure and tried to ignore the cars and trucks that slowed as they passed. She wished Titus were beside her instead of in the field while these strangers gawked, driving down the road and then coming back. Cars turned around at the dead end, where the remains of Titus Clay Sr.'s burned-out farmhouse stood. The barns were intact, full of hay and farm machinery, but of the house itself just two chimneys remained, surrounded by blossoming lilac bushes and hundreds of withering daffodils.

Drivers and passengers also rubbernecked as they passed the island, attempting to see Rose Cottage, but the leaves had come out on the black willows, and the eight-foot elderberry shrubs had filled out the understory, assuring privacy. Some cars moved barely fast enough to outwit the mosquitoes that zinged in through their windows. Kids waved into the fog, not knowing what might be nestled within it. People stopped at the Boneset Table and bought up the last few bundles of dandelion greens, lamb's quarter leaves for eating or toothaches, and spring tonic eggs that Donkey had put out. They walked along the road, and even farther in, to look through the foliage at various angles, trying to see the women.

They looked across the street at Wild Will's grand old place, still boarded up, and over the woven wire fence at Triumph and Disaster, especially the spotted jenny, Aster, who used to provide ass milk for children at christening time. The women gossiped with one another, frowning as they wondered aloud how Herself was recovering and whether she would be the same, smiling at the thought of Rosie's unpredictable and foolish ways. They noted that the sun garden hadn't been planted, mulched, or weeded, though the usual time to do so had passed. All Hermine had managed to do before being shot was to put her aloe vera plants out in their pots to revive for the season. Along the edge of the garden, overgrown perennials—lemon balm, mint, chamomile, St. John's wort, lavender—grew extravagantly.

After Rose Thorn's return, men still visited the gun club at the other end of Lovers Road, but they didn't fire as many rounds, and they found themselves standing in the parking lot upon arriving, talking to the other shooters about kids and the weather before heading in to the range, feeling both the excitement of the earth's renewal and the melancholy of time passing. Inside the gun range, too, they talked with each other more than usual, and then they conversed still

more before getting in their trucks to head home. Without mentioning Herself by name, the men tried to establish their innocence with
one another, mentioning where they were at ten a.m. that Saturday
Herself was shot. But even those who had an alibi couldn't feel certain
one of their own bullets hadn't gone astray. As they talked on about
their weapons, their wives, or their workplaces, they felt guilt bubbling up inside them, for all of them had shot incautiously, and a .22
bullet could travel half a mile. Even more insidious thoughts came to
some of them later in their beds: just as a man was falling asleep, he
might be jarred awake, certain that he had sighted, aimed, and fired
at the old woman. In the wake of the shooting, when the men shot
outside the range, in or near the Waters, their aim was careful, conservative, deliberate.

One evening, a week after Rose Thorn came home, Jamie Standish
found himself sitting in the gun club parking lot, trying to calm the
agitation that only worsened the discomfort in his feet and belly.
But he couldn't stop thinking about how his fifteen-year-old daughter had screamed at him again and then disappeared again with the
same boy who had knocked her up. Standish had been wondering
whether he should relent and allow his wife to sign the birth control consent, which seemed to him a way of condoning the girl's bad
behavior. These women, with their underground lives and mush-
rooming desires, made him feel powerless. His daughter had brought
that pregnancy on herself, and he didn't understand why God had
snatched away the punishment that could have redeemed her. That
new child would have weighed on his daughter her whole life, the way
his daughter weighed on him, and she would finally have to take some
responsibility and get serious about her place in this world.

He kept clipped to the visor in his truck a picture he'd carefully
torn out of a Bible storybook in the waiting room at the gastroenter-
ologist in Grand Rapids, a picture of Mother Mary in blue robes. He
took it out now and stared at the image of Mary surrounded by little children of all races and varieties, their little faces glowing. Those
different colored children all celebrating Christ soothed him. Mary's
eyes were downcast, her expression forgiving. There, on her breast,
was a place a man could rest his head. If only he'd had a mother like
Mary, generous and gentle and loving, instead of what he'd gotten—a

woman who was always chasing after some mean jerk she wanted to bring home with her to sit in Jamie's dad's chair. He wished his daughter, too, could have had a peaceful, soothing mother. These women in his real life just frustrated him. Maybe that was why he had shot Herself—but he hated to think he had been motivated by anything other than his need to protect the innocents.

After he finished shooting, instead of driving home, he sat in his truck in the gun club parking lot, slipped off his boots, and tipped his head back. He fell asleep like that and dreamed he saw a fish with a gasping mouth on the edge of the Waters. With his bare foot, he pushed the fish into the water, under the surface until it stopped struggling, and when it went still, the fish's body became a goo that clung to his toes. Then someone knocked on the window, and Standish startled out of his dream, and for a moment he thought he was being arrested. He swooned with relief to see the manager of the club, Joe Blank, standing outside his truck. He rolled down his window. If the manager had asked him in that moment if he'd shot Hermine Zook, he would have confessed, would have been glad to come clean in a simple, manly way. "Yes, sir, I did shoot the unholy old woman for her crimes against the Almighty," he would have said and offered his wrists for cuffing. Mary mother of Jesus would forgive him—that was all that mattered.

Instead, Joe Blank said, "Trouble at home?" Joe was known to be a hard-ass about gun club dues and regulations, but he said nothing about the pint of blackberry brandy between Standish's thighs—or about the image of Mary resting on Standish's knee.

Standish shook his head and tried to laugh. Something about the fish dream had deflated him, and so all the way home he had to work to rebuild his anger toward Hermine Zook. Even if she hadn't killed his grandchild, she'd killed someone's grandchild. He told himself he was sorry he'd missed the old woman's heart, which was what he'd been aiming for, but he wasn't feeling it.

AFTER ROSE THORN CAME HOME to Whiteheart, people asked Molly about her at the hospital and in the trailer court. Husbands and fathers remained outside late into the evenings, repairing cars and lawn mowers. They had more patience with their teenage sons than usual. Found themselves gripped by heartfelt hopes that their sons would want to know how to repair the kinds of machines, or at least bicycles. It was a shameful notion to the men that they were raising sons who would buy everything new and fill the junkyards and landfills with manufactured objects that just needed some repair and lubrication to be useful again. Their sons' youthful bodies seemed flabby and weak, but warm June nights made the men imagine they could redirect the barge of history. Some of them imagined their self-indulgent boys growing taller than them and more capable and less subject to the weakness of the flesh, because of the influence their fathers had imparted. Conversely, some of them wished their lazy sons would become more lustful and fruitful, fuller of life.

Mothers who were usually stern or impatient sat on the sides of their little ones' beds and listened to the details of their dreams, the scary monsters and underwater adventures. Some women pulled old photo albums out of the closet, ostensibly to look for photos of relatives who had passed or photos of Ada McIntyre, who had been moved from the hospital to Christian Comfort Care and was fading rapidly. They let their sleepy kids gather around them in their thin summer pajamas and take turns lifting the fragile pages. They squinted at the bleached-out gray-and-white square photos set into black glued-down corners on black pages. The images featured ancient people strangely dressed in thick leather belts and curious hats and heavy plain dress shoes and high heels and severe work boots, leaning against automobiles that resembled cartoon cars. Some women turning the pages of these albums caught the scent of peppery celery as they touched the photos of their grandparents, young then, standing before old Whiteheart Celery Co. signs. Every album of a certain age contained a postcard that Titus's great-grandfather had made and distributed as an advertisement, a painted photograph of Ada McIntyre as a sixteen-year-old girl in a white apron, holding against her belly a head of celery the size of a healthy year-old baby. Ada, the women noticed, had looked matronly even at that age. Bless Ada, who was fading from this life, and Bless Herself, who had survived being shot.

A good number of women still planted celery in their kitchen gardens, but it was a leafy green variety, stringy and leathery, easier to tend and more suitable for flavoring soups than nibbling raw. When people tried to grow the Whiteheart variety, most of them found the soil changed, no longer right for the crop. Ada had had some luck, but Herself was the only one who could grow the sweet old variety, in medicinal amounts in the island soil that wasn't ridden with fertilizer and pesticides. Mothers bought this celery when it appeared on the Boneset Table and fed it to their kids with peanut butter, the only way they'd eat it. These mothers hoped their kids could grow up feeling they came from a special place; they hoped they would have sweet memories of their families and of their hometown, even if many of them would leave soon, convinced they could find someplace better.

Many of last year's garden crops had failed, so this year, women rummaged around and found old seeds that had been saved and passed down with handwritten notes (*Lydia's famous yellow peppers—sweet*, or *St. George's bitter lettuce*). Prissy Standish remembered the Royal Burgundy pole bean seeds in the bottom of her kitchen drawer. She waited until her husband, Jamie, and their daughter were asleep and sneaked out to a secret fishing spot her father used to frequent on the western edge of the Waters and caught three bullheads by moonlight. She stunned them with a hammer, chopped them up with a hatchet on a stump, and buried the flesh with the seeds. Virginia Smith, Smiley's mother, picked the anchovies off her pizza and later, in secret, worked them into the soil of her mossy little kitchen garden.

At any mention of the lazy girl who had thrown over the best man in town—what a fool Rosie Zook was!—many women would shake their heads and smile. Lorena was lucky to have caught him! Whoever had heard of a grown woman who roamed the way Rosie did, outside of the Johnny Cash song, which made no sense anyhow? But when the rains came softly at night, many of them dreamed for the first time in a long while of dancing with men who, in waking life, would not dance, dreamed of dancing with their sisters the way they used to do as girls, before men were anything other than brothers and cousins, dads and uncles.

Titus stopped by the island every day to do some job for Herself. He wanted to help, he said, to be neighborly, but he swelled with an eagerness to get a glimpse of Rose Thorn. Meanwhile, Rosie slept or faked sleep, and, as the days progressed, Titus began to come later in the afternoon, to speak more loudly outside where he imagined she was in the cottage, and his scent grew musky with hunger. By the seventh day, after he'd filled the cowshed with hay and straw and bags of feed, when he was making plans for building a handrail on the bridge, he smelled like a wild animal. He wanted to drive a new well for them, he said, get them started on next year's firewood, though he should have been home replacing the exhaust and head gasket on his truck, if not helping Lorena in the garden.

People went to the Muck Rattler and sat inside that dimly lit room watching the door, waiting for Titus or Rose Thorn to show up—or, better yet, both of them together! When Titus was there, he watched the door, too, and wouldn't make conversation, but some people noticed him stroking his tattoo under his shirt sleeve. At home, Lorena wouldn't sleep with him, because he kept waking up panicked and calling out the wrong name. She spent a lot of time talking long distance with her relatives in Texas, and she and Titus fought over all kinds of things in addition to the phone bill, such as when to spray pesticide on the peach and apple trees, what time of day to water the garden, whether to keep some moth-eaten children's clothes they had found in a box, and after Ada died in the nursing home, they even fought about her funeral. Lorena thought Titus had turned selfish and callous. His desire for lovemaking sometimes came upon him suddenly and with a violence that scared her. And Titus himself began to see Lorena as too quiet, too sturdy, too practical.

TWO WEEKS AFTER ROSIE CAME HOME, Herself sat at the head of the table drinking the coffee Donkey had made with eggshells put in with the grounds. Because sleeping was healing, Donkey had been tempted to let Herself sleep into the afternoon the way Rose Thorn did, but the cottage was lonely with just Ozma for company, and Donkey wanted to remind Herself that she was needed, or she might just fade away, in the same way Donkey had threatened to fade away as a baby.

"Don't you want to sit by the road today?" Donkey asked as she peeled four slices off the hunk of bacon they kept in the refrigerator. "I can try to pin up your braids again."

"Not today," Hermine said. "I need peace and quiet." Her braids hung down on either side of her head like a girl's braids, like Donkey had worn hers when she was little. Every day Hermine said not today. Peace and quiet had been what she'd needed before when she was working on a remedy, but now she was only knitting—she'd figured out how to do it with one hand—and bathing in the sulfur pool, something she used to do occasionally but now did every day. If Donkey put herbs, bark, or merry in front of her, she would absentmindedly crush, crumble, or separate leaves from seeds, but she did not take the next steps necessary to create any fixes. It was as though she was a healer's assistant now rather than a healer, and to Donkey she seemed like a ghost of Herself. How much of her was left behind at the hospital, Donkey wondered, and how much had maybe been lost along the road between there and the island? She shuddered to think that some of the substance of Herself had been burned up in the hospital incinerator or taken to the church basement.

"Then what day? Tomorrow?" Donkey asked. "Are you mad because Titus comes to the island now?" Donkey had noticed Herself pretending to not see him doing the heavy work she used to do.

"It was bound to happen," she said, without apparent distress.

As the kitchen air filled with the smoky-sweet death smell of bacon, Donkey opened the door to the porch. The only saving grace of bacon smoke was that it covered the worrisome fishy scent that was especially strong in the morning while Rose Thorn slept. With both Donkey's arms employed in cottage work, there was little time for learning what topology was but plenty of time for ruminating about Rose Thorn's cancer. Could Herself be right, that it was better not to know some things?

Just then, Marshall Wallace's gravel delivery truck rattled past the Boneset Table, as it did every day at about 8:30, heading toward Whiteheart Farms, and Herself didn't seem to notice that either.

"Titus says Rose Thorn makes the lions and lambs lie down together," Donkey said, "but Molly says she lies around too much. Molly says I should get her out of bed early." Donkey got an idea of mentioning the cancer, and as soon as the thought landed, she felt Herself shut down and close her ears. Donkey lifted the scorched and wormy strips of bacon out of the frying pan and put them on a piece of a brown paper grocery bag. Then she stirred her oatmeal on the back burner.

Though lazy Rose Thorn didn't help much with the island work,

Donkey's load felt lightened by her mother's presence. Even when she wasn't with them in the kitchen, even when she was sleeping, she was a part of every conversation, part of everything happening on the island. She had been part of these things all along, Donkey realized, by her absence, by *not* sitting in her chair where she belonged, by *not* sipping coffee laced with Delilah's cream all day. The way negative and positive versions of a number had the same absolute value, the same distance from the zero point. The missing mother, the sleeping mother, the foolish mother was still the mother. Her mother's proximity now served as a bridge between Donkey and Herself, or at least a distraction against Hermine's strange behavior. Every afternoon when Rose Thorn finally bubbled to life and flowed into the kitchen like a clear, cool stream, Donkey felt a little breathless, thinking anything was possible on that day, even a cure for cancer.

"I'd keep my lambs away from the lions, that's what I'd do," Herself said, startling Donkey as she poured half the scrambled eggs into melted butter in a pan. She then poured the other half into the bacon pan for Herself, who added thoughtfully, "Maybe lions keep their promises not to eat your lambs just until they get hungry."

It was times like these that Donkey was sure Herself heard a lot more than she let on.

"Shouldn't you try again to make something for somebody?" Donkey glanced at the notes overflowing the Primrose bowl, some of them worn from Herself handling them. Rose Thorn had said if people want golden eggs, they shouldn't have cut off the golden goose's wing. "Maybe something simple for somebody's cough? Or some stomach water?"

"Make what you like. I'm busy today."

"They want you to make it," Donkey said. "And you don't look busy."

Herself reached for her own right hand with her left and then stiffened in frustration.

Later that morning, when Herself returned to the kitchen table after bathing in the sulfur pool, Donkey tried again, taking a folded piece of paper from the bowl. "I'll read you some notes," Donkey said. "This one says a lady has a bump she can't get rid of," Donkey said, though the request was really for an itch cream. "Do you want her to go to the devil-doctor?"

"Give me that one," Herself said. She held it briefly and then put it into the fire and clapped the door shut.

The notes were just paper, but they were weighing on Donkey. She was realizing she *could* make a few medicines herself, could gather some water in bottles, and that weighed her down even more. Earlier, she had already made merry poppins sleeping tea for Rose Thorn, with poppy juice and marijuana leaves from the plants behind the donkey barn. Plus turkey tail for cancer, though Herself had always said it didn't do much for the new cancers. She'd already cut and dried heaps of yarrow and nettles in her attempt to inspire Herself.

"You want to use the hand you gave me? You put that meat in the pan for goulash," Herself said. From the cupboard, she took some ground sweet peppers and a jar of green powder. Fever weed. A person would get sick if she ate that. Donkey moved it out of Hermine's reach, put it at the other end of the table. Was Herself testing her? Or did she no longer know oregano from fever weed? Yesterday Herself opened a bottle that held a tincture of poison sumac and smelled it. Donkey decided she would stop asking Herself to cook.

"Lucky for me I got only one grandchild who knows better than me," she said.

"Did you forget everything you used to know?"

"I never knew anything, Donkey. You're the one with the recipes. Cures just moved through me sometimes, gifts from Baba Rose, and I made them. And now I don't know what's moving through me."

The idea of not knowing anything spooked Donkey, but if she ever forgot what she knew, she'd have her notebooks to help her remember. The wall behind the cookstove was lined with cast iron pans hanging from hooks, and when Donkey took down number eight, its black circle of iron showed on the faded yellow paint, marking how everything in the finite cottage had a place. She poured bacon grease from the can into the pan. She pulled away the butcher's tape and unrolled the bloody mess of burger, still frozen in the middle and checkered with fat, into the heavy pan. Then she got stomach-sick the way she did every day while cooking for Herself. It was impossible to pick the meat out of goulash.

"Did Rose Thorn used to eat food?" she asked as she broke up the meat with a wooden spatula. She cut up an onion into chunks and added it and then sprinkled in pepper and oregano and parsley that she got out of the cupboard, approximating the amounts she'd seen Herself add.

"All my girls used to eat what I cooked."

"Titus says it's Ada's funeral today," Donkey said, sitting close to Herself again, in Rose Thorn's chair. "You always used to go to funerals."

Two days before, when Titus had told Donkey about the funeral, it hadn't struck her that Ada was dead for all ∞, but upon seeing Hermine's eyes brimming with tears now, Donkey began to cry.

"She was a dear neighbor," Herself said as her tears overflowed and streamed down her face. "She always helped us. When you were born, she helped, and never said a word about it to anyone. And she made very good pies."

"Ma'am, maybe we can give other people recipes to make their own medicine," Donkey said, pressing her T-shirt sleeve against her eyes. "I can write down the recipes for them. Maybe they can save their own lives."

"So now you're the great authority on life and death?" Herself said, and her crying stopped. "Well, you go ahead and give away Baba Rose's medicines to brutes and leave yourself with nothing."

"Granny, we can tell people the recipes, and we'll still have them. That's how you know something's true, if everybody can have it. Be logical, ma'am."

"Everybody can have your true things, Donkey? You're going to give yourself away to everybody in Nowhere like your poor mama? That's what Baba Rose did too. Every moaning, complaining devil-girl with a pebble in her shoe, every girl crying into her cuntshell was a precious sweetie to Baba Rose. That's the curse on this family. Soft hearts."

"You said Rose Thorn's curse is how she looks."

"Your mama is double-cursed. Let them all cry, I say. I threw sticks at the devil-girls and chased them with snapping turtles, but they all still came to Baba Rose like possums with their pouches. They took a nibble out of her every time until they ate her up. Next you'll give away this island to men and snakes and abandon all the souls still waiting here."

Hermine's inspired complaining made it seem she would start curing somebody any minute.

"You said you buried Baba Rose," Donkey said, encouraging her, "and the men tried to steal her bones, but they couldn't find her. And she died of a rattlesnake bite—and because of knowing too much."

"All the brutes in Nowhere have their aches and pains and buboes they want to get rid of, but I can't help them anymore," Herself said. "They killed Baba Rose, and now dear Ada. Let those people go to the hospital to be hacked to pieces by devil-doctors and then go home to live with betraying daughters and granddaughters who wake them up every morning and won't let them sleep." Herself nodded at the cooker, and Donkey knew to push the pan of meat onto the cooler part of the stove to simmer. Nowadays she knew what Herself wanted as well as she knew her own wants.

THAT AFTERNOON, Rose Thorn became restless to leave the island, and when she had only one coffin nail left, she took off Wild Will's bathrobe and put on her shirt and cutoffs.

"I don't want you to go to the Muck Rattler," Donkey said.

"If you'll keep me company, I'll sit over at Boneset, and maybe somebody will bring me some coffin nails," Rose Thorn said. "I need sunshine. And my books."

"Titus said I shouldn't leave Granny alone."

"That man doesn't know women," Rose Thorn said. "Women need to be alone. Otherwise, how are they going to put themselves back together?"

Ozma and Herself sat on the landing just outside the screened porch and watched them leave. Mosquitoes zizzed around in the shade, but Herself, Rose Thorn, and Donkey were wearing catnip, eucalyptus, and lavender bug dope, while Ozma had thick fur to protect her. Though they were only a few miles east of the mountains of paper sludge, the smell on the breeze now was of the sweet first-cutting alfalfa that Titus had just mowed in the field behind Wild Will's house.

As Donkey and Rose Thorn arrived at the Boneset Table, Donkey saw the sign that said "Baby killer" driven into the ground on a fence stake a few yards to the east for oncoming cars and trucks to see. It was hand-painted in red on white poster board, so Donkey could read it backward from the back side. She was unable to pull it out of the overgrown grass quickly enough to hide it from Rose Thorn, the way she'd hidden the last one from Herself.

"What's up with that?" Rose Thorn asked tiredly, as though crossing the bridge had worn her out. The women in this family might say they were sleeping to heal, but when Rose Thorn got up from sleeping so much, she was always tired. She sank down in Donkey's folding chair near the table.

"There was one before," Donkey said and tore the paper into shreds and broke the stake in two and put it all in the firepit, which was a few yards west of the Boneset Table, halfway to the big swamp oak, alongside the road. Before Lorena had moved in, Titus would sometimes burn junk wood and weeds in the firepit, and while he was watching the fire, he would play the guitar and sing. Donkey would sit and listen as long as she could, until Herself called her home across the bridge. Now Donkey would like to hear her granny's voice yelling loudly over the Waters.

"I love this town, and I hate it," Rose Thorn said and lit her last coffin nail. She exhaled a column of smoke. She stood up and moved the chair into the sun and stretched out her legs. She always unfurled like a flag in the sunshine.

"That's illogical." Donkey sat in Hermine's big wooden chair, which was heavy like a throne. There was a lot of extra room in it.

Two great blue herons flew overhead, their necks curved into snakes. By the time they disappeared into the swamp, Titus's truck came along from the direction of town, and he pulled over onto the shoulder across the road, in front of the Boneset sign.

"Praise Jesus and Jehoshaphat for bringing Rosie home!" Titus shouted when he got out of his truck. He pushed the door closed behind him but not hard enough for it to latch, so Donkey ran across Lovers Road to open it and slam it harder. On the dashboard she saw two packs of smokes, so she reached in through the open window, took one pack, and put it in her pocket. Titus always shared his coffin nails with Rose Thorn, so it wasn't stealing. As she walked back across the road, she imitated Titus's relaxed, long-legged amble.

"Why do you always have to drag poor Jesus into everything?" Rose Thorn asked. She grinned and squinted up into the sun behind Titus, who grinned too. The way he showed all his teeth, Donkey was briefly afraid he would eat Rosie up.

"I just—" Titus said. He took off his Allis-Chalmers cap to hold it over his heart. "I forget how it is to look at you, Rosie! Like a breath of summer! Like a cool stream on a hot day. It's like the world starting all over new again! How long has it been?"

"Six hundred forty-eight days," Donkey said. Although her mother faked impatience with Titus's flowery talk, Donkey knew she really liked it, apart from the godly element.

"Maybe next time, your sweet Lord could spring for a plane ticket instead of making me take the bus," Rose Thorn said, still smiling. Though she didn't move her arms, some ghost of her—her desire for him—was reaching out for Titus like a golden shimmer that extended beyond her edges.

"Three buses," Donkey said, looking from one rapt face to the other, not wanting to be shut out. This was hers, too, this shimmer when Titus and Rose Thorn were together, because she wanted Titus for a father as much as Rose Thorn wanted him for what she wanted him for.

"I don't care if you came by hook or crook, you're here now," Titus said breathlessly and then added as an afterthought. "For your family."

"Oh, my family does fine without me. I'm not much help with the nursing or the cooking."

"It's true," Donkey said. "She doesn't help."

Titus reached out to muss Donkey's hair but missed because he wasn't really looking at her and only touched her ear.

"You shine like the sun," Titus whispered. "Oh, Rosie. It's been too long."

"Naw, I'm more like the moon," Rose Thorn said. It was something she had always said, offhandedly, but she was realizing the truth of it. These days she was more a reflection of other people's light than a source of her own. "I hear you're engaged."

"Lorena is a good girl." Titus's neck and face flushed red. "She's a hard worker."

"Maybe you won't marry her now," Donkey said. She flattened some grass with her bare foot and then lifted her foot to watch it spring back up.

"I had some extra buttercup squash plants, String Bean," Titus said.

"I put them in the garden for your granny. Maybe you should go check on them. Weeds are growing up after that rain."

"Oh, stay, Dorothy. I feel safer with a chaperone," Rose Thorn said, blinking at Titus. Flirting. "You being engaged and all."

"How many squash plants?" Donkey said.

"Sixteen, I think," Titus said.

"Two raised to the fourth power and four raised to the second power." Donkey's observation added to the shimmer in the air.

She looked over at the island to see that Ozma had wandered away and was sniffing at the poison ivy at the edge of the landing. Next time, she would tie Ozma up to make sure she kept watch over Herself, who, without her hearing, might not notice trouble coming, might not even hear a rattling tail. And without her right hand, she probably couldn't catch or kill a m'sauga that dared to come onto the island—or dared to stay.

"Buttercup is my daddy's favorite squash," Titus said, casting his gaze pointedly toward the garden, hoping Donkey might take the hint.

At the mention of Titus Sr., Rose Thorn's stomach tilted toward nausea. She hadn't seen Titus Sr. since he'd raped her, and she hoped she would never have to see him again. She wondered with dread if he were coming to Whiteheart for Ada's funeral.

"My mama isn't strong enough to slice those big squash in the kitchen, though. Sometimes my daddy has to put them in a vise and use a hacksaw. I'll do that for you in September."

"Mama has a machete," Rose Thorn said. "I'm sure three generations of us can figure out how to cut a squash. With all due respect to your godlike father."

"We have five hands," Donkey offered.

"My dad's having some medical trouble, can't make it up here for the funeral. I know he wanted to come."

Rose Thorn gave a great sigh of relief. "Since you're here," she said to Titus, "maybe you can get my books out of the barn."

"We took good care of your books, didn't we, String Bean? Let's run and get them for your ma. Then I got to get ready for the funeral. I got ice in the truck."

Donkey fell in step with him, couldn't stop smiling at their going up the driveway, along the wooden part of the pasture fence and into the barn together through the side door. Had she been alone, Donkey would have climbed the wooden fence and entered through the pasture gate. "We kept them safe," Donkey said, surprised at how true these words seemed, though in fact, she'd put them out in the barn because they made her sad when she saw them in Rose Cottage.

"Why are you wearing that old jacket of mine when it's eighty degrees out here?"

"Seventy-eight," Donkey said, patting *True Things* in her left pocket. As they entered the barn, she asked, "How can you marry Lorena if you still love Rose Thorn?"

"Such unholy questions from the mouths of babes," he said, unlocking the tool room with a key on his chain. Donkey would have used the key that hung on a nail under the yardstick. She'd already tried the key she found in the caboodle, discovered it did not fit this lock. Inside the tool room were Wild Will's old pitchforks and shovels and hand tools. While they both stood there in the doorway, Titus said, "Are you doing what I said about the little shells?"

"Only one came, and I buried it." She had partially buried it, pressing it into the mosaic near the Boneset Table; it winked at her every time she walked past, asking her to pick it up and offer it for Hermine's consideration.

"Good girl," he said. "You said you'd bring me some sleep herbs."

Donkey handed over the plastic bag of merry poppins, from the batch she had made yesterday.

"You didn't mention this to your mama or granny, did you?"

Donkey shook her head. A deal with the man who was going to be your dad couldn't be a deal with the devil, however it might feel.

"*Bird rib* is a palindrome," Donkey said, hoping he would notice *dad* was also one.

"You don't say," Titus said as he picked up the big box of Oz books and gestured for Donkey to get the smaller one. Once outside the tool room, Titus put his box down to relock the padlock. Donkey held onto hers while she waited, nudging it up with her knee.

"I think Rose Thorn might stay this time," Donkey said, "and not go away again."

"That would be beautiful. For you and your granny, I mean." Titus began to hum.

Donkey was carried pleasantly along in his alfalfa and coffin-nail scent, and before she knew it, they were back across the road, standing before Rose Thorn like supplicants.

"Right here." Rose Thorn patted the ground beside her. "Bring them to mama."

Titus dropped his box, and Donkey dropped hers beside it, like father and daughter boxes containing twenty-three books between them, fourteen Oz books and nine assorted others.

"I've missed these stories," Rose Thorn said. "Half the time I end up reading some awful thriller. This is what I want. Adventures with some good comrades and worthy opponents."

"Rosie, I can feel my beans sprouting in all the sunshine you bring us. Nothing grows right around here without you."

"Easier to shoot women in the sunshine," Rose Thorn said with her eyes closed. "I figured I'd come sit out here and make myself an easy target."

Titus struggled to say something but then shook his head.

"In another town, shooting unarmed women might be considered poor sportsmanship," she said. "I just wish that if a man wants to shoot old ladies, he would shoot somebody else's."

"Rosie, we're all sure it was an accident. Your ma said so to the police. She said it was careless shooting, and a few of us went out and posted signs all over the edge of the property. If you don't think it was an accident, you should tell the police."

"You're sure nobody would do it on purpose?" Rose Thorn asked.

"I don't want anybody to shoot at us," Donkey said.

"No, String Bean, nobody's shooting at anybody, especially not at you," Titus said.

Titus studied Rose Thorn's throat and collarbone, modestly revealed by the sleeveless button-up shirt. Donkey could see now that she wore it because it covered up her cancer bump better than a tank top, but it also had the effect of making her look dressed up, fancy.

"Sweet Heaven, Rosie, you and I should talk about this alone," Titus said, nodding toward Donkey.

"I've been thinking a lot about that heaven of yours. Do you think the men get to keep their guns in heaven? Is that what your heaven's going to be like, guys wandering around with guns, shooting whoever they want? *Hey, I don't like the song. Let's shoot the harpist."*

"I won't go to heaven if people are going to shoot at us," Donkey said.

"String Bean, close your ears."

"I can't close my ears," Donkey said, although she wasn't sure that Herself wasn't doing just that. Today she'd seemed to hear everything Donkey said to her, even in a normal voice.

"Oh, Rosie. I think you're scaring somebody." He stepped close, as though he wanted to take Rosie in his arms, but since she was sitting in Donkey's folding chair, he only cast a shadow over her and gave the impression of a looming threat.

"The people in your church don't trust Herself to know what a woman needs, but they all want her medicine. And now you want my daughter to keep things from her granny."

"You're talking in riddles, Rosie. Why do you got to be so hard on a man?" Titus stepped back and looked at Donkey, as if for help. Donkey shrugged a guilty shrug. She slept with her mother now, and she couldn't stop telling Rose Thorn almost everything when they lay side by side, and if she didn't tell, Rose Thorn might just read it in her dreams anyway. In the single bed, Donkey had been pulled into Rose Thorn's dreams, those brilliant confusions, paths circling on themselves and getting nowhere, body parts trying to piece themselves back together into a whole.

"You didn't tell my daughter to throw away cuntshells?" Because Titus was no longer blocking the sun, Rose Thorn had to squint up at him. She wanted him close to her again, and she knew he felt it and wanted the same.

"I wish you wouldn't call them that," Titus said. "And you know that whole abortion business is a problem, has been for a while. It's better for everybody if she stops."

"Is it? Better for everybody?"

"You can't deny that if your mama makes a medicine for a woman, a beautiful voice might never be heard." Titus's voice rose to a high pitch at the end of the sentence.

Just then, Lorena approached from the east, returning from town, in her dusty sedan, a dark blue former police cruiser with Texas plates. The front doors of her car had been painted a flat navy, but Donkey noticed a sheriff's badge was bleeding through on the passenger's side. Lorena slowed and pulled off the road near the firepit. She got out, slammed her door, and stood leaning against the back of the car with her arms crossed. Her thick black braid hung almost to her belt.

"This must be Lorena," Rose Thorn said.

Titus startled and turned around and waved. Rose Thorn also waved, so Donkey did too. Lorena hesitantly waved back.

"She looks young," Rosie said.

"She's nineteen. I'm not breaking any law," he said.

"Titus Andronicus, great follower of the law. As I recall, that has always been important to you. It's a skill to be able to turn your passion on and off according to the rules."

"I'll be back, Rosie, and we can talk," Titus said anxiously. "You sure you don't want to come to the funeral, String Bean? I'll be playing some music."

Donkey shook her head. It would feel wrong to be at the funeral without Herself.

When Titus was across Lovers Road, Rose Thorn shouted after him, "Bring me something to drink when you come back!"

Donkey followed Titus with her eyes. "How come you always have to fight with him?"

"I can't very well make love with him out here," she said, "can I? There's no man in this world for me but him. It'll kill me if he marries somebody else, but I hope he does."

"Is that why you burned yourself?"

"I burned myself because I was tempted to say yes to being his farm wife," Rose Thorn said. "I had to wake myself up from his dream."

Rose Thorn opened the flaps of the bigger of the two boxes and extracted *The Road to Oz*. She blew away the hay dust and wiped the cover with her hand. Just then, a big-eared deer mouse leaped out of the box and ran up her arm, across her nut-brown shoulders and down the other arm. It jumped to the ground, landed spread-eagled, and ran off toward the bridge. Donkey knew well that frantic mouse language. Rose Thorn laughed and held up the book. The edges of the cover had been chewed by critters—maybe by that same deer mouse—and even the shaggy donkey depicted in raised ink on the cover looked more ragged than when Donkey had put the book into the box last year. Rose Thorn wiped the cover again, this time with her sleeve, and kissed the image of the donkey, even though they both knew mice pissed everywhere they chewed. Next, she extracted *The Lost Princess of Oz* and brushed mouse turds onto the ground. This cover featured Dorothy of Kansas arm-in-arm with a man-sized frog.

"*Should* we report to the police about a man shooting Granny?" Donkey asked.

"Just imagine that." Rose Thorn smiled and shook her head. "Imagine if we brought a couple of officers over the bridge to meet Herself. I just wish Titus would find the guy who did it and kick his ass. Peace at any price, that's your Titus. He'd take a cup of tea with the KKK Nazi party to keep things calm. He'd sing them a holy hymn and try to save their souls."

"Don't you want to know who did it?" Donkey asked. "I do."

"Hell no! I don't want to know anything about it. If we know, then we have to do something," Rose Thorn said, draping herself over the chair, one knee over the arm and one bare foot dangling. What a difference from the way Herself sat, straight-backed, filling her whole chair. If Herself was a full-grown black willow tree with a limb hacked off, then Rose Thorn was a vine that entwined with anything it could cling to and climbed up toward the light. Rose Thorn returned to *The Road to Oz* and traced the raised letters before opening it up. As her eyes fell upon the first page, as she became instantly absorbed in the words she'd almost memorized, Donkey felt the old pangs of jealousy. Her mother loved so many things—words on a page, Titus and Hermine, all the people of Whiteheart—and Donkey wasn't sure where she fit on that list.

While Donkey watched, Rose Thorn put her hand over the dense knot in her right breast, touched the pearl of venom she'd stored inside her own body. Rose Thorn could see her daughter watching.

"Here, sit with me, Freckle Face. Let's enjoy being off the island, even a few steps away. Isn't the sun nice?"

With difficulty, Donkey moved Hermine's big chair closer to her mother.

"Let's say I do marry Titus," Rose Thorn said. "First thing, he'd take me to the hospital and tie me down and let them carve a chunk out of me."

"You could keep it secret and not tell him."

"It's hard to keep a secret," Rose Thorn said.

"No it isn't," Donkey said, though she recalled how she'd almost told Herself about the cancer this morning. "Is that why you burned yourself? To keep a secret?"

"I think I burned myself to feel something on the outside. I'm sorry I did it. Now I think I have more answers than I had two years ago. Instead of burning myself, I'd say, *Let me think about that for a long, long while*."

"It was twenty months ago, not two years."

Rose Thorn thumbed through the pages of the book in her hand until she got to an illustration of Tip, the boy who carved Jack's pumpkin head and fished that head out of a river with a stick after it had gotten knocked off. "And if I had another baby with Titus, you might not inherit your granny's island."

"You can have a boy," Donkey said. "We can teach him not to trample mushrooms."

"Say, did you ever think to ask what if Jack Pumpkinhead's pumpkin head rotted off in April? What would he do?" Rose Thorn waited for her daughter to answer.

"He'd get a new one from the root cellar," Donkey said. "And Tip would carve a new face and put it on his neck."

"What if they were all gone, no more pumpkins?" Rose Thorn asked. "What if the mice got in and chewed them up. Then what?"

"Maybe somebody could carve him a better head out of wood," Donkey said, sinking into the luxury of her mother's attention, "so he didn't have to keep finding pumpkins."

"But then he wouldn't be a Pumpkinhead anymore, would he?"

Donkey thought she didn't care what her mother's head was made of, so long as she was here. She let her eyes travel over the mosaic of trinkets in the ground to the cuntshell and then got up and walked down the steps to look at Herself across the way, sitting safely there in a ladder-back chair, filling it up completely, while Ozma stood guard. Everybody was accounted for. Donkey returned to Rose Thorn and handed over the pack of coffin nails.

CHAPTER TEN

❧

Love, like hope, springs eternal.

DONKEY STAYED AT BONESET that afternoon and weeded the garden, collecting the dandelion greens and timothy to feed to Triumph and Aster, who were acting frisky and cranky. Seventy-two vehicles went to Ada McIntyre's home funeral and burial. Ada had written into her will that it wasn't to be held in the church. Rose Thorn sat across the road reading, halfway between the Boneset Table and the firepit. The first car leaving the funeral was a station wagon that slowed as it passed. The second car was a rusty white coupe with a blue passenger-side door. The driver beeped, and somebody waved from the back seat. Third, a man in a Chevy truck passed slowly and put two fingers on his forehead in a salute to Rose Thorn. She waved back like a flag to each vehicle, without looking up from her book.

The first to pull over, in a late model four-wheel-drive Chevy truck, were Titus's cousins on his mother's side, Ralph and Larry Darling. They stopped in the road and offered Rose Thorn a ride to the Muck Rattler. She glanced across the road at Donkey and invited the brothers to join her where she sat. Larry pulled his truck into the Boneset driveway between the garden and the pasture and parked there. They carried over a cold six-pack of cans and set it beside Rose Thorn's chair like an offering. She put *The Road to Oz* facedown, open, in the grass and twisted out one beer and handed it to Larry, twisted free another and handed it to Ralph, and then cracked one open for herself.

Next to arrive were two old friends of Rosie's, a stringy-haired man and woman, who pulled into Wild Will's driveway and parked there. From the back of that truck sprang two boys Donkey knew from the hospital, Roger's cousins, who'd run the halls with her there one day. As the two adults walked across Lovers Road, carrying their own folding lawn chairs, the boys ran to the edge of the donkey pasture. As the adults opened their chairs and sat down near Rose Thorn, the older of the two boys threw several rocks at Triumph and Aster, who were grazing, and missed. Donkey found a plum-sized rock of her own behind the blackberry spears along the driveway and stood and tossed it at the boys, hitting the little one, who then ran across the road crying, "Mommy!" Donkey sank back down behind the canes. The bigger boy picked up another rock, and, just as he was tossing it, Donkey reared up, threw a rock that hit him in his butt, and squatted again. He looked around but saw nobody. He waited and picked up another rock, and when he turned toward Triumph and Aster again, Donkey landed a stone on his shoulder. Finally, he shrugged and went across the road to join his parents. The donkeys were sniffing at each other and didn't seem to notice.

There was plenty of room for people to gather on the grassy shoulder on the island side of the road, but it was narrow enough that people naturally stayed close to Rose Thorn, arranged themselves in a semicircle around her. Most of them were blinking at Rosie as though they'd just come out of a dense mushroomy forest into sunshine.

A black Ford Bronco with rusted out wheel wells pulled up. A couple of plump women got out and sat on the ground near Rose Thorn. With a pang of jealousy, Donkey imagined they were twins, a female Tweedledee and Tweedledum in almost identical wine-colored dresses stretching over their bare pale legs crossed in the grass. They seemed happy to share a beer in the sticky heat, swatting at ground bees. When Donkey came close to them later, she caught a familiar moldy smell coming from their dresses, like the clothes in the closets in Rose Cottage if they didn't sometimes air them out by keeping the doors open. When there were fourteen people gathered there on the roadside, Rose Thorn accepted a joint somebody passed to her, and that skunky scent filled the air.

Ralph Darling said he was glad Titus Clay Sr. wasn't there, though he would have liked to see his aunt Mary. The Darling family grudge had not eased since they'd been forced to sell their farmland to White-heart Farms. At the mention of Titus Sr., Rose Thorn took a long swallow of beer to settle her stomach.

"I'd like to harness those donkeys," Larry Darling said. He and Rosie had been classmates, along with Whitey Whitby, who was there with his new girlfriend, Teresa. Rose Thorn hadn't graduated from high school with them, because she'd had too many absences. "I'd like to drive them around with a cart," Larry said.

When Rose Thorn did not immediately protest this idea, Donkey rose from the ditch across the road, where she'd been hiding, and shouted, "No! Say he can't!"

The whole crew turned and smiled to see the tall girl stand up among the cattails.

"My daughter's the boss around here now," Rose Thorn said. "She says leave the asses alone."

Donkey ducked back down. She liked that her mother had called her *my daughter* in front of them and deferred to her opinion; it made her feel cozy, like she was a part of things she'd never been a part of before. She was intrigued by these people but nervous without Titus there to make her feel safe.

"But they're no good for nothing," Ralph Darling chimed in. "Not since your ma beat that poor jenny nearly to death and she couldn't have no more foals. My ma's cousin Marsha said Old Red seen her do it. Everybody knows." His voice was a reedy whine. He'd been complaining about this situation for more than eleven years but was as surprised as anybody else to hear himself say the words aloud right here where Herself would have been sitting. But he had his principles. Even if killing an animal for food or to protect your property was okay—even drowning kittens that would overrun your place was sometimes necessary—to harm a domesticated creature for no reason was as wrong as kicking a sleeping dog.

"Your cousin isn't telling the truth," Rose Thorn said. "Herself aborted that foal to save my daughter's life. Dorothy would have died if she hadn't gotten that milk when I couldn't feed her. Better you were angry at me for not having enough milk."

Ralph Darling contemplated his round belly. He brushed some dog hair off his shirt—pits weren't supposed to shed, but his female, Ophelia, did. His older brother Larry had given him Ophelia on the condition that Ralph give him a litter of her pups at least once a year, pups sired by one of Larry's dogs. Larry was training the dogs to fight, but now that Ralph had a sweet-tempered female of the breed, he didn't like the idea of dog fighting.

"Well, then, I can't argue with a little girl's life," Ralph said. "Though some other people might not believe it. Why didn't she tell anybody that's why she did it?"

"My mother isn't one to explain herself," Rose Thorn said. "Maybe you noticed."

"She should've gotten another jenny," a woman said, "if this one won't foal."

"Why don't one of you get your own jenny?" Rose Thorn said with laughter in her voice. "Get your own ass milk."

"Is your ma ever going to make something for us anymore?" asked a skinny woman Donkey had seen regularly at the Boneset Table, but only from a distance. She noticed now that the woman's hands shook and that she had a birthmark like a forked tongue above her left eye. The woman looked around furtively, as though surprised she was the one asking.

"You think she's going to curse all of us now?" Ralph asked.

"Maybe you were the one who shot her," Rose Thorn said.

"Hell no, Rosie," Ralph Darling said, bristling. Then his voice became kind. "Of course not. We only heard about it after she went to the hospital. The guy probably doesn't even know he shot her. Half the guys around here can't hit the broad side of a barn."

"Well, she's only got one hand to work with now," Rosie said to the skinny woman with the birthmark. "That would slow any woman down."

"You could help her," the woman said.

"And maybe Herself will come out here and drink a beer with you all," Rose Thorn said.

"Maybe your girl could help her," the woman suggested.

"My daughter is sharp as a pencil. She doesn't want to be your medicine maker."

"Well, how come your ma drove Wild Will away?" Ralph Darling asked.

"You're upset about something that happened thirty years ago, before you were born!" Rose Thorn said. She laughed, so everybody else did too, including Ralph. "What a town this is!"

Across the swamp channel, Herself was sitting on the landing, ignoring the party. She was glad for the quiet and didn't mind being alone, grieving for Ada, waiting for what would come next in her life and her body. Ozma, however, was attentive, head up, taking in every word that sailed across the water.

"Your ma's always found a way to hold onto her land," Ralph Darling said, without thinking. "She won't sell it to nobody. I heard some people from Chicago tried to buy it. It ain't easy keeping a big piece of land."

Others in the group nodded, and a strange shift occurred. Without anybody saying so, a general consensus was reached: they did not resent Herself for all she had but, instead, they admired her. Rose Thorn reached out and squeezed Ralph's hand and smiled.

When Two-Inch Tony arrived, he handed Rose Thorn his half-pint of blackberry brandy and was surprised by his own generosity. She took a swig and, to his relief, handed it back. Another car parked across the road next to Ralph Darling's truck, and the man who got out of the driver's side had a guitar; the woman with copper-colored braids who got out of the passenger seat had a fiddle. They walked across the road and sat on the Boneset Table, and the man began to play, and Donkey felt her jaw drop. At first it seemed sacrilegious for them to sit where Hermine had always put her medicine and food, but the music filling the air was another kind of nourishment. Musical instruments were something they'd never had on the island. The man played a bright flowing melody, and the woman's notes fell in alongside, the sound of her violin keeping his guitar company, and even Triumph and Aster hung their heads over the fence to listen.

Donkey would have been uneasy in a room with so many people—she'd been uneasy in the past whenever she'd gone into the Muck Rattler to find Rose Thorn—but instead of sour carpeting and stale beer, the smells here were of swamp, grass, alfalfa, and dung. With cottonwood fluff hanging in the hazy sunshine, she felt light and breezy. And if Herself needed her, Donkey could run home in a minute. As the sun moved into the west, the shadows of the black willows and the big swamp oak lengthened, and Rose Thorn kept moving her chair out of the shade and into the sun to charge herself like a battery, and everybody else moved to circle her, even if it meant they had to shield their eyes with their hands or sit in the road. Nobody mentioned Ada McIntyre, as though they'd chewed and swallowed the old woman's life that afternoon, and now they were each privately digesting her.

Some women stopped in their cars and poked around the Boneset Table behind the musicians. They peeked beneath the table at the empty basket lined with a clean orange knitted blanket. One woman put a note in the money box right in front of everybody. Another, a woman who'd had trouble with her bleeding over the last few years, stopped by and slipped a note into the box more discreetly. She left a jar of strawberry jam with sweet foam on top, just the way Donkey liked it. Herself had always given the woman a two-mint tea with nettles, a recipe Donkey knew. She called it Menses Tea and had put a bottle of sulfur water next to it on the table for the woman's bath.

When Standish, who had been at the funeral with his wife, drove past the party in his truck, Prissy suggested they stop. Rather than slow down or pull over, Standish accelerated past the people gathered there, and Prissy called him a joyless asshole. He couldn't deny that he had been tempted to stop. The scene of the crime can bring back strong feelings, and even a man who hates his feelings is drawn to feeling them again, if only to know better what he hates.

A load of kids came by the Boneset Table in a station wagon with "Congrats Grads" spray-painted in canned snow foam on their back window. Three teenage girls got out and talked to Rose Thorn shyly, while two boys stood a few yards away from the circle. When Dickmon arrived with his wife, Hannah Grace, he adjusted his rectangular glasses and told the teenage boys to make themselves useful and get some firewood. To Dickmon, this looked like a party that would continue after dark, and somebody would want a fire, and boys were happier when they had a job to do. After they had gathered branches from the woods downstream along the road, Rose Thorn quietly offered each boy a beer from those that had materialized before her, which they accepted and shared with the girls, all of them standing apart in their own circle. Soon they got back into the station wagon and drove away.

An outdoor party was a great thing for the people of Whiteheart, because it didn't cost anything, and it felt a little like the satisfying work they remembered in their bones from an old life, one in which work and play were not separate. But they couldn't have managed the party without Rose Thorn, somebody who could have been anywhere but chose to be with them, somebody who needed them as much as they needed her. Rose Thorn had always liked a party; she grew brighter as more people gathered around her, and she glowed brighter when they left, as though it was not their presence she needed as much as the energy of their coming and going. Both Rosie's mother and her daughter were worthy of a lifetime of study, but Rosie craved the distraction of these other people she knew less well. What she hungered for most was Titus—his big shoulders and the heavy arm he used to drape around her, his musky grain smell, and even his willingness to argue playfully with her.

Without him there, Rose Thorn could only pick and choose what she saw in these other men of Whiteheart and piece something like him together from lesser parts. She had no right to Titus—she'd had all the chances in the world to marry him, if only she'd been willing to go along with his script. She might even have found a way to explain her daughter's paternity without lying. But she wanted him on her own terms, and she wanted him to trust her without an explanation. Out here in the sunshine, with Ada McIntyre respectfully buried, the world seemed to ripen with possibility.

At Rose Thorn's request, everybody—lions and lambs alike—raised a glass or a bottle or a coffin nail or a joint in a toast to Herself. The man with the guitar started up again, sang a folksong about a train, and a couple of women were slapping their thighs to the rhythm. The violin player took a break and drank a beer, enjoyed the dappled sunshine. Donkey lay listening in the ditch across the road, chewing and swallowing sour wood sorrel with its yellow flowers.

"We're praying for her," the woman with the fiddle said wistfully to Rose Thorn. She had used an island medicine to relieve her joint pain until a few weeks ago. She was enjoying being out here with her neighbors, but she needed that medicine badly. *And Lord knows*, she thought before she started playing again, *it is difficult to disentangle people from what we hope they will provide for us.*

"My sister really needs her stomach soother," a woman with sad eyes said to nobody in particular, "and the prescription drugs make her bloated."

The stomach soother she was referring to was made with peppermint, cabbage juice, honey, and chili peppers. Donkey considered making it to help that woman's sister. Why not help somebody if it was easy?

When Donkey first noticed Roger, he was behind her, half in and half out the cab of Larry Darling's truck. She thrummed to recognize his feet and legs sticking from the passenger-side window. She thrilled to see the scuffed white athletic shoes with blue stripes, which he wore with socks—also with blue stripes—even though it was a warm day. His appearance here made more seem possible, maybe even school. Roger flipped around and appeared upright inside the truck, where he lifted a rifle from a gun rack, stuck it out the window, and pointed it toward Triumph and Aster. Donkey stood up out of the ditch and ran across to the wooden fence, to put herself between Aster and a bullet. Roger startled visibly when he noticed her there, and Donkey feared he would fire, either on purpose or by accident. She could be killed right here and now.

"What the hell are you doing, kid?" yelled a man's voice.

Roger yelled, "Nothing!" He hurriedly returned the rifle to the rack.

Sitting in a cage in the bed of the truck Roger was in was Larry Darling's biggest brindle, Rocky, who might have been mistaken for a dog statue. When the wind blew, Aster's ears went up at the scent of the dog, and even Donkey could smell the dog musk. When the wind died down, Donkey got a shiver, thinking she sensed the dog smelling *her*, the way the Lindworm had smelled her at their first encounter. Her whole body was still thrilling with alarm at Roger's presence and with the violence just averted in the pasture, and somehow the dog made her feel it more. As Roger slithered out of the truck window, landing on all fours, Donkey climbed through the fence rails and up onto Aster's spotted back. The jenny was still shedding her winter coat, and Donkey's legs and seat were now covered with two-inch white and brown hairs. Aster stamped her foot hard at nothing Donkey could see.

Roger walked toward Donkey and Aster with a stiff-legged gait and then leaned against the fence. He pulled a can of beer out of his baggy shorts pocket and showed it to her through the rails.

"How tall are you?" Donkey asked. She knew he was eleven, like her, and he looked a little taller than he had at the hospital, though it had only been three weeks ago.

"Six feet tall," he said.

"No you're not," Donkey said. It struck her as curious that he would lie about something that could be so easily disproved. And then it struck her as funny.

"That dog's getting trained to fight in a pit," Roger said. He climbed up onto the top rail of the fence, about five yards away from Donkey and Aster. "They live next to us, and they have three pit bulls."

"A rattlesnake has pits for smelling warm blood," Donkey offered, needing to say something she was sure of. At the hospital they'd mindlessly run around, and she'd said anything that came into her head, but she was a little afraid now, with Roger so close to the island and able to get hold of a real gun. "*Sistrurus catenatus*," she said. "*Canis lupus familiaris.*"

From her perch on Aster's back, Donkey looked across to the cottage where Herself sat, ready to warn Donkey about the dangers of boys. Through the foliage, Donkey could make out only a smear of lavender color that was Hermine's shirt. She got a shiver, a curious sensation in her feet and hands, a fear that somebody might fire another bullet at Herself.

Then Titus's red-and-white truck arrived like a wind from the west and pulled into Wild Will's driveway, into a space they'd all unknowingly reserved for him. He got out and slammed the door, which did not shut all the way, and when he walked long-legged across the road, what passed through Donkey's body and the other bodies at the party was relief. Whatever he'd said earlier about Lorena's virtues, he was drawn to Rose Thorn as to a medicine to save his life, to save the life of the town. Now Rose Thorn and Titus were together the way they should be. Dickmon took Hannah Grace's hand, and she tried to smile at him, but the smile faltered, and she flushed. They had a babysitter tonight for their three girls, and they could take the long way home around the Waters as they hadn't done in years. The fiddler bumped shoulders with her guitar player at the Boneset Table, and they both remembered a song they hadn't played in a long time, and that remembering took such a hold of them that they slowed their playing in anticipation of playing that other song. Ralph Darling laughed loudly at something with one hand on his stomach, and most everybody else laughed at the sunshiny pleasure of the afternoon.

Perched on the top rail of the fence, Roger was a little above Donkey's eye level where she sat on Aster's back. He was watching her with a growing intensity—fear? His expression changed from its usual smugness to astonishment. His eyes widened, as if Donkey were growing wings on her shoulders, and he dropped the unopened can of beer to the ground. Before Donkey could ask what he was looking at, something hard hit her from behind, a hoof clubbing her right thigh and another hoof on her back knocking her forward hard onto Aster's withers and pinning her. Triumph was mounting Aster with Donkey trapped there between them! The jenny took a few steps forward, and Triumph's hooves slid down and dragged Donkey bodily off her mount like a ragdoll, and she landed on her bottom between his two front hooves in the soft dirt. She scuttled a few feet away as he jumped again onto Aster's back, moving out of range just in time to avoid the crashing hooves.

She'd seen the jack mounting Aster from the other side of the fence before, and Herself had told her once that Triumph, who weighed about 750 pounds, could be dangerous when Aster was in heat, but Donkey hadn't believed Triumph would ever hurt her. In truth, there had been so much going on that day that Donkey hadn't asked herself why the donkeys were behaving so strangely. Now she rose from the ground and, trembling all over, pulled up her jeans and straightened her army jacket. She picked up *Garden of Logic*, which had flown out of her pocket. She picked up the can Roger had dropped and climbed onto the top rail beside him, her heart pounding.

In the pasture, Aster kicked at Triumph with both back legs and then backed up into him. Her mouth opened and closed in an odd way, her eyes rolled back in her head, and her tail arched, and Donkey shrank away from Roger with a new kind of embarrassment. She was embarrassed for Aster—who had at first seemed merely annoyed and tolerant—for the way she was now both wanting and not wanting Triumph on her.

Roger cracked the beer open, and it exploded. When it stopped foaming over his hand, he took a drink and squeezed up his face and held the red, white, and blue can out to her.

She swallowed the warmish bitter foam and then gagged and spit. "Do you like that?" she asked with disbelief.

"Sure. Don't you?" Roger pulled up his socks.

Donkey shook her head no and handed the can back. She'd assumed she would like it—it was the kind of beer Titus drank. Roger took another small sip. He squeezed his eyes shut as he swallowed.

Triumph jumped onto Aster again, and when she moved forward, he slid off. His dark leathery equipment dangled, nearly touching the ground.

"Woo-hoo!" a man yelled from the firepit.

"Atta boy!" another man shouted.

"Like looking in a mirror."

"Reminds me of Titus and Lorena," Roger said. "I saw them once, in the barn."

"No," Donkey said, to block out the idea. But she had been reminded of Rose Thorn and Titus the same way.

Aster's mouth was now dripping drool. Her right eye was watering so much that there was a wet trail down to her jaw. She kicked at Triumph again, but everyone could see she didn't mean it. Donkey's heart filled with sympathy for her.

"What a magnificent piece of ass!" howled a man's voice.

"Teresa, don't look!" shouted Whitby, playing around at covering his girlfriend's eyes.

When a dump truck full of bank run gravel rolled by, the second load of the day, everybody's voices were drowned out briefly by the roar of the great machine. The truck slowed as the driver caught sight of the donkeys and honked his horn.

Blind and deaf to outside distractions, Triumph jumped onto Aster again, and this time Aster planted her hooves, and he finally succeeded in getting purchase. Unlike Triumph, Aster seemed aware of the noise coming from the crowd and the road, and her eyes blinked open and closed as if in confusion as she received her mate. The thrusting of Triumph's powerful satyr haunches continued for several minutes, during which Donkey didn't dare look at Roger. Without warning, before Triumph even pulled away from Aster, Roger tossed down his half-full beer, jumped down to the ground, and ran back to the truck where Rocky was caged. When Triumph was done, he slid off and backed away from Aster's dangerous back legs. Aster stood very still, her ears flattened and her legs shaking. Donkey climbed through the fence and approached her, but she snorted in a way that said she wanted to be left alone.

Instead of returning to the party, Donkey went back to the island, and she gradually began to feel an ache where Triumph's hoof had landed below her shoulder blade. That night she made out a blood-speckled hoof-shaped bruise forming on her right thigh. She couldn't tell Herself what had happened without admitting her own careless behavior, without revealing something about the men in attendance at the party, and whatever she said later to Rose Thorn was only in their shared dreams, where Triumph and the truck carrying the gravel were conflated into a heavy unstoppable force bearing down on them. Donkey left the bridge boards down that night, intending to sneak across and check on Aster, but instead—overcome by the events of the day and the waves of feeling emanating from Rose Thorn—she fell asleep next to her mother in the single bed.

THAT NIGHT, TITUS DROVE BACK to the island and found the bridge down. He crept across and tapped on the window of the little room off the kitchen of Rose Cottage. All day Rose Thorn had felt inflamed. Titus had never gotten close to her at the firepit, but she'd felt his hand grazing through his curly hair, his hand on a beer bottle, both hands on his guitar, and she'd watched his chest rise and fall with each breath. She had lain awake for an hour, remembering the alfalfa-sweat-diesel smell of him, and then turned the light back on and read some more of *Glinda of Oz*. The book's plot seemed to have been dreamed up just for her: an island submerged in a lake, and the only witch who can raise it and liberate its inhabitants has been transformed into a swan. Then tap, tap tap from outside. She crushed out a coffin nail and put the book on the floor facedown.

Without waking the sleeping daughter beside her, she slid out of bed and sneaked out through the kitchen. Titus was waiting for her on the screened porch, conjured from the shaggy bark of hickory trees, the hoots of great horned owls, the scent of cut grass, and most of all by the happenstance that Dorothy had not pulled up the bridge boards.

"You're really here!" she said. Being there together, with Herself asleep inside, felt exciting and reckless.

Titus put his finger to his lips, and Rose Thorn kissed the finger and then kissed his mouth and couldn't stop. Once she got a good hold, she kissed him for a long time, feeling as though she might dissolve into pure laughter and moonlight in his arms. A year and a half away should have weakened the power of them together. She pressed her face into his chest to feel what she'd always known, to know what was hers in him, what was his in her. This was the Titus that Rose Thorn hungered for, Titus in silence and darkness, the Titus who was not trying to save her soul, the Titus who was not asking her to commit to anything, not asking her to believe what he believed. And to be with him on the island!

They stumbled past the hollow sycamore where Rose Thorn had twice seen the tall gray ghost, past the poison garden and to the soft place inside the stone circle, where they scared up two does and a fawn, who bounded away, their upraised white tails bobbing like sprites, disappearing silently into the trees.

They fell side by side into the grass but could not lie still. They rolled over one another and lay where the deer had lain and kissed again softly at first and then with gathering force.

"Lord, how I've missed you," Titus moaned.

"Shhh," she whispered. "You stink."

"It's mosquito dope. Rosie, I died without you," Titus said. "Every day I died."

"Shut up."

"But I'm alive now. Look at me, with you. Resurrected."

Rose Thorn climbed onto him and kissed away the dope scent, grateful for it covering any essence of Lorena. She kissed away the thousands of miles she'd traveled and her own stubbornness and his stubbornness and every other damn thing that had ever gotten between them. Other people had tried to feed her, but this was the food she needed.

Before them stood the big mother oak trees with the galls like mismatched breasts, and in their branches a family of a half dozen crows slept, each bird with one eye open. Titus had brought a bottle of real brandy, not the candy-flavored stuff, and a pack of coffin nails, and they rested from kissing inside the stone circle with their shoulders touching and their hands moving over one another, sharing a coffin nail. When Rose Thorn crushed it out, she said, "We're together, Titus. It's real." She pulled his T-shirt off his arms and over his head and lay her cheek against the rose tattoo on his biceps. They wriggled out of the rest of their clothes as naturally as cream rises to the top of milk. But when he started unsnapping her shirt, she pushed his hands away.

"I have a cyst. I don't want you to see it."

The last thing Titus wanted to do just then was argue.

Rose Thorn heard rustling and felt she was being watched. She feared Dorothy had followed them outside, but it was the crows above them, rustling the leaves, and other island creatures shifting and slithering around them. Dorothy would have identified every one of the animal sounds, but they entered Rose Thorn's ears as a glorious buzzing confusion. What was happening now was as natural as planting seed in soil. Though Titus weighed almost twice as much as Rose Thorn, he moved onto her weightlessly, glided down like a heron landing on a branch at the water's edge, its neck shifting forward and back.

"Let's stay like this forever, Rosie," he breathed.

She didn't want to talk, for fear they'd talk themselves into seeing how wrong this was, how hopeless. Maybe there were two pairs of people there at once, one animal couple breathing one another in, alive in one another's skin, their destinies entwined so profoundly that they were one entity, so that nothing and nobody else mattered; the other couple was asleep for now, those stubborn, incompatible ruminators, separated by faith, wounded by the past, and skeptical about the future.

"Oh, Rosie," Titus growled, and she pulled his head down and kissed him.

The swamp groaned and gurgled around them and they both caught a whiff of sulfur. The snakes, crayfish and voles sleeping underground absorbed the couple's rhythm. Rose Thorn's life here on the island was the most familiar thing to her and also the strangest. Nobody else she'd met seemed to know what it was like to live so enmeshed with people in a place that you shared one another's dreams. Only rarely had she encountered Prim's dreams in California, but it happened anytime she and Prim slept on the island. If she and Titus fell asleep tonight, she wondered if she'd become mixed up in his dreams too; she already felt impossibly entangled with him.

"Oh, Rosie." He slowed, trying to hold off any change in the world. He didn't want to fall away from her; he wanted to stop time so the morning would never come.

"This is how I want to be forever," Rose Thorn whispered. "Kill me now."

"You kill me first," Titus said.

"That's illogical," she whispered and laughed and pushed the thought of her daughter away.

"Oh, Rosie," he sang from a melancholy prison song he liked. "Stick to the promise, girl."

"No promises here," she breathed.

"Lying with me here means you're promising me the world with you in it," he said and stopped his movement.

Slowly she began to pull him down again, and he resisted being pulled down, and so they created the perfect tension. Even as she wanted to die with Titus, Rose Thorn wanted to be alive now, wanted to survive as she had not wanted to since her biopsy two months earlier. Beneath her, roots were regrowing between her and the material world.

As soon as Rose Thorn felt herself letting go, Titus couldn't hold back any longer. He drove her hard and howled as he let go. He rolled onto his side so as not to crush her. They were both shaking.

"God, I love you, Rosie," Titus said, gasping. "I'll have to break the news to Lorena."

"Shhh."

"Marry me, Rosie. I don't care what happened before. You won't have to go to church. We can get married at Boneset. Dorothy will be our flower girl. You can make your own vows. We can live in the

Boneset house if you don't want to live at the farm. You can be close to your ma. I don't care about anything but you!"

"This *is* our wedding, Titus. We're already married."

"I mean really married."

"This is better. Just us. Here." Rose Thorn sat up and plucked a piece of marsh grass and carefully wrapped and tied it around his finger. He took her hand in his and studied the grass ring she'd made for him. He kissed the palm of her hand.

"None of what happened before matters now, Rosie." He pulled her hand over his heart, squeezed it a little too hard, like the gearshift knob in his truck. She wanted to believe it and watched him move carefully to preserve the grass ring. She snapped two snaps that had come undone on her top, and Titus was happy not to see an imperfection in the woman he loved.

"I want to give you a real ring," Titus said. "A diamond."

"I prefer my warm stone." She took the amber out of her pocket and showed it to him in the moonlight.

She wondered now if her tumor had formed last year as a protest when she had refused to bring her body home where it belonged. Maybe being here with Titus would cure it. Maybe Molly would touch her and heal her instantly. Maybe Herself would regrow her hand and Baba Rose would pass a secret recipe through her. Maybe Dorothy would forgive her for leaving and that forgiveness would heal all their wounds. Rose Thorn wanted to live now; she wasn't ready for the doctors and their knives, but in search of a magic potion to save herself, she would try to drink them all.

CHAPTER ELEVEN

—

There are all kinds of ways to save lives.

JUST AS THAT NIGHT on the island with Titus was the first of many nights Rose Thorn spent with him, the party was the first of many gatherings at Boneset that summer and into the fall, with Rose Cottage obscured by foliage and Wild Will's boarded-up house on its little hill a grand presence overseeing the goings-on. Every Saturday, and sometimes during the week, Rose Thorn sat at the firepit anticipating her visitors. Initially Donkey came along to keep an eye on her mother and also to watch the men, who had been kept from her all these years and who, as a result, were her new favorite area of study. She studied them, all sizes and shapes of them, their muscular movements, their T-shirts (and, on cooler evenings, flannel shirts) stretched across their chests and bellies, their cleanshaven cheeks and bristled jaws and beards and mustaches. They smelled skunky, musky, even soapy, each of them like a new animal species. She marveled at how each man spoke his own language, a low rumbling like Dickmon or a sharp, nasal tenor like Standish. Roger's voice was a broken changing sound, and she didn't know how it would end up. After a few weeks, Donkey enjoyed the parties almost as much as her mother did and looked forward to spending time in the company of the people of Whiteheart.

Soon after mother and daughter dropped into their chairs at Boneset on a Saturday afternoon, somebody stopped by bearing gifts of beer, food, coffin nails, stories, and songs. Within a few hours, voices and music drowned out the shots from the firing range. Rose Thorn shared every bit of food and drink and good feeling that came to her, and somehow there was always enough for everybody.

At the end of June, people were talking about how Lorena had loaded up her old Ford police cruiser and left town. Everybody liked Lorena and sympathized with her over Titus's behavior, but most folks felt that Titus's getting back together with Rose Thorn was a matter of putting things right.

Talking and laughing with the visitors helped Rose Thorn keep cool despite the heat of her desire, a fire she climbed into so often she felt scorched, even a little brain damaged. The heat of that forge distracted her, if not completely, from the cold truth: she was not the wife Titus needed to help on his farm, not a good mother for his future children. And then there was the coldest fact of all—the tumor in her breast.

All the visitors in attendance at the edge of the Waters—often dozens of people—brought to the parties their own personal histories and intentions. Whitby brought a desire to look out for Rose Thorn, to watch for any disrespect or threat of violation, and he was relieved whenever Titus finally got there. When, at the end of July, his girlfriend Teresa would discover she was pregnant, his protective feelings would swell to include both women.

After a few weeks, Standish started coming to the parties with his wife. His reluctance was feigned, since he was drawn there as powerfully as Prissy, though for different reasons. He brought along his angry confusion, but his emotions always softened at the sight of Rose Thorn. Though she had asked people to leave their firearms in their vehicles—or better yet, at home—Standish secretly carried a small hammerless pistol in his front pocket. He felt he had special insight into how crazy men could be and wanted to be ready to defend the group if anybody else showed up with a gun to make trouble. He'd grown so thin from his digestive troubles that the gun made an obvious bulge in his pocket, so he always wore an untucked shirt over his tee, either army green or camouflage. As soon as he and Prissy drove away from the party and he lost sight of Rosie, his anger returned. Why was he fawning over her with all the other fools of Whiteheart? She had not been a responsible mother—they all knew that—and now she just sat out in the road in short-shorts inviting outrageous behavior. So why did he want to be near her right down into the marrow of his bones? He knew the failing was in himself as much as in her.

In the first week of July, Larry and Ralph Darling brought a cord of firewood and stacked it near the firepit. Titus started mowing the grassy area around the firepit and up and down the edge of the road, and then across Lovers Road and around the garden and eventually all the way up to Wild Will's house, where the yard had been a kind of overgrown meadow. Though the planks and plywood still covered the windows of the Boneset House, on days when cars and trucks parked in the driveway, there was a sense that the house was occupied again. A few times Donkey caught sight of a ghostly gray man slipping behind the house or watching the party, and she could only assume it was Rose Thorn's bartender ghost, though Rose Thorn just smiled when she mentioned it.

Another man, one who introduced himself as a social studies teacher, brought Donkey a high school geometry textbook that contained two hundred and six proofs, and she worked through these logical stories for the rest of the summer, significantly increasing the number of things she could trust were absolutely true. She appreciated the book's convention of declaring the truth by writing at the end of a proof the Latin phrase *quod erat demonstrandum* or *QED*, "it has been shown," and she adapted it for *True Things*. In addition to copying into her notebook Euclid's proof that there are an infinite number of prime numbers (ugh!), she wrote: *Rose Thorn loves Titus*, plus *Titus loves Rose Thorn* and an arrow pointing toward *They should get married, QED*. She left her notebook open to that page sometimes where Rose Thorn could see it.

"Your daughter's going to be as pretty as you, Rosie," the social studies teacher said. He wore a button-down shirt and was clearly a liar, but he didn't seem like a man who would tie a kid to her desk. Donkey liked him.

"She's got no use for pretty," Rose Thorn said. "She's a genius. Sharp as a pencil."

"Well, I hope she's coming to school in the fall," the man said.

"Girls do what they want here," Rose Thorn said. "They don't like to be bossed around."

Michigan was a state where a parent could keep a kid out of a school with no explanation, but Donkey had been thinking more and more about how to go to school. She thought if Rose Thorn would stay in Whiteheart, at Rose Cottage, and get cured of cancer, she could watch over Herself, and Donkey might slither out in the morning and be back in the afternoon. She could milk Delilah and collect eggs before she went. If Rose Thorn and Hermine would sleep until she was home from school, maybe they wouldn't even miss her. Too many *ifs*, the problem was, and so little opportunity to work forward with certainty to a clear QED the way she could in proofs. She felt jealous of the textbook's authors, of how when they set out, they already knew what it was they were proving.

THE SECOND SATURDAY IN JULY, Donkey wore her straw cowboy hat to weed the garden in front of Wild Will's house. She felt comforted by the solid structure rising behind her, even if she wasn't allowed to go inside. Then she fed Triumph and Aster the good weeds and crossed the road to check the Boneset Table, near which Rose Thorn sat reading *Ozma of Oz* in a reclining wooden chair that had belonged to Ada McIntyre. She walked down the steps to look across and wave at Herself and Ozma on the island. Herself waved, and the dog thumped her tail on the landing in hopes that Donkey was returning. On most summer days in the past, Ozma would have accompanied Donkey on her island adventures, but she was now tied to a tree, guarding Herself, which was boring for her. Donkey returned to sit beside Rose Thorn in Hermine's upright chair and read *Garden of Logic* and write in her notebook. In the heat of the afternoon, a shy teenage girl came by on foot and offered to read Rose Thorn's tarot.

Rose Thorn moved her legs so the girl, Irma, could lay the cards out on the lounge chair. Irma held up a few of the colorful cards—a sun with rays streaming over a baby on a horse, a body dead with ten swords driven into its back—and Rosie said, "They're beautiful," and what she said ricocheted off the cards and onto Irma, whose arms and shoulders and neck were pale and damp, whose gray-brown hair fell in soft serpents around her pimpled face. Irma's posture softened, and she sat down cross-legged on the ground in a comfortable slump, and her voice became fluid. She laughed and swatted away flies, and Donkey gave her the jar of bug dope to rub on herself. The young woman drank from a silver flask of Southern Comfort she'd swiped from her aunt. She offered it to Rose Thorn, who took a small sip.

"You're so pretty," Irma said and blushed at the compliment reflected back to her in the silver flask. "My aunt calls these cards the devil's deck. I have to live with her now because my mom hates me." Though it was a statement full of hurt, she delivered it matter-of-factly to Rose Thorn, who nodded and smiled sadly, let the bitter truth of it blossom between the three of them. Rose Thorn squeezed Irma's shoulder and kept looking into her face until Irma cried a little and was ready to move on.

Irma cut the oversized deck of cards and placed two of them face up: the Chariot and the Empress. Donkey was interested in the numbers on the cards: seven and three, both primes. These were Major Arcana cards, which foretold important events, Irma said. The Empress card meant fertility, beauty, and femininity. That contrasted with the Chariot, which indicated victory, control, and intentions. Irma turned over a third card, a terrible gray tower on fire with people jumping out of it. Rose Thorn laughed at the stark image, which wasn't necessarily bad, Irma said, but meant upheaval and change. This card was number sixteen ($16 = 2 \times 2 \times 2 \times 2$), Donkey noted, the number of ounces in a pound and fluid ounces in a pint canning jar, and so much more. Rose Thorn raised her beer and nodded at Irma to lift her flask, and they clinked them together. "Here's to the chaos foretold!" Rose Thorn said merrily.

To some of the more conservative Whitehearters, exchanges like this one between Rose Thorn and Irma, and the spontaneous parties as a whole, seemed frivolous, even decadent, but Rose Thorn felt in her bones how natural and right it was to receive people at Boneset. She was helping Irma in this moment, had helped Whitby when he was devastated by a fight with Teresa, even helped Standish open his heart. The way Herself knew the pain in people's bodies and had healed them using her own arm, her own blood or breath, Rose Thorn felt the pain that lived deep in a person's bones. If Molly laid on hands, then Rose Thorn laid on her attention as she did now with Irma, as she'd done last week when a woman brought her grandfather who didn't get out much and who could no longer speak at all—and who seemed happy to just sit near Rose Thorn. She greeted everybody with friendliness, was honestly glad to see them, and people responded to being kindly received by becoming kinder and more generous themselves. Donkey watched these exchanges and felt confounded by how exactly they were happening. She could not write down recipes for laughter and sympathetic expressions and hand gestures and openness. But there was no denying that just as Herself had found the wisdom to soothe the symptoms for a particular contagious or insidious disorder, Rose Thorn was able to ease an endemic self-loathing.

Irma shuffled Rose Thorn's cards back into the tarot deck and invited Donkey to cut the cards. She presented her with the Moon (number eighteen) and the Ace of Cups (number one), a hand holding a bowl brimming over with golden liquid. Donkey liked the bowl, until the girl tapped her heart and said, "This is a lucky card. It might mean a baby."

"What if somebody has cancer?" Donkey asked, and Rose Thorn shot her a glance. Then Rose Thorn shook her head no with surprising firmness. Irma looked slightly confused until Rose Thorn smiled and reassured her.

Donkey's hands had itched to braid Irma's hair, as she braided Hermine's hair, but at her mother's rebuke, she ran away from the two women and brushed Aster instead. She'd been holding a grudge against Triumph for a month, since he'd bruised her with his hooves and humiliated Aster with his mating, but today she relented and used the curry comb on him too.

WHEN TITUS SHOWED UP LATER at the grassy clearing after working his usual twelve or more hours, he brought his big strong homegrown energy, and the party really began. Upon arriving, he rested his guitar on the grass beside Rose Thorn's chair and slipped both arms around her, picked her up, and held her in the air so she was above him, spun her around—she shrieked with pleasure—and put her back down. He could have stayed right there beside her, but in his generosity, he took a seat on a stump opposite her across the firepit and began to strum, so the town was held between the two of them. His rose tattoo bulged on his biceps in the evening sunlight. Its thorns, rattlesnake, blood, and moon had been covered by a long sleeve all winter and spring while Lorena was there living with him at

Whiteheart Farms. People came closer to the circle around the firepit, and somebody started the fire; within a few minutes several people were helping kids roast marshmallows somebody had had in their car. Several marshmallows were blackened in the flames, a few melted off the kids' sticks and sizzled on the wood, but the rest of them became perfectly browned caramelized melty sweetness. Two-Inch Tony's wife, Cynthia, produced a bag of peanuts in the shell that they passed around the circle. Vehicles continued to arrive and depart, containing and releasing bodies.

Once the children had all left the firepit, Titus said, "What do a virgin and a thinblood have in common?" Nobody answered.

"Just one prick and it's all over," he said, laughing. All of them laughed. Rose Thorn stood up and tossed a peanut at Titus across the flames, and he caught it, shelled it, and ate it and then resumed playing guitar.

Boneset had always been the intersection of the town and the island, a place where people brought their private complaints. The spirit of Hermine Zook, whose figure now sat a hundred fifty yards away, on the other side of the bridge, still hovered over them like the Holy Ghost. And though Wild Will's Boneset House was empty, nobody could deny its concrete-block foundation and hardwood framing were still straight and sturdy. That marriage and Hermine's healing had bound the town to the island for a long while, but now both Wild Will and Herself had withdrawn, and it was time for a new marriage and this new kind of healing. People were here to be part of a compelling story, and at the center of that story was Titus gazing at Rose Thorn across the fire or arguing theatrically with her. In a town where men and women were shy, where they relied on TV love or movie love or pop-song love, they watched Rose Thorn and Titus hungrily, emulated them. With the two of them together again, the hardworking citizens of Whiteheart were beginning to feel they, themselves, might have a chance at a great love. Rose Thorn and Titus knew their romance was bigger than they were, and though they had their own doubts and concerns for the future, for now, all was lightness and laughter, at least on the surface.

Ralph Darling followed Titus's joke with another: "What does a limp dick and a rattlesnake have in common?"

Somebody shouted the answer: "You can't fuck with either one."

Men flashed their wing bars like songbirds at these parties. Bald men posed in sunlight like mallard ducks to make their heads appear shinier. Young men wore tank shirts that showed their muscles. Extroverted men told outrageous stories about physical feats (*God must've helped me lift that four-wheeler off my niece—I couldn't have done it myself*); and about livestock and hunting trips (*Just don't ever pull the pin on a can of doe urine inside your blind, that's all I'm saying*); and about rescuing Old Red from certain drunken death (*Pulled him off the tracks at Rex Crossing not three minutes before the Twilight Limited came through*). They became more gallant in offering their seats or stumps or laps to the women who arrived. And the women, many of them, put on lightweight shirts or skirts that moved in the breeze and wore their hair down like Rosie's and relaxed and become more expansive and laughter-filled versions of themselves. As part of the natural variety and flow, there were a few women who behaved more like the men and some men who wanted to be breezy, and that was welcome too. Everyone flirted more on those Saturdays, not only with Rose Thorn but with one another, even with their own spouses. The smell of cologne rose around the fire. And even those townspeople who didn't come took pleasure in knowing they would be welcomed if they did, pleasure in imagining what they might have worn or talked about, even as they shook their heads at lazy Rose Thorn for having parties instead of weeding her mother's garden.

What most of the people of Whiteheart did not know for sure, what they did not dare ask God for fear of revealing a lack of faith, was about the value of this earthy life that they sometimes loved and sometimes hated. They wished their ancestors could come to them in sleepless hours and assure them that, beyond the long, dim scramble of making a living and taking care of every urgent thing, there was an importance in each breath taken on this earth as a human animal, a value not dependent upon a heavenly reward. On Saturdays, Rose Thorn offered them a few hours of freedom from that lonesome concern, a freedom from what was good or bad, holy or unholy; she offered them a sense that they were appreciated and interesting as individuals right now, and that their joy, sorrow, work, and pain mattered to others in their community the way a painting or a mosaic might matter if it was pleasing to look at. Rose Thorn's going away and returning told them they were worth coming back to, in the same way that a mariner's sweetheart judges her worth by whether her sailor comes home alive, though she could not possibly be responsible for a storm or a seiche that capsizes a freighter and drowns a crew in Lake Michigan.

No one but Donkey noticed that Rose Thorn was careful after her return to Whiteheart in ways she hadn't been before. She hardly drank alcohol, hardly drew on the coffin nails she held between her fingertips. Rose Thorn didn't understand it, but she who'd always drunk like a big man could sip a single beer for hours now and just watch the smoke from her coffin nails rise in coils and dissolve into the humid air or waft away on the breeze. Rose Thorn made sure not to lie, not to behave in a way that was casually cruel or dismissive. She sensed that any false behavior or unkindness could cause her tumor to breach its walls and spread throughout her body. She drank in what sunshine she could; she inhaled the fresh green fertility of the Waters like fine wine; and she loved every minute with these people, who were precious to her. She did not want to miss a moment, especially not with Titus, and she found a little of Titus in each of the guests. When her daughter was nearby as well, her joy became ecstasy.

Molly came by the island every other Saturday, one of her days off, to check Hermine's wound and to cluck over her. Herself did not respond to anything Molly said, and Molly continued to assume it was because her mother couldn't hear her. She usually brought Donkey something educational to read and some store-bought food she liked, such as peanut butter and saltines. While she had Donkey's attention, Molly continued her quest to get Donkey to eat meat. There was no doubt in her mind that the girl did not have enough protein in her diet.

Upon first arriving, Molly would shake her head disapprovingly at the roadside gathering, but she would stop by the firepit to talk to Rose Thorn before getting into her car to leave. She wasn't allowed to visit Roy on Saturdays, since he was focused on writing his Sunday sermon, so she often stayed for an hour or more, sipping juice or eating a takeout meal she brought in a Styrofoam clamshell, always trying and failing to get Rosie to eat something too. Rose Thorn and Molly always talked about Primrose, about how much they missed her. Both of them talked to Prim at least once a week now, Rosie using the phone at Titus's house. Prim keeping in touch with them was something new and welcome.

Donkey liked overhearing that Prim was a *workaholic* (Rose Thorn said she worked all her waking hours) and that she should move closer to home (according to Molly). Donkey saw that if Prim lived there in Whiteheart, she wouldn't be able to take Rose Thorn far away, and also that she might provide more books. Donkey was beginning to doubt that she hated Primrose; rather, California was the terrible thing. Apparently Prim worked now for an organization whose purpose was to save its clients from the death penalty. This was fascinating and frightening news to Donkey, listening in, since she hadn't known there was anything like a death penalty to be afraid of—a whole new way of dying, being killed by a terrible chair. Donkey wondered why Molly, a natural-born healer, couldn't smell her sister's cancer, that slightly fishy scent on Rose Thorn's breath.

While people were glad to see Molly every other Saturday, they were all a little more reserved in her presence and relieved when she left, as they would be relieved to dry off after a medicinal bath and pour themselves a drink. If they had to put up with Molly's company in order to bask in Rose Thorn's presence, they would happily do it.

Even after the first party, Rose Thorn saw that her company did the people of Whiteheart good. After that, she kept a certain mission in mind, to protect Hermine from the dangers of hostile feelings: if the people of Whiteheart would stop hating and hurting themselves, they wouldn't have to hate or hurt anybody else, in particular, Herself. Rosie didn't know who had shot her mother, and she didn't want to know—she wanted desperately to believe it was an accident. And what she wanted more than anything was for nobody to shoot at or near the island again.

Decades ago, when Wild Will had lived at Boneset, in that house on the hill, he'd protected Herself in his own way. He was a wheeler-dealer and a storyteller, and his words had been a conduit between the town and M'sauga Island. He invited men to sit with him and converse and admire his wife from a distance, through the prism of himself, even offering the men her medicines. In this way, he presented Herself as a concept worthy of contemplation, as well as a convenience to the town. Rose Thorn did the work differently, by showing both the men and the women in Whiteheart that the island and the town were one whole place, with a shared history; they belonged together. Wild Will had done his work with his eloquence and his authority, while Rose Thorn's instrument of persuasion was simply her presence and her attention, and that was why she was exhausted at the end of an evening of doing what looked like nothing.

DONKEY FOUND HER OWN WAY to create goodwill in the community. During the week, she made what minor medicines she could, and along with cartons of herbed eggs and bottles of spring water, put them out on the table every Saturday morning. The first time she made bug dope, she used pennyroyal, catnip oil, and peppermint, and Herself reached for a jar in the cupboard and then leaned over the bowl to add crumbled poison ivy leaves, something she would usually cook for a long time and then add to the batch in minuscule amounts. After the mixture cooled, Donkey dumped it out near the compost pile and made another batch to hide away. And while Donkey was making a popular stomach soother that called for a whiff of watered-down hemlock tincture, Herself, with great earnestness, put in a bounty of the stuff. To a batch of foot balm, she offered a generous amount of itch weed. In Hermine's original medicines, there had often been a hint of poison cooked into a big batch, and Donkey saw how Herself had, at the very least, lost her sense of proportion; at worst, she was trying to hurt or sicken people. As for the medicines that now appeared on the Boneset Table, neither Rose Thorn nor anybody from the town expressed any suspicion that Donkey was making them. She made them while Herself and Rose Thorn slept, when she usually would have been reading and writing in her notebook.

If Herself was a mystery to the people of Whiteheart, she was, after losing her hand, a more particular mystery to Donkey. When Donkey questioned her about the poisons she gathered and tried to use in excess, Herself said, "We need this, don't we?" Donkey was hesitant to toss away or burn anything Herself had gone to the trouble of collecting, but she worried that Herself might add poisons to food or drink unbeknownst to her or anyone else, so when Herself brought home bundles of poison sumac and hemlock and fresh poison ivy, hundreds of times the amount they could ever use, Donkey hid the poisonous bounty under the house and the regular useful poisons out of sight in the left-hand caboodle.

One evening, Donkey knelt to reach down inside this caboodle for a pinch of boneset for a sweating medicine, and there she brushed against the feathery softness of the Lindworm. She startled and began to pull away but then reached down again and touched the soft scales just barely and let her pinkie linger there. Slowly, the m'sauga moved out of reach. Donkey sat cross-legged on the floor with her heart pounding, feeling inexplicably happy that the creature was still there in the cottage and still alive. The pencil wound had not killed her, and today she had chosen not to bite. This powerful creature, her *Sistrurus* sister, had stayed with her.

Donkey shone a flashlight down into the hole and caught sight of a tiny patch of chocolaty mottled snakeskin.

"Rose Thorn has cancer," Donkey whispered to the snake. "And I want her to go to the doctor." Telling the secret to the snake felt good. She fingered the key hanging there as she considered what else she wanted. "As soon as Rose Thorn and Granny get better," she said, "I want to go to school."

ON THE SECOND SATURDAY IN AUGUST, in the early evening, while the adults were distracted by sampling somebody's homemade cherry wine, Roger and his cousins tore loose the plywood from the big south window of Wild Will's house. With her heart pounding, Donkey watched the sheet of wood fall to the grass with a whoosh, heard somebody's parents call out just then that it was time to go home, and watched Roger and the others run back to the firepit and pretend nothing had happened. Donkey had always been forbidden by Herself from even asking about the house, let alone approaching it. If Herself could have tossed the house in the swamp, she might have done it. It was the next Saturday, before any other kids arrived, that she braved going back. She brought out the stepladder from the barn, put it into the rosebushes, and climbed up to find the window frame was studded with broken glass. She went back to the barn for a couple of burlap oat bags, which she used to pad the ledge before she climbed inside. The window opened into the big dining room. She'd never before seen such a big ornate table with carved legs. Donkey wasn't sure what purpose it served to have a special indoor dining room instead of just eating in the kitchen, until she realized that the house had no screened porch.

The wood floor in the dining room was mostly covered with a rug patterned with flowers and curlicues, with some evidence of footprints, probably from Molly. Molly's grand dream was to move Herself into the Boneset House and sell the island altogether. Rose Thorn insisted that wouldn't happen. The wood showing at the edge of the room was dark and dusty, but when Donkey knelt and wiped it hard with her jacket sleeve, the planks, though dark, became as glossy as the floors at Rose Cottage right after they were waxed—another job they hadn't done this year. The high ceilings were draped with cobwebs so thick and dusty they were opaque in the light coming through the one open window. Against the wall there was a tall, wide bookshelf with glass doors holding leatherbound volumes.

Donkey opened the sideboard to find several folded tablecloths, ivory colored with lace patterns. She put one on the table, right over the dust, and then she set the table with the bone-colored scalloped-edged dishes from those cabinet shelves. Why hadn't they taken some of this stuff to Rose Cottage, where everything was wearing out? Here were forks with straight tines, not tines that had been twisted by being slammed in the drawer, spoons with silver bowls instead of bowls worn through to the brass, teacups without cracks. Looking around the spacious room with all its beautiful and useful things, Donkey wondered for the first time if Molly might have the right idea.

She walked through the dark kitchen and put her hand on the knob of the back door, which was not boarded up, and the knob turned in her hand. She realized she could unlock the deadbolt if she wanted to and leave the Boneset House that way, rather than climb back out the window. She said to the spiders in the dark kitchen, "I'm off to school. See you later!" and then listened for a response until she heard a sharp creaking upstairs. Rose Cottage was an old granny of a house, with nooks and crannies and sighs and groans, but even the complaints this big house made were precise and austere.

In Donkey's imagined scenario, each morning when she left for school, Titus would head out to get on his tractor, and Rose Thorn would sit at the huge dining table drinking her coffee with honey and cream. She would spend her lazy days reading the dozens of books moldering on the shelf in the dining room. Donkey returned to look again at the table she'd set. She'd put down only three plates. Her body thrummed with guilt. Herself couldn't be left alone on the island—she might just go to sleep and never wake up—and she'd sworn to never live in Wild Will's house. Donkey knew that even thinking about moving in here was duplicitous, a betrayal, another side effect of the snake blood she'd taken in.

She crept into the next room with the slow movements she used in approaching a kingfisher's muddy bank nest. After a lifetime surrounded by the softness of the island and the rough-hewn, sagging cottage, Donkey wondered if she might be more logical living in this stately place with its straight lines and exact angles. And there in the dark before her was a set of steps like none she had ever seen before, an elegant wide stairway with a curved wooden banister ending in a big wooden ball. A house with an upstairs was a mysterious thing for a girl growing up in a one-story cottage. As she crept up the carpeted stairs, they creaked like a new kind of musical instrument. She had a little flashlight in her pocket, but she preferred to navigate by the shards of light entering through the cracks between the boards nailed over the windows.

The first bedroom had heavy drapes covering the boarded-up windows, and dust lay thick on the hardwood floor and the wool rug, strewn with bits of leaves and mouse dung. Light came in through the top of the window and lit up a graying bedspread, wrinkled as though a body had briefly lain there. Donkey had explored the second floor of the hospital, but this second floor was something entirely different—it seemed like a house above the house. She would have liked to look out the window and see her mother and whoever else was arriving at the party from this high and unfamiliar vantage point, but there was no view to be had here, and she moved down the hall to the next room.

Upon entering, she first saw light coming through a crack between two boards on the window at about eye level. She began to move toward it, hoping to look out and see Rose Thorn in her lounge chair. And then she saw she was not alone. A figure, tall and colorless, was silhouetted in front of the boarded windows. The light coming in had messed up

Donkey's ability to see in the dark, but she sensed the figure turning slowly toward her. Another eleven-year-old girl might have run, but Donkey's inclination was the same in that moment as when she had seen the m'sauga or the crayfish: to move closer to know better what she was seeing. This ghost—it had to be a ghost—had a beard covering most of his face, a beard that grew high on his cheeks, almost to the bottoms of his eyes, and hung down over his throat and collar. Gray hair hung down onto his shoulders, under a cap of the sort engineers on trains wore. A work shirt that might have been gray-green hung off his skeletal frame; his work pants were caked with dried swamp soil. He was taller than she was. Donkey had imagined a ghost would be wavery, made out of something resembling coffin-nail smoke, but he seemed solid enough to touch.

"Hello, wide-eyed child," the ghost said finally, with a sad smile mostly hidden by his beard. Donkey wished he'd cover the window so her eyes could adjust and see him better. She smelled the swamp on him. "You're a tall girl."

"Are you Rose Thorn's bartender?" she asked. "Her ghost?"

"An interesting question," he said, and ran a bluish hand over his beard. His shirt cuffs were threadbare, disintegrating. He wasn't muscular or slick or lively like the men she admired—he might creak like the Tin Man when he moved—and yet she was drawn to him.

"You don't sound like a ghost," she said, stepping closer.

"What does a ghost sound like?"

"Very logical. Sharp as a pencil," Donkey said. "And he would know topological graph theory."

"I'm not that kind of ghost," he said and laughed lowly.

"Rose Thorn has cancer," Donkey said. "And I don't want her to die. And I don't want her to go away."

Alarm registered in the ghost's figure, a stiffening, though she'd assumed ghosts were all-knowing.

"And I want to go to school. As soon as everybody is okay and doesn't need me so much."

Donkey heard a yelp then, from downstairs, and kids' voices—they must've just arrived at the party. She pulled back her hand, realizing that she'd been reaching toward the figure. Another scream from downstairs, bloody murder this time, as though a kid had seen a rattlesnake.

Donkey turned and ran down the staircase and found a curly haired girl about four years old grinning and shrieking both, with blood on her suntanned downy little arm. The feed sack Donkey had laid over the broken glass in the window frame was on the floor beside the child. There were three more little kids right behind her at the window, on the stepladder. Donkey ordered them in a stern voice to get down off the ladder, and then she opened the kitchen door and walked the little girl outside and down the steps. To distract the four kids, she took them to the big barn, where they sat on bales of hay. Donkey washed away the blood on the girl's arm to reveal scratches, but the blood continued to flow. Donkey picked some yarrow leaves, chewed them up, and put the chaw on the deepest cuts until the bleeding finally stopped, while the other kids watched solemnly. Then she braided everybody's hair that was long enough to braid.

Donkey wanted to go back and find the ghost—she had so much more to tell him and ask him—but the kids followed her, clung to her, so she took down the yardstick that always hung on the barn wall and taught them to measure. While she wasn't watching, the girl with the scratches climbed into the donkey stall, and Donkey had to rush in and grab her before Triumph or Aster stepped on her by accident. Donkey then taught all the kids to stay out of the donkey stall and pasture as Herself had once taught her. One by one, she grabbed them by the shoulders and stomped their insteps.

"It will hurt a lot more," she told them loudly, over their cries of pain and disbelief, "when it's donkey hooves stepping on you."

Each of the kids screamed and ran away after their lesson but then came right back.

"He looked very real," Donkey said to her mother later when they were alone. "Like a real person."

"Ghosts are real, aren't they?" Rose Thorn said, smiling at the confusion of the thing.

It didn't take more than a few days for Molly to notice the missing plywood over the window at Boneset and have Titus replace it and lock the back door. It also didn't take long for Donkey to try the key she'd found in the left-hand caboodle. It didn't fit in the front door at Boneset, but it turned in the back door deadbolt, and with some jiggling, the door opened into the kitchen. No wonder Herself had stored the key with the powerful and poisonous medicines. Donkey stepped inside and inhaled deeply the dusty, woody, bookish scent that was already familiar to her. After that, she ventured into the big house every chance she got, but found no gray ghost waiting there, only the ghost of a future evoked by the table set with three plates. She felt the snake blood bubble in her veins as she put the key back in her pocket and willfully got out a fourth plate, a fourth fork, knife, and spoon.

DONKEY MISSED SHARING EVERY EXPERIENCE with Herself the way she used to before having a life off the island. Just a few months ago, Donkey had reported her every move to her granny, but over the course of the summer, she'd become aware of what Herself wouldn't like: any discussion of men and certainly anything to do with Wild Will's house. She told Hermine what was growing in the garden at Boneset (since returning from the hospital, Herself had not once crossed the bridge) and assured her that she was keeping the Babby Basket tidy, but otherwise she shared few of her experiences. Donkey hungered for conversations with Herself, but now that she had to pick and choose what she told, talking didn't feel natural, and in those silences, a sadness grew between them. Neither Donkey nor Herself had mastered Rose Thorn's art of creating polite or intentional conversation. Donkey especially missed arguing with Herself, but now she didn't even dare to disagree with her, for fear that Herself would be upset and not want to live or else be mad and not forgive her, the way she had gotten mad at Prim, Molly, and Rose Thorn. The worst was not sharing Rose Thorn's secret about cancer, but whenever Donkey thought she might spill the beans and betray her mother, Herself went deaf again. When Donkey once asked outright, "What if somebody has cancer, ma'am?" Herself didn't respond, didn't even say, "Send her to the devil-doctors."

One afternoon in August, Herself suggested Donkey can some green beans with her—somebody had left a bushel at the Boneset Table—and Donkey's heart sank. "But today's Saturday. I want to go with Rose Thorn."

Herself said nothing, but her left hand slowly moved to her right forearm in a terrible way. Donkey realized how leaving the island for all those hours—sometimes six or eight hours—left Herself paralyzed. Ozma made a groaning sound from the floor. Donkey knew how much Ozma missed her when she left the island for the day—even the chickens missed her, because she didn't let them outside to peck the ground—but somehow she hadn't realized the same about Herself. Before this summer, time had seemed open and endless, but now it was something to be thought about and portioned out.

"We can do it tomorrow," Donkey suggested, but she must've spoken in the wrong voice, because Herself didn't seem to hear.

When Rose Thorn called Prim each week on Titus's barn phone, Donkey sat nearby on Titus's old Ford 8N tractor listening to the different tone in her mother's voice, a contented sound, like a dog being petted, her words cleverer and more opaque than usual. Before each conversation, Rosie asked Donkey if they should invite Prim to come visit, and Donkey said, "Will you go to the devil-doctor?"

Rose Thorn's unspoken answer, so far, was one Donkey couldn't argue with: *Not yet, Freckle Face. Soon enough I'll be in their clutches, but just let me breathe free a little longer.*

CHAPTER TWELVE

Freedom has a cost.

ON THE SECOND TO LAST Saturday in August, Jamie Standish pulled into Wild Will's front yard and parked his blue diesel Ford truck next to Larry Darling's white Chevy with the dog cage bolted to the bed. On the left side of Standish's bumper, a sticker said, "I'M PRO-LIFE!" and on the right side, "YOU CAN HAVE MY GUN . . . WHEN YOU PRY IT OUT OF MY COLD DEAD HANDS." Larry Darling's bumper stickers said, "IF YOU CAN READ THIS, YOU'RE TOO CLOSE" and "I LOVE CATS. THEY TASTE JUST LIKE CHICKEN." If Molly's Buick sedan had been there that day, her bumper stickers would have countered with "SUPPORT GUN CONTROL" and "SANE CAT LADY."

Even before pulling the key out of the ignition, Standish tipped up a bottle of peppermint schnapps. He took a long swig, though it made his belly burn. He couldn't tell anymore when he was hungry or thirsty. After the schnapps, he took a big swallow of minty Pepto Bismol. Then he got out of the cab, patted the pistol in his front pocket.

"Good boy, Rocky," Standish said to the dog in the cage in the back of Larry's truck. He knocked on the side of the truck bed as a test. Rocky stayed still. When Standish caught sight of Roger ducking down behind the tailgate, he said, "You're not making trouble, are you, Rodge?"

"No, sir," Roger said.

"Good boy," Standish said. "Don't mess with Larry's dog. He's in training."

The red-and-white Herefords, way off in the field, ignored the party as usual, but Triumph and Aster were standing at the fence line with their ears pointed forward, watching the pit bull in the cage. They were always prepared to chase a dog or coyote out of the pasture if necessary or kick it if it wouldn't leave on its own. In this way, they protected Titus's cattle too.

Donkey had moved around the front of the white truck by now to get a good view of Standish. His boots were tied loosely, and he walked in a mincing way that told Donkey his feet hurt with each step. She wondered if it would help if he took off his shoes and went bare-foot like her; he probably needed to build up some calluses.

"You aren't making trouble, are you, Rodge?" Donkey said, imitating Standish's tenor voice and capturing his nasal tone pretty well. It was the first time all afternoon she was able to make Roger laugh.

"That guy's truck is a piece of shit," Roger said, imitating other men he'd heard. He climbed into the bed of Larry's newer truck, moved around the dog cage, and peered through the back window, into the cab. The dog didn't turn his head but stayed still with tensed muscles.

A third truck, one with a camper top, was blocking Donkey's only view of Rose Cottage, and so she had to imagine Herself sitting outside on the landing with Ozma tied to a tree nearby, both of them small in the distance. Maybe Donkey would go home early from the party today and take Ozma up to the sulfur springs and soak with her. Roger jumped from the bed of the white truck across a four-foot span into the bed of Standish's truck, landing with a thump and falling against an engine block that was dripping oil onto a piece of plywood. He wiped his hands on his pants. Then Roger jumped back again to the white truck, just as Donkey was climbing over the tailgate. He fell onto the dog cage, rattling it. Rocky growled.

"I have a dog, Ozma," Donkey said, looking into Rocky's face. "She's eleven years old." Rocky's eyes darted around, and his tongue came out and began to flap in rhythm with his panting, a kind of dog air-conditioning.

"Rocky just mated with a bitch," Roger said, seeming to enjoy saying that word. "Now she's going to have puppies."

"He says he wants out of his cage." Donkey saw how the dog was sweating. The sunlight was diffuse through a glittering haze, but there was no wind, and the dog would have preferred the shade.

"You don't know what a dog says."

"Yes, I do. He doesn't want to be in there," Donkey said. Like Granny had said, a cage was no place for any creature, especially with nothing to drink or eat. "He's thirsty."

"They're going to sell the puppies for five hundred dollars each."

Roger's two younger boy cousins were messing around near the Boneset Table, where their mom was feeding a note into the top of the locked box. People used to be furtive about putting notes into the box or looking on the table for what they needed, but over the course of the summer, they began to do these things openly, without even looking around to see who might notice. Donkey figured she knew what this woman wanted by the stiff-kneed way she was walking. Shrinking tea with nettles, which could be drunk or applied to skin. Donkey had been putting a half dozen cures out a few times a week—including a garlicky ointment for foot fungus and a tonic with honey and peppermint and a few other herbs that would make people cough junk out of their lungs—all from recipes she'd written in her notebooks over the years.

Donkey knew she was being deceitful by letting people think Herself was back to fixing fixes, and she thought it must be the snake blood that allowed her to take pleasure and pride in secretly being the one who could heal people now. She had always paid attention to the amounts of money people paid, but she'd never known before now how much it mattered. She kept the money down in the caboodle with the poisons, saving it for electric bills and taxes. She worried that, along with her right hand and her hearing, Herself had lost the ability to see into the future. Donkey could imagine a future in which their food ran out, in which they didn't have money to pay these bills. Donkey had never appreciated it before, when Herself had done the worrying and left Donkey's mind free to measure and calculate whatever interested her.

Donkey saw now what Roger's little cousins were doing bent down by the Boneset Table. They were squatting on the mosaic there, prying loose half-buried objects with sticks. Then one cousin stood up and tossed something down the bank and into the swamp channel, and soon the other kid did the same. As though objects there were nothing special, even though they had been placed there carefully by island girls over many decades. What would these boys do when they discovered the Babby Basket?

Donkey stood up next to the dog cage and shouted, "Stop doing that!"

The boys froze and glanced her way with narrowed eyes, and she felt the dog go rigid. The dog's hyper-alertness spooked Donkey, sent a shiver through her.

She glanced over at Rose Thorn, who was laughing with Titus. A heavy feeling came into her from the dog that said death could come at any time. Rose Thorn might be in danger right now. Standish had a gun. All men had guns. Even the reverend had a pistol for shooting raccoons, according to Molly. Titus was right there next to Rose Thorn, but even he couldn't stop a bullet once it left the chamber. Some man here today might have an argument with somebody else that would set him off or put him in a mood. Maybe that was why Rose Thorn was not as worried about her cancer as Donkey was, because she knew another kind of death was closer than death from a lump in her breast. And it wasn't just bullets that could kill a person. Cars could do it too. There were dead animals on Lovers Road all the time, usually squirrels and woodchucks and rabbits, but once, a coyote and twice, cats.

To Donkey's relief, the boys' mother heard her shout and stopped their digging. Donkey let her heart pound down and took in the details around her. Sitting with Rocky made her think of a kind of death penalty for not paying attention. She might be crossing the bridge one day, and somebody would aim and shoot, and she'd fall in the quickmuck and sink to the center of the earth, and nobody would care whether she ever learned topology. If a man was in a shooting mood, he might shoot Molly on the bridge while she was huffing and puffing and complaining about there not being a handrail. Donkey felt a dreadful camaraderie with her family members as she imagined each of them gunned down on a whim. Bullets could pass through walls. They weren't even safe inside Rose Cottage.

"Earth to Dorothy," Roger said and kicked the cage to get her attention. The dog growled again.

She bent down and whispered to the brindle dog, eye to eye, using Hermine's voice and the words Herself used to say right before making a fix: "*The beggars are a plague on us. They take and they take until there's no more to take.*" Donkey was satisfied by the dog's angry growl.

Roger kicked the metal cage again, jostling Rocky, who vibrated in response.

"He doesn't like that." Donkey had learned that Roger liked to make noise and sensation, liked to agitate the environment around him and change the landscape. This behavior was predictable, she supposed. This was why Herself didn't want men on the island. They would break branches and slam doors and crush mushrooms under their boots. They'd jostle nests and crack birds' eggs. At the parties, Donkey noticed men absentmindedly working the ground with their boot heels to make a flat spot where they were standing; she noticed how they tore up the grass with their truck tires.

"You are a very handsome dog," Donkey said. So different from loose, soft Ozma. "Your muscles shine."

A loud crack startled Donkey and Roger, and Rocky tensed so his brindle coat became a swollen coat of muscle. Aster froze and Triumph stomped. A man had broken a live branch off a willow across the road with much to-do. He wrenched it free, stripping a long tongue of bark off the trunk in the process. He tossed the branch onto the fire to a wave of complaints, and then the green leaves began to smoke. The man laughed, felt better after having made his mark, and the party resumed. Donkey could have used that willow bark for a cure.

Another man, older than the rest, was sitting on a stump whittling a little animal shape from a hunk of wood with a pocketknife. Donkey had once pocketed a little bird he'd left behind. The man was short, and his gray beard was close cut, but in his ancient calmness, he resembled the ghost Donkey had seen upstairs in the Boneset House, and she felt a pang of longing. He talked and listened to others at the party as though the carving he was doing was nothing. Herself used to knit that way but now, with only one hand, knitting demanded her full attention. Maybe Donkey would go sit near him. Then Jamie Standish approached Rose Thorn, and Donkey crouched down again, even though Standish wasn't looking her way.

Donkey growled in imitation of Rocky, and the dog growled back.

Set me free, Rocky said. She listened to the dog's anger and sadness, which reminded her of the Lindworm held captive in Hermine's bucket. Wishing to free that snake had eventually led to the loss of her granny's arm, no denying it. If she had let Herself deal with the snake without interrupting, Herself wouldn't even have been on the porch when the bullet came through the screen. *Nobody hears me,* Rocky said. Donkey put both hands on the sides of the cage, and the dog shivered. His shadowy coat was like a summer evening when the late sun slanted through cattails, making everything appear both dark and golden, when turtles settled in for the night and frogs thrummed. Rocky wore a tight leather collar studded with steel spikes. Ozma didn't have a collar, and that was why Donkey used baling twine to tie her on the landing so she would stay to guard Herself.

"I can't let you go free," she whispered to Rocky, "but I'll get you some water."

At the sound of her voice, the dog's growling vibration increased in intensity. His desire for freedom swelled into his stillness, so that he was stretched even more tightly against the muscular shell of his body, which was yet another cage, one he had grown himself but could not shed, and its rigidity echoed the rigidity of the cage, bolted to the rigid truck body. Ozma was soft, always stretching and yawning and sighing and groaning and rolling over, her old muscles loose in her skin. Even in sleep, she moved her paws as though swimming or walking. This dog's hardness was thrilling to know—it was so solid it might be measurable. Donkey ran to the barn and returned with a small plastic bucket of water for him.

Donkey had spoken to and petted dozens of dogs she'd seen jogging along the road or poking around for food at the edge of the Waters; some of them were traveling dogs, males chasing the scent of females in heat, while others had mysterious agendas they did not share. The cats she met were usually more elusive, hiding out and hunting until Molly saw the signs of their presence and trapped them and took them home and saved their lives all by herself. But dogs were valued in a town that knew them as man's best friend, and usually the loose dogs who appeared on Lovers Road were reunited with their owners or else were taken to the makeshift shelter Smiley Smith's mother had set up, where they were quickly adopted.

By now Roger had worked the white truck's back slider window all the way open, and he moved a shotgun and rifle out of the way and lowered himself headfirst onto the front seat.

"Ow!" he said, when he clunked his head on the gearshift knob. His voice had a hitch in it.

"Ow!" Donkey said, imitating the yodeling hitch. The dog growled again, a powerful sound. She slowly undid the top latch of the cage and whispered, "Now you just stay there, and I'll give you this water." She hoped it would ease the ache for freedom in the dog's vibrating muscles.

"You better leave him alone," Roger said, his face appearing between the two long guns he'd replaced in the truck window, the rifle above and the twelve-gauge shotgun below. "You'll get in trouble."

Laughter rose across the road, along with complaints about the smoke from the live willow branch and its leaves. Donkey held the door of the cage closed with her shoulder as she wiggled the bottom latch. The dog focused on her hands. And when she flipped open the latch, though she was leaning all her weight against the door, it burst open. The bucket flew out of her hands, splashing water into the air and all over both of them. Rocky surged through the swinging door and scrambled over Donkey, scratching her with his toenails. And then Rocky was gone, bounding over the tailgate and onto the grass, running toward the Boneset Table.

"What the hell?" shouted Titus from across the road. "Roger!"

"She opened the cage!" Roger called out the truck window. "I told her not to."

Donkey jumped over the tailgate and ran after the dog, who continued like a bullet toward the boy cousins, as though he might trample them for tossing objects from the mosaic into the Waters. But when they jumped out of the way, the dog kept on, down the wooden steps. Toward the bridge.

"String Bean! No!" Titus shouted, his voice pleading for the thing to be undone. Donkey ran across the road in pursuit.

"Whoop!" and "Whoa!" shouted the folks gathered around the fire, folks as much in awe of Rocky's wild run as they'd been at the sight of Triumph mounting Aster. The guitar music became faster and more urgent, imitating the dog's pumping legs, which made folks laugh.

Rocky was down the steps now and onto the bridge. When Donkey was halfway down the wooden steps, she saw, on the landing in front of the cottage, Ozma still tied to a tree, saw the alarm in Ozma's body as the old dog struggled to her feet.

Ozma strained against the twine, moved to protect Herself from the incoming dog, while Herself stood and searched for her stick. Rocky flew up the stone stairs and leaped from the top step onto Ozma, and the force of the collision knocked Herself back into her chair. At first, Rocky on Ozma seemed something like Triumph mounting Aster, but then it wasn't. The pit bull bit deeply into Ozma's fleshy neck and held on. As Donkey ran up the stone steps, she saw Herself sawing through the strained twine with the little knife she carried. As Donkey reached the landing, Ozma tore herself free from Rocky, revealing a bloody wound on her neck. Ozma ran toward the Moon Palace. But then she paused to look back at Herself, and in that moment, Rocky lunged again, this time locking his jaws on her hip.

Donkey finally reached them. She found a stick and beat Rocky with it until it broke across his back. Then she kicked him with her bare feet. The sensation of her foot meeting the hard muscle was like kicking a creature who was half dog and half giant millipede. Sweet, slow, gentle Ozma yipped, cried out in pain and shock, snapped at the air behind her, but she was too old and stiff to reach her attacker.

Standish, in his camouflage and his loosened boots, was the first person to run down the stairs toward the island after Donkey, his limp temporarily gone. He saw where help was needed, but when he stepped onto the bridge, he saw Herself on the island, her one-handed body full of rage, and his feet wouldn't obey him. Then Titus pushed him out of the way and ran across the bridge, mumbling his prayer. Titus took the steps up to the yard two at a time. Standish should have been able to follow him, but his feet ached again, and his boots felt frozen to the ground. Herself descended the stairs on the other side of the bridge with surprising speed before Titus ascended. As other men, including Ralph and Larry Darling, joined Standish on the landing, Herself then managed, one-handed, to engage the apparatus that lifted the bridge boards, so no other men—and not even Rose Thorn—could cross after Titus.

When Titus reached the knot made by the two dogs, he grabbed

Rocky's back end and yanked again and again, his tattooed muscles bulging. Donkey saw what his pulling was doing to Ozma. She felt how the pit bull's grip on Ozma was stronger than whatever held Ozma's old flesh and bones together. If Titus continued what he was doing, Ozma would be pulled to pieces.

Donkey punched Titus, grunting with the effort. "Let go! Let go!" she shouted.

When he finally did, Ozma lurched forward toward the swamp. She dragged Rocky along a few more feet, through a crayfish pool and toward the sandy place where ant lions hollowed out their traps.

Titus was looking back at the men on the landing. "Control your dog, Larry!" he yelled loudly.

"Rocky, come!" Larry called over and over, but he couldn't see that Ozma somehow kept moving across the narrowest part of the island, miraculously dragging Rocky a few feet at a time, toward the water. Now she plunged over the edge of the bank and slid into a little lagoon of soupy quickmuck, with Rocky tumbling and scrambling along with her, his teeth still sunk into her hip.

Ozma moved through the muck, paddling more than walking, pulling Rocky through an open channel, toward the Old Woman River, where the mud would gradually open up into flowing water. Donkey sank down onto the bank and began to slide down after them, but Titus grabbed her from behind and held her as she kicked and squirmed to escape him. She had caused the event now unfolding, and she had to stop it and save Ozma. Desperately, she fought to get away from Titus. She wished for the Lindworm to appear and bite Rocky; she wished it to call on the other m'saugas of the swamp to rise up and attack the pit bull.

"Why'd you let him out?" Titus asked, his voice and his face filled with his puzzlement. He was holding her now with what seemed like little effort.

"Let me go!" Donkey squeaked. She renewed her struggle. "I have to get Ozma."

"She'll come back," Titus said. "She's a smart dog."

"What if she can't?" Donkey continued to squirm against his grip. "What if I killed her?"

"You didn't mean to hurt her, String Bean. It was an accident."

"But I did it!" Donkey began to sob. She hadn't tried to free the pit bull, but she'd wanted him to be free, had unwittingly wished for it, no denying it, because she couldn't stand his being trapped in a hot cage. She kept struggling, but she didn't want to get away from Titus anymore. She wanted him to put his arms around her and hold her tight. As the dogs moved into the distance, Rocky's head went under the mud entirely; Ozma's nose was barely visible above it as she paddled toward the open water to save her life. She'd had trouble walking these last two years, but she'd always been a strong swimmer. Rocky's head surfaced briefly and then went under again, but still he did not let go. He held onto Ozma with a determination that made no sense.

"If I let you go," Titus said, "will you promise not to go tearing off into the swamp? You'll get stuck out there, and then we'll lose you too."

"I wish Rocky bit me instead!" Saying this made Donkey's bones ache and renewed her sobbing.

"No, you don't, String Bean. You'll just know better next time." Titus let her go slowly but held her hand as they stood and moved along the bank, watching as Ozma's coyote-colored fur disappeared, as the brindle's coat blended with the colors of the marsh.

While Donkey held Titus's hand, she felt that she and Ozma were under his protection.

"You have to be here when Ozma comes back," Titus said. "Do you see how smart she is? Rocky will have to let go or else drown."

"Can't you shoot Rocky?"

"My gun's in my truck, String Bean."

"That skinny man, Standish, has a gun in his pocket," Donkey said. "I saw it. He can come over the bridge and shoot him."

Titus stared at her before saying, "If he tries to shoot Rocky, he might hit Ozma. He's not that good a shot. Neither am I."

Donkey wondered what the point was of all the guns if nobody could use one to save a good dog's life. She continued to watch, to call out to Ozma as she dragged the pit bull farther into a deeper stream of water. The two animals disappeared behind a marsh island, heading downstream. A crow commented loudly from a branch fifty feet above but didn't let on what it saw.

She hoped Rocky did drown. She wanted that mean dog to suffer and then go into the endless forever ∞. She wished these things so hard that she momentarily forgot to wish for Ozma to survive.

Titus loosened his grip on her hand, and she pulled away, but then she didn't know what to do with her freedom. She moved downstream along the island's edge and kept up her search until the bank leveled out before a flat slough of sedges and horsetail. If no one would stop her, then she would go to Ozma, even if it meant she, too, would be lost. She stepped off the edge of sandy dry land and moved defiantly into the muck, moved farther out, feeling it surge up over her calves, her knees, and then her thighs. But she didn't know which way to go, couldn't even see where Ozma was. When she fell backward and sank up to her waist, she had to pull against a clump of sedges to extract herself. Finally she was able to slide on her bottom back to solid ground.

Titus watched from twenty feet away, ready to jump in and grab her again if she got into trouble, but what Donkey saw in him was his knowledge that what had happened to Ozma was her fault. He probably didn't even want to be her dad anymore. As she slogged back toward Rose Cottage, he said, "Are you going to be careful now?" She nodded, and he returned to the landing, where, after getting a nod from Herself, he discreetly activated the mechanism to lower the bridge planks. Donkey wiped off as much mud as she could and climbed into the nearest big tree, a swamp oak, but she couldn't reach the crow's tiptop height, and she saw no dogs at all through all the leaves.

Meanwhile, Larry Darling had left the landing on the Boneset side of the bridge and was driving his truck slowly along Lovers Road, calling his dog. People walked along after him, carrying their beers, their voices echoing his, as if it was all just another story somebody would tell. The noise they made meant Donkey couldn't hear anything from the Waters. After fifteen or twenty minutes, the call rose up from down the road that Rocky had returned. Some of them celebrated that prodigal's return, while others admonished him for his disobedience, and Donkey heard a yelp and a clang as Rocky was locked again inside his cage. Then she heard the truck rattle past on the road. It didn't seem fair that Rocky was going home to eat dinner, with Ozma hungry and alone in the Waters somewhere.

"It's really not your fault, honey," Rose Thorn said when she came across the bridge to find Donkey. Donkey wanted it to be true, and she wanted to be soothed, but she'd seen her mother soothe so many people this way with her gaze and her touch that it seemed too cheap and easy to accept her sympathy. After what she'd done, Donkey didn't deserve soothing. Later that evening, when Rose Thorn was in bed, she called into the kitchen for Donkey to join her.

"I won't sleep," Donkey said. But she gave in finally and lay beside her mother on the condition they leave the bedroom window and door open and the kitchen door open to the porch to hear Ozma's return. Her mother's voice was a balm, and her arm around Donkey was a stronger balm. Donkey sniffed and said, "I'm just going to lie here awake until she comes home."

But she betrayed that good dog once again by closing her eyes and sleeping deeply all night long.

In the morning, after waking Herself, Donkey went out to the Moon Palace and discovered, beyond it, on the trampled grass, the beloved body. Ozma's last act had been to drag herself back onto the island; she had tried but had not been able to make it to the door. Her coat was soaked with mud, her haunch bloodied, and a flap of flesh hung down from her neck. Killed by Donkey's desire to help a devil-dog from Nowhere who should have meant nothing to her; killed by the foolish soft heart Herself had warned her about. Donkey lay down with Ozma—not dissuaded by the blood or the coolness of the body—and wouldn't be moved away. She'd seen many dead animals, and Ada, her friend and neighbor, had died, but never had death come so close to her heart as this; nothing else had proved so conclusively the awfulness of ∞, QED. She saw how the awfulness of death could even make life seem not worth living.

That afternoon, as Donkey continued to lie on the grass hugging the fly-ridden corpse, the situation began to worry the adults. Titus came to the island and lifted her from the dog's body. She hit and kicked Titus for doing it, but once he had set her on her feet, she was glad to be released from her vigil. Together they buried Ozma by tying rocks to her body and sinking her in the quickmuck on the downstream end of the island, where Herself also wanted to be buried. Rose Thorn hugged Donkey, and they cried together as Hermine and Titus stood close by. Donkey knew she would bury everyone she cared about, one after another. This island was finite, but the death it would contain would be infinite. Without the people and domestic creatures she loved, the island, even with all its plants and wild animals, might not mean anything to her. For now Rose Thorn was close by, comforting her, but Donkey felt her wanting to move toward Titus. Donkey had long imagined the three of them together as a family, but Rose Thorn and Titus's romance had an exclusivity that kept her on the periphery.

A week later, Titus brought a new girl puppy to the island, a fawn pit bull mix with blue eyes and a pink nose and white feet—a gift from Ralph and Larry Darling, acquired at great expense, for the promise of one of Rocky's pups. At first glance, Donkey saw Rocky's abominable square head, but soon she saw beyond that. With its sweet, alert gaze, its plump squirmy body, its raised ears, the puppy was a perfect creature; but Donkey didn't deserve another dog, and the island was too dangerous. A tiny unknowing puppy could be killed the same way Ozma had been, maimed the same way Herself had been maimed by somebody with a gun, ravaged by cancer or even by Donkey's own misguided wishing. She shook her head against the puppy and clasped her hands behind her back, refused to accept the little creature, even going so far as to let the puppy drop to the ground instead. She steeled herself against the whimpers, knowing if she held the little body, she wouldn't let it go again.

"This dog might be helpful, and she could protect you and your granny," Titus said. But Donkey shook her head again.

When Titus had taken the dog away, Herself blinked like a crow opening its second eye and said, "Let's make a pie." She took Donkey's hand and held it tightly. And once again, in that moment, she was the granny Donkey had always known.

"Ma'am, I let that devil-dog go. I betrayed Ozma, and I betrayed you, ma'am. I called Molly, and she took you to the hospital. I'm sorry, ma'am." She stopped just short of admitting she'd been going into Wild Will's house.

"Pie would be a good thing," Herself said. "I think you didn't eat all the blueberries."

Donkey tried to resist that comfort she didn't deserve, but she loved pie too much.

"Your mama will make the crust," Herself said. "You know it takes a lazy woman to make a good pie crust."

Molly came over for lunch and, instead of making Donkey talk about *The Lion, the Witch, and the Wardrobe*, cleaned the kitchen and shared boring gossip from the Church of New Directions (which Rose Thorn called the Church of Nude Erections), and Donkey took comfort in the healing pool of her presence. With coffin nail pinched between her lips, occasionally pausing to sip coffee, Rose Thorn stirred the lard and flour mixture lazily, rhythmically with the pastry cutter until it turned pebbly. Then Herself pressed it into a mound with one hand, and Donkey took over and as gently as possible formed two disks and then rolled those flat. Rose Thorn stayed with them in the kitchen instead of moving to the bed to read as Donkey mixed together blueberries from the freezer, sugar, a little cornstarch, and lemon and filled the bottom pie shell with it.

Just when Donkey felt soothed, she looked around the room, from her mother to Molly to Herself, and experienced another horrible moment of remembering that all of them would die and be dead forever, like Ozma. But as the kitchen filled with the sweet scent of the pie baking, a feeling of relief came with it. All the human women she loved were still alive right now in this finite moment. Even Prim was alive, somewhere in California—though Donkey wasn't sure yet that she loved her. After dinner, Donkey and Herself and Molly each ate a piece of pie in the kitchen rather than on the screened porch, because it was cozier. Rose Thorn pretended to nibble at a sliver. And then Donkey ate another piece.

The next morning, Donkey woke up exhausted. She opened the cupboard and shone her flashlight down into the left-hand caboodle, looking for the Lindworm as though searching for her own secret angry body. She smelled the mushroom musk but couldn't see anything among the jars stowed there. She even reached down, slowly, risking her arm in exchange for the feel of the silky skin, but she found nothing alive. By lunch, she had finished the rest of the blueberry pie. For days after that, she searched the island but couldn't locate that coil of life threaded through all the other life. At dawn and dusk, hundreds of twisted roots at the water's edge tricked her with their serpent shapes.

CHAPTER THIRTEEN

—

Zero is not nothing, and infinity is not everything.

TITUS AND THE OTHER Whiteheart farmers brought in their crops in September and October, and their harvests were surprisingly large, especially considering the dry weather in May and June. In backyard gardens, the potato crops were especially good, mostly because they were big specimens, but a good number of the tubers had grown into grotesque bulbous shapes like gnarled old fairy-tale men and women, and people were inclined to photograph these figures instead of eating them. They shared the images in church and posted them on the Dollar-Mizer bulletin board, although they saved the pictures of a few erotic-looking spuds for private showings at home or at the Muck Rattler.

There was a superstitious feeling about these curiously shaped root vegetables, but nobody could remember whether they portended illness and death or fruitful marriages or violent weather. Without a right hand, Herself couldn't hold one and make a pronouncement, and she just told Donkey to cook them. Molly had *no time for such nonsense*, and Rose Thorn only laughed with pleasure whenever she saw one. Though Donkey's limited readings in topology assured her that all potatoes were essentially the same, she was nonetheless made uneasy by their profound asymmetries and was reminded of the tumor in Rose Thorn's breast. Also, she was painfully aware that there was no way to make sense of their proportions without resorting to calculus; all she could do was weigh them with a fish scale and draw the most interesting ones in her notebook.

At this time, rabbits and white-tailed deer overran the town, and though hunting season did not open until November, some of the men found opportunities to shoot deer on the sly and hang them inside their garages to tenderize the meat, which they processed themselves on their tool benches. Everybody so inclined ate lean venison in great quantities during the autumn and ate the livers of all animals; they even fried and seasoned the livers of store-bought chickens instead of feeding them to their dogs.

The parties at Boneset grew quieter after the incident with Rocky, but people kept gathering there, and, after a few weeks, Larry Darling even returned, with the cage in his truck empty. Donkey couldn't stay away from even one gathering, but she was more watchful of possible dangers. Though she still liked studying the men, she once again felt afraid of talking to them, especially after Two-Inch Tony told her he was sorry about her dog, and she burst out crying violently, uncontrollably. After that, people were cautious in what they said to her. Often she sneaked into Wild Will's house to watch the parties from a distance, from the bedroom where she'd seen the ghost, strangely comforted to think he might be watching over her, like Titus was.

In September kids didn't come to Boneset as often, because of school and sports and band practice. The evenings grew too cold for Rose Thorn to sit outside after sunset, even wearing Titus's jacket, even sitting next to a roaring fire. Titus was busy during harvest season, often working late into the night, and on many days, he didn't have time to stop by. He found himself fondly recalling Lorena, who could drive a tractor and a truck and who would have thrown all in with the big harvest. She had been sturdier and steadier than any hired man and had never complained. In those long hours, Titus sometimes tried and failed to see Rose Thorn ever becoming the wife he needed to keep the business afloat. A farmer could never truly relax, even in a bountiful year. Bounty drove prices down.

Donkey picked the warty green buttercup squash Titus had planted and stored them in the root cellar under the right-hand caboodle lid in the kitchen. She dried what mushrooms they didn't eat—golden oysters and Indian oysters were plentiful—and even canned two dozen quarts of tomatoes, as well as made apple butter, which was easy if you froze it. They had already canned two bushels of green beans. The coming of the chilly weather seemed to Donkey like ∞ approaching, but Herself was still distracted and lost in thought most of the time and didn't seem too concerned about how much winter preparation went undone. While Rose Thorn slept, Donkey inspected the cancer bump in her breast, noted that it did not appear to have grown. But the *Garden of Logic* chapter "Zero Is Not Nothing, and Infinity Is Not Everything" had taught her that incremental change adds up; by looking every day, she may have rendered herself insensible to gradual changes in the tumor. Whenever she mentioned it, Rose Thorn still said something along the lines of, "I'll know when it's time to tell someone. For now, let's both just keep wishing it away." Donkey did wish it away, wished continually and with such single-mindedness that she gave up wishing to go to school, gave up wishing even for Titus to become her father.

In *Garden of Logic*, Professor Schweiss showed her a way to solve impossible math problems. Donkey read and reread the following passage from the chapter "Imaginary Numbers Are Real":

> If we need a new kind of number to solve an equation, let's just assume it exists. Let's give that new kind of number a name and study it. If we want a number x, such that $x^2 = -1$, let's call it i so that by its very definition $i^2 = -1$. That means $i = \sqrt{-1}$. Now go ahead and do whatever you like with your new number, my friend.

Donkey loved how A. Schweiss called her *my friend*, and she imagined a group of mathematicians somewhere in the world who were friends and who discussed numbers and equations together. In response to Professor Schweiss's friendly invitation, Donkey wrote, with some trepidation: $(x^2 + 1) = (x - i)(x + i)$. In other words, there was a factorization of a polynomial that she'd thought—she'd been certain—had no factorization. But Schweiss said a solution for x to the equation $(x^2 + 1) = 0$ was $x = i$. She imagined this fresh new number i arriving in the Babby Basket, the wool blanket tucked around it. Though the origin of i was suspicious, this foundling turned out to be very useful in calculations, and so Donkey tried inventing a cure for the cancer that same way, out of thin air, calling it *Z-fix*. After assuming *Z-fix* existed and could cure Rose Thorn, it was just a matter of finding the herbs and mixing them up the right way. In pursuit of *Z-fix*, she tried looking at plants the way Herself used to, studying each to see how it looked, felt, smelled, tasted. She put leaves in her pockets, slept with roots under her pillow, heated and cooled them, and occasionally she found something to add to a stomach soother or a foot ointment, but she soon accepted that she wasn't like Herself; she didn't work from intuition or from a mysterious wisdom that originated in her bones or was whispered to her by a ghost. Donkey was a logical healer—if she was a healer at all—working from recipes, from known qualities and quantities, performing small experiments and making small adjustments.

She still checked the Babby Basket first thing every morning, in any weather, for a new number or an herb she hadn't known about, but the most she ever found there was a pair of tiny orange kittens that Molly came and picked up. Maybe Donkey would eventually stumble across something miraculous growing in the swamp, but, like Rose Thorn's imagined visit to the doctor, it would probably come too late. Herself, meanwhile, had redoubled her harvest of poisons. When Donkey asked her why, she said, the same as before, "We need this, don't we?" This refrain made Donkey wonder if Herself might be in search of a cure the same as Donkey, in her mysterious way. All Donkey could do was keep moving the illogical and dangerous herbs out of the kitchen.

Whenever Donkey saw Rose Thorn reach down beside her chair or bed for the loyal dog who wasn't there, it reminded Donkey again of Ozma's soft, thick fur, her velvety head, her gentle mouth. Ozma's absence was like the loss of summer warmth, the loss of a recipe for a healing tonic, and Donkey felt as though she was responsible not only for the dog's death but for the onset of the cold weather. She felt a chunk of icy winter forming inside her belly and held it silently and secretly, because when she tried to talk about Ozma, everybody insisted over and over that it wasn't her fault, even though it was. She didn't understand how people could lie this way. Did they really think a lie could make her feel better?

Rose Thorn sighed whenever the cold winds blew across the Waters and against the windows, and Donkey knew she was longing to leave. Before this year, Donkey thought the California warmth was all Rose Thorn wanted, but now she saw how Prim was part of that longing, how Rosie needed to talk to Prim on the phone more often as more time passed. Rose Thorn sighed when she saw Marshall Wallace's dump truck and other trucks and cars go by on Lovers Road, and Donkey could imagine her mother's desire to see Prim eclipsing even her desire for Titus. In dreams—hers or Rose Thorn's, she didn't know which—Donkey saw her mother sitting with Primrose in the kitchen of Rose Cottage. When Donkey asked her granny's opinion about these dreams, Herself only said, "Women should do what they want," but she seemed happy to hear about the vision.

Donkey became alarmed when Rose Thorn stopped drinking merry poppins tea altogether, saying she didn't care for it anymore. One October afternoon, Rose Thorn didn't touch her coffee with honey and cream, and she went on to refuse sustenance all day. Donkey finally admitted to herself that the only way to keep Rose Thorn from running away to Prim might be to bring her terrible aunt there, to M'sauga Island.

"It's okay if she comes," Donkey said to her mother the next afternoon. She put a cup of coffee before her. "Granny had a dream of four babies in wool and four coyote pups nursing."

Rose Thorn laughed a little wildly.

"Promise you won't go with her to California this time."

"Winter in Whiteheart?" Rose Thorn gazed into the cup Donkey had handed her. Finally she picked it up and sipped and swallowed. "Okay, I'll stay. It'll be an adventure."

It was a few days later, the night before the first freeze, that the Lindworm took up her brumation under the house. Donkey smelled her there, and then, by shining a flashlight down into the hole, was able to locate her, snug against the drainpipe, warmed slightly by the cookstove. Maybe it would have been better if she'd never learned how soft that Lindworm's skin was, because knowing how it felt made her want to feel it again, and the snake was lying just out of reach.

JUST BEFORE A CAR PULLED UP on the shoulder of Lovers Road at 5:03 p.m. on Halloween, Donkey was in the kitchen with Herself and Molly, the three of them looking at the pie Molly had brought from the church bake sale. Herself lifted the plastic wrap with one finger and sniffed the pie disapprovingly. The masking tape read "Hermine's Blackbird."

"For crying out loud, Mama," Molly said, "so what if somebody copied your pie? You're a local legend, what do you expect?" Molly pulled off the plastic wrap entirely, and Donkey smelled cinnamon and cloves and raisins. "Why do you have to be so negative about everything? People in Whiteheart are interested in you, Mama."

"Why do you have to be a negative number?" Donkey said, imitating Molly's voice, only in a lower register. She'd noticed that Molly had somehow gained all the weight Herself had lost since the hospital. Both women were still shaped like the nested dolls, but now Herself could have fit inside Molly. Today, for Halloween, Molly wore a plastic headband with leopard-spotted cat ears in her short blond hair.

"Are you sure she can't hear me?" Molly asked. "Sometimes I think she's just stubborn."

"I won't eat that if there's birds in it," Donkey said.

Herself heard most of what Donkey said and almost nothing Molly said. With Rose Thorn, it was a mixed bag.

"You're being silly, Dorothy. Prim named it that because your grandpa liked to think he was Old King Cole. Maybe there were supposed to be four and twenty ingredients in it."

Herself had never made this complicated pie for Donkey.

Donkey was watching the road, and she now saw a reddish car pull in near the Boneset Table. She put on Titus's jacket and flew barefoot out the door, across the bridge, and up the steps to examine the shiny low-slung vehicle breathing out purplish smoke. The cars and trucks that passed on Lovers Road usually groaned or squealed or blubbed or coughed, but the engine of this car with Illinois license plates purred like a big smug cat.

The engine cut off. Although she was afraid, Donkey crept closer and closer to look in through the driver's side window. The woman inside, her aunt Prim, turned toward her then and broke out into a grin so wide that Donkey imagined being eaten. Still she crept closer, to get a better look.

The window glided down. "Hello, my lovely!" Prim said.

"Thank you for *Garden of Logic*. It's the best book ever," Donkey said, and she turned and ran back across the bridge, rattling the boards under her bare feet.

"Terrible Aunt Primrose is here!" she panted as the screen door slapped shut behind her. Molly was holding the kitchen door open. "Granny, her hair is white now."

"Why don't you put shoes on?" Molly said. "It's forty degrees out there. And why do you insist on calling her terrible?"

"It's forty-three. And she still has a witch's bump on her chin," Donkey said breathlessly. She didn't know why she felt so happy.

"You just saw her a year ago."

Donkey shook her head, held up two fingers. "Two years ago. And I was only five feet tall then. I'm as tall as she is now."

Prim had called the hospital room daily while Herself was there this year, but the last time Donkey had seen Prim in person was when she'd swept in to spring Rose Thorn from the hospital. She'd tried to convince Donkey to come with them to California, and Donkey had run away from her and watched from a distance as she and Rose Thorn departed the building. The mole on her chin had been as dark as dried blood that day; now it was a flesh-colored bump big enough to cast a little shadow in the car's interior light.

"Pack your suitcase, Donkey," Herself said. "Your aunt is here to take you away."

"I don't have a suitcase. And I won't go!" Donkey said in her low voice. It had been so long since Herself teased her that Donkey didn't catch on right away.

In anticipation of Prim's visit, Herself had behaved erratically, no denying it. This morning she'd eaten the breakfast Donkey made for her, and then she got up and made a second helping of the same eggs and bacon and ate that too. Donkey hoped this meant she would start cooking for herself more often. It was true that she was using the stump of her right arm to push and hold things more and more now, and her one-handed knitting was getting faster. Yesterday and today she had managed to tie her braids up on her head for the first time since being home from the hospital; she let Donkey add a few extra hair pins to make them straighter.

"For crying out loud, Mama," Molly said loudly. She dropped the peeler onto the potatoes and shook her head. "I'd better go out there and get her."

"Maybe we'll send some milk home for your aunt's cats," Herself said, grasping the handle of the milk pail with her left hand, weighing the thing, reacquainting herself with the feel of it. Donkey wanted to reach out to take the pail in her own hand—she was the milker now—and she started to say no, that they needed all the creamy milk for Rose Thorn and that they should freeze any extra for when Delilah dried up (she was supposed to calve in late April or early May), but Herself shushed her with a look. Herself seemed to be up to something, and Donkey wanted to know what it was.

"That's considerate of you, Mama," Molly said. Molly seemed confused, too, at this glimpse of the old motherly Hermine. Donkey spent enough time with Herself to see how she often rose to the occasion when real mothering was called for.

Molly put on her puffy jacket, which Rose Thorn had once remarked looked like a flotation device, and trudged down to the bridge. When Donkey started putting on her chore boots, Herself took her right hand.

"I'll milk tonight, child. You stay here."

"You can't milk with one hand," Donkey said, making a side-to-side milking motion with two hands, even while Herself still held onto her. Donkey's hands were big, her fingers much longer than Hermine's.

"Now you're the great authority on what I can and can't do," Herself said. "You want to know the truth about things, well, you'll learn more truth by listening to your aunts. Stay in Lazy's Room and make use of those big donkey ears of yours, and don't make a peep."

"Should I tell you what they say?" Donkey had been duplicitous plenty often since the Lindworm had arrived, but this was the first time Herself was encouraging her to be so. The second hand of the clock seemed to be going around too fast, and the table looked crooked on the floor tiles, though Donkey had lined it up perfectly when they'd pulled it away from the wall.

"Too much quickmuck under the bridge for me, but you should know," Herself said.

"What if she tries to take Rose Thorn away?" Donkey said, backing up into the little bedroom off the kitchen.

"Then stop her. What good is all that logic you carry around if you can't use it to take care of your mother?" Herself dropped Donkey's hand and pushed her the rest of the way into the bedroom with the milk pail and closed the door so the latch caught.

Donkey listened to Herself head down the hall with the pail in her hand and the egg basket in the crook of her right elbow. Then she sat cross-legged on the floor so she could peer through the bedroom key- hole into the kitchen, feeling the cord connecting her to Herself stretch- ing like twisted fabric. Her feet tingled in their desire to follow Herself to the cowshed. Could Herself even pull a bale of hay from the stack with one hand? Would she knock down three or four bales by accident and leave them blocking the way? Donkey grabbed the door handle, but then she heard the clop-clop of boots like hooves on the steps leading to the screen porch and stayed put behind the closed door.

Titus had super-gripping size-thirteen boots and was "sure-footed as a mule," Herself said, and Molly took small, careful steps in her thick rubber-soled clogs. This clop-clop of wooden heel on wood was confident and steady, proving Prim had no fear of falling into the quickmuck or being shot. Rose Thorn said Donkey was morbid for worrying about them being shot as they crossed the bridge or any- where else. Donkey didn't know how the rest of her family took ∞ in all its forms so lightly, especially Molly, who admitted that people died at the hospital all the time. Already Ozma, the best and most loyal friend Donkey would ever have, was gone forever. And once you had witnessed ∞, how could you not think about it all the time? The heels clop-clopped onto the screened porch. The big door whooshed open, and cold air flooded the kitchen, even crept under the bedroom door. Only then did Donkey notice her left-hand pocket was empty. She'd left *Garden of Logic* on the table with her crayfish shell sitting on top of it. She'd glued the claw back on herself, at the wrong angle.

Through the big keyhole, Donkey could see only glimpses, and she had to piece her aunt together like a puzzle over the course of the next hour. Primrose seemed every inch the White Witch, as tall as Titus in her heels, with a pile of gray-blond hair (not actually white, as it had looked in the car) clipped at the back of her head. Two thick strands cascaded over her temples and curved under her chin. Her eyebrows were distinct and dark in contrast to her hair. She wore a belted red coat, its crisp fabric covering her narrow hips without wrinkles or visible pleats, and clean dark jeans with flair bottoms that partly covered her boots, so that what stuck out were two disconnected sections— toe and heel. Those high-horse heels could have pinned Donkey down as effectively as the heavy-footed schoolteacher Rose Thorn had conjured up. (Donkey startled at this thought. Had Rose Thorn invented a cruel schoolteacher in Prim's image to scare Donkey away from school?) Though it wasn't cold in the house, Prim hugged herself as she walked over the kitchen tiles. With one hand, she reached out and touched the handles of cupboards and drawers, the backs of chairs, the dusty window ledge. Her presence felt like a kind of thunderstorm, and everything she touched emitted jagged red lightning sparks in response.

As Prim studied the familiar landmarks of the cottage, she became aware she was holding her head the way Herself used to hold hers, proudly, defiantly, as though rising above something, above some high-water level from a past flood. She wandered into the hall, her boot soles shushing on the moth-nibbled rug. She still felt strong and capable of anything—like Herself, she might milk a rattlesnake, snap its neck, and devour it before breakfast, or else drive the whole species from the island with a command; maybe she could make mushrooms pop out by tapping the soil the way Herself used to do.

"Where's old Baba Yaga?" Prim asked, feeling she was speaking from a great height. "I swear, when I was a girl, this cottage used to be on chicken legs."

"She's milking the cow with Dorothy," Molly said. "How long are you staying?"

"I have a flight out of Grand Rapids in the morning." Prim lifted the twenty-inch-long cast-iron fire poker from a hook next to the cookstove and felt the weight of it in her hand.

"Why would you come for one day? Why don't you stay longer?"

"Don't want to turn into a pumpkin, Moll," Prim said. "And I have to work on Monday, a lot of paper to shuffle before then."

"I hate how you and Rosie always just take off. You don't even say goodbye."

"You supposed to be some kind of pussycat with that getup?" Prim asked.

"I dressed up for my patients. I thought it would be festive to leave it on," Molly said, swaying her bottom to wave the cat's tail she'd pinned on a wire to her belt.

Prim knew there was a part of Molly that wanted to *be* a cat, really, wanted to sit on somebody's lap purring, to be something she could never be on this island, or in this town, where she was too powerful and too substantial a person. She watched Molly splash the potatoes she'd peeled into a pot of water and set them on the cooker. The thin aluminum pan made popping noises as the water began to heat. Her sister Molly did her best to seem ordinary, to seem not as magnificent as she was.

"Look at that mince pie on the counter," Molly said. "I got it at the church sale. The lady told me it was made with Mama's recipe. She even calls it blackbird. Isn't that something?"

"The son of a bitch's favorite," Prim said, grinning, reaching out with the fire poker toward Molly's belly. Any mention of Wild Will made her feel deliciously mean.

"Oh, please, let's not talk about him. Let's all just get along for a few hours."

"Someday we'll all be drunk enough to talk about it," Prim said. She was pretty sure she was the only person in the family still in contact with him; over the last thirty years, she had come to terms with him in a way nobody else had. She preferred him in his diminished form.

"That's one thing this family needs, isn't it? More drinking," Molly said. "Rosie has been having these big drinking parties every Saturday, out there half the night." She pushed away the pointy ash-end of the poker and smoothed the front of her sweater where—below the cross pendant she wore on a chain—a jack-o-lantern grinned. The sparkles in the weave looked like the tears that came into her eyes when she argued hard. "We'll reheat this pie after we take the other food out."

"It's been a long time since I got to poke somebody this way," Prim said, circling Molly. She poked Molly between the shoulder blades, and Molly yelped and turned around.

"Stop doing that."

"At work, I have to poke with my wits. This is nice." Prim poked the center of her own palm and looked at the sooty spot. She wiped her hand on her jeans and hung the poker back up. She was beginning to loosen her coils and feel at ease in this space she knew better than her own body, though she hadn't set foot here in two years. As much as she admired the Pacific Ocean, it didn't soothe and nourish her the way the Waters did. "I'm sorry, sister. Thank you for all you've been doing for Herself and Rosie and Dorothy. I am grateful, even if I don't say it often enough."

"Oh, the whole thing was horrible," Molly said, turning away from the potatoes, so her cat tail brushed the hot cooker. "Mama was in bed in a pool of blood. She could have died. I don't know what she put on her hand and arm, but her flesh was melted."

"Maybe it saved her life," Prim said. "Who knows?"

"Oh, stop it. If anybody should know better about her nonsense, it's you. Or what's the point of all your Ivy League education?"

"Does there have to be a point?" Prim clop-clopped around behind Hermine's chair to the window. She picked up the binoculars and looked through the willow branches toward the Boneset Table as she used to do as a girl. The familiar view felt reassuring, and she put them back down. She turned and yelled toward the room in which Donkey was hiding.

"Rosie! Get out here!" By the time Prim clopped over to the door in her heels, Donkey had slipped under the bed, knocking over her mother's ashtray. Prim pushed open the door and switched on the light, and Donkey lay quietly with her heart pounding against the floor, smelling coffin-nail butts and the bitter citrus of the Osage oranges they kept under the beds to repel insects.

"She's in Mama's bed," Molly said. "She drinks all night and sleeps all day."

Prim turned off the light and closed the door. She pounded on the wall behind the sink. "Get out here, Rosie! I wish I could sleep like her and Mama—or Daddy. He slept like the dead."

"Listen, before anybody gets back," Molly said, "I need you to know what's going on. I scrubbed this floor, I poured straight bleach on it, and it still won't come clean. This place isn't safe anymore—and it certainly isn't sanitary."

"She ought to replace these tiles," Prim said. "What are they, 1920? Probably asbestos."

"Living here like it's the nineteenth century. She almost died. And to get hit by stray bullets—these men don't care if it's hunting season or not when they're in the swamp. I'd like to jam up all their damned guns. And who doesn't call the doctor right away when they get shot?"

"Our mother," Prim said, a little prideful. She could imagine arguing a case while bleeding out, waiting until after closing arguments to go to the doctor, if she'd go at all. Then she grasped the oven handle with her bare hand and yelped and pulled away. She went to the sink and ran water over it. The pump began to run. "I've forgotten the joys of country living."

"And don't drink the water out of the tap. It's poison, probably." Molly opened the fridge and took out the two-quart glass jar. "This sassafras tea is made with water I brought from home. It's got cinnamon too."

"Titus should drive her a new well. How far do you think you'd have to go down to get away from the paper-mill waste?"

"It's his fault Mama's here at all. I had it all set up for her at Christian Comfort. Then we could have moved her to Daddy's house. The church still wants to buy the island."

"Rosie tells me you and Roy Blaisdell are seeing each other again."

"We're taking it slow," Molly said.

"You've been dating for what? Twenty years? Twenty-five?"

"Not continually," Molly said. "What I'm saying is I had everything set up for her, and Titus shows up at the hospital to drive her home, and Dr. Hunt starts telling me about patients' rights. Me! I wanted to tell him he could hobble his supercilious ass across the bridge and bandage Herself every day after he gets out of work." Molly took the plastic tub of fake butter out of the fridge, snapped off the lid and put it on the table. "Nobody cares about infection or clogged arteries in this family but me. You and Rosie criticize me, but you'd both have let Herself die."

"Oh, she's not going to die," Prim said. "She's too tough to die."

"You two have your heads in the past. She's old and frail. She's what, eighty? And now, she's going deaf—forget about a hearing aid. She doesn't want to hear."

On the other side of the wall where the frying pans hung over the cookstove, Rosie lay tangled in soft sheets, blanketed in the scent of lavender, holy basil, and cedar. She'd been dead to the world for hours and now roused to the sounds of voices she loved, the voices of these exasperating saints: the pleading, defensive voice of Molly, desperate as always to shape their family into something acceptable to the wider world, her yearning perfectly balancing the prickly, caustic song of Primrose, who would nonetheless give her last breath to rescue anyone, even a stranger. When Rosie lived with Prim by the beach, she never got enough of her company because Prim was always working to right some wrong. Prim couldn't just sit calmly even long enough to drink her morning coffee without getting indignant about something she read in the paper. Herself used to be the same in her own way, always working on a fix, day and night. Now Herself was more like Rosie, just trying to be Herself in a world that saw being yourself as nothing.

To hear those two voices together, here on the island, was to luxuriate in an old ballad she only remembered in fragments. She slid out of the bed and flowed toward her sisters, the way water seeks its own level. Soothing the town was easy compared to soothing the big personalities of the women in this family.

Prim's ears pricked, and her eyes brightened. Donkey crawled out from under the bed and squatted on her haunches to look through the keyhole again.

"I'll be damned," Rose Thorn said as she reached the kitchen threshold. She adjusted Wild Will's flannel bathrobe around her torso. "It's Regan and Goneril, the wolf and the fox."

"Cordelia! In the flesh!" Prim clopped over to wrap her in her long arms. "Oh, I've missed you, my girl, missed your sharp tongue and tooth. Come back home with me. We can go now, before the battle-ax gets back from the cowshed."

Even when Prim let go of her, Rose Thorn couldn't stop smiling. She wanted to sink into the healing waters of her family; she wanted this as much as she sometimes wanted to get away from them. People in the community were aware of her intense feelings for Titus—*that* caught their interest—but she loved every member of her family as passionately and outrageously as she loved him. She embraced all of their mysteries so hard that she often needed to rest as a result.

"What are you harpies cooking up?" she said now.

"Poor Jesus, you get more beautiful every time I see you!" Prim said and hugged her again. "You ought to stop doing that, Rosie. You're calling too much attention to yourself." While the exposed part of Prim's chest blushed with emotion, any change in her cheeks was covered by makeup.

"What are you fishwives plotting?" Rose Thorn asked.

"The downfall of the regime," Prim said, stepping back. "Pull up a chair."

Rose Thorn slid into the nearest chair at the foot of the table. She straightened the collar of her robe and patted the pocket. She produced Titus's silver lighter, flipped it open, and flicked it until a flame sprang forth. It was a homunculus of Titus himself, with a cross on one side and a rose and thorn etched on the other. "Either of you got a coffin nail for me?"

"I wish she'd quit," Molly said to Prim. "She's going to end up with emphysema or lung cancer. I've told her a thousand times."

At the utterance of the word *cancer*, the kitchen air ruffled. The spiders inside the cupboard and under the table tucked their legs up. The m'sauga under the floorboards buzzed. Rose Thorn's hand went to her breast, involuntarily, and Prim reached up to the mark on her own face.

"I'm no quitter," Rose Thorn said when she could breathe again. She forced a smile.

"Did she tell you she's back with Titus? Even drove his fiancée away," Molly said. "What's he going to do when you make a fool of him and leave again, Rosie?"

"Did I say I was leaving?"

"You always do," Molly said.

"I sure hope you're leaving," Prim said. "Promise me you're not planning on staying here forever to marry the Prince of Whiteheart."

Rose Thorn laughed and sparked the lighter to evoke Titus with its flame. She had her own worries about the situation here. Titus, for sure, but her daughter more so. The girl worked too hard, took everything to heart, especially the death of dear old Ozma, but Rosie didn't know how to share her concerns in a way that would do more good than harm. Prim and Molly were so sure that Dorothy had to go to school, but Rose Thorn could see how school would just pile more work on the girl. And worse, it would split her in two; she would have to be one person at home and another at school. Rosie wanted her daughter to know who she was before she went out into Nowhere, where terrible things would happen to her. It was hopeless to try to protect a girl—better you equip her to protect herself. If Dorothy could feel certain of who she was and what she wanted of the world, if she could be confident in her skin, as none of the rest of them had been after a childhood on the island, she could make her way anywhere, do anything. Molly and Prim didn't take this line of thinking seriously, didn't ever take Rosie seriously, no more than Herself ever had.

"I think you're just torturing the poor guy," Molly said. "That's what I think. Titus wants a family. He wants to settle down."

"You marry him, you're stuck in this place," Prim said.

"I'm already stuck, wherever I am," Rose Thorn said and laughed. Talking about Titus was easier for all of them than talking about Dorothy. "I try being with any other guy, and it's nothing. And then I come back and get a whiff of him."

"Well, smell him all you like, Rosie, but don't marry him," Prim said. "And don't get yourself knocked up."

Rose Thorn said, "We're careful." She was as careful as a woman who refused to go to a doctor could be. "How about you, Prim? I thought you were going to have that carbuncle taken off this summer."

"Your beauty mark," Molly said smugly.

"Moll, you don't think it's cancer, do you?" Prim asked, startling the room again, plucking the deplorable word right out of Rose Thorn's breast. "A doctor said it looked like nothing five years ago."

"You went to a doctor?" Molly said, puffing herself up a bit. "I thought I was the only one in the family who would."

"I had a client who was a doctor, and he said it didn't look like cancer."

"I thought you only represented hardened criminals."

"He was a back surgeon, Dr. Hunter Bell, killed a drug rep. He told me I had an exemplary spine," Prim said. "Seriously, Molly, will you look at it?"

"You ought to have it checked. Maybe it does look bigger. Or a little different. If it's symmetrical, it's not usually a problem, but it's hard to say."

"I need some of Mama's salve of last resort."

"Don't even say that," Molly said. "I've seen terrible burns from bloodroot salves. I think that's what Mama put on her arm that melted her skin."

"Maybe you're like Zeus, and you'll pop Athena out of your face," Rose Thorn said. "Or it's a Siamese twin waiting to hatch. Mama's still waiting for one of us to have another babby. Whatever she might say to the contrary."

"She's too old to take care of a babby," Molly said. "You both have to see that."

"Babby!" Prim shrieked. "I forgot how this island talks. I saw the Babby Basket out front. Is that fire in the cooker still Baba Rose's guiding light?"

"As much as it ever was, I suppose," Molly said. "The fire went out while she was at the hospital, and she's still furious with me about it."

"Is she still wearing her necklace of lost souls?" Prim asked. That time, as soon as the words left her mouth, she felt she'd taken a joke too far.

Molly shook her head tiredly. She opened the firebox door and used the poker to agitate the logs inside. She told herself she was unaware of the difference between the reliable old fire and the new inconstant one that Dorothy had repeatedly restarted, but she did sometimes feel an unfamiliar cool breeze in the kitchen, and the fire seemed to need more tending. She fed in another split piece from the box Dorothy kept full under the window.

"Just go have it checked, Prim. I'm sure Southern California is full of dermatologists," Molly said. "Maybe you can find one who disfigured a movie star."

"Please, Moll, put your hand on me. Heal me the old-fashioned way." Prim grabbed Molly's hand and tried to pull it up to her face.

"Don't *you* start," Molly said, pushing her away. "You're as bad as Mama. Sometimes I think you want to end up like Herself, an eccentric old woman."

"You're the one who should be worried about becoming Mama. I think you've gained more than a few since I saw you last." Prim pinched Molly's formidable biceps through her sweater. "I definitely don't want to get in a fist fight with you."

"Not everybody wants to be anorexic like you two. But the reverend and I are going to start walking together for exercise."

"You call him *the reverend*?" Prim clop-clopped over and bent down and hugged Rose Thorn again, long enough that Rose Thorn started to laugh. "Rosie, how about you come back with me tomorrow? You and Dorothy. She has to be curious about the wide world by now if she's read all the books I sent her."

On the other side of the door, Donkey lost her balance and tipped back onto her bottom. She'd thought any plan of kidnapping would be a secret thing; she hadn't expected Prim to come out and say it. She crawled on hands and knees back to the keyhole and sat down.

"Maybe she doesn't ever have to leave," Rose Thorn said. "Maybe she can always stay here. She's the youngest, after all. Take over the family business."

"Stop it, Rosie. She has to go to school," Molly said. She opened the oven with a potholder and poked a meat fork into both buttercup squash halves cooking under tinfoil, one stuffed with sausage and sage and the other with butter, apples, black walnuts, and cinnamon. She pressed the side of the fork against the chicken Titus had brought them last night. Herself had been inspired to guide Dorothy through stuffing it, and a little extra stuffing was in a pan on the shelf below. As she closed the door, the sausage, cinnamon, and chicken smells wafted into the warm room. "She's already getting eccentric."

"Says the lady with thirty cats," Rose Thorn said and flicked the lighter, creating and snuffing out flame after flame. "You're in the wrong town, Molly. This is a dog town. A dog gets forgiven for his crimes here. A cat has to pay the price for every transgression. Meow."

"Is it really true Mama isn't seeing people at Boneset anymore?" Prim glanced toward the window again, was comforted to see the red of her rental car.

"I think it's for the best if she stops," Molly said. "The mood isn't right anymore. People are riled up. That dirty business of hers has tainted any good work she might incidentally do."

"Rosie says you've gone pro-life on us," Prim said. "I see ninety cats in your future."

"I'm not against all abortions. I'm just against Herself having anything to do with it," Molly said. "I'm saying this for her sake, too, not just for a baby who might not be born."

"Women are people, too, Moll. It's not just about babies," Prim said.

Molly touched the tip of the poker to make sure it wasn't too hot. Then she reached out and poked Prim in the back. Prim jumped, and Molly gave a self-satisfied grunt.

"Watch it, this is a new jacket." Prim swiped at her back. She plucked a bit of bramble off the red belt and tossed it into the stove's flame and watched it burn before closing the firebox door. "This place gets all over you, doesn't it?"

"Has Mama said anything else to you, Rosie? About what she plans to do?" Molly asked. She pushed her tail out of the way and sat in Hermine's chair.

"Do about what? About you wanting to sell her island to Nude Erections?"

"Why do they want it?" Prim asked. "Shouldn't they buy a store-front or something?"

"The reverend—I mean, Roy—says it'll be a prayer outpost. Christ on the Waters."

"What the hell's a *prayer outpost*?" Prim asked. "Is that where they put up a giant cross that ruins the view for miles around?"

"I doubt they'll do anything with it. Certain people just want us gone," Rose Thorn said, reaching down as she spoke to scratch her bare ankle. If her hair had fallen in her face this way while she was sleeping, Donkey would have brushed it back. As Donkey was having the thought, Prim reached out and tucked the hair behind Rose Thorn's ear. It hit Donkey like an electric shock how Prim loved Rose Thorn too.

"I don't want to talk behind Mama's back or anything, but this is our chance to talk about what comes next," Molly said from her perch at the head of the table, opposite Rose Thorn. She wiggled in the chair to free her tail.

"I want to talk behind her back." Prim went to the cupboard behind Molly and grabbed both handles. Donkey prepared for her to reveal the Lindworm, but that did not happen. She opened the doors and rearranged a few bottles but didn't see what she wanted and closed them again.

"Rosie, you could say you and Dorothy are moving to Daddy's house," Molly said. "She can't do by herself here."

"Why don't you take Mama to live with you and your cats in White People's Village?" Prim asked.

"Don't call it that. You know I hate that. There's a black family now. Or half black. The stepdad's black, and it's not an issue. And his wife Nancy's going to have a baby, and it'll be black. Nobody even cares. Or almost nobody. And Dorothy knows she's always welcome to live with me."

"Dorothy should come with me," Prim said. "She should see a new part of the world. I couldn't wait to get away from here when I was her age."

"She's not an easy girl," Molly said.

"Poor Jesus, save us from easy girls," Prim said.

"Dorothy knows where she's safe, right here with Mama," Rose Thorn said.

"If she doesn't get hit by a stray bullet," Prim said.

"You want to take her to LA to stop her from getting shot?" Molly asked. "Rosie and Dorothy and Mama can live across the street right here. Daddy's House is way nicer than this place. Just needs to be scrubbed and aired out and some glass replaced."

"I don't live in LA, Moll," Prim said.

"My Freckle Face knows you're both trying to send her away from her birthright," Rose Thorn said.

Molly now looked to Prim for support. "Rosie and Mama make everything more difficult. Mama told Dorothy that people at the hospital are brutes and devil-doctors, and I had to make a joke out of it when she repeated it."

"Maybe she knows a devil when she sees one," Rose Thorn said, flicking Titus's lighter some more. "I wish I did. She's safer here, even if somebody shoots across the bow once in a while. There's nowhere in this country men aren't shooting at women, far as I know. Even the supposed holy men concealed carry. And Molly's sleeping with the enemy."

"Roy's not the enemy," Molly said and swallowed. She rose from Hermine's chair to check the potatoes. "And speaking of Roy, Rosie, I wonder if I could get some of your sleep medicine for him."

Rose Thorn laughed raucously. "You don't believe in Mama's medicine."

"But some herbs do help a person relax a little. He said Titus shared something Herself made for him, and he thought it helped."

"That son of a bitch! He gave Rev Roy my merry poppins!" Rose Thorn said, smiling at his name on her lips. "Traitor! Does your reverend know it's marijuana and opium poppies?"

"Only trace amounts, I'm sure. Everybody has challenges." Molly leaned over the boiling potatoes, inhaled some steam to clear her sinuses. She wished her sisters would trust her that there was something worthy and noble in Roy, best glimpsed when he broke down in despair, which nowadays was about once a week. She loved him best when he accepted, if briefly, that he was an ordinary man. It was true that his ambition could be taxing, but he honestly wanted to heal and help the souls here in Whiteheart.

"They want the island because they want more m'saugas," Rose Thorn said. "You can't take the snake-handling out of that church. I don't care what they say."

"That's all in the past," Molly said. "Nobody's handling snakes. Certainly not Roy."

"The past is where all those men live," Rose Thorn said. "Titus told me there's a hidden room under the church basement that nobody knows about. Where they used to do secret things. That's probably where they took Mama's hand."

"Stop about the hand. It was incinerated, like state law requires. I'm just thinking there's a future we can all live with. Mama sells what she can, and she can afford to live in Daddy's house. You know she hasn't got any Social Security. That's all I'm saying." Molly drank down her sweetened sassafras tea and poured more. "The truth is her amputation site hasn't healed all the way. It's been five months, but it could still get infected. And she keeps bathing in those swamp pools—it's not sanitary."

"You just want to tie Mama up with a neat bow," Prim said. "Tuck her away, so you don't have to worry anymore. Maybe you want her to start going to church."

"You bitches," Molly said. She opened the door to the cooker and slammed it with a loud *clank*. "You're so critical, but you'll be out of here, and I'll be stuck taking care of her."

Rose Thorn said, "I'm not planning on going anywhere."

"You always leave!"

"Well, you know Mama's not selling the island," Rose Thorn said. "And she'll haunt us if we try to sell it when she's dead."

"We couldn't sell it anyway," Prim said. "The island belongs to our youngest girl."

"It belongs to all of us. I mean, after," Molly said. "Unless there's a will."

"Oh, there is a will," Prim said. "You ever seen her signature? *HZ* with a long tail, ends in snake rattles like Daddy's."

"If you helped her make a will, you're not doing Dorothy a favor saddling her with this property," Molly said.

"Let *her* sell it to the church then," Prim said. "Then she'll have money to go to graduate school. I'm already putting away money for her college."

Molly huffed into her boiling potatoes. "I might as well tell you both, the taxes aren't paid on this property. She gave me money in September, and I paid for Daddy's house, but I put the rest against the hospital bill. Don't look at me that way, Rosie. I work with those people every day, and they all think she's got money buried in the ground."

Prim took the fire poker off the hook and offered it in an open hand "You are the greater witch by far, aren't you? I hand over my wand to you, Almira Gulch."

"Oh, put that away," Molly said. She looked intently at her own pink fingernails, then hid them behind her back. "You two don't understand what it's like. All I do is worry. And you know Dorothy doesn't eat right, and Herself won't make her. Rosie either, as you know. There are so many problems with this situation that you want to ignore."

Rose Thorn clicked Titus's lighter open and shut faster. She was hoping she could share her thoughts about Dorothy's education with them. Maybe they would listen if she chose her words carefully. Just then she sensed Dorothy's presence, and, sinking into that feeling, she turned around and saw through the keyhole of her bedroom door something that was not empty air. She smiled in confusion, sent the girl her love. She was always glad to see her daughter, no matter what, no matter her own uncertain feelings.

"The hospital could get a lien against her property anyhow, and she'd lose it that way," Molly said. "I don't see either one of you offering to chip in. Nobody helps me around here."

BY THE TIME THE FOOD WAS COOKED, Herself had still not returned from the cowshed, and the small kitchen had become a rich and humid confusion of roasting chicken and other smells. Rose Thorn turned off the overhead light, sat back down—in her own chair this time—and lit the lantern Donkey had filled with paraffin oil. The three shiny blond heads leaned toward the lamp flame. With steam and a bit of black smoke swirling, the image conjured a fairy-tale vision, with Rose Thorn's long tangled hair splayed across her back so voluminously it could have wrapped around all three of them. Together, these sisters were one creature with six arms and legs, animated by flame, not subject to the earth's gravity as much as to one another's. Herself usually stomped and huffed and stabbed the floor with her snake stick to announce her comings and goings, but now, just as the sisters were organizing to retrieve her, she materialized with her milk pail in the kitchen as though out of the steam and smoke in the air. The three-headed monster that had solidified before Donkey's eyes now became three separate women again. Rose Thorn grinned. Prim blanched. Molly gasped and stood from Hermine's chair.

"The Fates are conspiring," Herself barked, her voice chopping the kitchen air like a machete. All the life in the room—the spiders in the corners, the mice in the dresser drawers, the moths in the cupboard, the Lindworm under the floorboards—thrilled at her voice. Her herbal scent blended with the dinner smells. She had not managed to make a fix in five months, but with her braids arranged in a crown, she still appeared to the world to be full of healing. Watching through the keyhole, Donkey rejoiced at the sight of the milk in the pail—of course her granny could milk Delilah with one hand!—and felt the force of these four women in the same room for the first time in years. All five of them here in the cottage together was like and unlike the scenes from Hermine's dreams: a pile of babies nestled in lavender wool, a spreading oak full of complaining crows, a coyote mama tending to her pups underground, and somewhere in the background, a dam threatening to burst.

"Which of you three is going to snip the thread that ends my life?"

Herself said grandly. "Isn't one of you supposed to have the scissors to end this trial?"

Molly held up a jar of string beans, one of the old blue-green jars with bubbles in the glass. "Should I open these?" she asked.

If Herself heard the question, she didn't answer.

Prim got up and walked around the table, trying to look proud, but she shrank as she passed behind Herself. She took off her red jacket to reveal a long-sleeved sweater of the same color. She hung the jacket on a peg next to Molly's puffy bruise of a coat, and by comparison Prim's was a small, sharp wound, a narrow blood-soaked passageway, maybe a dangerous escape route to another island. In the bedroom, Donkey curled her bare toes; her heart pounded. After all the strange things she'd heard, she didn't want to leave the bedroom until Prim and Molly were gone, but the smell of vegetables cooked with butter and cinnamon was luring her out. She was starving. And *Garden of Logic* was out there.

"Such richness I created in the world by raising you all up to be just who you are," Herself said, with relish. "And here we all are, together again."

Rose Thorn started laughing, her part of an extravagant four-part harmony.

"Oh, we'll all be together again at your funeral, Mama." Prim's voice softened after the word *funeral*. She regretted saying it and hoped Herself hadn't heard.

"Your hair is going gray, Prim," Herself said gently, tearfully. "I never believed my girls would grow old."

"Not true, Mama," Rosie said with a grin. "You always reminded us we're dying, day by day."

"My hair is ash-blond, and I paid good money for this color," Prim said, feeling choked.

"You two need to see each other more often," Molly said, trying to regain her balance.

Despite herself, Molly felt jealous of her mother's irritated attention on Prim. She focused on sliding the long beans from the jar into a saucepan, careful not to break them. Dorothy liked them whole. Then she got out four chipped egg-yolk and moon-colored serving dishes and put them on the counter. While the others watched, she pulled the chicken from the oven and then the glass cake pan with the two squash halves, too, pretending everything felt normal. Molly wanted this meal over so she could go home to her cats.

"I'm glad you could finally step down off your high horse to come home, Prim," Herself said, breaking the silence. Those who didn't know Hermine's dreams might have thought she hadn't wanted Prim home, but Donkey and Rose Thorn knew otherwise. What even they didn't know was how it felt to be Hermine now, readying to relinquish her power and distribute it among them as she had always known she would have to do one day. After a minute of enduring Hermine's gaze, Prim broke out in a sweat, her forehead shining through the makeup.

"I make my own home. But thank you for reminding me about my horse. Could somebody please go feed my high horse?" Prim fished in her purse for a tissue.

"We've got nothing but donkeys around here," Herself said. "Come out here, Donkey! Come out, my girl!"

Donkey scooted backward and rose up onto her knees, ready when Herself pushed the bedroom door open to reveal her. All eight eyes were wildly alive and focused on her.

"Why didn't you witches tell me she was in there?" Prim whispered loudly.

Herself stood there smiling, pressing her cuntshell necklace into her breasts with her hand. She'd never loved her Donkey girl as much as she did in this moment.

"I looked in there. She must've been hiding," Prim said.

"I didn't know," Molly said. "She always does chores with Mama."

If only Donkey could have slowly streamed into the room like mist, slithering through the keyhole to add herself to the company as that invisible observing zero she'd been a minute ago! They wouldn't stop staring. Hermine reached for her heir to the island, took Donkey's hand.

"A little snake in the grass!" Prim exclaimed, but she smiled with an open mouth when Donkey stood up to her full height, a head taller than Herself. Prim fell in love with the girl again as she'd fallen for her every time she'd laid eyes on her. The girl in her new form was the solution to a problem Prim didn't even know she'd been working on. She grinned at Donkey's awkwardness; she seemed clumsier and more innocent than Prim had ever been. Had any of them ever been so willowy and shy as this girl? The confusion and distress on Donkey's face, her misery at being exposed, only added to her charming perfection. Prim blotted tears with her makeup-stained tissue, and more tears of joy came. The girl looked a little like Rose Thorn, though not in any attribute—her hair was redder, her skin freckled like Prim's own skin. Rosie never would reveal who the girl's father was, knowing that Prim would drag the man through the legal system and Rosie along with him. But in this moment, unforgiving Prim found a kind of forgiveness, or maybe it was gratitude, for that awful man. Dorothy Rose Zook, however cruelly conceived, was perfect.

The full reality of motherhood had not struck Prim until she became a grandmother, when she first met Dorothy at age two. Now this girl was so full of promise and desperately in need of every bit of Prim's knowledge of the world. Saving people from the death penalty did give her life meaning, but in this moment, she knew she would press the button to send a killing surge of electricity through any man who even looked sidewise at this girl. Twelve years ago, Prim would have done anything to get Rose the abortion she'd said she wanted, and now she would do anything to save this girl the smallest pain.

Molly turned away long enough to lift the greasy chicken from the pan and onto a serving platter. She set the platter on the table atop a brass trivet decorated with rattlesnakes.

Donkey squeezed Hermine's hand for comfort and, with the other, touched *True Things* in the pocket of Titus's army jacket. Rose Thorn continued to smile at her, enjoying the confusion of the moment. Once Molly got the meat on the table, she turned her attention back to Donkey, looked at her with an expression different from her usual irritation, as though she might listen if Donkey said something. Hermine's smile was the most unexpected element of the moment, a smile that held pride for Donkey and for all of them. No longer a deaf woman with a missing limb, she was a woman with eight good ears and eight extra hands.

Donkey felt the snake blood racing through her veins. She tried to be logical, to think of right triangles and cubes inside bottles with space between them, but her brain short-circuited. She felt too small to contain all that was in her, and those cubes became smaller and smaller until they liquefied. She was a test tube rather than a bottle, and she overflowed, not with the rich new truths she'd heard sitting there behind the door, but instead with what she'd needed to say for so long, and she said it in a voice as low as a massasauga's purr, the voice from the Black Lagoon: "Rose Thorn has cancer in her breast. Please help her! I don't want her to die!"

CHAPTER FOURTEEN

The truth will set you free.

ALL FOUR WOMEN LOOKED at Donkey in astonishment.
Prim emitted a sound like a screech owl's sad whinny, and
Molly dropped a wooden bowl full of rolls onto the table she'd
set with plates and silverware. Rose Thorn, her secret exposed, let her
jaw fall slack. Herself moved to the head of the table and sat down
in her chair with a splashing *oof*. All the threads that had softened
and loosened between the four women instantly knotted themselves
into a dense, tight fabric. Donkey was struck by how what she'd just
added could not be subtracted. How once you picked a mushroom,
snapped the head from its underground body, or once you'd accidentally stepped on it and crushed it, you couldn't unpick it or uncrush
the thing—it would never go back to how it had been.

Prim said, "I don't know where to start." She bent down beside Rose
Thorn, who sighed and, reluctantly, pulled aside her bathrobe to show
everybody her whole pointy little breast and the bluish knuckle there.
Though Donkey had inspected the pale breast and its dimpled lump
every morning while her mother slept, she felt as though she were
finally really seeing the horror of it. Only Titus could believe that was
a cyst, and only because he wanted to believe it.

"This is what I didn't want to hear," Herself said quietly. She reached
across the corner of the table and took Rose Thorn's hand.

"Oh, my girl," Prim said and knelt between Rose Thorn and Herself.

"We shouldn't assume anything yet. You'll have that looked at,

Rosie," Molly said, making her way to her chair on the opposite side of the table. "Monday. Now everybody, sit down and eat."

"Mama, only you can heal me," Rosie said quietly, and Molly shook her head in distress.

"No, I can't," Herself said with a sigh, as though she were sinking into a pool. "Only the devil-doctors can help you, Rosie." Hermine understood, with a jolt, why she'd been gathering poisons all over the island these months—it wasn't to bring back Baba Rose. Rosie needed a new kind of poison, one not even Baba Rose had been able to make. The worst thing about the new cancers was that there wouldn't be enough time for a cure from the Waters to work, even if you made one to try.

The crow roosting with her family above Rose Cottage opened her other eye to see the light coming from the kitchen window. That see-all, tell-nothing bird decided right then to stay the winter on the island, even if some of the others went south. Spiders shifted in their webs; some crept out from under the boxed ends of the kitchen table to listen and fret.

"These squashes look delicious," Molly said, because somebody had to say something. She reached across the table with her serrated knife to saw the buttercup halves each into quarters, the dense orange flesh and leathery green skin. She cut carelessly, so the cinnamon apple mixture of one big half spilled out into the glass baking dish and mixed with the greasy sausage mixture from the other. Molly then deftly sliced into the breast of the chicken, sliced again and again. She ripped off the thick outer slice, with the crispy skin, and put it on her own plate. She took a bite of chicken and chewed hard and swallowed. "Everybody, please sit down, and let's talk about this."

Donkey's heart continued to pound with her own venomous betrayer's blood. Her mother had forgiven her for many things, but Donkey didn't know if she could hope for forgiveness this time. She noticed that her book and crayfish had been moved to the far end of the table, and she picked them up. She placed her notebook carefully beside her plate, put *Garden of Logic* on top of it, and on top of that, her crayfish shell. She slipped into her chair next to Rose Thorn without looking at her. Normally, she faced a blank wall while she ate, imagining equations, but now she would have to look at Molly frowning and chewing.

"Prim, please sit," Molly said. "Rosie needs a biopsy. Then we'll know what's going on."

"She already had a biopsy," Donkey said. She glanced at her mother's hands clutching Titus's lighter in her lap. Then she glanced at her own fork. Molly had given her one with tines so twisted she might not be able to eat without damaging her mouth.

Molly stabbed the chicken on her plate. "Then why didn't you tell me, Rosie?"

"Why didn't you tell *me*?" Prim said, still kneeling beside Rose Thorn.

Donkey got up to fetch a straighter fork and then sat back down but noticed that her moon-colored plate was cracked and repaired with glue, so she got up again to replace it with one that was only beginning to crack. She thought of the good dishes, the straight forks at Wild Will's House.

"Because I knew everybody would be upset," Rose Thorn said. "Now I just need a drink. Please, a drink, somebody." She tugged her hand out of Hermine's, shook Prim's arm off her shoulder. "You're all making me nervous."

"Mama, did you know about this?" Molly shook her head toward Herself and angrily applied fake butter to a roll.

Hermine felt herself flushing, alive with all the energy flying around the table. "I didn't know," she said, but it wasn't exactly the truth. She'd known. She'd known in her bones if not in her mind or in her missing hand. Her bones had heard it from Rose Thorn's own mouth on the porch all those months ago, even if her ears had shut it out. Maybe she'd known it even before Rosie had arrived, and maybe it had been the source of her fog during the last year, the fog that kept her sleeping all morning if Donkey didn't wake her up, the feeling of her heart slowing, her arteries clogging. She'd been trying to dream a cure. She hadn't been faking her hearing loss—she'd never faked anything in her life—but she'd slowed the rate at which words could penetrate her mind and distract her from her task. And instead of dreaming an herbal cure, instead of dreaming of Baba Rose, she'd kept dreaming of her daughters coming together.

"And Mama, why can you suddenly hear every little thing?" Molly asked. "You haven't heard anything I've said for five months."

"I've already heard too much," Hermine said.

Prim moved behind Herself and took her seat against the wall, across from Rose Thorn, while Hermine sat with her own failure to find a cure. She'd never trusted her girls as healers before—not even Molly, especially not Molly, who was too brutal—but she'd have to trust them now to work together to cure Rose Thorn. Her hand was shaking, both of her arms. Her whole body trembled.

"Do you know what kind of . . ." Molly asked, trailing off. "I mean, how far along?"

Rose Thorn laughed. "You mean, is it a boy or a girl?" Despite herself, Rosie was still glowing.

Hermine saw what it was to be Rose Thorn, that she was bright even when she was miserable, with no ability to draw the curtains or staple up plastic over the windows or send out a fog to stop her from transforming with her light whatever was around her. Anybody could see her and head toward her or take aim. Hermine hadn't acknowledged the power of this light before, hadn't guided Rosie in using it. Rosie had been her lazy helper for years, and before her was Molly, and before Molly was Prim. Hermine always had a girl with her, a helper, but she'd not valued any of these girls enough, and before Donkey came along, she had not really even listened to them. Baba Rose had tried to teach her about the wisdom of youth—that was why only the youngest could inherit the island—but Hermine had not really believed in it. She'd been certain that Baba Rose had all the wisdom, forever, no matter who came after. She'd stayed focused on Baba Rose, even as she'd grown old, ignoring the clumsy and tentative wisdom unfolding before her and even inside herself. Her girls had needed her encouragement, and she hadn't been able to give it. And so her girls, these powerful sources of energy, were pointing away from her, away from the island, toward things as absurd as law and math. And now Rosie's life was in their hands.

"Rosie, I hate doctors too," Prim said anxiously, "you know that, but I agree with Moll this time. We can do this. We can all get you through this."

Prim accepted the bowl Molly was offering and pulled four long green beans onto her plate. Herself took a watery heap of broken beans, and when the bowl came around to Donkey, she picked out the eight unbroken ones and lined them up according to length, with the smallest at the outside of the plate, so that none of them hung over the edge. When Donkey bit into one, she tasted cinnamon and cloves from the aroma of the pie that was now warming in the oven. She took two quarters of the squash, wiping the sausage grease off the skin with a blue-and-white cloth napkin, hoping nobody would notice her doing it.

"You're all ganging up," Rose Thorn said. "Mama, tell them they can't make me. Tell them I can say no to their treatment until I'm ready. Women can do what they want here."

Herself reached out with her fork and took a slice of chicken and put it on her plate. Then she took something out of the chest pocket of her work shirt—a caustic bloodroot that she had dug out of the ground the previous morning—and set it next to her plate. She'd been glad to tune out the brutes of Nowhere with their unpalatable requests, but she shouldn't have done the same to her daughters. She now had to will herself to listen carefully, to catch every nuance of this problem to which she had no solution.

"You do not have a right to not get treated for cancer," Molly said. "Even Mama knows there's no medicine in the Waters that wouldn't kill you in the process of curing you. It's bad enough I have to watch you starve yourself." She wiped her eyes.

"I might know best for myself. Please consider that," Rose Thorn said. "And I'm not starving. I can barely button my jeans." In truth, she didn't know what was best. Already she was not feeling quite the same, and she'd assumed these last few months it had been the cancer telling her not to drink, to go to bed early—and yet, there was an edge of euphoria, too, as if cancer might not be all bad.

The next step, according to the doctor at the cancer center in Laguna Beach—apart from paying the $2,200 bill for the biopsy—was cutting out the tumor, and then there would be radiation every day for six weeks. But Rose Thorn knew what she couldn't endure, not yet: the controlled violence of the hospital, a bed under fluorescent lights, all that would have to be endured without privacy, without a beer or a coffin nail or a cup of merry poppins tea, nurses bustling in and out, angry at her for resisting anything they demanded. When she'd delivered her baby, she'd been so young, she'd barely fought them, but in the psych ward two years ago, she had resisted. The shackles they had put on her had kept her on her back so she couldn't sleep, spread-eagled her for the doctors and anyone else to inspect, to do with as they would. The nurses had straightened out her blankets, tucked them tightly over her feet and shoulders to give the illusion that she was there of her own free will.

She wasn't saying never to treatment, but she needed to come to it in her own time—it wasn't something she could make herself do for other people—and she understood that her own time might seem like too late to them, might even truly be too late to save her life. Something like this had happened when she was pregnant. When Herself hadn't given the medicine to start the bleeding again, Prim had made her an appointment at a family planning clinic. Three times, Rosie had said she would go. Just not yet. The time wasn't right and wasn't right, and then it was too late. Women in this family were supposed to do what they wanted, but often the most Rosie could do was figure out what she didn't want. Not deciding was a decision in itself, she knew; it possibly allowed some other larger, wiser version of herself to make the decision, or that was how it felt anyway.

"Molly's right," Prim said in a measured way. "Let's eat first."

"You know she hardly eats," Molly said, tears now pouring from her eyes, "Look at how thin she is."

"You keep saying that, but she's always been thin," Prim said. "Looks like she's gained a little weight since she's been here. She looks fine."

Donkey wished they wouldn't talk about her mother as though she wasn't right there.

"I'm sorry, Mom," Donkey whispered. Rose Thorn seemed small in her chair, while Donkey felt like Alice grown grotesque and clumsy, with a long snaking neck, so her head stuck out of the chimney.

"Damn it," Rose Thorn said to Donkey, "I could have told you this would happen."

Donkey shrank back. She hadn't seen her mother angry like this since two years ago in that hospital bed, and then the anger had been directed at Molly.

"I guess I raised a daughter with a mind of her own," Rosie said, without looking at Donkey. The rage she felt toward the girl shocked her too. The truth was, when Rose Thorn came back this time, she'd wanted to tell Herself about the cancer; she'd even said it aloud, intending for Herself to hear. But when that hadn't worked, she'd been relieved. And once she'd decided to keep it secret, she'd become entrenched in that secrecy, invested in it, whatever the consequences.

"You did right to tell us, Dorothy," Molly said.

Having Molly's approval felt like proof to Donkey that she'd done something terrible. But if it meant the cancer would be cured, it would be worth it. She glanced at Herself, whose fork trembled as she lifted a bite of squash to her eighty-year-old mouth. Before now, everybody had said they didn't know how old Herself was. Why had they lied?

After that, Molly ate in angry silence, flushing and reddening, opening her mouth to speak but then shaking her head and remaining silent.

Prim attempted small talk: "How were Ada's peaches this year?"

"She's dead," Donkey said, and her eyes watered.

"I'm sorry. I forgot," Prim said. "So, do you think they have a decent math teacher at the middle school?"

Donkey shrugged, stared at her crayfish.

Rose Thorn took alternating sips from two glasses, one containing eggnog, and one full of homemade tomato juice with vegetables and herbs in it. When the smell of the heating pie began to overwhelm them, as they were finishing their meal, Herself nodded to tell Donkey to take it out of the oven. Donkey was glad to have a job, glad to have the clove-nutmeg-cinnamon scent waft hotly in her face. She wished she could cut it into seven equal pieces the way Lorena did, but now Lorena was gone, and Donkey could never ask her how she'd done it.

"It's settled. Monday we go in, Rosie," Molly said, blotting her lips with her napkin.

"We have all night to talk about this, Moll," Prim said.

"Maybe you do, but I have responsibilities at home. I can't stay here all night," Molly said. Her agitation continued to grow.

Herself sat as still as a great mound of earth, but they could all feel the countercurrents flowing inside her—her belief that women on the island did what they wanted and her desire to cure her daughter of cancer. And so much more.

"Well, I don't appreciate your playing deaf, Mama," Molly spat. "Seems like I'm the only one not in on the joke, as usual. Everybody but me is so clever and mysterious."

"I'm not going to the doctor tonight," Rose Thorn said. "Tonight, somebody needs to get me a drink. Or I'll walk to the Muck Rattler and get one. Don't you have something in that purse for me, Prim? Or are you as bad as the rest of this sobriety society?"

"Sorry, honey, no rattlesnake in this pot," Prim said, patting the leather bag she'd hung on the back of her chair. "Just a cough drop. I have to drive to the airport early in the morning."

"I thought we could at least eat breakfast tomorrow, you and me," Molly said to Prim. "You say you want me to consult with you about things, that you want to be a part of this family."

"Yes, I need to go get a drink." Rose Thorn stood up. First she would look in the hollow tree—but then she remembered that no new bottles had appeared there all summer. She looked around uncertainly. The cancer in her cells didn't feel separate from this conversation. Molly and Prim's bullying was a part of the cancer, their eagerness to send her into the clattering, fluorescent, chemical hospital horror show. That even Herself was willing to send her there was evidence of a cancer in this family.

Herself reached over and took Rosie's hand, pulling her back down into her chair.

Then Donkey had an idea. She moved around the table to the tall cupboard behind Herself. She opened the left-hand door and crouched there. The women watched her lift the hatch of the left-hand caboodle and feel down under the house, past where the key hung when it wasn't in her pocket. She inhaled deeply the familiar mushroomy musk, and then, one by one, she pulled out the jars of useful poisons hidden there—feverweed, poison ivy leaves, bloodroot juice—and set them on the floor. As she put the salve of last resort—with the bloodroot flower painted on the red lid—next to the others, she felt Prim's eyes on her. She reached farther in, to the ground level, her entire arm's length. Her fingers closed around what felt like a snake shed, which she let fall, thinking she'd try to get it later, and finally (she was pressing her shoulder into the floor now) the whiskey. As she lifted the bottle out, her knuckles brushed against the feathery scales. She lingered there until she felt the Lindworm tense her muscles. When Donkey quickly pulled away, she almost lost her grip on the bottle. She drew the caboodle hatch back into place.

"Somebody's been holding out on me!" Rose Thorn said. "My own baby!"

As Donkey held the dusty round pint bottle out to Rose Thorn, Prim moved behind Herself and deftly intercepted it. Also, without anybody but Donkey seeing, she grabbed the salve of last resort and dropped it into her purse. Donkey hoped she knew to be careful with it.

"Is this Daddy's whiskey?" Prim asked, cradling the bottle before looking closely at it. "It is! Never thought I'd see another bottle of this. Daddy's favorite medicine! I made this label myself!"

"I really don't think we need to add alcohol to this dinner," Molly said.

"Give it to me," Rose Thorn said.

Prim sat down with the bottle and used her thumbnail to slice through the wax all the way around the stopper. She produced a Swiss army knife from her purse, pried a corkscrew from its folds, and extracted the cork from the neck of the bottle with a dull pop.

Molly shook her head. Though she'd meant to stop eating, she served herself more of the stuffing that had not been inside the bird. Rosie's refusal of medical treatment was causing all the anger she'd stored up her whole life to brim over.

"Mama!" Molly shouted suddenly. "Why are you just sitting there? Tell Rosie she has to listen to us."

"Molly, you can't force somebody," Prim said.

"Yes, I can!" Molly said.

"Moll, let's just discuss it calmly," Prim said. "Rosie will listen to reason, I'm sure."

Hermine felt herself dissolving into these women she had raised. They could speak for her, speak better than she could from all the points of view. If she put her trust in Molly's anger and Prim's arrogance, in Rose Thorn's love of life's chaos, she could relax. She was starting to feel loose in her joints, and she knew she needed to come apart and be reassembled, like the sultan in the story "The Bronze Ring" who needed his bones boiled—Donkey had read that story to her dozens of times—but she didn't think it should be happening now. She squeezed the bloodroot in her hand to release a tiny amount of crimson poison into her skin. She couldn't give her daughter permission to die, even though she wanted that right for herself.

"You don't give us any reason to trust you," Molly said to Rose Thorn. "Look at your arm. You have a fight with your boyfriend, and you burn through your own skin."

"It wasn't a fight," Donkey said quietly. She was afraid of what she'd unleashed in Molly.

"Mama, you can tell Rosie," Molly said, her voice rising in pitch. "You did it before when she wanted to— She asked you, and you said no. If you'd gone along with her back then, we wouldn't have Dorothy! We could have lost Dorothy if you'd gone along with her that time!" she shrieked. "Can't you be on our side, Mama? Tell her she has to get treatment."

"Poor Jesus," Prim mumbled. "The big guns."

Donkey did her best to close her ears. She thought about spherical geometry. Professor A. Schweiss said new rules applied when lines didn't stretch out into ∞ anymore but just wrapped around a finite planet. On a sphere, according to Schweiss, lines crossed in surprising ways. The rules and theorems were different. Donkey had always thought her birth had been welcomed by all the women of the island, that she had been wanted. But if Rose Thorn had wanted to throw her away, if she had never wanted Donkey to begin with, then it made sense that she always went away and left her.

Rose Thorn said to Donkey, "You know I love you. I was confused back then."

"Oh, shit," Prim said and put down her fork. "Molly, what the hell? Dorothy, your mama was very young. We were afraid for her. There were complications."

Herself nodded at the pie, directing Donkey to bring it to the table and cut it. Donkey carried the chicken to the counter and put the pie in its place. The flesh was dense—the apples had been minced to the size of raisins—and Donkey sliced with such force that she knocked the pie in its pan off the rattlesnake trivet. She served her mother last, on a small, cracked plate the color of egg yolks. Once a piece of pie sat before each of them, the deafening scent of spices filled the room from wall to wall, floor to ceiling. Donkey felt all of them watching her now instead of Rose Thorn, and she pushed her fork into the triangular pie tip. When she touched it to her tongue, she tasted a dense explosion of cinnamon, nutmeg, clove, allspice, and ginger. As she chewed that first bite, she thought she would have preferred blueberry or peach, or even plain apple, but as she took another bite and then another, the more she wanted it, the more she realized her body had hungered for this pie forever. She ate the whole piece in two minutes and afterward felt slightly intoxicated.

"I'll come while you're in the hospital," Prim said, splashing a little more whiskey into Rose Thorn's coffee cup, though she hadn't yet drunk what she had there. "Or you can come to California and recuperate at the beach. You won't even have to work at the Sea Cave. You can just relax."

"She'll have to have radiation," Molly said. "She's not going to be lying in the sun."

"You come, too, Dorothy," Prim said. "Come with us and help your mom recover. You can go to the same school your mama went to. You get to choose your own curriculum. Rosie read books, but you could do math."

Donkey shook her head no. Right now she'd even say no to math. She felt the heat of anger rising in her. It wasn't just Aunt Prim who was terrible—they were all terrible.

"This is exactly what I was afraid of," Rose Thorn said. "That everything would become dreadful and serious. And sad."

"I'm not crying," Donkey said when Rose Thorn looked at her with sympathy. "I just have something sharp in my eye."

"Aren't you going to eat my piece of pie?" Rose Thorn whispered. That was why Donkey always served her mom sweets, so her mom could give them back to her. But Donkey shook her head. Instead, she lifted the last piece from the pie pan and put that on her plate. Rose Thorn blinked back tears and wrapped her piece in the tinfoil that had been over one of the squash halves. She thought she would give it to Titus, whose love of pie was famous.

Molly and Prim planned it all out as Rose Thorn sat silent, now and again wetting her lips with the whiskey. Prim agreed with Molly that Rose Thorn would start treatment at the hospital in Grand Rapids. But if it didn't seem adequate, they'd fly her to the cancer center where she'd been diagnosed. To hell with the cost—they'd go into debt.

"And Daddy's whiskey seals the deal!" Prim banged her cup on the table like a drunk.

"That's the last bottle of whiskey," Herself said. "I was saving it for him."

Rosie took out her warm amber stone and put it on the table-cloth between her and her daughter, a gesture of forgiveness. Normally Donkey would have picked it up, but she couldn't do the normal things now, not yet, even if her hand itched to hold it. Instead, she pulled *True Things* into her lap and held it in both hands.

"Well, to hell with him," Prim said. "We're drinking him up once and for all."

"Is he dead?" Donkey's eyes filled with tears.

"He's not dead," Prim said. "Don't worry."

"Are you sure?" Molly asked. "You sound sure."

"Yes, I'm sure. Unless he died in the last three months."

The whole room, people and spiders and Lindworm, perked with interest. Herself stopped breathing momentarily.

"So you like that book?" Prim asked, nodding at *Garden of Logic*, still on the table. "I'll send you the author's brand new one when it comes out. I think it's called *Calculus for Kids*."

"I don't want that one," Donkey said.

"What's the matter with you, Dorothy?" Molly said. Her eyes were still watering. "She takes that book everywhere. She loves that book. Say thank you."

"I already said it."

"I know the woman who wrote it," Prim said. "If you come out to California and visit me, you can meet her. You've never met a mathematician, have you?"

A female mathematician? Donkey wiped at more tears of confusion. She lifted the crayfish and put her notebook on top of *Garden of Logic*. When she put the crayfish back, she positioned it so it faced Prim, but the claw stuck accusingly back at Donkey. She felt duped again. She'd all along imagined A. Schweiss as a man, with muscles and powerful intentions, proving theorems with the confidence of driving a truck or shooting a gun, somebody who could see a dog in a cage and not want desperately to let it out. That was how she wanted math—and life—to be. She'd seen Schweiss lay out problems logically, without apparent struggle, move from beginning to end without anything getting in the way. But if Schweiss was a woman, she might have struggled along the way like Donkey to be logical, recording everything with care, never quite feeling certain about anything beyond what she could measure or calculate on the page. Maybe A. Schweiss even had things in her life that got in the way of doing math, like two terrible aunts, like a mother and a grandmother she wanted to keep alive even more than she wanted to solve equations. If Schweiss was a woman, how had she come to accept ∞ enough to include it in so many chapters?

"If you come with me to California, you can probably be in a class of nerdy kids who like this stuff as much as you do," Prim said, studying her, maybe ready to run around the table and grab her if she made a move to escape.

"Would you like that?" Rose Thorn asked, but Donkey's head was spinning. Maybe A. Schweiss hadn't been wanted by her mother either. Maybe she'd almost ended up a cuntshell on a necklace, same as Donkey.

"So it's agreed, Rosie?" Molly said. "Before we change the subject. I'm not getting up from this table until we have an understanding."

"Maybe you can just hit me on the head with a hammer and rouse me when it's all over," Rosie said.

"It doesn't have to be a drama," Molly said. "People go through this every day."

"Will you tie her to the bed?" Donkey asked, avoiding Rose Thorn's gaze. She realized A. Schweiss could get the same kind of cancer as her mother, and if she did, Donkey was almost sure A. Schweiss would go to the doctor.

"Nobody's tying anybody to a bed, Dorothy. And we're out of the Dark Ages. It's routine surgery, lumpectomy," Molly said. "As long as it hasn't spread."

"What caused it? That's what I want to know." Prim took another bite of her pie and drank down the whiskey in her teacup. "Why Rosie? If it's the farm chemicals, why not me? I'm eighteen years older. Or you, Molly? You've got huge boobs."

"You're wishing cancer on me, Prim?"

"Of course not. But it's got to be the chemicals in this place," Prim said, splashing more whiskey into her cup. "The PCBs and PBBs. Remember that fire retardant in the cattle feed at the Farm Bureau? Our old milk cow, Bambi, ate it, and we drank the milk."

"There isn't always a cause," Molly said. "And it's not a death sentence. Ada McIntyre had breast cancer twenty years ago, and she had a lumpectomy, and it never came back."

"But she's dead! Ada's dead!" Donkey shrieked. And Ozma was dead. And if there had been another milk cow before Delilah, she was dead too.

"Mama, you still haven't said anything. Don't you think Rosie should go to the doctor?" Molly spoke loudly and exaggerated her mouth motions as she'd been in the habit of doing with Herself.

Rose Thorn said, "I'm right here, everybody. And so is Dorothy."

"I guess our precious lastborn is old enough to hear everything tonight," Prim said.

Herself was crying as she took Rose Thorn's hand and kissed it. Then she took Prim's hand and kissed that. She let it go and reached out for Molly's hand and squeezed it. Molly started crying again at the strangeness of the act. They were all quiet for a while.

"Mama, that was your pie, all right." Prim said after she had swallowed the last bite from her plate. "It was rich, but I didn't even taste the meat."

"Meat?" Donkey asked.

"Just a little bit," Molly said. "Don't worry. It won't hurt you to get a little protein."

"Are you a vegetarian? I was one for a while too," Prim said, wiping her eyes, glad to change the subject. "It's just a little beef and suet, nothing much."

Donkey looked to Herself, who was still teary-eyed, and then to Rose Thorn, who shrugged with a sympathetic expression. Donkey hated them one by one. Witchy Prim, who was easy to hate out of habit. Molly, who had tricked her into eating meat by bringing this sweet-smelling pie. Herself, who'd made a slave out of her right arm. Rose Thorn, who'd wanted to kill her before she was even born. The smell of the pie still filled the kitchen, and now it was sickening. Donkey welcomed the hot springs of anger inside her; she wished she'd swallowed more snake blood, enough to make her powerful and dangerous. She should have grabbed hold of the m'sauga and brought her out of the caboodle and held the angry body up for everyone to see. She looked at the crayfish shell, sitting on top of *True Things*, and pounded her fist down and smashed it.

"Dorothy!" Molly said, and Donkey hit the crayfish two more times to crush it to shards.

Prim said. "At least you know how to get mad. Took me until I was thirty."

Donkey was shocked at her own illogical behavior, destroying one of her favorite things. Her heart pounded as she brushed the bony shards into her teacup like eggshells for the next day's coffee.

"Let's all have a family toast before the brutes get out their shackles and scalpels." Rose Thorn ignored her cup and took a swig right from the whiskey bottle and passed it across the table to Prim, who took a drink. Then Prim held it out to Molly, who shook her head.

"Come on, sister." Prim said, slurring a little. "A taste of the old man."

"I especially don't like it when you put it that way," Molly said, but she tipped up the bottle and took a small sip for their sake, gasped and shivered. "Poor Jesus, how can you drink that stuff?" She handed the bottle back to Primrose, who passed it over to Herself. All three daughters watched as the old woman lifted the bottle with her left hand.

"Here's to the wisdom of my daughters. Including you, Donkey." She took a long drink, let the whiskey burn her lips, her tongue, and her throat, all the way down. A few drops fell down her chin, and her reddened eyes watered a little more.

"Mama's drinking!" Rosie leaned her chair back on two legs to get perspective.

"I've got a daughter who drinks so I don't have to," Herself said grandly. "And I've got a daughter who saves me from getting up on my high horse. And another who would put me in a nursing home. And my Donkey, who won't let me sleep."

"Do you want a little taste, Freckle Face?" Rose Thorn asked. "You won't like it, if you don't even like beer." She took the bottle back from Herself and held it toward Donkey, who looked to the head of the table. Herself shrugged.

"If you want to know what makes so much trouble for your mama, you go ahead," Herself said.

The bottle, warmed by all the other hands, felt natural in Donkey's paw, and the smell was of island smoke and rotting wood and sweat and sulfur water, plus the scent of the pie hanging in the kitchen air. Donkey studied Rose Thorn, had a thought of her dying; she tried to imagine not caring, but she couldn't do it. Molly and Prim and Herself cared about keeping Rose Thorn alive as much as she did. Already the passion of hating them all was trickling away.

Rose Thorn said, "Just take a tiny sip. It's a big night. A lot of things got said."

"A bad idea," Molly said. She slathered the last roll with fake butter.

"She's eaten Mama's boiled pokeweed for eleven years," Prim said. "This can't hurt her any more than that. Dorothy, make a wish to your mama's health."

Donkey saw how together, they were the cure for cancer, the *Z-fix*. Together, they would save her. She tipped the bottle up, closed her eyes, let whiskey flood her mouth like milk, if milk were fire. It burned her tongue and throat, and the vapor even burned her lungs. She didn't expect such pain from something her mother loved so much. The glass mouth of the bottle knocked against her teeth. She'd wanted to punish them, but the whiskey burned all the way down to her belly for eating the meat, for making the wrong wishes, for sending Herself to the hospital, for telling Rose Thorn's secret, for letting Rocky out of his cage, for freeing the m'sauga. The whiskey felt like the cruelest father in the meanest fairy tale. It woke up her chest and belly and burned into her skin from the inside. The pencil lead burned under the skin of the hand that held the bottle. She had done terrible things, no denying it; she shivered and took a second drink to stifle the cough rising in her, swallowed again to redouble the hurt she needed to feel.

"Oh, poor Jesus!" Prim said and struggled to stand. "Stop her, Rosie!"

Donkey felt grit, and then something solid in the back of her throat. She swallowed hard. She'd forgotten about the junk she'd seen settled at the bottom of the bottle.

"Whoa!" said Prim, grabbing the bottle away. "You are Rosie's daughter!"

Donkey choked and collapsed into coughing. She let herself fall against her mother and Primrose, who'd gotten between them. Her whole body shivered.

"Now she's going to be sick," Molly said. "Maybe you should try to throw up, honey."

"She drank the rattle!" Prim said, holding up the empty bottle. "Swallowed it whole! Wild Will used to do that."

"You didn't tell me there's snake in that stuff," Molly said. She made her way around the table to tend to Donkey.

Donkey coughed more, coughed until her face radiated heat. She wanted to blame someone, to say she'd been tricked, but she'd done this illogical thing to herself.

"Are you going to be sick, Freckle Face?" Rose Thorn asked, squeezing her shoulders. "It's okay if you are. Might be better to get it out."

When Donkey tried to pull away from her mother's embrace, she knocked *True Things* and *Garden of Logic* to the floor, along with her moon-colored plate, which did not break. As Prim picked everything up for her, Donkey began to feel dopey. She wasn't sure what happened next, but soon Prim was supporting her, lifting her back up into her chair. They were talking loudly all around her, joyfully attending to her, laughing at her boldness, offering her cool water, sassafras tea, and her notebook and *Garden of Logic*, glad for the distraction.

Normally, Donkey would have pushed them away, even run to escape their touch, but then Molly laid both hands on her face, and Donkey felt a soothing warmth, a settling. And after that, all the hands in the room were on her, and it felt like the *eureka!* of discovery. They were no longer five separate bodies in a kitchen but five flowers growing from the same root; whether she hated or loved them wasn't relevant to their work together. Donkey's vision blurred until they all seemed wrapped up together in fog and spiderwebs. Any talk of Donkey being special and precious didn't mean anything, because she was not even separate from them, just the youngest part of the family monster—and a monster was what it would take to cure Rosie.

Donkey knew now why Herself dreamed of having her daughters gathered together—because such distance between the parts of a whole was unnatural. Donkey didn't notice she'd collapsed again until Prim and Rose Thorn pulled her back up off the floor. Together, they carried her down the hall, through the living room, and put her into Hermine's bed. Donkey could have sworn she heard Ozma's breathing on the floor beside her, or maybe the Lindworm was buzzing under the floorboards to keep her company.

FROM HERMINE'S BED, moving in and out of consciousness, Donkey heard them all in the living room, words upon words, angry and subdued words alternating with laughter. And her own name, repeatedly. Parts of the conversation swirled around in her body, along with the lavender and sweet basil, before she deciphered the meaning.

"Rosie, eventually you'll have to tell her who I am."

"Oh, Prim," Molly said. "There's no hurry. Why do you have to disrupt lives? She doesn't need to know everything. She's already upset."

"The girl does math," Prim said. "Don't you think she'll eventually figure out our ages?"

"The rest of the town hasn't figured it out," Rose Thorn said.

"She's smarter than the rest of the town," Prim said.

"I don't see why we have to face every truth. You told me, and it took me years to believe," Rose Thorn said. "Even to understand. And I still don't understand."

The words, at first, confused Donkey. She already knew old women didn't have babies—they discovered them in baskets, or in cabbages, sprung from sorrow. A stranger had brought Prim to the Boneset Table forty-seven years ago and left her to be raised by Herself. Molly, everyone knew, had come from Herself and Wild Will. And Rose Thorn had brought Donkey, of course, everybody knew that too. But what Prim and Rosie were saying now was that Prim had brought Rose Thorn to M'sauga Island. This new knowledge knocked Donkey into a swirling eddy. It was too much to get used to immediately, but in her dizzy half-sleep, she came to see her mother as more like her, another foundling without a father, something like the sister she'd always wanted. She couldn't forgive her mother completely yet, but she knew she would.

Before Molly went home, she came into Hermine's room and touched Donkey's forehead and cheek, her exposed shoulder; she ran a hand over her arm, and Donkey's stomach settled. Molly said nothing, just held Donkey's hand until she fell asleep. When Herself came to bed, Donkey luxuriated in her granny's arms in a way she had not done since Herself had lost her hand.

Nobody but the spiders and the Lindworm heard the conversation between Rose Thorn and Primrose in the kitchen just before Prim left in her rental car. It had taken Prim many years to realize she hadn't escaped motherhood by leaving the island. Not until Rose Thorn herself was pregnant did Prim realize how profoundly she'd failed the girl. At least she should have taught Rosie about the dangers of men, should have prepared her to defend herself. Prim didn't want this cycle to continue. Could she possibly leave California and return to this backwater to help raise her granddaughter? Would she even be welcome here? She had things to teach the girl that nobody else could, things not written in the books she sent. A girl needed a hundred weapons merely to defend herself against the brother, the father, the friend, even before considering how to defend against the stranger.

"Aren't you going to take me with you?" Rose Thorn asked. She was sitting at the kitchen table watching Prim pull on her red coat.

"Not this time." Prim saw that the best hope for curing Rose Thorn's cancer was for her to stay here with Molly. She took her purse off the back of her chair and checked that the salve of last resort was still there. "And maybe Dorothy *should* stay here. I can't stand thinking of her ever going into the world."

"You must still be drunk," Rose Thorn said.

"All that matters now is that you get well, Rosie." Prim heard tiny seeds of snow pelting the kitchen windows. She would have to be careful on the bridge.

"I guess I do want you to tell me about Wild Will," Rosie said. "Did you notice how Herself seemed happy when you said he was alive?"

"Now? You finally want to hear it, or you just don't want me to leave?"

"Just tell me how it wasn't rape. Tell me how you could *want* to do that with someone who raised you, your own father."

"If you think Wild Will actually raised anybody, if you think he was some fine father figure, you aren't seeing the real picture. Anyway, I wasn't like you, Rosie. I wasn't some naive romantic girl. I wanted experiences, adventures. And I was furious with Mama. Once Molly was born, I was nothing to her. She loved Daddy though. And Daddy was an exotic stranger to me, living over there in his high house across the road. Maybe I wanted him because she wanted him."

"Was it more than once?"

"Of course it was. Nobody but you could get knocked up in a one-off. Yes, I had an affair with him, after I left this squalid cottage and moved in at Boneset." She put her purse over her shoulder. As she stood there in front of the door, preparing to leave the island for Nowhere, she was straightening out her spine, getting taller, looking more like a lawyer. "We can talk about this any other time."

"Does Mama know everything?"

"Of course. Why do you think she wants to break me down and crush me into a powder?"

"That was because you wouldn't come home. You weren't the one she banished. I don't think she's angry with you anymore. Something's different in her." Rose Thorn studied Prim. "And maybe it's not so bad to be crushed," she said.

"I'm afraid of that too. Afraid I won't mind it. That everything I've done to get away from this place isn't worth anything. But I've saved four people from the electric chair. Four people are alive who would've died." She waited for Rose Thorn to respond, because what she'd said didn't have the effect she hoped for, didn't even resonate in her own mind. Saving lives was meaningful work, but maybe there was something even more critical she was neglecting by being so far away. She unclasped her barrette, caught up some stray strands of hair and refastened it. "And Molly's the one who can save you right now. You have to let her. I don't know how we'll pay your hospital bill, but we will." Prim hugged Rose Thorn and left, slipping around the door and closing it behind her without letting too much cold air in.

From Hermine's bed, lulled and deafened by snoring, Donkey didn't hear Titus arrive. He tapped on the window, and Rose Thorn invited him in. They made love in a tangle of blankets in the little warm room off the kitchen—something they'd never done. Donkey did not hear Rose Thorn afterward begging Titus to defend her against Molly and the doctors, did not hear the conversation that left them both angry and in tears. Instead, Donkey lay dead asleep in her granny's arms, dreaming that Rose Thorn would be healed by the other four-fifths of the family. It was a bully's dream, that Rose Thorn's small fraction would not be able to resist the power of the rest.

CHAPTER FIFTEEN

◦

Love isn't everything.

ONCE UPON A TIME, the next morning to be precise, November first, when Donkey was 4,200 days old, she awoke to the sound of mooing and a layer of white frost on the ground. She hurried out into the bracing cold with the milk pail, hurried to the cowshed on legs that felt somewhat disconnected from her body. As she milked, she woke up into a new kind of dizzying sickness, worse than the flu she'd once caught from Molly. She steadied herself by pressing the top of her head into Delilah's soft flank, feeling as though she'd been liquefied and churned about and then stuffed back into her translucent freckled skin. Rose Thorn, who had never blinked an eye when Donkey and Roger had stolen beers from a Boneset party, had not told Donkey how miserable and sad a morning felt after drinking alcohol. Shards of last night's conversation pricked her as she squeezed right-left, right-left, sending fine streams of milk into the pail. Her dulled brain was finally understanding why Rose Thorn wanted to go to California—not just for the sunshine but to be with her own mother, Prim.

As Donkey milked, Delilah lifted her ears at the sound of Titus's cows murmuring in the Boneset pasture across the road, and for the first time Donkey appreciated how Delilah was lonesome. She'd always thought they were protecting the cow by keeping her safe here on the island with them, but Delilah had the company of no other cattle, did she? No bull even came to breed her—they brought a bull's sperm in a plastic syringe. Though her paddock was big enough to walk around in, and even graze in, it was a prison, as was the whole island. If Delilah tried to escape across the bridge, she'd break the boards and plunge into the quickmuck and sink. Delilah didn't know her mother or grandmother. She'd been taken away as a calf and then raised by Herself, all the while hearing the others in the distance that she couldn't touch or know. Delilah gathered a breath and bellowed, as if to confirm the truth in Donkey's thoughts. When Delilah had birthed a calf two years ago, Titus carried it away into Nowhere, and, Donkey, feeling the cow's distress, had for a few weeks slept in the cowshed to comfort her. Thinking about that time, Donkey's hands failed her, and she could barely squeeze out any more milk. Maybe she had never really heard what Delilah was telling her. Had she ever even heard Ozma? Or anyone else? She watched her breath blossom in the cold stall and dissipate around Delilah's warm body.

On her way back to the cottage with the pail of milk and a basket of brown and white eggs, Donkey was gently slapped awake by the cold air. Near the poison garden, she startled at a sight as exotic as a m'sauga—something from a fairy tale, something she'd seen only a few times in her life. She lay on her belly and inched closer to the wingstem stalks to see ribbons of ice exuded from the burst-open stems in the shape of a coiled serpent or a complicated rose or a swirl of elegantly whipped cream. A frost flower! The sight took her breath away, but as she leaned in closer, her breath returned, and the flower made of ice melted, dissolved into fog.

The dried seeds still hung on the wingstem plant, whose roots Herself had often boiled to make a tea that gave relief from problems of women's bleeding and childbirth pain, and so Donkey tapped them into her open palm and put them in her coat pocket. She could come back and dig up the root before the ground froze solid and make a fix to help a new mother. She stood too quickly and felt so dizzy and nauseated that she had to put the milk pail down again.

Inside Rose Cottage, after she strained the milk, Donkey woke up Herself, who said a strange thing before she was fully conscious: "Can you piece me back together, child? Can you reassemble my bones?"

"Wake up, ma'am. You've had too much medicine."

"I don't know if I can move this river," Herself said. "I'm too old and tired. Check the basket, Donkey. Maybe somebody left a babby. Look under the cabbages."

"It's winter, ma'am. Be logical. There are no cabbages, and the basket's always empty, but you can have my arm today." Donkey said it, as always, but she felt tired at the thought. She also was reminded how seeing frost flowers growing from the burst, ruined stems of flowers that had once been alive could make Herself melancholy, the way a cuntshell did. "I don't feel good, ma'am."

Herself heaved up out of bed, put both her big feet on the ground, and stood. Though she'd taken only a sip of the whiskey last night, she now swayed; her hand reached out and brushed the bed covers as though searching for something she'd lost. She followed Donkey into the kitchen, and instead of waiting for the girl to make coffee, she put five scoops of grounds into the percolator basket. Then she picked up the teacup that usually contained yesterday's eggshells, emptied it on top of the coffee in the basket, and pushed down the lid. Except that it wasn't eggshells. Molly had tossed those out to use the teacup for supper. It was the teacup containing the shards of the devil crayfish shell. Donkey opened her mouth but then closed it; she was in no hurry to tell people things when there were so many things they hadn't told her. The softness she'd felt with Delilah hardened a little bit. She would not tell about the frost flower either.

Maybe Herself would have made her own breakfast if Donkey had waited, but she needed to keep busy. As she made bacon and eggs for her granny—her *great*-granny—and oatmeal and eggs for herself, she spoke loudly. She let the pan clank on the cookstove and let the fork hit the side of the metal bowl as she scrambled the eggs. She wanted Rose Thorn to wake up and feel sick and uneasy with her, but Rose Thorn resisted the call. Donkey watched Hermine drink *Cambarus diogenes* in her coffee, as easily as Donkey had drunk the tail of *Sistrurus catenatus* last night.

"If Prim's my real granny, then who is my real grandpa?" Donkey asked Herself at the breakfast table, with Rose Thorn's chair empty between them. But she might as well have been talking to the Lindworm, because Herself just pressed her cuntshells against her chest as though the strand were holding her together.

A crow dropped a hickory nut. It hit the roof with a clang. The nut had been stolen from a squirrel's nest, and now it would become food for a mouse, who would have to gnaw through the tough shell to eat the nut before itself becoming food for a rattlesnake.

"And why did Rose Thorn want to kill me?" Donkey asked. She felt Herself finally come awake at this question.

"If she'd really wanted to kill you, you wouldn't be here," she said. "That's what I think, but she didn't come to me. My daughters have to go away and make all their difficult decisions without me."

"But she asked for the medicine?"

"Your mother weighed and measured whether to have you. If she hadn't, then you wouldn't know if you were wanted or not." Her eyes suddenly filled with fear. "Where is your mother?" she asked.

Donkey checked the little bedroom off the kitchen, saw that the tan backpack was not on the dresser where it had been last night. Neither was Rose Thorn's warm stone on the table where she'd left it. Donkey opened the refrigerator and saw that the piece of pie Rose Thorn had wrapped in tinfoil was also gone. So was Titus's jacket from the hook where it usually hung, the jacket they shared. "Maybe she went to see Titus. Maybe she's going to marry him," she ventured, but she didn't feel hopeful about this theory.

After dishes, she ran down the road and found Titus, but her mother was not with him. Titus called Prim's number and left a message for her to call him when she got home, but Donkey didn't want to believe her mother had left with Prim after promising not to. She searched Rose Cottage, under every bed, behind every chair and couch, and inside every closet. She lifted the rug at the foot of Hermine's bed to see if there was a new trap door under it. Though they had no wardrobes, she searched their closets for secret passageways and looked closely into the bathroom mirror for an opposite world. There'd been no tornado or hurricane or earthquake to shake somebody into another dimension, no rabbit hole opening big enough to swallow a woman. She flicked on the light in the right-hand caboodle, stuck her head inside, and confirmed that the root cellar contained only potatoes, squashes, pickles, and some medicinal roots.

Rose Thorn's scent—a mixture of honey, smoke, coffee, cancer, and old Oz books—still emanated from the room off the kitchen, but there was no denying that Rose Thorn's presence was dissipating moment by moment. Donkey searched the henhouse—taking time to hold Big Scratch and Billina in her arms to listen for any messages—and then the Moon Palace and the hollow snake-barked sycamore, where she hoped to find her mother curled against the cold or calling out for Titus or looking for a bottle, though no new bottles had appeared there since last year's mold-speckled one. She shouted into the hollow tree, but the mulch inside the trunk absorbed the sound and gave back nothing. She ran to the end of the primrose path, past the poison garden to the stone circle where she'd spied on Rose Thorn and Titus that summer and to the sulfur pool where Herself bathed. She crunched over the frozen soil to the top of the island where the spice bushes grew, but she saw only crows above her in the trees. Those birds kept watch even in their sleep, but they would never say what they'd seen, even when Donkey begged them to. There was no new sign of a disturbance on the island; if Rose Thorn had fallen off the bridge and into the muck, she'd done it without a sound, without a splash or a broken branch or a muddy handprint.

That afternoon, after Donkey had searched the whole island a second time, Titus came over and said that Prim had called back from Laguna Beach to say Rose Thorn had not gone with her.

"I'm glad she's not in California," Donkey said, but she wasn't sure. Rose Thorn in California was something she could have imagined and settled her feelings on: the sadness, anger, and desolation she'd felt whenever her mother went away. Now, as she looked at Titus, the realization bloomed like breath in the cold air between them that they had no idea where Rose Thorn was or whether she was safe. Knowing how Prim must be worrying, too, gave Donkey a desperate feeling of connection to Prim that she hadn't known before.

Titus spent the next day searching for Rose Thorn in Nowhere, and other people joined the search. He stopped by Rose Cottage in the evening to assure them that *our beautiful Rosie* was not passed out on a picnic table outside the Muck Rattler as she had been one afternoon two years ago, nor was she in a ditch along the road between the island and the bar or between the bar and town or between town and the highway, where she might rest if she got tired while walking. For days, he neglected his work and searched the roadsides and checked in at taverns within easy driving distance. Donkey got tired of his reports about nothing. They already had plenty of Rose Thorn's absence on the island and didn't need Titus bringing more. The song of Rose Thorn's quiet snoring, her swishing and slithering along the hallway, her feathery footfalls, her drinks sloshing inside pint canning jars—all of that was gone, along with her light, the glass shards of her laughter, her conviction that Dorothy was precious and as sharp as a pencil.

After a full week of searching without much rest, Titus tripped over a rusted set of box springs somebody had abandoned in a ditch, and he ended up in the hospital with uncontrolled bleeding. After he was released, a few days later, he stopped coming to the island all the time, and so, like the last time Rose Thorn had left, Donkey lost both her mother and her best chance at a father.

The not knowing was the hardest part for the people of Whiteheart, too, though they might not have said so. Without knowing where she was, people had nowhere to stockpile their hope that she would soon return. Without being able to envision her in California with haughty Prim, they couldn't imagine her leaving that sunshiny place and coming back to them, and, as if to intensify their gloom, sunlight barely penetrated the cold fog for the first weeks after her disappearance. Donkey felt a camaraderie with everybody who wanted Rose Thorn safe and accounted for, but that feeling did little to alleviate her distress. In the face of sympathetic neighbors, Donkey longed for the simple fellowship of Rose Thorn's summer parties. She even missed the sound of the gravel truck going down the road—deliveries had stopped when the ground froze.

On the winter solstice, Donkey and Herself usually made sweets and laughed at silly jokes and stories, but by the time the day arrived, they'd run out of honey and sugar, and Molly forgot to bring any. Nobody laughed but woodpeckers on that day, and those birds laughed stoically, with dread, as the air grew bitterly cold.

"She's wherever she wants to be," Herself said while Molly wiped out their refrigerator, which Donkey thought was clean enough.

"I want her to be here," Donkey said and waited for Herself to chide her. In the past, the idea of Rose Thorn being where she wanted to be had provided solid ground for Donkey's sadness to rest upon. "What if she's inside a wolf, ma'am? Did you think of that?"

Herself reached into her pocket and squeezed a bit of snakeroot she'd dug up before the ground froze.

"I don't hate Prim anymore," Donkey said.

"Well, I should hope not," Molly said, without looking at her.

Herself took Donkey's hand, even though she'd just been handling poison.

"Maybe Rose Thorn was eaten by a talking lion," Donkey said, tugging her hand away. She wanted to argue, but Herself wouldn't argue at all anymore. "Maybe she's underground, ma'am, waiting for us to dig her up, and we're not even looking for her."

Herself only sighed, and Donkey felt a gap open between them. Arguing would have distracted Donkey from seeing the truth, how whenever she tried to save somebody, it came at a terrible cost: Calling Molly had cost Herself her hand; Rocky's freedom had cost Ozma's life (she still choked into tears at this thought). By trying to save her mother, Donkey had driven her away. In resisting cancer treatment, Rose Thorn was just trying to be herself, the way Jack Pumpkinhead resisted any head but a pumpkin head. Donkey had tried to take off her mother's beautiful human head and fit a wooden head in its place.

Donkey felt Rose Thorn being subtracted from Rose Cottage, from the island, over and over in waves throughout the ensuing weeks, and that feeling was a reminder about another danger of wishing. Even if you got what you wanted for a while, losing it later might hurt even more than not having gotten it in the first place. Rose Thorn hadn't helped with cooking or cleaning, but her presence had made those things easier. Without lifting a finger, she had spun straw into gold, and she had made Donkey and everyone she encountered interested in what could happen next.

At the end of December, Donkey gave what money she had set aside to Titus for the taxes, but he said he would pay them from his own money. However, when he went to the county treasurer's office, he found that Molly had already paid the taxes in full. Also the clerk told him that Primrose had called and attempted to pay the taxes that Molly had already paid. Donkey was ever more cautious about what she told Herself, and since she had never mentioned that the taxes weren't paid, now she didn't mention that they were. Still, there was the electric bill every month, and the future felt terribly uncertain, so Donkey continued to make as many fixes she could, letting Molly and everyone else believe Herself was making them. Before Molly's revelation, she hadn't realized that going to the hospital cost so much money; while she was comforted that Prim and Molly would help pay for Rose Thorn's treatment, Donkey thought she should save money too.

With Rose Thorn gone, Donkey assumed Molly would renew her efforts to make her go to school, and she readied herself. School would be a respite from watching Herself spin a cocoon of sad thoughtfulness around herself. Herself had given up searching for Baba Rose and seemed instead to want to be with Donkey every minute. But Molly was laid as low by Rose Thorn's departure as Donkey and Herself were and could think only of her healing plans. When Molly came to the island to discuss *Pippi Longstocking* with Donkey, she apologized and said the book had been a bad choice and then cried for a long time into her hands at the kitchen table. Donkey didn't dare mention how much she liked the book, how easy it was to read, how she'd cried for Pippi with her father at sea (he was gone for what seemed like ∞) and her mother dead. Molly didn't notice that Donkey referred to the character as Ippi, a palindrome. In fact, Donkey had tried to salve her own grief by sleeping like Ippi, upside down, with her feet on the pillow.

"She can't do this to us," Molly said, her face tear-stained. "Just disappear. Prim is losing her mind. Sometimes I wish I didn't have a little sister."

"You don't," Donkey said. "You have a niece."

"Well, I guess I can't blame you for knowing things," Molly said, standing up from the kitchen table, straightening herself out, getting ready to leave.

"When we find her, will you tie her to the bed to make her get cured?" Donkey asked hopefully. She'd been rethinking Molly a lot since Rose Thorn's disappearance. Molly was at least half right about school and Wild Will's house, which Donkey still visited, even though it was cold as a tomb inside, too cold even for factoring polynomials. Maybe she was half right about tying people up to cure them. The idea of Molly being right made her feel upside down. "If I find her asleep somewhere, maybe I'll tie her up."

"Let's not think that way, Dorothy. We can't force her to have treatment. Oh, why does everybody in this family have to be so stubborn?"

That evening, doodling in her book of *True Things* in the henhouse, Donkey drew a snake who had eaten another snake just barely smaller than itself and so was entirely full, from tip to tail. Then she decided that this snake-eating snake would actually be inside another snake, a rattlesnake, so she drew a third snake around it. And she knew that a king snake, immune to venom, would eat a rattlesnake, so she put a fourth snake around the others. She considered then that the snake doodle moved back in time: Before the biggest snake could eat the second-biggest snake, all the inside eating had to have happened already. What she had drawn could not logically be older snakes eating younger snakes but precisely the opposite. The younger snake grew up big enough to devour the older snake, who'd already devoured *its* elder, and so on back in time. The nested dolls Rose Thorn had given her were perhaps not mothers with babies inside them, but babies grown large enough to eat their mothers. All her life she was afraid of Herself eating her, but maybe there was—also or instead—an opposite problem.

AS THE WINTER SETTLED UPON THEM, Hermine's dreams became so powerful they traveled down the hall, even sent tendrils outside the cottage to the cowshed where Donkey milked Delilah. Herself dreamed bears (*Ursus americanus*) giving birth in dens, coyote pups *(Canis latrans)*, baby rabbits (*Sylvilagus floridanus*), and nests of tiny m'saugas. Once, there was a cup overflowing. In her own dreams, Donkey saw Herself wrapped in mummy's sheets or a silken cocoon or, once, fermenting in a pickle crock. When Herself was awake, she often moved slowly as though newly aware of her surroundings, but occasionally she had the urge to spin her snake stick in a playful way with her remaining hand. That winter she requested more and more wool yarn from Molly and knitted as many crooked blankets as she could. Her voice sometimes moved from high to low registers, reminding Donkey of Roger's. Herself began cooking again, slowly at first, making different dishes, some with more beans and little or no meat, so that more often than before, Donkey ate what she made. Even stranger than wanting Donkey with her every minute, Herself began asking Donkey how certain foods were made, and she was willing to use teaspoons and cups instead of just pinches and handfuls. It was as though she were just learning to cook, was maybe even imitating Donkey.

When Donkey was sad during the day, she had Delilah and the chickens to comfort her, but sometimes she woke to a lonely ache in the middle of the night. Instead of going to Hermine's bed to be overwhelmed by her big dreams, she dragged her blankets into the kitchen and lay on the floor by the stove above the Lindworm. If she concentrated, she could feel the snake's coils pressed against the drainpipe that was warmed by the cookstove. She sensed how the snake endured the cold by slowing its heartbeat and its breath, and she tried to do the same. She took pity on her sister, *Sistrurus catenatus*, banished to live under the house, but she also kept a heavy weight on the lid over the caboodle.

Molly and Titus had spread the word about Rose Thorn's cancer throughout Whiteheart, and a ragged handful of men began gathering at Boneset on Saturday nights again, and sometimes during the week, in a sort of vigil. When Molly saw them there, she told them to put out their fire and go home.

"There's no damned reason for them to sit out there," she said. But for Donkey, their coming made sense as a way of honoring her mother. Donkey had hungered for the men's voices and the social life she'd gotten used to, with surprises and gifts and funny comments and stories. The men went home after Molly scolded them but came back the next week and kept coming. Even later, even when they behaved badly, Donkey didn't mention them to Molly.

When the gatherings ran past dark, she sneaked out onto the porch wearing Wild Will's big barn coat to listen to the men shout and rage and mutter. She left the boards of the bridge in place so she could sneak up close and watch the fire light up their faces. They seemed angry in a way they hadn't been before. When they muttered about Rose Thorn and her cancer, they settled into dreariness, embarrassed by how foolish they'd been all summer and fall with their music and dancing and laughter. They decided that nothing short of witchcraft could have made them forget about the impending winter. Damn Rose Thorn for getting sick. Damn her for running away and abandoning her responsibilities—wasn't it her responsibility to get her cancer treated?—while the rest of them had to stay and worry and endure!

From a crouched position on the sloping bank where the man in camouflage had once lain with his rifle, she listened to the men's stories about Whiteheart's fathers and grandfathers, listened to the men grumble about wives and daughters who confounded them, heard men rail about how much better things had been when Goliath Paper paid decent wages. Donkey ignored the men's bitterness and enjoyed the sweat and fuel smells that wafted from them. Ralph Darling's big belly had grown since the summer and now looked like a pregnancy; Standish reminded her of the pit bull when he was still in his cage, solid and still but with a ripple of tension underneath his skin. On the rare occasion that Dickmon showed up, he puffed out his chest and stolidly absorbed everything, his mind always working to put two and two together so the world made sense. Whitby was the only one taller than her, was the person who reminded her most of Titus, in Titus's continuing absence—he came by only once a week now—but Whitby never broke into song or pretty language the way Titus did. Two-Inch Tony was still eagerly trying to please. Smiley, old enough to be the father of most of the others, was the concerned old woman of the group, for if there is no woman, one of the men has to play that role.

Donkey sneaked even closer to the group one night, studying the men from behind a willow tree. When she fell asleep in her crouching position, she woke herself up by tipping over loudly into the crunchy snow. Ralph Darling caught sight of her, and she held her breath. A squirrel or a fox or a coyote would have run, but she slowly stood and revealed herself.

"That Rosie's daughter?" Darling said, patting his belly. "Look, it's Rosie's daughter. You don't want to put a curse on us, do you?"

"Aw, don't say something like that to the girl," Smiley said. He'd just closed the bar and was sipping a coke, though he knew it would keep him awake long past the time he wanted to be asleep. He'd given up alcohol at the request of his mother, who was tired of him coming to work at the Muck Rattler hungover and complaining. But being sober made it harder for him to go home to an empty house. "How you doing tonight, Dorothy?"

"Are you spying on us?" Standish asked.

Donkey stayed frozen so long the men began to smile and laugh. The same way the women in her family had laughed at her in the kitchen when she emerged from the bedroom after spying on them through the keyhole.

"You sure are a tall girl!" Smiley said. "I hope we're not keeping you awake."

"We're not going to bite you," Whitby slurred drunkenly. "Come talk to us."

She approached cautiously. She knew the men, knew their names, but she had never talked to them without her mother there.

Whitby, sitting on a round of firewood, felt moved by the girl's shyness—she reminded him of a long-legged fawn—and he lunged for her, grabbed her, pulled her onto his lap and held her there with both arms. She kicked and squirmed, but after his years of farm work, he was able to hold the girl there effortlessly, and after two forty-ouncers and most of a bottle of blackberry brandy, he didn't feel the pain of her kicks.

"Let me go! I'll tell Titus!" Donkey felt her eyes roll back in her head as she strained to break free, the way Aster's eyes rolled back when she tugged hard against a rope wrapped around a post. However, even as Donkey struggled to get loose, she felt alive on Whitby's lap; even as she fought against his hold, she fought the temptation to soften into his arms. He smelled musky and like fuel and heat. "Titus, help me!"

Whitby didn't want to hurt the girl. He hadn't even meant to grab her that way, but when she called out Titus's name, he held her tighter. He wanted her to sit there and listen to him. She was Rose Thorn's daughter, half made of that woman. As for the other half, he wanted to shout it, tell the men they were idiots for not knowing what he knew. And the girl should know who her father was, should know what her mother had gone through to bring her into the world. If she would stop fighting him and sit still in his arms, he could whisper to her that he was sorry, so sorry he hadn't helped Rosie. But how could he justify having withheld the information for twelve years? No one was likely to believe him now about Titus Clay Sr., who had always been revered by the people of Whiteheart and who was now, in his afflictions, pitied too. He squeezed the girl tighter.

He would never have grabbed Donkey if Titus had been there. And Dickmon, if he had been there, would have stopped Whitby right away. But now it had to be Smiley who said, "Cut it out, Whitey." Then

Smiley dribbled some coke on Whitby's ear, which was sticking out of his stocking cap. "That's enough."

Whitby let Donkey go. "I was just screwing around," he said, wiping his ear with his collar and flushing deeply with shame. He had no conscious impulse to hurt women or girls—the opposite, really—and he didn't know why he'd grabbed her, maybe the same reason he'd shoot an animal that startled him. He wasn't like his uncle Titus Sr.—he wasn't! She was just a kid, but she was about as tall as he was, and she hadn't seemed like a kid on his lap. She smelled of a kitchen fire and herbs, womanly, and her bottom was more substantial than it looked from a distance, firm and rounded. And there was no civilized way to explain how a woman struggling—a girl, even—made you want to hold onto her, at least until she heard you out. If he could have grabbed and held Teresa before she had left for Tennessee, he would have done it, but she had packed her things and gone while he was asleep. As though what was growing inside her was all hers.

"Fuck this place," Whitby said and watched the girl return to the island, watched her lift the planks of the bridge to lock them out. How the hell did that thing work? Those women didn't care about anybody but themselves! Nobody cared how a man felt in this town! He strode to his truck and got his chainsaw out of the bed. (In winter, the men all kept their chainsaws in the backs of their trucks in case a tree fell across the road during a winter storm.) Whitby pulled the cord and revved the engine—it started on the first try. He was the first to start cutting that night.

IN THE HOMES OF THE PEOPLE OF WHITEHEART, things were also going badly that winter. Women severed the tips of their fingers when they chopped vegetables for stews, and accidents occurred with cutting and grinding machines. There was a man south of town trying to keep warm in his car after his furnace broke down, and he was asphyxiated by carbon monoxide. For many, sleep did not come easily. Every time Reverend Roy lay down without having taken the island sleep medicine, he was plagued by worries and disturbances of the soul. If he did succumb, he often dreamed that the Waters were taking over the town, rising up through the subbasement of the church, filling it with snakes and flowery perfumes. He feared he would suffer so long as women lived on that island in defiance of God's plan as he understood it. He did not wish Rose Thorn to die of cancer, nor did he let himself wish for Hermine Zook to give up the ghost in any unnatural way, but if God saw those things fit, then that child could be taken from the island and brought up in a prayerful household, his own household perhaps, if he and Molly decided to take on the burden of raising her together. For the sake of the child, he and Molly would marry, and as a married woman, Molly would be less resistant to seeing Whiteheart as the pious place it was always meant to be. She would no longer be torn between the two poles of church and family but could be wholly with him. Without those cursed cats. He knew he should instead maintain faith that God would show the mother and grandmother the light, that they would change, but his waking dreams were often of that willowy girl living under his auspices, subject to his guidance.

That winter, Whitehearters—adults and children—were ravenous as ship rats, but they grew impatient with cooking. The Dollar-Mizer store had to order record numbers of cases of macaroni and cheese, and the gas station sold as many frozen pepperoni pizzas as the distributor would provide. As a result, the whole town became constipated and sluggish, suffering through the winter without ease or grace.

Up on the roofs of trailer homes and small vinyl-sided shacks, satellite dishes leaned out from weatherheads, and inside, big TVs glowed in dark rooms. The TVs stayed on because when people sat in silence, they felt awash in shame over they couldn't say what. They pulled curtains across their windows so nobody could look in; or they stapled flattened cardboard boxes into the window frames to insulate against the wind, which blew from all directions that winter; or they covered their leaking roofs with blue tarps and were grateful for the way the tarps hung down over the windows. Though they were all watching the same police procedurals, medical dramas, and reality shows as their neighbors, they did it alone. Irma took up watching TV and smoking coffin nails with her aunt and let her tarot cards lie in the bottom of her underwear drawer, wrapped in that purple rayon scarf threaded with gold.

Though the people of Whiteheart felt angrier than usual during their waking hours, at night they become strangely languorous. Softness and gauze filled their dreams. Grown men orgasmed in their sleep as they hadn't done since they were teenagers. And the next morning, these confusing emissions dredged up shame, so the men accelerated in traffic and smacked their misbehaving children a little harder or even used a belt. A surprising number of men still owned the belts they'd been beaten with as children by their own angry fathers, and they were now drawn to these historical objects more than ever. Even when these men managed to keep the hard edge all day, at night they found themselves weeping in the shower before bed, desperate for the touch of a spouse, a child, a pet—any living creature. Many women got pregnant that winter, including Two-Inch Tony's wife, Cynthia.

The dogs of Whiteheart, meanwhile, wanted to get away from their people and sit outside at night, barking into the distance to keep warm and to make their existence known to other dogs, yearning for a pack of their own kind. They longed to demonstrate their dominance over or submissiveness to one another, to snuggle and nose and mount and bite one another, but the most they could hope for that winter, straining at the ends of their chains, was to hear one another and be heard.

Fuel oil was so expensive that year that many families had to keep their thermostats at fifty-five or sixty degrees, and if kids sneaked out of bed during the night to turn the heat up, they got smacked. The reason for the high prices was a military conflict fought halfway around the world, in a country many of them hadn't even heard of. More than a dozen local boys from Whiteheart and Potawatomi fought as volunteer soldiers, and after one of them died by friendly fire, the town's hatred of that heretofore unknown enemy increased exponentially. Everybody attended the closed-casket flag-draped funeral to show support for the grieving parents—the largest funeral since Ada McIntyre's last summer. The flavor of grief was more bitter than sorrowful, and in the spirit of wreaking revenge upon that foreign nation that had cost this dear, familiar life, a half dozen more young men traveled to Grand Rapids the next day and joined the US Marines.

In the Michigan state government, environmental protections were relaxed, and the plans to clean up the mounds of paper-mill waste in the Waters were delayed for lack of funding. The legislature justified these decisions by saying they would instead institute tax breaks to benefit businesses, though no business in Whiteheart benefited from the lower taxes. The Whiteheart post office closed that winter, so everybody now had to drive eight or ten miles around the Waters to the Potawatomi branch, and people missed talking to their neighbors while waiting in line. Teenagers, always the most creative and innovative members of any community, learned how to cook methamphetamine over burn-barrel fires. A handful of girls cut themselves secretly with razor blades for the rush of sensation it gave them, and one boy shot himself in the head with his father's pistol because of how some other kids talked to him at school. He didn't die, but people said maybe he should have, given how he ended up.

At the Muck Rattler, over a discussion of whether Aster might be pregnant—there was a hint of swelling, just enough for speculation—somebody resurrected the old story of how Wild Will had decided to breed pony stallions to donkey mares to get hinnies, the opposite of mules. As the story went, he'd had trouble getting the stallions interested in his jennies, and one day he showed up at the bar with a condom half the length of his arm. This receptacle for collecting a pony's sperm elicited many clever remarks. The reminiscence provided more laughter that evening than the story merited.

There was a black-and-white photograph behind the bar: Wild Will in a military pith helmet, leading a tall, handsome black mule loaded with heavy machinery, namely a Howitzer tube with muzzle and breech covers. When Two-Inch Tony's brother, who was visiting, asked about the picture, Smiley was happy to tell again about Wild Will's military service during World War II, and there was a sense that the anger of the town was settling into its own kind of sentimentality. The old stories were the stories that defined who they were, a people who admired and appreciated great men. Young Willy Zook had been a soldier in the 612th Field Artillery Battalion, charged with bringing American firepower to Burma, which was under the control of the Japanese. The road between India and Burma was impassable for tanks, trucks, or personnel carriers, so Wild Will's Brigade (5332nd) led Catalan mules burdened with the trappings of war hundreds of miles through mountains and jungles into enemy territory. Nobody ever got tired of hearing this story; even Herself had had a copy of the photograph until she tossed it into the swamp. Though they'd seen the grainy photo dozens of times, this time they all looked closely, noted the similarity between Wild Will and Rose Thorn—the eyes and eyebrows, the cheeks.

WHEN WHITBY FIRED UP HIS CHAINSAW that Saturday night and began biting into the bark of the grand old willow tree nearest the Boneset Table, the one with the four-foot diameter trunk, he felt so scrambled and confounded and frustrated, he hardly knew what he was doing. He couldn't have said why he had to start cutting any more than he could have said why he'd held onto that kicking, screaming girl for so long. Now Smiley shone a flashlight on Whitby's machine and said, "Maybe that's not a good idea."

"It's the best fucking idea I've ever had," he said.

His inability to do the right thing twelve years ago had poisoned him, and now he knew he could not escape what he'd been running from ever since. Titus Clay Sr. had shown him something true and terrible about men, and Whitby had tried to resist becoming terrible, and now the terrible thing possessing him made sense. Teresa had seen it in him, and that was why she'd left. With his new Stihl chainsaw, with all that beer and liquor in his blood, he embraced his ruin. He had a rattlesnake by the tail and was whipping himself with it, whipping Teresa, whipping Rose Thorn, who had let herself get raped and who, by running away, taught other women to run away too. He stood tall, revving his machine, whipping the whole confounding world.

Ralph Darling and his brother Larry got their chainsaws from the backs of their trucks, and the three men worked together. When Two-Inch Tony felt the momentum of the group tip toward taking action against the tree, he got his Jonsered and fired it up. If Dickmon had been there, this wouldn't have happened. And Titus, with a joke or a funny phrase, would have prevented Whitby from even thinking about it. Smiley and Jamie Standish stood back and observed.

"Maybe Smiley's right, Whitey," Standish said finally, but his voice lacked vigor. He could have left—Smiley too—but they wanted to stay with the tribe, if only to witness the story unfolding. Standish was jealous of the camaraderie between the four men driving their blades into that thick old tree, removing wedge after wedge of the trunk on the swamp side, trying to assure it would fall in that direction. He hadn't known until now how he had been changed by all his rumination about having shot Hermine Zook. He was like the man in war who'd dropped the bomb on a village and who, by that act, had gained a special knowledge of right and wrong. But what could he do? Grab Whitby's chainsaw? Put his body between the man and the tree? That wasn't how men in Whiteheart treated other men. Judging men was God's business. Anyhow, his voice didn't stand a chance against the buzzing of four machines. Might he have afforded Herself the respect, the benefit of the doubt he offered these men now? How about all the other women who had ever confounded him? Could he choose not to judge his wife and daughter? His mother? He felt himself teetering on the cusp of something profound, and the sense of tipping over into it nauseated him.

What had seized Whitby so fitfully, and the others to a lesser degree, exaggerated by alcohol, was a certainty that felling one of the great willows blocking the view of Rose Cottage had always been their dream and desire. Though none had realized it until tonight. After about forty minutes of work from various angles, the seventy-five-foot black willow creaked and groaned like the oldest giant in the Waters being roused. All the men marveled at the power being unleashed. To keep up his courage, Whitby had to pause to take another drink. Too late, the men understood that the tree might not fall the way Whitby intended, since the life in a tree, like the soul in a person, is not fully knowable. The tree could fall in any direction, across the road, on the men, on their trucks. Though they'd done their drunken work that evening without consideration of God's plan for the tree, only their own whims, they all whispered, awestruck, out into the darkness, "God, don't kill us. Please, God, let Thy will be done, but spare us!" All six men gave themselves over to God's will as they ran down the road alongside the pasture where Triumph and Aster stood alert. The tree cracked and crunched and plummeted toward the swamp, and the men were breathless, electrified with God's greatness and how it coincided with their own boldness. The giant tree landed in the swamp channel with an earth-shattering crash and a slush and a suck and a shudder, as they told themselves they'd known it would. Because it did not crush any of their trucks or their tools, didn't even take out the bridge or the power line connecting the island to the grid, the men felt reassured that God must be on their side.

The asses in the field absorbed the quaking of the earth and froze with their muscles clenched, listened to learn if this was the end. The six-month-old donkey fetus—now weighing about eleven pounds—shuddered and shifted for the first time in Aster's belly. Turtles stiffened in their winter tombs and waited. Woodchucks and rabbits shivered in underground caverns. Coyotes yipped across the Waters. Under the kitchen floorboards, the Lindworm twisted and writhed and fell away from the drainpipe as her world vibrated. Donkey awoke in terror on the kitchen floor. Without turning on any lights, she opened the kitchen door and slipped onto the porch unseen. She'd gone to sleep with her body still trembling, thrilled at being held by Whitby, made hyperalert by the smell and feel and easy strength of the man. From the porch, she heard the men cheering into the cold night and saw the top of the giant tree stretched a quarter of the way across the swamp channel, just east of and parallel to the bridge. Donkey sneaked down to the dark bridge in bare feet, listening to the men's footsteps and voices across the way. She couldn't calm her heart. She listened for Titus's admonishment of the men. He must be waiting, she thought, for the best moment to appear, to speak up, to make sense of this, to put the situation to rights.

Donkey went back inside to check on Herself and found her still asleep on her back, her timeworn face peaceful, her hand and stump moving rhythmically as though knitting. It was as though no happenings in this world—not even something so close to where she lay—could touch her anymore.

"LET'S TAKE ANOTHER ONE DOWN!" Larry Darling barked, but nobody joined in, and soon the men fired up their trucks and, one by one, drove away. Whitby was the first to leave, peeling out and fishtailing to get away from the scene of the crime, his new Stihl saw (its chain dull now) bouncing around in the bed of his truck. He didn't dare think about the meaning or the effect of what he'd done but focused instead on the grandness of the act. No denying he'd done something big, in the face of all in the world that belittled him. No matter that he felt awful, worse than before. No matter that he imagined women crushed under the tree, calling out for any good man to save them. He reached under the seat and pulled out another pint of blackberry brandy.

Standish was the last to leave. His stomach and esophagus burned as he leaned against his truck. When the others were out of sight, he fell to his knees and puked up a watery mess of what he'd drunk that evening. He feared he would never make restitution for his crimes against the women of the island, for he, too, had thrilled at the toppling of the tree.

He prayed to Mother Mary, guardian of trees and flowers: "I'm sorry! Forgive me, Holy Mother." And he imagined forgiveness washing over him, as Jesus's forgiveness never had.

IN THE MORNING, when Donkey came outside, she trembled at how the landscape had changed, at how clearly she could see Boneset now, and, more frighteningly, how the island was laid open to the gaze of the people of Nowhere. The trunk of the willow tree stretched like the beginning of another bridge between Boneset and Rose Cottage. Donkey blinked herself awake into a new way that M'sauga Island could be ruined: men could erect their own bridges across the swamp channel, so they could come and go as they pleased.

When Molly saw the tree down, she called the police, who came and took pictures, but nothing else happened. Molly also discussed the matter with Titus, who admonished Whitby and then Standish and Smiley when he found them at the Muck Rattler. That evening, he came to the island and stood with tight lips and a hard jaw that wouldn't soften.

"I think those guys were just blowing off steam, but that was a bad thing they did," he said. "That willow won't even be good firewood."

Donkey shrugged like she didn't care. She didn't know why the men would do what they had done, and she couldn't enjoy the confusion of it the way her mother might have, but she didn't want the men punished. She just wanted them to go back to being nice, fun, the way they were when Rose Thorn was there.

"But maybe you ought to bolt that door at night, just in case," Titus said, nodding at the two-by-four above the kitchen door. "Will you do that for me?"

Donkey nodded, afraid of what he might do or say to the men. He took the two-by-four down and made sure she knew how to fit it into the brackets. He showed her how the door couldn't open into the kitchen with it engaged. Before he left, he said, "And you be sure to pull the bridge up after I leave."

She was relieved when the men quietly returned the following week to resume their vigil, but she kept her distance from them. They behaved better after that, with the downed tree always serving as a reminder of their worst selves.

At this time, a flood of notes requesting cures came to the Boneset Table, as if the women in Whiteheart, upon learning about the downed tree, feared that the island would no longer be a source of healing, and they bought anything Donkey put out, stocking up for the future.

Unbeknownst to Donkey or the people of Whiteheart, on New Year's Eve Lorena called Titus to tell him she was pregnant, had been since June, and to ask did he want one more chance? The following week, Lorena quietly returned to Whiteheart and moved back in with Titus, and together they attended Sunday services at the New Directions Church. While her pregnancy was joyful news to the members of the congregation, it also meant the people of Whiteheart had all reached the end of a book they had been reading for years—some of them, their whole lives—the great romance they'd known firsthand. Now people knew for sure they'd been made fools of.

CHAPTER SIXTEEN

Rose Thorn always goes away.

N FACT, ROSE THORN hadn't left Whiteheart at all. She hadn't fled by car or plane or river ferry or even on foot but had remained right there in the swamp, brumating the way snakes, turtles, and frogs do to survive the winter, keeping still and watchful. She was warm and safe and even nourished, meditating upon her hardworking daughter and her powerful, embittered mothers. No denying it, she had a wealth of mothers—even her daughter mothered her. Fathers were another issue altogether. She meditated on the hurts and pleasures of the people of Whiteheart, too, but mostly she relived every moment she'd spent with Titus; in the absence of other intoxicants, thoughts of him made her lose track of everything else for long periods of time. Though she knew he was unable to see her as a person entirely separate and different from himself, the simplest thoughts of him made the cells in her body hum. He loved her too much to let her die, he'd said, and the whole town loved her too much, and so, like the women in her family, he'd be willing to shackle her to a hospital bed and force a cure on her. As if they all weren't dying!

She didn't *want* to die—far from it. Like the other women in her family, she wanted to save lives—her own included, all things being equal. Her ability to save other people from their rage by simply reflecting their own light back onto them could only be sustained with energy that had to be replenished. By sunshine, by love, by liquor. But she didn't know how to use that power of reflection on herself. She'd saved all her own bitterness for just one person, and she never had to see Titus Sr. again. Her hating one man proved she was capable of hate, and that made her love for the rest of them more meaningful by contrast. Didn't it? Until the cancer, she thought she'd found a balanced way to live.

The tumor was a small rooted truth worthy of contemplation, a knot she needed to untangle, and it told her she needed a new way to live. Each cancer was distinct, unique, the doctor had told her when she was diagnosed. Her cancer was her own, and it had formed slowly, over years. She imagined it woven of strands of the unexpected and inexplicable violence she had endured at Titus Sr.'s hands, strands of what had happened between her and Titus since then, the ups that sustained her and the downs that sent her on the road and into Prim's arms; there were strands of her own confused motherhood, sisterhood, and daughterhood in that fibrous mass. There was the chemical pollution of the swamp, along with her own drinking and smoking.

And one additional poisonous strand: Prim's *adventure*—or whatever it was—with Wild Will at age seventeen. Rose Thorn had long known and accepted that Prim was her mother—after a willful period of refusing to hear that truth. But she hadn't wanted to talk about it, and fatherhood was a big part of why. Of course Wild Will was her father—her paternity was written across her face. But rape would have made more sense to her. If she were a child of rape, then her molestation by another of the town's great fathers could have been part of a family tradition. Prim herself had arrived as a babbling infant in the basket under the Boneset Table. Perhaps her coming into the world had also been the result of a violation too painful for a birth mother to endure. It was harder to comprehend that Rosie herself might have been conceived out of something like love.

Doctors could cut the cancerous knot out of Rosie's breast, but she feared the loose ends that would remain, places where new knots might re-form. Or worse, surgery might release some venom from the serpent inside her and infect the other women near her, infect even her daughter, who accepted all burdens. Throughout that long winter, Rose Thorn let herself stay with these irrational feelings. She knew nobody outside her own body could have followed her along the paths traced by these thoughts. Molly would demand she explain herself and then not listen to her answers before handing her over to the medical authorities. Rose Thorn understood the urgency—Molly wasn't wrong—but to let them cut her open now was to disregard all she felt. Contrary to what everyone thought, having surgery now might be throwing away an opportunity to heal.

The morning she left the island, she walked east along Lovers Road until she found an animal trail leading into the Waters. She followed a ridge of solid ground as far as she could and then crunched through the skim of ice, soaking her canvas tennis shoes, searching for the cave carved into the side of a little hill—surely it was no more than a half mile away from Rose Cottage, as the crow flies. If she could just sit alone awhile, her head would clear, and she would know what to do. Years ago when she'd found the hideout and told Herself about it, Herself referred to it as the Fox Den, though clearly it had been hollowed out by human hands.

The first time Rosie stumbled upon it, many years ago, she thought it looked like a quiet place to sleep off a drunk. But three years ago, she'd gone searching in the Waters again without telling Herself, looking for the ghost bartender who'd silently handed her a pint of brandy on the island. The same gray figure, she was pretty sure, had helped her across the river after Dorothy was born. She'd found the den those two times but had not found it a dozen other times, maybe because she wasn't drunk enough or maybe because the contours of the Waters changed year by year, heaving and sinking and sprouting new maples, white cedars, and ash trees that flourished in the waterlogged soil.

She was looking for a hummock rising out of the wooded swamp. There, she'd twice found a piece of rotting plywood propped against the rough opening in the humped-up earth. She'd pushed aside that crude door and climbed through into a cool room with a dirt floor and walls, a room about eight feet square, a little smaller than the bedroom off the kitchen at Rose Cottage, with a ceiling barely high enough for her to stand. With the help of a flashlight, she'd made out timber rafters interspersed among tree roots. There'd been plenty of evidence of previous habitation: The first time, a musty hardcover book of Kipling's poetry, in which she found the phrase "If you can meet with Triumph and Disaster," which made her laugh for a long time in that echoey little room. That was how she'd learned where the donkeys' names had come from. The next time, her flashlight lit upon *The Old Man and the Sea* with the pages accordioned out with moisture. The first time, there was a stiff flannel shirt draped over a bucket, and the second time, an abandoned canvas chore coat size extra-large hanging on a hook carved from a root. Tin cans of beans and meat were stacked in a corner on a table made of a piece of wood set atop two more buckets. Both times, someone had been there, but not recently.

For years, Rose Thorn had assumed the tall gaunt figure she saw in the Waters was a ghost, because Herself would never allow a man to stay in her swamp. It was only after Prim's assurance that Wild Will was alive that she considered there was one man Herself might allow to stay at precisely that distance from her.

It was after Rose Thorn gave up looking for him and sat on a cold rotting log that the figure appeared in the distance, walking a zigzag path toward her through the forested swamp, looking grayer and thinner than the last time she'd seen him. Perhaps in her fear of freezing to death she had conjured him from swamp grasses, frozen blue clay, and muskrats. She was hugging herself in the insufficient shelter of Titus's army jacket—it wasn't a winter coat—and the sky was pelting her with tiny granular bits of snow.

"Why don't you wear a hat?" he asked in a ghostly voice.

He guided her a short distance to the little hill and through the new plywood door, south-facing, which now had a plexiglass window covered in milky plastic and a handle made from braided and knotted baling twine. Grapevines had been hanging over it as camouflage. The familiar underground room smelled of moldy dirt, but now the ceiling was covered with sheets of tin bolted to the rafters, and new log poles were propped vertically at the sides and in the middle of the room, supporting the ceiling. He invited Rose Thorn to sit on a pallet padded with three folded wool blankets. She took off her wet shoes and sat down. Morning light came through the window in the door and fell on her softly. There were four bricks warming on top of a propane heater, which had a flame she could see through a vent hole in the side. He adjusted the dial, and the flame quivered.

"It warms up in here pretty quick," he said and put two of the bricks in front of her on the floor, inviting her to put her feet on them. He lit an oil lamp with a plastic lighter and then pulled a wooden milk crate into the small circle of light and sat facing her. With her feet on the warming bricks, she wrapped her arms around her knees.

She'd never seen him up close—close enough to see the dirt in the creases around his eyes, fox-colored like hers. It was something like staring at herself in a clouded mirror.

"Looks like you fixed the place up," she said, nodding at a framed botanical print of bloodroot hanging from one of the crude log supports. On the other side of the room was another similar print, but it was too dark to see what it pictured. Boneset, maybe.

"Thought I might make it more habitable. That's why I got this heater, thinking I might stay here for a while."

"Very homey."

"Usually I just come to Whiteheart for a few weeks a year," he said, in no hurry. "But I met your daughter this summer—"

"You stay away from her," Rose Thorn said, her blood pulsing painfully in her fingertips, which had gone white from the cold. "Anyway, she thinks you're a ghost. And so do I."

His laugh in response was like hers. A little reckless.

"Seeing her gave me the idea I might want to stay here. Maybe she needs a grandfather."

"Is that really who you are?"

Smiling, he took off his oily chore coat, rolled up his sleeve, and turned so the lamp lit up his strong, stringy arm: the rose, the rattlesnake, a drop of blood, and a crescent moon.

"Anybody can get one of those." But Rose Thorn couldn't hide the thrill it gave her to see the faded original of Titus's tattoo by flickering lamplight. On his other arm, he revealed a cursive name: *Hermine*. At the sight of that second tattoo, every cell in Rosie's body opened up. She noticed the air was becoming warm, almost comfortable, and the mustiness was fading with the cold.

Before meeting him in person, after a lifetime of hearing about him, Rose Thorn had thought she should condemn him and have a second man to hate, but that wasn't how it felt. It would be hard work to hate him. It worried her that she might not even hate Titus Sr. if she met him under similar circumstances.

"You're my first houseguest," Wild Will said.

"Here's your housewarming gift." She opened her backpack and handed him the slice of mince pie she'd meant to give Titus last night.

Wild Will unwrapped the tinfoil and smelled it before he lifted it like a sandwich and ate it in small bites, very slowly. Halfway through, he offered some to her. She shook her head.

"Herself didn't make it, but Prim says it's her blackbird pie," Rose Thorn said.

"It's good, but it doesn't have her whiskey in it."

"Sorry, Prim and I drank the last of it."

"That's okay. I gave up the booze anyhow," Wild Will said. "A year ago, when I woke up half froze to death in a boxcar in Nebraska. Parked on a siderail. I wish I'd given it up earlier. I'm seventy-six years old now, a little late to start seeing the world clearly."

"My tough luck," she said. It interested her that he was younger than Herself.

"You and Prim should give it up," he said, flattening and folding the tinfoil for reuse, the way Herself always did. "You might be drinking away more than you know." He got up and put the tinfoil with a small collection of pans, pots, and bowls on a table in a shadowy corner of the room, next to what looked like a Coleman camping stove with a single burner. There were four glass jugs of water on the floor nearby.

As Rose Thorn's eyes adjusted, she noticed a little shelf unit nailed crudely together, entirely filled with pint jars and jelly jars. Later she would discover most of these jars were filled with honey. Wild Will sat back down on the milk crate, looking less like the muscled man in the photo in her dresser drawer and more like one of the sinewy rattlesnakes dangling from that man's grip.

"A spirit rises up from the swamp to tell me to give up spirits," Rose Thorn said and laughed. She might give up drinking, but she was not ready to give up the promise of drinking. She liked that he didn't insist on talking too much, liked that there were long silent pauses between everything they both said. If she decided to condemn him, she could do it at her leisure. "I guess I won't come here looking for booze anymore."

"Is it true what your daughter said? You have cancer?"

"What? Did that child tell everybody?"

"She must've figured a ghost could keep a secret. You need to go to the doctor." He didn't seem to notice that he was crying a little.

"I should hate you, but I can't seem to muster it." She moved her feet around on the bricks, which were starting to cool. "It seems pretty shitty what you did with Prim."

"You don't seem like one to judge."

"Maybe now's a good time to start. People in this town might hate you if they knew."

"They might. They might not."

"I can't believe you're so casual about it. Even if it wasn't rape, it was all your fault—you were the adult."

"That's true."

They were both silent for a long time, so long that Rose Thorn thought she would fall asleep sitting up.

"If you're my father, maybe I should ask your fatherly advice."

"Sure. Anything you want to know."

"It's nothing to do with you. Titus asked me to marry him again last night, even though I'm the exact opposite of what he needs. He should hate me, but he loves me."

"You got a problem with a guy loving you? You think you're the only one who gets to love somebody for no reason?" he asked.

They spoke as though Wild Will had always been part of her life, and maybe he had been. Donkey had said, "You have Wild Will, even if he's gone." And she was right: Even the absent father was the father, after all. The empty father's house was still the father's house. Herself could have torn that big house down, but she hadn't.

He took away the cooled bricks and brought her two warmer ones. When she took off her wool socks and put her bare white feet on them, he said, "Don't burn yourself," and fetched a piece of canvas to put between her skin and the clay.

"My daughter should hate me too," Rose Thorn said. "I can't even look her in the eye, I feel so guilty about leaving her. I feel like every-body in this town should hate me." She was surprised at how easy it was to say anything in this underground place. "They're all about motherhood, and I couldn't mother my child. I still can't. They're all about hard work, and I just can't work like they do. They're all about God, and I don't believe in God."

"You are what you are." He shrugged. "Maybe they all appreciate that."

"I'm not, though. I'm not what I am. I'm just pieces of whatever I am. Every time I'm around Titus, I dissolve. Herself crushes me. Prim's just as bad. Even my daughter tears me to pieces. I swear I have to sleep fourteen hours a day just to regain some semblance of myself."

"Sleep is medicine," he said. "Herself always said so. Everything she said turns out to be true. She cursed me to live as a woman. For twenty-eight years I cursed her back and stayed drunk. Now I'm interested. She finally got my attention. What's that mean, *live as a woman*? Here's my latest effort." He fetched two books from the side of the pallet away from the heater and handed them to her: *To the Lighthouse* and *Madame Bovary*. "Not really my cup of tea."

"One of those is written by a man," Rose Thorn said and laughed. It felt good to laugh. She kept hold of both books.

"Maybe living like a woman means I should take care of you," he said.

"It's a little late for that, isn't it?"

"Maybe not. Do you think Herself wants to see me?"

Rose Thorn laughed long and loud, until she felt dirt cascade from the wall, until she remembered about the whiskey. Herself had said she was saving it for him. And hadn't Herself smiled at the news that Wild Will was alive?

"I wish I could protect her," Rose Thorn said. She thought he must not know that somebody had shot Herself. "From what people think."

He nodded. "I'd like to see Molly too. You know I've visited Prim a few times in Laguna Beach to apologize. She's forbidden me from seeing you. She said I'd upset you."

"She's forbidden me from doing lots of things. I do most of them anyway. Watch out for Molly or she'll tie you to a bed and torture you like she did me," Rose Thorn said. After a while, she added, "In her defense, she was trying to help me. I'm not easy to help."

"Women do hold a grudge," he said.

IT TOOK A FULL DAY IN THE FOX DEN, sitting beside the heater with its comforting blue flame for Rose Thorn's feet and fingers to turn pink again. She didn't ask, but Wild Will assured her the heater was safe, that the fumes exhausted out a pipe that disappeared into the ceiling. She figured out that anything she put on the flat top of the heater dried quickly.

Wild Will went out that night, and Rose Thorn slept without dreams on a camping pad atop the pallets in a tangle of the three wool blankets. In the morning, light came in through the plastic on the window, and Wild Will returned with a store-bought bottle of cranberry juice and a plate of rabbit he'd roasted on a charcoal fire outside. Rose Thorn refused the meat but took the juice from his hand. Then he sat down on his milk crate again, using her face as a mirror as she'd done with him last night.

"After thirty years," he said, "seems like Herself would at least want to talk to me."

Rose Thorn laughed, though she shouldn't have. "Your own daughter, Daddy!"

"She was my *step*daughter. Not my flesh and blood, not Hermine's either. And I didn't really know her before she came to live with me." He said this calmly, must have gone over and over his reasoning. "Even Molly, my blood daughter, I hardly saw her. Doesn't Herself still hide your daughter away from everyone else?"

"Titus is like you. Very focused on the begetting. The technical aspects of fatherhood. As you know, Herself is all about the raising."

"Your daughter looks like that family, you know."

"See how you are?" Rosie shook her head. She cracked open the cranberry juice, which emitted a little puff of air. "My daughter happens to be a gift from God."

"Thought you didn't believe in God."

"How *could* I believe in a God who uses a devil to deliver a gift?" She took a long drink, but the juice was too cold and shrank her insides. She put it on top of the heater next to the bricks and watched Wild Will eat. He ate the meat with the same intensity as Herself, only he didn't use silverware. He crunched through the rabbit bones with his teeth instead of using a little hammer to break them. "I suppose you think a rapist has rights to his offspring."

"I didn't say that. And I'm sorry about what happened to you. Prim told me you won't say who it was. But maybe fathers do want to help out, even terrible fathers." He paused and held out a piece of meat on a delicate bone. "Sure you don't want some of this? There's a fork here somewhere."

"You know people here still talk about you all the time." Rose Thorn glanced over to where the pots and pans were kept. She knew there was an artesian well outside, knew he could warm water in a pan by putting it on the Coleman stove or the heater. Did he do dishes and laundry in a bucket? "They'll probably have a parade for you when they hear you're alive."

"I'd rather you didn't tell anybody I'm here," Wild Will said.

" 'All the proud fathers are ashamed to go home,' " Rose Thorn said. "Somebody said that. You know people are going to see you if you stay," she said. "Maybe they've already seen you."

"If they do, they don't trust their eyes. The night clerks in the beer store over in Potawatomi know me as a hobo. I told them I sleep under a bridge."

"So I'm finally meeting the troll." Rose Thorn laughed. "I knew it was real."

He laughed, too, and wiped his mouth on a dirty worn-out cloth napkin that matched the checked blue ones from the cottage. He must've swiped it from their clothesline. "I don't interest anybody, not like this. There are all kinds of folks other folks don't see. Maybe if you stop being beautiful, they won't see you either."

"Nobody sees you here because they're afraid of Herself." She let his last comment sink in. It would happen eventually if she survived her cancer: her looks would fade with time, and she would have to find another way of being in the world. And Herself was not so fearsome as she used to be, and even the old painted skull-and-crossbones signs all around the Waters were fading away. That would mean more change; people might start trespassing, poking around.

When Wild Will finished eating, he wrapped what was left of the rabbit bones in the tinfoil and tucked them away, to dump them out in the Waters later, away from the Fox Den.

"I used to regret what happened between Prim and me, but I don't anymore. I'm looking at you and seeing something beautiful. You remind me of my young handsome self."

"Fuck you," Rose Thorn said. How dare he take pride in her. At the idea of Titus Clay Sr. taking pride in Dorothy, a wave of nausea moved through her. She could keep her daughter hidden away on the island, but she couldn't protect the girl from what she was made of. Rose Thorn's own body was the scene of two crimes, and there was nothing here to distract her from that sickening truth. She couldn't even look off into the distance, because she couldn't see through the milky plastic on the window. If both Wild Will and Titus Clay Sr. had not been terrible men, her daughter, with all her genius, wouldn't be in the world.

She picked up one of the Osage oranges she'd found beside the pallet bed last night—they were in the cottage too, to repel insects—and held it to her nose to smell the bitter citrus. This was how you could give a brute the high ground, by allowing that the issue of such a crime—the beautiful child—mitigated the crime. How could a woman accept the gift and not be a little grateful to the giver? No one like her daughter had ever existed, Rose Thorn was sure, and the family's need for the girl's peculiar and particular brilliance could not be overstated. Not for a moment could she imagine a world without Dorothy. This certainty, along with her love for her child, made her feel complicit in the pain the man had inflicted on her. Or maybe because of Rose Thorn's hatred of Titus Sr. there was a part of her that had resisted fully embracing her daughter, even as she loved Titus, another child of the rapist, without reservation.

She threw the Osage orange at Wild Will, and it hit him in the chest. Though he'd seen it coming, he hadn't lifted his hands or turned away to protect himself. He coughed out a breath and held his hand over his heart.

After a long while she asked, "With all your love of begetting, have you got any idea who Prim's parents are?"

He soberly shook his head no. Then, after considering the question, he laughed. "Royalty, I imagine. Almost certainly."

THE NEXT MORNING, Rose Thorn asked if she could stay. She didn't want to leave the Fox Den until she figured something out, and she felt safer there than on the island, where the women in her family had the power to make her doubt her own mind. Both father and daughter were allergic to explaining themselves, and neither put any demands on the other. Both preferred to live for the day as it unfolded, and so neither thought to get a message to those who might be worried. And they quickly found a routine that suited them both.

Wild Will slept on the pallet during the day, on his back, dead to the world except for his snoring. He did his fishing and hunting and swamp-crossing at night, while Rosie slept on the pallet. He returned every morning with food and drink and sometimes a twenty-pound tank of propane. During the day, Rosie took the plastic off the window to feel the morning sunshine on her face, and he slept on. By sunlight and by the light of the oil lamp, she reread *Madame Bovary* and *To The Lighthouse*. She came to love the middle part of *Lighthouse*, in which the house is empty of bodies and conversations for ten years, gently decaying and gathering dust. Didn't houses—and people— need to just sit after all that had happened to them and inside them, to prepare for what would next transpire? How long would Wild Will's house have to stay empty after what had happened there between him and Prim for it to be ready for something new? Was her daughter's sneaking into the Boneset House part of the something new?

As for Emma Bovary's compulsive desires and poor mothering, Rosie felt an awful sympathy.

She wished she had *My Ántonia* with her; the Shimerda family lived in a space even more primitive than this dirt room and without a good heater. She wanted her Oz books, too, but there was also a pleasure in being away from them, in hoping she would return and read them again.

Wild Will had stored black walnuts and hickory nuts, wild rice, and dried fruits inside various jars and buckets to keep critters out of them, and he prepared and cooked the animals he killed, using many of the skills he'd learned from his wife. This summer he'd found some abandoned honeybee hives near the gun club, but he hadn't had proper straining equipment, so the product he'd put into the jars was dirty (the jars weren't very clean either), but it tasted good, and he had a lot of it. Rose Thorn was surprised at the variety of blood-colored juices he brought her to drink, some from the store (cherry, cran- berry, once pomegranate!) and others homemade (tomato and grape) with seeds, though he couldn't have canned them himself—not here anyhow. Without other people or coffin nails to distract her, Rosie found she was hungrier; she started eating some of Wild Will's preserved fruits and then some sharp cheese he bought. He offered her a bottle of vitamin pills one day, a caretakerly gesture she thought hilarious. Of course, she realized, this was probably his way of reminding her of her cancer, something he'd promised not to bring up.

She warmed up a pot of water from the artesian spring outside every evening to wash up and brush her teeth, and she washed her articles of clothing one at a time when they needed it, drying them by the heater. On the island, her daughter had washed her clothes in the wringer washer, and she'd always felt guilty about it, and about all that her daughter did for her. If her daughter asked little of her in return, what she did ask felt impossible: stay in Whiteheart and marry Titus.

One morning Wild Will showed up with a small milk goat, white and brown, and said they could make their own cheese. His hands turned out to be way too big for the dwarf's teats, and he was surprised that Rose Thorn didn't know how to milk. Their fumbling first efforts frustrated the poor nanny, whom Rose Thorn named Scraps, after the patchwork girl in Oz. They never did make cheese, but Rose Thorn drank the milk she could extract into a saucepan and slept with her arms around the creature; though it grazed outside all day, she insisted it come inside at night. By some miracle, the goat rarely urinated in the Fox Den, preferring to do so outside, and Rose Thorn swept up the berries of goat manure every morning and tossed them onto a compost pile. Sometimes she dressed in Wild Will's insulated clothes and oversaw the goat's grazing.

In the Waters, there were areas that never froze, and a goat could make breakfast, lunch, and dinner from bushes and swamp plants and a little supplemental feed. Maybe it was the light through the leafless trees while she was outside with the goat or maybe it was the solid food; in any case, despite the cold, Rose Thorn began to feel better. Her cravings for booze were gone. She still craved coffin nails, but since Wild Will wouldn't buy them for her, that craving was weakening its hold on her. She'd gained some weight while living at Rose Cottage, probably from her daughter's infusions of cream and honey, plus eggnog, and now she could no longer button or even zip her jeans. She wished Molly could see her.

Wild Will's compulsion was toward work and improvement, and with Rose Thorn there, he found reason to make the place nicer—

installing bricks in the floor a few at a time, almost all the way through the room, excavating dirt at the back to create an alcove for the pallet. He found some abandoned wooden fencing near the brick pile and constructed a low-lying Moon Palace nearby. This industrious man, after all, was the template for all the hardworking men of Whiteheart.

AS WEEKS TURNED INTO MONTHS, Rose Thorn's body finally revealed to her the secret it had been keeping. The noise inside her became audible and then grew louder and more insistent than the imperceptible gnawing at her breast. It was a stretching and swelling in her belly, the explanation for her new hunger. She realized what had been growing there since this summer, what she'd assumed was the cancer or indigestion.

She meditated through the horror, moved through the dread, and gathered herself up to a kind of numbing acceptance of what a pregnancy could mean. She had to tell Titus. More than anything, he'd wanted his own child, and now, despite their precautions, his will had been done. She thought of their wedding ceremony in the stone circle on the island, the grass ring on his finger. A nauseating euphoria crept into her. This child could have a father, a good father, who would care for and protect and raise up his child. Titus's love was powerful, and for a child of his own, that love would be unconditional. Rose Thorn knew Herself wanted a babby, would never stop wanting a babby, but her reign was coming to an end. Rosie would give the baby to Titus and surrender herself in the bargain. She would marry him the way he had always wanted and live with him at the farm. By doing so, she would also give Donkey what she wanted—a family with Titus at its head. Dorothy would go to school, and Molly would be relieved; Prim would have to stop complaining about Titus if they were married. Peace would reign. As she worked her way through these possibilities, she felt often in her pocket for the amber Titus had given to her, the reassuring warm stone.

Hadn't this been the direction she'd been headed all along? Wasn't this the melodramatic turn in the story of Titus and Rose Thorn that people had been waiting for? Ask anybody in Whiteheart. She would deliver this child to Titus, even if it killed her. All the better if it killed her, for the town could use a martyr who was a mother instead of a

soldier. Baba Rose, who had died for these people—died from knowing them too well—had almost been forgotten. Rosie hoped Dorothy
could forgive her for dying, if it came to that.

Regardless, Titus's child would be loved and favored in a thousand
ways, maybe even by Titus Sr., that blind ghost, if he had the nerve
to visit from Florida. No doubt he would love his long-anticipated
grandchild. Rose Thorn feared she would not be able to sustain her
hatred of him if that happened. She marveled at how her body had
worked contrary to her intentions.

Maybe there was even a way of trading in her pumpkin head for
something more solid, a head full of the kind of sense Titus needed
in a wife. She could imagine the wedding feast—the party to end all
parties, the whole town rejoicing! In these months underground, she'd
missed other people. She was tired of ruminating; it didn't suit her. The
momentum of that party and the presence of Titus would carry her
along so she wouldn't have to think too much about it. While she was
pregnant, they would not make her get cancer treatment—even Molly
wouldn't force radiation or chemotherapy on her until after the birth.

One cold midnight she put her few belongings in her backpack,
plus a jar of the dirty swamp-flower honey as a gift for her daughter. She bundled up as best she could and sneaked away while Wild
Will was out on his nighttime rounds, checking his fishing and trap
lines. She left a note telling him she was going to Titus. She walked
the now familiar path through the swamp back to Lovers Road, imagining the arms into which she would let herself fall; she would not
resist but would give herself entirely to Titus and his vision and their
life together.

When Smiley's van pulled out of the dark parking lot of the Muck
Rattler, she hid in the ditch. This time she needed to see Titus before
seeing anybody else. She cut through the field behind Wild Will's house
to avoid being seen by the men gathered at Boneset—Titus was not
among them. She continued another mile and a half on feet growing
numb with cold, until she passed the peach orchard. In the driveway of
Ada McIntyre's house, which Titus had moved into after Ada's death,
she saw Lorena's retired police cruiser with its Texas license plate, the
striped blanket covering the front seat, the rosary beads hanging off
the rearview mirror. Rose Thorn walked over the glazed snow to the

shoveled walkway leading to the back steps. She peered through the glass of the storm door, through the porch, all the way into the kitchen, where she saw the fluorescent light of Ada's gleaming white electric Kalamazoo stove. Under a blue-and-white dishcloth on top of the stove was something the shape and size of a pie. On the porch, she saw something else, an old-fashioned wooden crib. Inside it were plush toy animals and a crocheted blue-and-yellow blanket.

She moved silently back to the driveway, got into Lorena's car on the passenger side. The key was in the ignition. On the floor she found a flattened pack of Pall Malls that looked empty but had one coffin nail left in it. Pinned up in the visor, she found a business card, and in the dome light she read the name and address of an obstetrician in Grand Rapids. She turned on the key, pushed in the car's lighter, and when it popped out, she lit the coffin nail on the glowing orange coil. She let the cab fill with curls and coils and finally a solid fog of poison. She smoked the thing down to its butt and crushed it out in the car's clean metal ashtray.

Her feet were like blocks of ice as she walked back along the road to the Boneset Table. The men were gone now, but they'd left a few empty bottles. (If there'd been any liquor remaining, she would have drunk it.) Their heavy footsteps had worn through the snow to reveal the mosaic of stones and shells and glass. She studied the men's grand work, the downed willow tree, which revealed the windows of Rose Cottage to anyone on the road. There was enough moonlight reflecting off the snow to show her that the bridge planks had been taken up, so she couldn't slip across and into her old bed. The cold of the earth was moving up into her knees, making them stiff.

There were a half dozen jars of medicine on the Boneset Table, mostly herbal teas, and no waters or eggs left out overnight to freeze. Like everybody else, she assumed the fixes were Hermine's work. Under the table, on its hook, was the Babby Basket, still waiting, with its knitted blanket made of soft orange wool. She wouldn't deliver a child to curse Titus in his new life; she wouldn't bring another child to the island to be raised by Herself in old age, however much Herself wanted one. She wouldn't put that burden on Dorothy or displace her daughter as the youngest and most precious. It was not fair to bring forth a life to serve as a bridge across a deep gulch. She would ask

Herself for what she needed one more time. Nobody in this world had a right to more of her than she could bear to give. If she could get out of this mess alive, she would take the energy and expense that she might have spent on a new child and spend it trying to better care for the child she had.

She found the jelly jar of honey in her pack and unscrewed the lid, then took from her pocket the gold-flecked amber, which she pushed into the cold, thick honey, so Herself would know who had sent the message. Then she worked to pry up from the mosaic in the frozen ground the object she needed. When it wouldn't come free, she lay on the ground and breathed on it to melt the frozen surface. She wiped the cuntshell in the snow and then sucked it clean. She pressed the cream-colored shell against her throat in hopes that it would speak for her, and then she stuck it into the honey in the jar and replaced the lid. She put the jar in the basket under the table, covered it with the orange blanket. If Herself ignored the request, Rosie would come back and beg in person.

Rose Thorn's feet were bluish when she returned to the Fox Den, and it would take a full day of hot bricks for them to regain circulation. Wild Will returned after she did, at dawn, and was unaware that she had gone out or that she went out each night after that to check the Boneset Table for the medicine she needed.

CHAPTER SEVENTEEN

We love best those for whom we suffer most.

ONKEY FOUND THE JAR of honey in the Babby Basket—a curious place to find food—and opened it that morning, because they had run out. She was used to honey that was cleaned and strained, and she didn't know who would have given them this dirty honey with shredded bits of honeycomb visible through the glass, along with a few crushed bees, and something like powdery pollen. She and Titus had harvested honey this summer, as usual, from Hermine's hives behind the barn, and Donkey had added it to everything her mother drank, and now it was gone. The cream too—pails of it had gone to sustain Rose Thorn instead of being made into butter they could freeze for when Delilah was dried up.

Donkey unscrewed the lid and dug her spoon into the honey. Only then did she see that stuck in that viscous stuff was a terrible object the size of the tip of a finger, creamy white, humped on top, and curled in on itself as if holding a secret in its ridged underbelly. Something she'd promised Titus she wouldn't bring to the island. Herself straightened her spine as if sensing the presence of the object in her kitchen, and Donkey quickly put the whole spoonful of honey into her mouth. She meant to hold the cuntshell there until she could spit it out in private and carry it back to the Boneset Table, where she would embed it in the ground with the others she'd never delivered to Herself.

"What's that?" Hermine's hand snaked out to grab Donkey's

arm. All morning she'd been moving slowly, but suddenly she was like quicksilver.

"Honeycomb," Donkey said and swallowed. Swallowed as easily as she'd swallowed a rattlesnake tail from the bottom of a whiskey bottle, as easily as she'd swallowed the snake blood licked off her wrist. Herself watched Donkey carefully as she drank some water to unstick the thing, but it caught and stuck again and again as it traveled down her throat. She took a big bite of unbuttered toast and swallowed that.

"I'm not crying, ma'am," she choked. "I just got something sweet in my throat."

What she saw next in the honey, what she might have scooped up in her next spoonful, was her mother's gold-flecked amber stone. She put the lid on the jar and let her heart pound down.

"Is that how you're going to eat honey now?" Herself asked, smiling. "Like a bear with a spoon?"

THAT NIGHT, DONKEY DIDN'T SIT QUIETLY and squeeze her biceps as Herself would have done upon receiving such a request. She didn't wait for a ghost or a dream to tell her what the souls involved needed. Donkey's dreams since the tree had come down were great swirling affairs filled with paths and secret passageways and bridges and stairs up and down. When the women of her family appeared in these dreams, they were trolls under the bridge, Lindworms in caboodles, grotesque figures in hidey-holes, and they spoke animal languages she no longer understood. She didn't share Rose Thorn's request or let it move through her but held onto it the way her belly held onto that cuntshell.

Her mother was alive and nearby. And her mother was pregnant. Like Delilah. Like Aster, who was just starting to show. Unlike those animals, though, Rose Thorn wanted to get rid of what she carried, just as she'd wanted to get rid of Donkey.

Donkey was certain she knew better than Rose Thorn, knew better than to end a life that could bring Rose Thorn and Titus together, all of them together at last. Donkey also thought she knew better than Herself, who had continued collecting poisons that Donkey had to dispose of, though the poisons seemed to be more carefully selected now and gathered in smaller amounts. Donkey would not give her mother a medicine to end a baby, but she was afraid if she put nothing out in response to her request, Rose Thorn would simply turn to Primrose. Donkey needed to put out something that would bring her mother home. What Donkey concocted was made to deceive—was maybe her greatest deception so far.

Donkey's fix contained no fringed rue, no celery seed, no pennyroyal, no bloodroot, no venom or antivenom. It contained nothing that would kill or diminish anybody, neither baby nor mother. Instead, she put in peppermint, chamomile, and lavender—masculine herbs—and also included strands of Wild Will's bathrobe and one of Titus's hairs, all of which would assure her mother would give birth to a baby boy. The last thing Donkey added was her own blood, tinged with the snake's. She put it all in a clamshell lined with a length of snake shed, which was how the fix for start-the-bleeding was always delivered. Though Herself would have simply sealed the clamshell with paraffin, Donkey also used a little duct tape. She wanted Rose Thorn to think Herself had made the medicine, so she wrote no note. She wrapped the clamshell in the orange blanket, set it in the Babby Basket, and hung the basket on its hook.

Donkey wrapped herself in all her blankets that night and slept on the screen porch despite the late January temperatures falling into the teens, but her mother's light footsteps didn't awaken her. In the morning, the clamshell was gone, the wool blanket tangled. Instead of waking Herself and making breakfast, Donkey ran down the road toward Ada McIntyre's house. Though Titus's name was on the mailbox now, though Ada had been buried more than six months, Donkey still didn't see it as Titus's house. She hadn't seen Titus for almost two weeks now. She would tell him that Rose Thorn was having a baby, his baby, that they could be married. Finally.

Ada's house was lit up, but Donkey heard a tractor rumbling farther down the road, so she kept going past the barn, toward the cranberry bog on the north side of the road, a flat watery place she had visited often when she was younger to talk to frogs and to try to catch a glimpse of Titus. Ada and her grandson Alan couldn't harvest the bitter berries with machines but had to do it by hand while pumps churned the water. From the time she was six, Donkey had helped with the work, a thrilling several hours during which water and red

berries splashed around her knees. Ada had let her take as many cranberries as she and Herself could preserve with sugar.

She now saw Titus a few hundred yards away on his old Ford 8N,
which he used for moving dirt and snow. The machine was choking
out thick white exhaust as it chugged atop what used to be the bog
but was now solid ground dotted with hillocks. All those truckloads of
bank run gravel, two or three loads a day throughout the summer and
into October, had been dumped near the road. In the dim morning
light, Titus had his back blade down and was dragging the gravel off
one of dozens of mounds and spreading it out over the bog.

Donkey hadn't been down here since Ada died, and she was stunned
by how the whole landscape had changed. What used to be part of
the Waters, a lowland cove that was flooded more than half the time,
was now part of a great flattened field, strewn with clumps of frozen
sand and thawed mud. Snow still covered the ground elsewhere, but
the bog mud, below the gravel, warmed the surface so it didn't freeze
entirely, and the snow was melted across much of it, revealing the
harrowed ground. It looked to Donkey like the surface of the moon,
238,900 miles away. What remained of the bog was now a hundred
yards farther out, where the native highbush cranberries still grew.

When Titus saw Donkey, he waved and drove to meet her. He got
down off the faded red machine.

"You're up early, String Bean." He was looking tall and strong in a
new black winter-weight Carhartt jacket. He was infused with some
new grandness, as though he were the king of something. "Your
granny okay?"

"What are you doing?" Donkey asked, approaching cautiously.

"Lorena and I are going to bring in some topsoil and grow a big garden here, put in a crop of celery and see what happens. Won't that be
something to see, acres of it here? Celery after all these years!"

"You and Lorena?" Donkey asked, her chest constricting.

"She's been back a few weeks, String Bean. We got married yesterday at the courthouse. I was going to tell you when I saw you next.
We'll have a big wedding in the summer, but for now we just wanted
to make it legal for the baby."

Donkey's eyes opened wide, and she had to blink away the cold.

"When she left at the end of June," Titus said, "she was pregnant.

She's giving me one last chance. I can't blow it this time. She and I'd been talking about planting a celery field for a long time, and now it's happening."

He reached out to muss Donkey's hair, but she stepped back out of reach. Her hand went rubbery and she dropped the amber on the ground. She quickly picked it up and wiped it on her jacket. She held the warm stone out to him.

"You said you'd pray for Rose Thorn to come back."

"I pray for her every night. For her safe return and for her soul. I pray for her to be delivered home, one way or another." Titus looked briefly at and then away from the stone he'd given to Rose Thorn.

"What if Rose Thorn wants to have a baby?" Donkey said. How could he not notice how the warm stone was glowing like something alive? "Then you could marry her."

"I'm married now." Titus took her hand in his and squeezed it around the stone. "Don't look at me like that. You know I've looked for your mama and waited for her. I've turned myself inside out, but she doesn't want to be with me. We tried and tried and couldn't make it work. Nobody ever tried as hard as your mama and me, but she's let me know she wants to be free."

"But she always comes back." Rose Thorn could show up dead in the swamp for all his prayer specified. "Do you love Lorena more than you love her?"

"I love them both. Just like you love both your granny and your mama. And your mama's left us, so we have to take care of them who stay. I'm worn out, String Bean. I can't wait this time. My responsibility is to my baby and to Lorena." He let his gaze fall upon the ravaged acres beside them. "And I think this will be for the best. Please don't cry."

"I just have something cold in my eyes."

If Rose Thorn stayed gone for a hundred years, Donkey would still miss her and hope for her to come back. So would Herself and Prim and Molly. She squeezed her mother's heart and put it into her pocket.

"It's what I've always wanted, String Bean, to be a dad. What do you think of that? Due in April. Before Delilah, I guess."

"But you're supposed to be my dad," she said. As the palindrome spilled with her breath into the cold air, she realized her mistake in saying it aloud.

"Oh, I wish I was. You know I've always wished I was."

She wanted to protest, but it was too late. Until now her certainty of his becoming her father at some future date had been something she'd held aloft by wishing and hoping. Titus couldn't deny a thing she hadn't said. Saying it brought her world crashing down. Like Herself getting shot and then shackled at the hospital, like Rose Thorn's cancer, like Ozma's ravaged carcass. Her conviction about Titus was a coin she'd kept in the air, and it had just landed on out-of-luck. Her and Titus's wishing together hadn't been strong enough. She doubted he'd wished as hard as she had. In one fell swoop, his freckles were no longer her freckles. His big ears were not her ears, no matter the resemblance. Professor A. Schweiss was a fool to put stock in an imaginary number; just because you needed a thing didn't mean you could just make it up. Donkey would sink that book in the swamp.

"String Bean, are you okay? We're still friends, aren't we?"

The sun was losing its pink color, going gray-white behind her, lighting up the mess Titus had made of Ada's beautiful bog. Donkey's life seemed less safe than it had a minute ago. She could have yelled Titus's name all night, and he wouldn't have saved her from Whitby. Or a bullet or anything else.

She should have been glad to know the truth once and for all, but she felt wrecked and alone, too tall and unsteady—nothing like Titus's big solid figure. She took another step back and tripped a little. When she looked down at what had grabbed her, she saw a coiled mess of something like cable or rope, but it was a tangle of snaking roots snagged and torn apart by the tractor's back blade. And before her, upside down, was not a chunk of wood as she'd first thought, but a frozen map-of-the-world turtle with a gravel-scuffed plastron. She tipped it over with the toe of her boot to find its shell cracked all the way across and guts coming out its back. Titus was always saying, *Thou shalt not kill.* If he was with Lorena, Rose Thorn would not be protected either. If she had a baby, it would be his *responsibility*, but a man in Whiteheart couldn't have two wives.

"Are you okay, String Bean?"

As Donkey turned to run, her feet sank into the stony sand. As though she'd grown heavier since trekking out here, each step threatened to sink her. When she got back to the pavement, she looked back at her sunken footsteps and wondered how many dead animals lay trapped beneath these thousands of tons of fill dirt, how many had been crushed and were dead forever, for all ∞, in their dens and burrows: turtles, muskrats, snakes, frogs, ground-nesting birds. How many animals would not emerge in spring? For Titus, she'd been reading the Bible. For him, she'd endured its terrible stories of women ruining paradise—Delilah, Salome, Jezebel, Eve, Lot's daughters. Women around here might run away from paradise, might not even see that it was paradise, but it wasn't women who ruined it.

Titus waved goodbye and climbed back onto his dieseling machine, and Donkey saw another way that her island could be destroyed. The people of Whiteheart could dump gravel down the bank until the swamp channel was filled, and then they could just walk across the Waters— there wouldn't even be an island there anymore.

She returned to the donkey pasture, to Disaster, beginning to swell in pregnancy. Everybody was pregnant. Rose Thorn should come back and be pregnant with them, to hell with Titus. Aster let herself be hugged and nuzzled by the girl whose life she'd saved so long ago. After a brief hesitation, Donkey embraced Triumph too.

When it began to snow, Donkey ventured up the long driveway to Wild Will's house and unlocked the kitchen door with the key she kept in her front pocket. She'd visited every few days since the first time she'd gone inside. She now searched the dark high-ceilinged rooms for Rose Thorn or the ghost. While she sat at the dining room table with its ornately carved legs, she imagined she could feel the soft snow falling on the roof. She wished she could replace the plywood with glass so she could see the flakes falling. According to A. Schweiss, snowflakes were always hexagonal, but Donkey had inspected enough of them to know they weren't perfectly symmetrical. Molly had stopped talking about them moving into the Boneset House, but Donkey still wondered if there was a way she could live in two houses at the same time.

THREE MONTHS LATER, Delilah began to calve early. When Donkey went out with the milk pail, she found her down in the paddock, and the flattened snow around her was evidence that she'd already been down for hours. The previous calvings—two years ago and four years ago—had gone smoothly, if mysteriously, and in the morning, on the straw of the cowshed there had appeared a sweet calf. Part of the job of a midwife is to be the graceful carrier of the possibility that death can arise out of birth, but Donkey kept wishing and working long after Herself said they should give up. With her long, thin arms, under Hermine's instruction, Donkey managed to extract the premature calf from Delilah's womb, but both calf and cow died on the frozen ground that day. Delilah had never asked for insemination. By impregnating her, they had killed her.

Herself tried to comfort Donkey, but she was as distraught as she'd been when Ozma had died. Herself tried to stay awake to keep her company but fell asleep at the kitchen table, and Donkey had to help her to bed. Later, Donkey lay on the kitchen floor, feeling the slow heartbeat of the Lindworm on the drainpipe, unsure what she could stand to write in *True Things* when nothing seemed certain except Delilah and Ozma dead forever, Herself and Rose Thorn headed in the same direction, and Titus destroying Ada's cranberry bog. Each time she squeezed the amber stone, though, she felt the sweet, sharp ping of the cuntshell she'd swallowed, almost like a joke. It was still in her belly, would not dissolve or pass. She didn't know how Herself could go around with twenty-eight shells agitating around her neck, let alone how Baba Rose had carried a hundred. Donkey hadn't chosen to carry that shell inside her, any more than her mom had chosen to get pregnant.

Donkey regretted tricking Rose Thorn with the clamshell. She'd been so angry at her mother for leaving them again, so angry at her request, that she'd forgotten how much she liked Rose Thorn, loved her, even if she didn't always want to say it. Life was fun, and somehow easier, when Rose Thorn was there. Rose Thorn made peace where Herself and Prim created battles; she saw value in people in a way Molly couldn't. How easy it would have been—Donkey saw, on this cold night—to have done something nice for her mother, such as adding wingstem leaves to her trickster medicine to give her some comfort, but she hadn't even done that. Donkey had callously overlooked just how much her mother did *not* want to have a baby. She couldn't deny the cruelty she had wrought in taking away Rose Thorn's choice in the matter.

CHAPTER EIGHTEEN

We're all dying.

ON THE THIRD SATURDAY in May, not long after midnight, strange warm winds rose from the southeast. Six sleepless men of Whiteheart, a perfect number of men, gathered at Boneset. Dickmon didn't know why he was there, why he wasn't home sleeping beside Hannah Grace, but he'd woken up and hadn't been able to settle back down. When he got out of his truck, he saw that Whitey Whitby, Jamie Standish, Smiley Smith, Two-Inch Tony, and Ralph Darling were already there, milling around a burning-down fire, listening to a barred owl call out from the Waters, "Who-who? Who cooks for you?"

"Not Cynthia," Darling said, and laughed.

"What are you talking about?" Two-Inch Tony asked.

"That owl says, 'Who cooks for you?' That's what it's saying. Cynthia still ain't cooking you a pot roast."

"Very funny." Tony wondered why Cynthia would tell her brother about the argument they'd had, and he didn't know why pot roast had become a point of contention in his marriage. He'd even tried cooking one himself, and when it came out like shoe leather, it became a new part of the joke. The red-headed Darlings all stuck together, that was for sure. Tony felt unease crawling up his spine and suppressed a shiver. "This wind feels spooky."

"My grandpa always said a warm east wind is an old man's wind," Darling said. "Makes an old man think he should go off somewhere."

"Old Red was a philosopher, all right," Whitby said. He'd meant to add a derogatory comment, but the statement, as it stood, felt true. He wished there were an elderly eccentric like Old Red in Whiteheart now; Whitby would listen to an old man just being himself that way.

When Dickmon's father used to feel restless this time of year, he'd go out and fix some farm equipment to prepare for planting, but Dickmon worked at a machine shop in Kalamazoo. He'd gone to the garage, intending to reorganize his workbench, but found he didn't want to be alone. Instead he'd done something he hadn't done since he was a teenager: he drove his truck along the edge of the Waters with his windows open and his headlights off.

Darling looked Dickmon over and said, "You out for a jog, man?" and the other men laughed.

Dickmon wore his lightweight Dickies jacket over blue-and-gold athletic shorts with some tennis shoes with stripes that Hannah Grace had bought him, an outfit he wouldn't usually wear in public. He hadn't even realized he was headed to Boneset, but here he was.

"That's how he dresses for success," Whitby said, and they all laughed again.

"Want to make sure I don't get a gut like yours, Ralph."

Standish laughed along with the others, but everything spooked him now, even this warm wind. He was afraid of his wife and his daughter, both of whom argued with him on every point. Afraid that they would storm out one day—they stormed out frequently—and never come back, leaving him in an empty house full of guns. He was afraid of how much he loved them. He was afraid even of getting angry with them, because when he was angry, he wanted to drink, and a few times when he was drunk, he'd thought about shooting them both and burying them in the woods. When he'd sobered up, he hadn't been able to forget those thoughts. No more than he could forget shooting Hermine Zook. Nothing had been easy since that day. His chest and belly had become so constricted with the fear of being arrested or of God punishing him that even taking a breath was hard. His good intentions no longer seemed to outweigh the gravity of his bad actions. Any misstep in his life could take him down, and he was starting to think that doing himself in would be the best thing.

Whitby had to do some work for Titus in just a few hours, before church, and he knew he would regret staying up so late, but he hadn't slept well these last few months, and might not have slept tonight even if he'd tried. In January, he'd convinced Teresa to come back to Whiteheart to have their baby, said they'd get married. He'd gone ahead and bought a trailer, a nice one. He thought their baby, Magnolia, would keep Teresa there with him, but after three months, she returned to her family in Tennessee, this time with Magnolia. She'd left a note to sum up their three years together, including the line: *I don't know what's stopping you from being a good guy, Whitey, but something sure is.* He'd refused to marry her as he'd said he would, and he couldn't bring himself to say out loud that ever since Titus had married Lorena, the whole idea of marriage had soured in him. He liked Lorena fine—everybody did—but Titus marrying her was a betrayal, and it made Whitby feel he'd failed Rose Thorn again, wherever she was. Teresa was right to feel slighted, caught up in Whitby's shadow, something that had nothing to do with her personally.

These sleepless men were drawn to Boneset, to the edge of the Waters, to M'sauga Island. They'd had remarkable times there, sitting with Rose Thorn on warm summer nights; coming occasionally, clandestinely, to meet with Hermine Zook over the decades, when they'd needed something. Uneasy times, like when they'd taken down that willow and when Rocky had killed the island dog. They'd all dreamed about the island over the years, focused enough attention there that they found it was harder to stay away than it was to just give in and head over.

Below the thin layer of perpetual fog that was not dispelled by wind, the frogs and insects of the Waters hummed, chipped, croaked, and buzzed so loudly in the night that the men had to raise their voices a little to be heard. That was why they didn't hear the creature approaching before seeing it on the road. Even after all these years, even after a few beers, Darling still had the best eyes.

"That a coyote?" he said.

"Who's that?" Standish called out. He walked purposefully to his truck, opened the door so the light shone in his eyes and ruined his and everybody's night vision. He returned with his rifle.

"Put that damned thing away," Dickmon said. "How much have you had to drink?"

"A forty-ouncer." Standish let the rifle hang loose over his shoulder

on its sling. In fact, he hadn't had anything. He'd been taking a stomach medicine he'd gotten from the Boneset Table, and it was helping
a little, so long as he didn't mix it with alcohol. He was humbled and
ashamed every day that the old woman he'd hurt so badly was helping him.

"Aunt Ricky Dicky from the Temperance Society thinks we all drink
too much," Whitby said.

They all watched a human being form out of fog and pollen and
hope, wearing Titus's army jacket, which hung nearly to her knees,
and muddy little tennis shoes with no laces.

Two-Inch Tony, who was leaning his hip against the Boneset
Table, felt a stirring in his own waters. He thought of Cynthia, who'd
gone to bed angry. She hadn't meant to get pregnant again. Their
younger child, a son, had been born thirteen years ago, and they'd
both thought two kids was enough, but they hadn't been careful.
Apart from lovemaking—which they still enjoyed with surprising
frequency—Cynthia wouldn't let him into the bed now because of the
way he clung to her in his sleep and muttered about God knows what,
so he was stuck hugging a throw pillow on the couch, yearning for her.
Maybe he'd go get some Sweetwater's doughnuts for her and the kids
and make a pot of coffee before she got up. She'd ask him if he'd gotten
a job, the way she asked every day, as though a regular job was what he
needed. She worked as a clerk at the gas station, but she didn't understand how it would be for him to go to work for somebody else. On
every hourly wage job he'd ever had, other guys harassed him about
being short or for having a limp. Guys called him stupid so much that
he sometimes believed he was.

"She came back to us," Standish whispered, his heart surging
with fear.

The approaching figure swerved and slowed and waddled and sped
up again. Under the jacket, she wore loose-legged denim overalls, cut
off unevenly at the ankles.

"Rosie, is that you?" Smiley shouted.

Rose Thorn stopped and paused as though she might turn and go
another direction, but then she continued toward them. In fact, she
hadn't been aware it was a Saturday night, when the men were most
likely to be there.

"Of course it's Rosie," Dickmon said, smiling. "Don't you got eyes in your head?"

"Hallelujah, I see the light!" Smiley shouted.

"Right. I knew she'd come back," Two-Inch Tony said.

"She always comes back," Dickmon said.

Tony hadn't known. None of them had; they'd only wished. It was late into the night now, but it felt like the day was starting over.

"What are you carrying there?" Smiley asked. He jogged toward her. Since he had given up drinking, he had a lot more energy.

"Hell, can't you see she's pregnant?" Dickmon said, now overtaking Smiley. He wanted to relieve her of some of her load, but she was empty-handed. The only way to unburden her would have been to pick her up and carry her.

The air around and between the men became electric, as though half-submerged dreams of growing and sprouting and making love were spreading under the thin layer of fog. Coyotes crept from their hollowed-out tree stumps to sniff the air; foxes lifted their noses, stretched their limbs, and trotted across fields; turtles flipped themselves right side up; snakes slithered from under rocks to await the dawn. Nearby, a mallard hen anxious about the men's presence stood from her nest and pulled some downy feathers from her breast, dropped them onto her eggs, walked a few yards, shat, and returned to sit again. Dickmon took Rose Thorn's arm, but that was an awkward gesture, more suited to helping an old woman up a set of stairs. Rose Thorn sat down heavily on the willow stump. All six men clustered around her.

"How far along are you?" Whitby asked. "Should I go get Titus?"

"She's all the way along," Dickmon said.

"Is that a technical term, Dickmon?" Whitby said. "All the way along? How'd you get to be an authority on every damned thing?"

"You got one kid, and I got three," Dickmon said. He could've added, *I know how to treat a woman so she don't run off.* But he was trying to stop being so cranky.

"Rosie, you're big as a house," Darling said.

"Almost as big as your gutbucket," Whitby said.

The men pressed closer, like drones buzzing around their queen to warm her, stealing her breath in the process. She was grateful when

Dickmon pushed them back to give her some space. She wanted to get away from these annoying and frustrating men to figure out what came next, but she also loved them profoundly, loved their uncertainty and clumsiness, their earnest desire to help, their loyalty. They were like overeager storybook dwarves in their various stages of inebriation, and they needed her love and appreciation—and their neediness exhausted her!

"You look tired," Smiley said. "Anybody got something for Rosie to eat?"

"I got jerky. It's homemade." Standish pulled a little plastic bag from his pocket and pressed it into her hand, but she wouldn't close her fingers around it, and he had to pick it up off the ground. Standish was reminded of how Herself had not accepted his note requesting healing all those years ago. Instead, the old woman had wanted to hold his hand, and he'd yanked himself free of her, couldn't let himself be held that way, not back then.

"Let me rest." The tears streaming down her face spooked and shushed the men.

The stump she sat on was sprouting green suckers, some of them two feet long, and all that new life, as well as the life inside her, made it impossible to sit there comfortably. Wild Will had been trying to convince her to go to Herself before things got urgent, but some kind of ambivalence had been holding her back.

"I'm sorry," Whitby said. "We shouldn't have cut down the tree. We got a little out of control." Apologizing felt good.

"That's right, you shouldn't have," Standish said.

"Should somebody go get Titus?" Two-Inch Tony asked, and several of the men glared at him.

"He's married to Lorena," Darling said. "They got married in January."

Rose Thorn instantly broke into sobs.

"I'm sorry," Standish said, following Whitby's lead. For nearly a year, he had been trying to shape his crimes into one solid, comprehensible body, and apologizing was on his mind. Apologizing for something he hadn't even done was a start. "I'm so sorry. Sorry as I can be."

"Willows grow out of stumps all the time," Darling said. "It'll regrow."

"Maybe only take fifty years, and half of us will be dead by then,"

Dickmon said, because it was true, and because he could no longer hold back his natural crankiness.

"Right. We're sorry about that tree." Two-Inch Tony repeated the community sentiment, not wanting to be left out of the apologizing, since he too had buried his chainsaw in the willow trunk and shouted, "Yee haw!" as it fell into the swamp. "We got carried away. You're not mad at us, are you?"

Rose Thorn paused in her sobs only to hold her stomach and pant.

"Where'd you walk from?" Smiley asked. "You should've called somebody."

"Let her rest," Dickmon said. "You don't have to talk, Rosie."

Rose Thorn groaned as her whole body contracted. She kicked off her canvas tennis shoes, so her feet were bare on the exposed roots around the stump. And then, in a whoosh, fluid darkened the legs of her overalls. Right here! This evening she'd left Wild Will a note saying she was going to Herself. She'd changed her mind again and again as she walked toward the island, and even now that she was here, she didn't feel sure she wanted Herself to take charge this time. Her hands slipped all the way up inside the sleeves of the army jacket. The men gathered more closely around her. They meant to soothe, but they were smothering her.

"We'd better drive you to the hospital," Two-Inch Tony said.

"Or maybe you'll have the baby here," Darling said. "You can put it in that basket."

What she wanted was Titus, but she couldn't have him and couldn't piece him together from these other men. She leaned over her knees and moaned. When the pain relented, she stood and gathered her resolve. "Get out of my way, you clucking hens. I'm having this baby on the island, how it's supposed to be." *Even if it kills me*, she thought.

Even as she tried to push them away, they were sure a woman had never needed their help and attention more than this, and they stayed close.

"Your daughter takes up the boards at night," Smiley said. "You want us to shout and try and make her come out?"

"Don't go shouting. You'll scare her," Whitby said. "I'm afraid we scared Dorothy one time. She's afraid of us. I'm real sorry about that, Rosie."

"We didn't scare her," Ralph said. "You did."

"Don't you dare wake her up," Rose Thorn said. She didn't want Dorothy to see her die in this process. Not Herself either. Maybe what she wanted, if she couldn't have Titus, was to die alone, the way Ozma had, in the dark of night. But she also didn't want to die, because she wanted this baby. If she hadn't wanted it, she would have taken the clamshell medicine, which now sat, duct-taped shut, in a corner of the Fox Den. Both she and Wild Will understood, had even discussed, the naturalness of Herself midwifing the child and trundling it away. Rosie knew that even if the baby lay beside her on the island, it would belong to Herself. These thoughts of separation from the new child were as painful as her contractions. But going to the hospital was an even worse option.

"Maybe we can find some more boards for the bridge," Smiley said.

"I got an eight-foot two-by-four in my truck," Darling said.

"Titus could bring some more boards from his place," Whitby said, forgetting they wanted to avoid the difficult subject of Titus. "Or maybe there's something in the Boneset barn."

"The hospital's got the machines and pain meds to help you." Dickmon wished Hannah Grace were there, but she was sleeping peacefully at home, she and the three girls tucked in their beds.

"You heard her, man," Standish said. "I'll get you over to the island, Rosie." He was glad Titus wasn't there to stop him. Even glad there was a ten-foot chasm to cross, glad for an opportunity to risk his life for Rosie. He would risk his life for his wife and daughter anytime they'd let him. He said, "It can't be as deep as they say."

"Heard it goes down to China," Darling said.

"I'll get you over there," Standish said. "So your ma can help you."

The other men were made nervous by the mention of Herself. Nobody had laid eyes on her since Rose Thorn had left, and nobody had spoken to her for long before that, and her absence made her seem more frightening. To these men, who had not seen her grow quiet and contemplative, she was still the Hermine Zook with a powerful right hand that could curse a man if she decided she didn't want to cure him. They could only imagine the power of her anger over the tree they'd dropped.

"We'll help you get over." Two-Inch Tony added his intentions to the collective spirit, and when he imagined the others were overcoming their fear of Herself, he overcame his, not realizing he was the first to manage it. After all, he hadn't grown up with a fear of Hermine in his bones but had only acquired it after moving to Whiteheart and marrying Cynthia. When Rose Thorn lurched across the mosaic and toward the stairs, the group of six moved right behind and around her, crowding her as she sweated and huffed. They were so close that her feet barely touched the wooden steps as she descended. As a beekeeper will tell you, drones huddle close to a queen for one of two reasons—to save her or to kill her and make way for a new queen. These men only knew they were finally close enough to breathe Rose Thorn in.

When they reached the bridge, they halted and held Rose Thorn within the cage of their bodies. All six of the men had joked about crossing the bridge at one time or another. Now, as they hesitated, Rose Thorn slipped out from among them to lumber a few steps alone. Standish closed his eyes as he stepped onto the redwood boards right behind her. Just like that, and the others followed. When Standish grabbed her arm to slow her down, she yanked away, and they both had to regain their balance. The bridge was so narrow they had to go single file. At each step, the men hesitated but kept on.

Rose Thorn stumbled across the planks her bare feet knew so well, and as she reached the last floating barrel before the gap, she almost stepped right off into the quickmuck. Standish grabbed her from behind in a bear hug around her breasts, above her big belly.

Dickmon shouted at the cottage, "Hey, somebody come out here! Lower this bridge!"

"Shut up!" Rose Thorn snapped. "Don't you dare wake them up. And let me go," she huffed over her shoulder at Standish.

She dropped down into a sitting position, and it was Standish who lost his balance and tumbled into the quickmuck. He bellyflopped, and his rifle flew off his shoulder, disappeared under the thin layer of fog. By the time he righted himself, he was up to his ribs and still sinking. He wiped the mud off his face and groped around for his rifle or anything else to steady or preserve him. When Rose Thorn tried to slip into the mud beside him, he used both hands to push her back up onto the bridge, sinking himself deeper in the process. "Come on, you guys, help me! Somebody hold her."

After all these years, Whitby finally heeded the call to action. He stepped around to the other side of Rose Thorn, right into the mud with his work boots on, as if stepping into a little stream. He was the thinnest and tallest of the men, almost as tall as Titus, and he went into the quickmuck like a fencepost, up to his armpits. "Damn it, I forgot about my pistol. It came out of my holster."

"You know that Winchester's the only thing I have from my dad," Standish said. "Take hold of Rosie so I can find it, Whitby. Shit, I just stepped out of one of my boots." When he realized that looking for the missing boot would mean submerging his head in the muck, he instead slipped out of his other boot, too, and both socks. It was easier to move barefoot in the cool mud.

Watching from the landing, Dickmon knew the smart thing to do would be to find some planks, but Rose Thorn wasn't going to wait for him to go rummaging around in the barn, if he could even get in.

Darling was the next man to jump into the swamp channel, and when he did, he splattered mud on everybody and almost knocked Whitby and Standish off balance. Smiley slid in right after, crying, "Oh, Lordy, save me from my folly!" Somehow the four of them caught hold of Rosie as she slid in and held her up above the surface of the quickmuck. Two-Inch Tony joined them, entering the channel as gracefully as a swimmer just in time to grab her bare foot. Because he was shorter than the others, he was soon up to his chin and had to turn his face up like a flower.

"That rotten egg smell," Darling said. "Man, that's strong."

"Sulfur," Dickmon said from the landing. "There's sulfur springs around here." He had to stop himself from saying all he knew about sulfur springs, that back in his grandfather's day, before there was any kind of bridge to the island, people came to *take the waters*. Instead he shouted, "Keep her out of the mud, man!"

Dickmon had taken a lifesaving course as a member of the volunteer fire department and was trying to piece together what was relevant to this situation. Now that Rosie's water had broken, she had to stay clean down there, that was for certain, and that meant keeping her out of the mud entirely. Also, any second, one of the drunken men could go under and not come back up. He didn't want to be in charge, but he saw that the situation had taken a turn. Lives might be at stake, and somebody needed to keep a cool head. Hannah Grace would think he was crazy, but there on the landing, he took off the tennis shoes she'd bought for him and took his pistol out of his jacket pocket and slid it partway inside his left shoe. He took off his shirt, folded it inside his jacket, along with his gym shorts, tied it around his head like a sultan's turban, and checked that it would hold. He'd seen the trick in a Western in which some men and their horses had to swim across a river, and he wanted to be presentable on the other side, in case he had to plead the men's case to Hermine Zook: they weren't trespassing, just trying to help. After some consideration, he took off his undershorts and stuffed those into his headdress as well. Then he said aloud, in the direction of home, "Sorry, Hannah. I'm going in."

Though the men only wanted to help her, Rosie struggled automatically against their hands, against what felt like restraints. She writhed against Whitby's grip on her arm and ribs, and this time he knew it was the right thing to do to hold onto a woman and not let her go.

Dickmon slipped off the bridge in a controlled way, just in time to catch one of Rose Thorn's arms before it went in the mud. When his clothes tilted slightly on his head, he straightened up, and the tucked ends held, and only his glasses, the new bifocals, fell off his face and disappeared into the quickmuck.

Smiley's ear was pressed briefly against Rose Thorn's swollen belly, and he rather enjoyed the sloshing swamp sounds he heard from every direction. Maybe he would get married after all, he thought, get himself a pregnant wife to spend his downtime with.

Darling slipped and lost hold of Rose Thorn's leg, and, somehow, Two-Inch Tony managed to throw his arm out of the mud and catch it, briefly sinking up over the bottoms of his ears. His heart pounded in fear of such a drowning, but he pushed on. They all pushed forward through the pudding-thick quickmuck with Whitby, Dickmon, and Standish supporting most of Rose Thorn's weight. When she finally realized how precarious her position was, Rose Thorn stopped struggling. They only had to carry her ten feet, across the gap in the bridge planks, but it was slow going in the mud, and awkward to carry a person that way, and they had to constantly shift and try to move as one creature to keep her above the surface.

Though three of the men were married and four had children, they all felt, in carrying out this task, as intimate as they had ever felt with other people. They usually avoided touching each other, but focused as they were on saving Rose Thorn, their hands and arms brushed against each other's bodies, they stepped on one another's feet, and they did not recoil. Whitby recalled the hours last summer he had helped change the transmission on a combine harvester, lying on the ground between Titus and Lorena, smelling their sweat, the three of them holding the weight in place as Titus tightened the bolts with a ratchet. Darling recalled one hot night decades ago when all the men and women in his family hurriedly unloaded a truck and wagon of hay minutes before a thunderstorm, handing off bales to one another and stacking them in the barn, banging into each other, so close they were inhaling one another's breath along with the hay dust. Tonight these men knew they were doing good and important work holding Rose Thorn above the mud, and their tenderness toward her allowed them to be tender even with one another.

Standish, his hands in the small of Rosie's back, reflected on how, all his life, he'd tried to help women, tried to hold them aloft—his mother and sister, his wife and daughter. In heaven, it would be different. A man would help women, and the women would be grateful and not make him feel bad for giving a damn about them, wouldn't look at him with suspicion in their eyes and accuse him of trying to control them. In heaven, a man would give everything he had to a woman and be appreciated for it. He wouldn't be possessed by anger, not even by righteousness. But he saw how this desire to help didn't compare with the simple way Herself was helping him by making the stomach medicine, without asking for anything in return—no appreciation or thanks beyond the twenty dollars he left anonymously in the cash box. With this thought, he redoubled his determination to help Rosie, in any way she wanted to be helped.

They finally managed to heave Rose Thorn up onto the island side of the gap in the bridge on her hands and knees, where she crawled forward over the boards, panting. Of the men, only Two-Inch Tony, whose arm muscles were developed from his flatwork and whose body was light, was able to grab hold of the frame around the oil barrel and haul himself up onto the bridge behind her. The other five men slogged through the quickmuck alongside the bridge to the island shore, gradually rising up out of the swamp channel into tangled poison ivy and grape vines. As she neared the end of the bridge, a contraction shuddered through her body. The men paused thigh- or knee-deep in the muck, waiting until the wave crested and subsided before moving forward again. Tony's arms were outstretched just inches behind her, ready to grab her hips to keep her from falling into the channel.

Rose Thorn crawled across the flagstone landing and up the stone steps. The men followed, wiping and shaking the mud off their bodies and their clothing. All their lives, they had known the Waters from the vantage point of dry land or a boat on the Old Woman River. They had known the smells of methane and sulfur that rose up and diminished in the air, but if they had ever stepped into the wetlands, it was with the protection of tall boots or even rubber waders. The men had not submersed themselves in the swamp this way before, a way that allowed them to know the crust of the planet so soft under their feet. The difference between these ways of knowing was the difference between knowing that love existed and falling in love themselves.

Standish emerged in his briefs. He'd lost weight this last year, so the mud had dragged the loose hunting pants he'd been wearing right off his body. Along with his pants, he'd lost the hammerless pistol he carried in the pocket. As he walked out of the mud, which squeezed between his toes, his feet felt good, better than they had in years.

Rose Thorn had managed to rise up onto her own two feet at the top of the steps, but halfway between the porch and the Moon Palace, she fell to her knees again in the grass. The crow who had stayed all winter woke on her nest above them and watched the commotion. She spread out her wings to better cover her eggs; she was awaiting sunrise, when her mate or one of her grown children might bring her some worms, or maybe a baby starling.

Though the men had not exactly been invited to the island, there was no denying they'd proved their loyalty, shown their mettle getting Rose Thorn this far. They'd waited their whole lives to be of service, and now they stood waiting to be thanked or told what to do. Rose Thorn, however, was not thanking them or even acknowledging their presence. On her hands and knees now, she seemed as much animal as woman.

"Where are you, Titus?" she cried.

"He's home with Lorena," Darling said. "She had twins. Two boys."

At this, Rose Thorn moaned as though caught in a leg trap. The fact of twins doubled her pain. She growled and began to rock back and forth. When another contraction seized her, she grabbed hold of Whitby's leg for support.

"Can't you shut up, Ralph?" Whitby said, wishing he'd done a better job wiping the mud off his pants and boots.

"Rosie, why don't we get you inside?" Smiley said.

"No!" Her certainty seized her, came even before her understanding why.

"You want to stay out here, Rosie, I'll stay with you," Standish said.

"Herself will probably kill us," Darling said. "Is she going to kill us?"

"Say your prayers, boys," Whitby said. "We're at death's door."

"Titus, you bastard!" Rose Thorn said, from her belly. Her love rose up in her like a release of warm healing vapors, as if in response to her bodily waters being released downward. She didn't know why she should love Titus even more for marrying Lorena and having babies with her. Her pain came with a relief that Titus had settled his fate, relief that she was no longer responsible for his joy or sorrow. Relief that it was not up to her whether Titus lost or kept his family farm. She tore his jacket off and pushed it away.

"Are you too hot?" Dickmon asked, adjusting the neck of his own T-shirt. He had rejoined the group fully dressed in the dry clothes he'd carried across the channel. He'd used his undershorts dipped in a sulfur pool to clean himself. He knelt on the grass at Rosie's side.

"We need somebody, Rosie," Smiley said. "Your ma or somebody."

"We could sure use some help here, Rosie," Dickmon said soberly, though his head was spinning as though he were drunk. The warm wind was picking up again.

She said, "No."

Last time Rose Thorn had had a baby, her thought from the beginning was that she'd give the baby to Herself, for the good of everyone. That is what would happen again if Herself arrived on the scene.

"She said she don't want to go in," Standish said. "Why don't you listen to her?"

"Nobody's answering the door," Smiley said, calling out from the screened porch where he'd knocked again hesitantly. "They must sleep like the dead."

The other men were relieved at this news but also spooked.

"You wake her up, she'll put a hex on us," Whitby said. "Anybody know what room the girl sleeps in, so we can knock on the window?"

"That poor girl's already afraid of you," Dickmon said. "One of us geniuses should go lower that bridge and go back for help." He'd almost said *you geniuses*, but he was sensing the importance of them all working together to save the situation.

Darling and Whitby returned to the bridge and tried to find the controls, but it was still too dark to see anything.

"Maybe we're all dead already," Standish said. Maybe they'd all crossed over into a strange hereafter, a far cry from what they'd been promised, as believers. More like what they deserved.

Rose Thorn moaned and grabbed a handful of grass. She wanted to have her own baby this time, a baby created by love, a baby she wouldn't give away, but she didn't know if she could do it.

Standish knelt next to her. "I'm sorry," he said. "I'm sorry about everything." His heart broke as he said it. He was so sorry. "I was possessed by a devil," he said, forgetting Rose Thorn didn't know what he'd done.

"Rosie, is there a water spigot outside? We need clean water," Dickmon said. "Whitby, go find a spigot." He knew what his father would do with a Holstein cow calving, but Dickmon's father didn't know women as well as he did. Funny how that realization bolstered him. He'd been with Hannah Grace in the hospital and paid close attention; he'd prepared for that by reading about delivering a baby in the handbook from the fire department. He looked around at the faces in the dark and was glad he'd lost his glasses, so he didn't have to see how lost they felt. Also, he thought his being unable to see clearly allowed Rose Thorn some modesty; as if in response to this thought, she kicked off her big overalls. She now wore only a big V-neck T-shirt, which he discreetly pulled down over her hips. He was trying not to touch her skin with his hands, worried that they might not be clean enough.

Whitby found a bucket near the spigot, and then he found a clean tablecloth, two sheets, and two towels hanging on the clothesline. Two-Inch Tony brought over a bottle of rotgut alcohol thickened with aloe vera that they used for handwashing in the Moon Palace. Dickmon washed his hands in the bucket and used a sheet to wipe the mud off Rosie's pale legs. It was spooky to see Rosie without a suntan, a ghost of the woman they loved. He soaked a towel in the strong-smelling rotgut and wiped everything again. They got a sheet folded in half under her and put the soft cotton tablecloth over her and, on top of that, Dickmon's own jacket, which she soon pushed off her body.

Over the course of the next two hours, at intervals, Smiley went inside the screened porch and knocked on the kitchen door. Once, he even tried the doorknob, which turned, but the door was barred from the inside. A few times, he went around and pounded on the windows facing the road, but he didn't dare brave the darkness to go all the way around to the far side of Rose Cottage, where he would have found the back door, leading into Hermine's room, unlocked.

Throughout the chaos of the delivery, Standish held Rose Thorn's hand. She squeezed his fingers so hard they lost all sensation, until he didn't even feel her nails dig into him. He didn't flinch at her curses; his wife and daughter cursed him too.

Though the other mud-streaked men sat nearby uttering a chorus of soothing words in quiet voices, they mostly let Dickmon talk Rose Thorn through the pain and confusion. He spoke to Rosie on behalf of all the men in a practical, deferential, forward-moving language they hadn't realized they knew. More than once, he told the men to go across and call Molly, but none of them could figure out how to lower the bridge, nor would anyone venture into the muck again. In truth, none of them wanted to miss out on the birth. Whole lifetimes passed for the men witnessing, with wonder and horror, Rose Thorn's hellacious journey, until, at last, the baby, with a high-pitched scream, entered the world. As the men wept in the darkness, they moved apart enough that none of the other men could see them. The new baby wailed quietly on Rose Thorn's belly, covered with the blue-and-white checkered tablecloth. Over that, Whitby spread the army jacket Rose Thorn had tossed away. At last, Rosie let go of Standish's hand, and he shook it out.

"Hey, you didn't tell us. Is it a boy or a girl?" Standish asked Dickmon, who was the only one who could have gotten a good look at the baby's parts.

But Dickmon, after spreading his own jacket over Rose Thorn's legs, had fallen back onto the grass, his arms out to his sides, panting, his heart racing. He was unable to speak.

After a while Smiley said, "Dickmon's fainted. What do we do now?"

"I saw something down there, so it's got to be a boy," Two-Inch Tony said. "Rosie, can we look?"

"Go to hell." She was barely touching the baby with her fingertips, letting gravity hold its weight in the bowl of her pelvis, just above where it had been all these months. She was shaking, trying to figure out her feeling of wanting. Was it for the baby? Was it separate from her desire for Titus? She needed to stay right there and know it.

"That's supposed to be the first thing you know," Smiley said.

"Dickmon, wake up, you know-it-all asshole," Whitby said, nudging him with a foot.

The crow on her eggs thought no bird in her right mind could have slept through that, but still none of her family members had brought her anything to eat. She was tempted to go find a meal herself, a frog maybe, but she decided to be patient. She let one eye close.

Dickmon's breathing had slowed, and his eyes were now closed. The sun would rise soon, and the relentless warm wind kept on warming them, ruffling the wispy layer of fog forming and reforming over the Waters. The men blinked and looked around, waiting for the next thing to do. Whitby crouched nearby, hoping to peek under the jacket and tablecloth at the baby tucked away. But when he reached out, Rose Thorn said, "Leave me be."

Standish, who sat at Rose Thorn's shoulder, keeping guard, gave Whitby a warning look and said, "You heard her."

"One of us should go find Molly," Darling said. "If she don't want her ma."

"Right," Two-Inch Tony said. "She lives in the Village."

Darling looked up and caught a tiny glint of the pink sunrise reflecting off something just behind the Moon Palace.

"What's that?" he said, elbowing Whitby.

Whitby jumped a little. "Scared the fuck out of me."

"Who's there? A witch?" Standish said, craning his neck.

It was Donkey, who had watched it all. She'd been sleeping with Herself when she heard the commotion. She'd barely been able to swim up out of the communal slumber and slip from her granny's arms. She had sneaked out the back door into the warm wind and watched as, to her relief, no bridge troll materialized to claim the men or Rose Thorn as they crossed the channel. What an illogical idea, a bridge troll, and yet her body still recoiled from it every time she crossed between dusk and dawn.

Now she sat hugging her legs behind the Moon Palace, wearing only a long T-shirt, one of Wild Will's, tie-dyed orange with bloodroot. There was no denying that her mother was dying, but Donkey didn't know if it was happening at a faster rate than usual. From behind the woodpile, she had watched the six-headed mucky monster rise out of the swamp, covered with duckweed, and deliver Rose Thorn to the island first and then deliver the baby. Donkey had watched the terrible ordeal with the same fascination as she would have watched a giant *Cambarus diogenes* molt. She'd been in awe of Dickmon's strong, soft voice; she admired how Standish was pressing a towel to her mother's forehead.

"Your granny sleeping through this?" Smiley said.

Maybe Donkey should have woken Herself, but she had heard and listened to Rose Thorn's insistence that she wanted nobody but Titus. The baby's short burst of crying was too high-pitched to wake Herself, and maybe she would keep sleeping, as usual, until Donkey woke her. Six men on the island—she couldn't imagine waking Herself up to this.

"Is she even alive?" Ralph Darling asked.

Donkey nodded.

"She comes out here, I'm running back through the mud," Whitby said.

The men looked to Dickmon—the night's leader—for a final opinion. His eyes were open now, reflecting tiny crescents of light, but he remained silent and motionless.

"Is he even breathing?" Whitby asked.

"You alive, Dickmon?" Darling asked. "Hey, he's crying."

"At least he's shut up for a while," Whitby said. "I'm tired of being told how stupid I am."

Though Herself wasn't there in body, she was there in spirit, Donkey thought. The absent granny, the sleeping granny still dominated and determined almost every aspect of the situation, demanded the quiet respect of the men.

"Go get us some hot water, Dorothy," Smiley said. "You can help clean your ma up."

"Are you crying, too, Standish? What the fuck's the matter with you guys?" Whitby asked as he wiped away his own tears.

Donkey, too, was crying, and she was glad to obey Smiley's order, glad to get away from Rose Thorn and the confounding creature she herself had brought into the world by taking away her mother's choice. She ran around to the back door and entered quietly, beside Hermine's sleeping figure. It didn't make sense that Rose Thorn hadn't wanted Herself there for the birth. Herself knew everything about babies. But Donkey had taken away Rose Thorn's choice before, and she wouldn't do it now by waking the old woman. As Donkey ran water into the steel milk pail, she tried to be logical, tried to focus on a few true things—all equilateral triangles were similar to one another, just made bigger or smaller, like the painted dolls were copies of one another, like the stack of wooden bowls on the counter, like snakes within snakes, if she drew them that way. She put the pail on the stove, added three pieces of split wood to goose the heat, and shut the firebox door quietly. It would take at least twenty minutes to heat the water.

When she'd learned geometry from a library book at age nine, no men were allowed on the island, and parallel lines never crossed, but Professor A. Schweiss said people who lived on a round and finite planet needed a different geometry. Lines on a sphere didn't necessarily go on forever. On a planet, lines could cross each other in surprising ways as they wrapped around it. Maybe Titus could help Rose Thorn now, even though he couldn't marry two women. Whenever Rose Thorn had come home, Titus had always come to her. He had always been happy to see her, and she'd always wanted to see him. No matter what either of them said beforehand.

As water droplets hissed on the iron cooker, Donkey went out again through the back door, then ran down the steps and onto the bridge, brushing past Darling and Whitby on the landing, hoping the men wouldn't find their way inside. With the men watching, she reached down under the flagstone ledge, inside the canvas cover. She pulled the lever out and began turning it, cranking rapidly, around and around, dropping the planks slowly. It was easier lowering the bridge than lifting it. The men watched the three-plank section descend, weightless.

As soon as it clicked into place, in the pinkish half-light, Donkey ran across the bridge and up the steps on the other side and along the road, not caring about bruising her bare feet on the stones she couldn't see well enough to avoid. She knocked on Ada McIntyre's back porch door. She'd seen Titus even less often since the babies had been born, and she'd avoided meeting the babies altogether. Titus shuffled out in slippers, and Donkey felt weak in his sleepy presence. She still wanted him to put his arms around her and be her dad, even now.

"Rose Thorn wants you," Donkey said. "She keeps saying your name."

"Are you okay?" He stepped outside and shut the door behind him. He put his finger to his lips. "I'm trying not to wake up Lorena. She finally got to sleep."

She nodded. "Can you come right now? For Rose Thorn?"

"Oh, String Bean. I can't this time," Titus said. "Lorena's got to sleep, and I can't leave the boys. I'm sorry."

"But she wants you." Donkey was suddenly out of breath again. Her initial logic had been wrong, she realized. She had planned to tell about the baby, but she stopped herself. She didn't know the new rules. Her world slipped sideways, and she ran back to the road without explaining, leaving Titus whisper-shouting after her.

She slowed and tried to catch her breath as she approached the island. She was used to seeing men's trucks parked along the road at Boneset, but seeing men on the island in the pink light of sunrise was shocking all over again. Men moving about on the grass and the bridge and the landing, men like prehistoric creatures, like *Castoroides*, the giant beaver of the Pleistocene, who probably crushed all kinds of precious plants and ferns when it lumbered out of the water and onto land; two-hundred-pound *Castoroides* stopped streams and rerouted rivers. Donkey hurried down the steps and halfway across the bridge but had to wait while Two-Inch Tony and Whitby put the boards back down. They'd been fussing with the mechanism and weren't quite sure how it worked yet.

"Keep cranking it!" she whisper-shouted.

Before the planks were even secured in place, she ran across them and up the steps to find her mother still breathing. Dickmon, that sturdy and reliable father of three daughters, remained on his back. When Donkey stood over him, he winked at her and smiled. She ran from him, back around and into the cottage, marveling that Herself was still asleep. The water on the cookstove was warm now, and Donkey lugged it out onto the grass with some clean cotton cloths. The body of men parted to let her kneel beside her mother, as though she had some special power, at least in the absence of Herself. Now that there was enough light to see, Donkey began washing the residue of blood off her mother's arms and legs, as much as she could without lifting the tablecloth or the baby under Titus's jacket. She wanted to curl up like the baby beside her mother's body and hide away, but she wanted to be with the men too. The inert creature was humped up like a box turtle. Donkey was sure it had been alive when she left for Titus's, but now it appeared to move only as Rose Thorn's belly heaved.

"Let your daughter see the baby, Rosie," Smiley said.

"Can't we all just take a peek?" Ralph Darling said.

"Leave Rosie alone," Standish said. "Dorothy too."

"Your mama's going to have to make us all godfathers," Smiley said.

Talked to this way by the men, about something so important, Donkey felt herself thrum.

"I'd cut the cord if I had my knife," Standish said. That too had disappeared into the quickmuck with his pants.

Rose Thorn took Donkey's hand and held it, and both were soothed.

"Why don't you want to tell Herself?" Donkey whispered. She sat cross-legged close beside her mother; when she leaned down to hear what her mother might say, it felt as though she and Rose Thorn and Dickmon had all been shot and were lying low to avoid the next round.

"I'm afraid she'll take the baby," Rose Thorn said, a confusing answer. Of course Herself would take the baby. She knew babies, and nobody else could be trusted.

From the bridge, Two-Inch Tony could be heard saying, "This machine is ingenious. Wild Will was a genius." He was happy to confirm a community opinion. After experiencing the mysterious wonders of Rose Thorn's flesh, the men on the bridge were relieved for something mechanical to appreciate, an apparatus they could master.

"Are you dying?" Donkey whispered. "I want you to stay alive."

"We're all dying, right?" Rose Thorn said.

"Shouldn't we go call Molly, then?" Donkey asked.

"I'm so tired," Rosie said. "Just let me sleep a minute."

When the men finished playing with the bridge, they could have returned to Boneset. But they climbed back up to the island and milled around some more, investigated the Moon Palace. Smiley bent down and looked under the screened porch to study the stone-and-mortar foundation he'd only ever seen from a distance.

"Dickmon's like a lady with the vapors," said Smiley, returning to nudge him with a toe. "And damn if his shiny gym shorts aren't still clean."

Dickmon swatted half-heartedly at Smiley's foot, proving he was awake, if exhausted.

All her life Donkey had seen men gaze over the swamp channel jealously, while they talked to Herself at Boneset or when they drank beer at the firepit. Even Standish, watching the island in camouflage clothing a year ago, had had an air of longing. Now that these men were here, it was a kind of relief for all of them. Donkey imagined them carrying bags of chicken feed, bales of straw, firewood. She saw them driving a deeper well, down below the pollution from the paper mill, so the water from the faucets would taste better. Putting up a railing on the bridge so Herself could walk across it again. Or at least showing Donkey how to do these things. She imagined men stopping other men from shooting at them. So what if the men opened the doors too wide and let the heat out and walked off the paths with their heavy boots? So what if they broke the doors by slamming them? They could also repair the doors. Surely the men wouldn't stomp *all* the mushrooms or cut down *all* the trees. Donkey heard Two-Inch Tony rattling the door of the Moon Palace, trying to get out, and she hoped he wouldn't rattle it loose. He shouted for somebody, but no one moved to help him. Donkey didn't want to let go of Rose Thorn's hand yet. She thought if she listened harder to the men, she could learn to be more like a man herself, and then Rose Thorn wouldn't need Titus so much.

The big willow clogging the channel was evidence of the damage men could do, but maybe they would be different if they were allowed on the island. Maybe they would learn to be a little more like women. They wouldn't have to start fires here the way they did at

Boneset; they wouldn't have to burn the rotting wood where hen-of-the-woods mushrooms grew. Donkey would have to tell them about all the special care the island needed. Every crevice and swollen place needed a certain treatment—different in spring than in summer or fall. There were nesting sites to watch out for, broken places in a tree's bark that could be sealed with goop to help the tree survive. The women who had lived on the island all this time moved carefully, tenderly, because there was so much to lose. But what if the men figured out where Baba Rose was buried? Nobody could stop them from digging up her bones. And her cuntshells, which needed the protection of the Waters.

With every minute that passed, the men were growing more bored. They began poking into corners, lifting buckets, kicking at rotted wood that housed toads that ate slugs and ants or contained nests of carpenter bees the island plants needed for pollination—bees that would take up residence in the side of the wooden cottage if somebody didn't leave wood on the ground for them to inhabit. The crow was circumspect above them, but the rest of the creatures of the island held their breath in the presence of the men. When Tony finally rattled loose the lock and got out of the Moon Palace, he slammed the door behind him so hard that one of the boards cracked. The screen door to the porch banged when Smiley released it, threatening to shake itself apart. Donkey couldn't stop the men if they really wanted to go into Rose Cottage. Though Donkey felt she might be ready to live with men, she felt sorrow and fear for Herself and for the whole tender, delicate world they'd protected here for so long. As much as Donkey had warmed to the men, she was more sure than ever they had to be gone before Herself woke up.

Once again, Standish dipped a piece of towel in the warm water and patted Rosie's forehead with it. Donkey wanted him to stop—the skin on Rose Thorn's forehead was beginning to look red and irritated—but Rosie didn't seem to mind.

Standish paused and met Donkey's gaze. He didn't look away. "You know it was me, don't you?" he whispered. "Who shot your grandma. I know you saw me there. I am very sorry."

Donkey noticed how thin and rough his face was, how raggedly shaved, and how tired he looked. Here was a man who was lost without his foot balm, his stomach water. Back when he'd spied on the island, he'd looked strong and certain. Donkey hadn't known he'd been the shooter, but she wasn't surprised. She knew she should have been immediately angry with him. Titus had always said if they had an idea who the shooter was, they should call the police, but Rose Thorn was right that police would be as bad for Herself as doctors had been. Donkey glanced down at her mother.

"I'll turn myself in if you want me to," Standish whispered. "I'll go do it right now. Do you want me to go?"

"You son of a bitch," Rose Thorn mumbled. She'd heard what Standish said, but her unstoppable forgiveness was already flooding her, flowing out of her and into him like lubricating oil. She was too exhausted to not forgive him, even for such a heinous act. And because she couldn't help herself with the baby breathing on her belly, because she had neither booze nor Titus to distract her, because she felt so much love for her daughter Dorothy, she let something else happen: She felt herself forgive blind old Titus Clay Sr. for what he'd done to her. She gave a great sigh and squeezed Donkey's hand and let go of what she'd held so tightly for so long. She wouldn't forget what he'd done, but in this moment full of life, she had to let that go to make room for new things.

"Maybe you can help us," Donkey said to Standish, "with firewood. And you can try not to break things while you're here."

"I can help you. I want to help. I'll bring venison too. Whatever else you need," Standish said. "I'll help with anything you want, Rosie. I'm sorry. I just got thinking about how innocent those babies were that were dying. It made me crazy."

"Don't be a dick, Standish," Rosie whispered. "Just keep your guns out of here."

"I lost my dad's rifle in the muck. And my handgun. I'm going to miss those."

"I'm sure you'll find another one," Rose Thorn said. Her eyes were barely open, but they were trained on Donkey, her beautiful daughter.

"Oh, I got other ones at home."

Donkey heard snoring from Dickmon, and as her eyes lit on him, she noticed movement beyond him. There, on the pale curving roots of a swamp oak, the sun lit up something beaded and richly colored.

A rattlesnake, a small young one, but with as much venom as one that was fully grown.

"Do you want your warm stone back, Mama?" Donkey whispered. "Your heart? I got it in my pocket."

"You keep it safe for me," Rose Thorn said. "You hold onto it."

There was a screech and a cough from the road as Molly's Buick jerked to a halt. Then her voice sounded over the swamp channel, shouting, "What are all these damned trucks doing here? I've got to be at work in an hour!"

The men hushed.

Molly's nurse shoes squeaked all the way down the wooden steps. She paused on the landing when she saw Dickmon's pistol tucked into an athletic shoe along with a white sock, all kept carefully dry. Titus had called her, said something was happening at Rose Cottage, said Rosie was home. She'd been unable to sleep last night, had lain awake, replaying an argument she'd had with Roy. The cats, too, had been restless because of the wind. She went ahead and kicked the gun off its safe perch, kicked it over the edge of the swamp channel into the mud, where it began to sink among the skunk cabbages.

"Goddamned stupid guns," she mumbled.

CHAPTER NINETEEN

———

It's hard to be a person.

W HEN MOLLY APPEARED OUT of the pink sunrise at the top of the steps, the men backed out of her way. Donkey stood up from the grass but did not leave her mother's side. "She's over here," Donkey called out.

"I can't see a damned thing." Molly's nurse shoes squeaked even on the dew-covered grass, and Donkey wondered if her aunt had just gotten used to the sound. Molly stopped when she saw the bodies, first Dickmon's. "I don't expect to see you with these rabble-rousers, Mr. Dickmon. Why are you lying on the ground?"

Dickmon sat up abruptly, as though Molly's addressing him had snapped him out of a trance. He looked around and blinked, unsure where he was, unable briefly to process language. More than happy to relinquish his leadership to a medical professional.

Donkey admired the ease with which Molly situated herself among the men, how she didn't even register shock that they were on the island. Donkey had heard Molly talk that same way to patients at the hospital, *mister this* and *mister that*, demanding compliance.

"Look, Molly, I'll bet you're surprised," Whitby said.

"Why are you running around in just a T-shirt?" Molly asked Donkey. "What is going on here?" She finally noticed Rose Thorn's state of repose, noticed the hump on her belly. And the blood on the sheet and in the grass all around her body. She collapsed onto her knees beside Rose Thorn, who dropped her arms and let Molly uncover the baby.

As soon as Rose Thorn allowed Molly access to the child, she sighed in exhaustion. Her eyes closed, and her head lolled toward Donkey, who knelt beside her again.

The men gathered behind Molly, wanting to see the baby through her eyes, wanting Molly to tell them they'd done good work, that the baby was healthy.

"She wouldn't go to the hospital," Dickmon said. "We wanted to take her."

"Poor Jesus, Rosie." Molly fished in her smock pocket for her glasses and shone her flashlight over the baby's body and little smushed face. Molly's energy began warming the mother and child. With busy hands, she felt the baby's pulse, causing the baby to start crying again. She gathered the skin temperature by pressing the backs of her fingers against the baby's neck. This was how she'd learned to work in nursing school—not like her mother, not holding someone's hand and waiting for some soul message but reading a body's clear signals. Here, she did as best as she could, according to a set of rules she knew and trusted, the way Donkey trusted adding and multiplying. She lifted the baby and held her out toward Donkey.

"You've got a little sister, Dorothy. You're going to have to hold her for me."

"I don't want a sister," Donkey said. "It's supposed to be a boy." That was the medicine Donkey had made, even including her own snake blood. If she were going to have a sister, the sister would need to be older than her, not younger.

"Put out your arms." Molly didn't seem to hear what Donkey had said. "Don't be afraid. Just be careful of her neck and head," Molly said, still proffering the baby.

"I thought I saw something hanging down like a boy," Two-Inch Tony said.

"It's not fair," Donkey said. She'd already lost so much—Titus, Ozma, Delilah, a strong and capable granny. She'd lost her mother over and over again. Now, Donkey would lose her inheritance. She would no longer be the youngest or most special girl.

"Put out your arms now and pay attention," Molly said. "I need you a hundred percent right now, Dorothy."

Donkey, on her knees, reluctantly offered her arms and let Molly place the package there, wrapped in Titus's jacket.

"Now support her head," Molly said.

"That head will fall right off if you're not careful," Darling said.

"For Christ's sake, Ralph," Dickmon said. "Do you have to say every damned thing that comes into your pea brain? You're doing fine, Dorothy. Just put your hand under there. Hold her close." He reached over and adjusted Donkey's hands. But she didn't want to bring the baby close.

"We were fine while you were asleep, Dickmon," Darling said. "We were fine without you knowing everything and calling us assholes for the last hour."

"Right," Two-Inch Tony said.

Molly felt Rose Thorn's forehead and shook her, jostled her with increasing vigor until she roused and complained. When she opened her eyes, everyone relaxed at the sight.

"Mom, did you take the medicine in the clamshell?" Donkey whispered.

"I didn't take it, honey."

"How come not? You asked for it."

"I needed to have it. I needed to know I could take it if I wanted to."

"I wish it could be a boy," Donkey said. She still supported the baby on her knees, stiffly and away from herself, the way she'd hold a turtle or a cat who might claw her.

"Oh, Rosie, what are we going to do with you?" Molly discreetly pulled down the collar of the oversized V-neck T-shirt Rose Thorn still wore to reveal the bump that knuckled its way out of her breast. Rose Thorn smiled. Standish studied the exposed part of the breast and then looked away, red-faced, though he'd seen plenty more than that during the delivery.

"Now that there's a baby girl," Rose Thorn said. "You can go to school, Freckle Face."

"I don't want to go to school," Donkey said. "I want to have the island."

"I can die content now," Rose Thorn sighed.

"No, don't die!" Donkey said, loudly enough that the baby began howling. The baby's energy electrified Donkey. She was called to attention to do something, but she wasn't sure what—she wasn't ready to soothe the baby, and so she studied the wrinkled red face in the pink light, watched the arms barely moving but reaching for her. She wanted to pull her close, sort of, but she'd held enough animals to know that you had to be careful. Also, she wasn't sure she wanted to keep the baby; if anybody should die after all this, it should not be Rose Thorn but the baby, who had caused Rose Thorn so much pain. Donkey's arms were getting tired from supporting the creature out away from herself. She noticed it was still connected to Rose Thorn by its thick greasy cord like a long tail.

"Nobody's dying," Molly said. "And I highly doubt any woman in this family is ever going to be content either."

"Everybody's dying," Donkey said, under her breath.

Molly placed both hands over Rose Thorn's ears and then moved them down her neck, to her shoulders. Then she felt her ribs, her belly, her hips. She traced her sister's arms with her plump palms and fingers and finally squeezed both of Rose Thorn's hands. "Nothing seems wrong, Rosie. You're not swollen. That's good."

Molly's being there—her simple, sensible actions—made the situation less mysterious. A woman had had a baby. Women had babies every day. Some men had helped her.

"It's just my heart that hurts," Rose Thorn said and sighed.

"You mean Titus," Molly said. "You know, I've loved a man longer than you have, and I have to move heaven and earth to get the kind of attention you get from a dozen men when you drop a cigarette butt." She shook her head. "Rosie, I don't know what you were thinking going through this alone, not telling anybody."

"I'm not alone. I've got the best minds in Whiteheart here with me."

"You do occasionally bring out the best in the men around you," Molly said, "along with the worst. Where have you been all this time?"

"I've been with Daddy," she said.

"Oh, really?" Molly said skeptically.

"We conjured him up that night with the blackbird pie and whiskey," Rose Thorn said.

Holding the baby, Donkey wondered if it might be better for everybody if this new little sister fell into the swamp and disappeared before

Herself saw her or even knew she existed. She still hadn't gotten the right grip on her when she felt something gush forth, a horrible slimy bloody mess. It seemed to come out of all three of them, but really it came from Rose Thorn. The glistening mass slithered in the weak morning sunlight.

"It's a Lindworm!" Donkey shouted and closed her arms like wings around her sister to protect her. "A terrible troll!"

Her left arm squeezed too hard and made the baby cry, but her right arm, Hermine's arm, knew exactly how to hold the baby, who, as soon as Donkey pulled her in against her chest, felt very alive and warm. Her right arm flooded her whole body with the feeling that she had never known a greater joy than holding this sister, for whom she must have been waiting her whole life. Donkey knew she couldn't drop such an alive thing into the swamp, like a turnip. And its head, *her* head, wouldn't fall off her neck as easily as the man said it would. Donkey could feel that this curled-up baby with its big head was well put together. She estimated that she weighed six pounds. A perfect number of pounds. At the same time, she saw that what had just come out of her mother was not alive at all; it was nothing but the afterbirth.

"You've seen a placenta before, Dorothy," Molly said calmly. "Just hold onto the baby now, and be careful. Somebody want to get me some alcohol? And a piece of string."

Dickmon produced the cord from the waistband of his shorts. They'd used up the whole bottle of aloe-thickened rotgut to keep clean during the delivery, but Darling handed over a nearly empty bottle of ginger brandy he'd managed to keep in his pocket as he'd moved through the mud.

"For once I wish you men drank something stronger than cough syrup," Molly said.

"Do you want me to wake Herself up?" Donkey asked. "She'll be mad if we don't."

Molly thought for a moment. "Let's not wake her up yet. And let's be quiet, everybody. You keep the baby warm, but don't smother her." Molly fumbled in one pocket and then the other and pulled out a beat-up little packet containing a single-serving alcohol wipe. She opened it and wiped clean the blades of the surgical scissors she took from her right-side pocket. Without hesitation, she tied Dickmon's string around the cord tightly and snipped through the cord as tough as any animal's tendon. She tied it off. Donkey stood holding the baby against her chest, a baby no bigger than most of their hens, smaller than Big Scratch, but somehow as grand as everything in the world combined. She opened the jacket a little to allow the baby to breathe and ran a finger over a bit of exposed belly. Wherever she wasn't sticky, she was rabbit-soft. Donkey decided that as well as being the perfect weight, she was also the perfect length.

Molly glanced around at the men, as if judging and finding each lacking. She said, "Now you big strong men can help me stand her up."

Again, Donkey marveled at how her aunt managed the men, as though they were ordinary, as though their being there was ordinary.

"Dorothy, you keep hold of that baby. Follow right behind us. I can trust you, can't I?"

Warmth emanated from the baby. The wind had calmed, and the morning was beginning to feel cool. Donkey adjusted the jacket around the baby so she could share Donkey's warmth. When the baby's cheek was against her neck, she felt an electric shock resonate inside her belly, the sense that a new cord was connecting them and then thickening.

"I guess this will be your island," Donkey said. "Herself can teach you a lot of things when she wakes up. She's been waiting for you." She had a growing sense that this baby was just what her family needed. Another girl, so that the five-headed family monster would now have six heads. "I'll teach you which mushrooms to eat. And give you clothes I can't wear anymore. I'll teach you math."

The pinkish light from the east lit up the new baby. The old Mother's Moon to the west, obscured by clouds, was waning. The next moon would be the Rose Moon. A person could change her mind about things. It wasn't illogical to change your mind when you got new information. Like that the earth was round and didn't stretch out forever to ∞.

"I think your name is Rose Moon," she whispered to the baby.

"Maybe this means everything will be like it was before," Standish said. "I mean, before Herself got—you know. Won't it?"

"Let's focus on Rosie and this baby, for crying out loud," Molly said. "What is the matter with this town?"

Standish felt suddenly aware of his nakedness. He wrapped the towel he'd been wiping Rosie with around his waist like a skirt.

"Herself must be hard of hearing," Darling said. "Rosie was screaming."

"If she wakes up, we'll never get Rosie to the hospital," Molly said.

"Don't wake her," Rose Thorn said. "Not yet."

Molly looked surprised and relieved.

"Do you think your name is Rose Moon?" Donkey asked the baby. "That's what I think it is."

Molly and the men gathered around Rose Thorn, and the men hoisted her to a standing position while Molly somehow managed to slip her back into her overalls. The pant cuffs were still wet where Smiley had washed the mud off them at the spigot, but Rosie didn't complain. Whitby pulled the denim straps up over her shoulders, tied a knot in each side to shorten them more. Rose Thorn began to glow brighter as the men assisted her in taking her first steps toward the bridge. Like before, her feet were barely touching the ground. She was a queen bee again, but now she found breathing easier.

"Oh, Molly, I was so scared," Rose Thorn said. "I think my bones have melted."

"You did good, Rosie. Now let's get everybody checked out at the hospital."

"I'm your *sis*, that's my palindrome," Donkey whispered to the baby, while keeping her distance from the men. The baby's whimpers turned into sobs. "Okay, you can be *sis* if you want. And it's okay if you cry. There's flowers on the primrose path. I can show you. You'll be surprised when you learn who your granny really is. Some people are afraid of her, but she's not so bad." The baby smelled milky, as though she'd been bathing in milk, as though Rose Thorn were made of milk instead of flesh. "You and I are *Homo sapiens*. We all are," Donkey said. This sister seemed lighter when Donkey held her close. "We have to be careful on the bridge. And I might study calculus. Then I'll show you how to figure the area of curves." While holding Rose Moon, ∞ didn't seem an impossible idea. And what was calculus but a lot of tiny glimpses of ∞? She wouldn't have to learn it all at once.

As Donkey descended the stone steps behind the men, she saw Titus descending the wooden steps on the other side, coming toward them. Her heart thrummed in the old way, though her brain knew better now. He wore the same thing she'd seen him wearing earlier, his plaid pajama pants, a flannel shirt over a sleeveless undershirt, and soft slippers that shushed on the wood. His bare ankles showed. He didn't pause to pray before he started across the bridge.

"Go plant your field!" Darling yelled to Titus from the island landing. It seemed right to razz Titus now. He hadn't been there for the baby, whatever the reason. Somehow his failure to show up had become the other men's own modest triumph. Darling, with the greenish-gray mud of the swamp dried on his shirt and pants, stood in front of Rose Thorn, blocking her from view. "To hell with us. I mean, to hell with you, Titus."

"What are you talking about?" Titus said.

"Keep moving, Titus," Standish said. "We've got to get Rosie across."

"Jesus, Rosie, it's really you. Why's everybody here?" With Titus on the bridge, everybody on the island side had to wait. "What's going on?"

"Guess you're late to the party," Whitby said.

"Titus, you're the source of this trouble," Molly said, "as far as I can see."

Titus joined them on the landing. "Rosie, talk to me," he said.

As soon as he was off the bridge, Molly pushed him aside and dragged Rose Thorn onto the planks, followed closely by the others.

Rose Thorn reached out to Titus, and their fingers met briefly before being knocked apart by the helper bees.

"Keep moving," Dickmon said.

"Titus, you help Dorothy with the baby," Molly said.

Whitby was the last of the other men to step back onto the bridge. "We're all godfathers of your baby, Titus," he said.

Titus turned and looked at Donkey holding Rose Moon above him on the stairs. She was whispering into Rose Moon's sticky head, counting, "Seven, eight, nine . . ." and being as careful as humanly possible descending the steps she'd set foot on nearly every day of her life. Titus looked again toward Rose Thorn, being hustled across the bridge without him, and then back at Donkey. Could this really be his child? After a decade of desperately wanting his own children, had he been blessed with three babies at once?

As Donkey's foot touched the landing, she said the word *eleven*.

"You're shivering, String Bean." Titus took off his flannel shirt and put it over Donkey's shoulders, and with this distraction, he lifted Rose Moon up and away from her, leaving her arms empty. When Donkey realized what had happened, she felt windswept and stupid for letting Titus take one more thing from her. She let the flannel shirt slip off her shoulders and fall onto the bottom step behind her.

"Oh, she is mine, all right! I can feel it. Rosie had my baby!" Titus brought the infant into an easy cuddle in his bare arms. He'd been cradling babies for more than a month already.

A light breeze blew through Donkey's empty arms, carrying the scent of rattlesnake. And there was the Lindworm, behind Titus, pulling her body into a coil. In the pink light, Donkey could see the pencil wound on the snake's side. Her dappled skin blended into the poison ivy leaves and vines at the edge of the landing. Titus stepped back, and the Lindworm froze, tensed.

"Oh, my sweet Lord. My Rosie had my baby," Titus gushed.

Let him get bitten, Donkey thought. This man who had never given a damn about her, never cared enough about Rose Thorn, not really. Let him get bitten for stealing Rose Moon out of her arms! For refusing to be her father. The Lindworm pulled her triangular head back, ready to defend herself. The buzzing of her tail joined the bird songs that filled the morning soundscape, and right there at the edge of the island, a few green frogs plucked banjo strings in alarm. Donkey imitated the purring sound to let the m'sauga know she'd been heard. Titus was nobody to her, and she didn't care what happened to him.

Only that wasn't true. Titus, now gazing into Rose Moon's face, was somebody to her. He was her sister's father. He was her sister's protector, if not her own. This made him her ally. With that realization, a whole spider's web of connections breathed to life. The men who'd come to the island were her sister's father's cousins and friends, her sister's deliverers and protectors. Donkey could no longer be the precious thing—she was too tall, too independent-minded, too full of lying snake blood—but she could hold and protect this precious thing, and she needed help. This baby might be cared for and protected not just by the women of the family but also by Titus and all these people who'd helped her come into the world.

Donkey reached out and tugged on Titus's arm to move him toward her, away from the snake, but he resisted, his attention affixed to Rose Moon.

Rose Thorn stopped halfway across the bridge. Loudly, clearly, she said, "I'll die without him."

"Rosie, you're not going to die of love, for Chrissakes," Molly said, tugging her back around. "We have enough drama without that."

"Just don't fall, Rosie," Whitby said.

"We'll save you if you fall," Standish said. All the men were getting restless at being trapped on the bridge in a line behind Rose Thorn, who began to move again, slowly, toward the end of the bridge, without any response from Titus, who was still transfixed.

Molly might sound callous, but Donkey realized her aunt was finally implementing her plan; they would get Rose Thorn to the hospital to save her from cancer.

The sky was lightening, and Donkey saw there was another small m'sauga on the downed willow tree, hanging off a branch, among the suckers that had sprung from the trunk, and she wondered if it had swum out from the island. Another snake, this one fully grown, lay coiled on the bank of the swamp channel, a dozen yards away, resembling a colorful pile of dung. It seemed Herself had been right when she said Donkey would let the island be overrun with rattlesnakes and men. During previous springs, Herself would have traversed the island by now, tapping her stick and calling out for m'saugas to stay clear, and Donkey hadn't thought of doing such a thing herself. None of the men had noticed the snakes, because they didn't really know the landscape, what was straight, what was curved.

Titus stepped from foot to foot, bouncing the baby gently. And the Lindworm behind him began to buzz again.

"God blessed us with a girl," he said. Females, while they could be carriers of thinblood, would not be afflicted by it.

"Titus, bring our baby!" Rose Thorn shouted from the far side of the bridge. She had only one more span to cross, one more place where there might have been a troll, if you believed in trolls.

"You stay and take care of your granny," Titus said to Donkey. He stepped back again, almost bumping the Lindworm, who drew its head back like a stone in a slingshot. "This baby's going to get the best care possible."

Donkey knew any snakebite could kill Titus, even if the venom wasn't strong enough to be deadly. And without Titus, Rose Moon would have no father. Or worse, a bite might startle him, and he might, as a result, drop Rose Moon into the Waters. If she didn't drown, she might be bitten by a m'sauga, whose bite could kill a baby. As Donkey felt Titus gather himself to step back again, right into the coils of the snake, she fell onto her knees at his feet. She reached past his slippers to grab the m'sauga by her slender neck. She knew how to hold the head, had seen Herself do it dozens of times, but before she could get hold, the Lindworm curl-whipped around and sank her hollow fangs into Donkey's bare wrist.

She'd known the blood and smelled the meat, and now at last she knew the electric release of the venom. It burned through her veins like rattlesnake whiskey. And now that she'd finally given in to the euphoria of being bitten, she invited the snake to empty herself into her. She wanted all the burning venom in the world for herself. In this way she could keep Rose Moon and the rest of them from being bitten. And this was how she would carry the power of the island with her wherever she went in the world—to school, to the Boneset House, to California, if she decided to go there. Her own blood would become the antivenom, as Wild Will's had been.

After the Lindworm withdrew its short fangs from her flesh, Donkey held the snake against her body as passionately as she'd held her sister, her grip on its neck now perfect. She slowly stood up before Titus. She knew what Herself felt like now, eating all the town's truths in one swallow. When the m'sauga folded back her fangs and tried to drop to the earth, Donkey kept holding the silky, muscular mottled body against her belly. She lifted the coils to her chest.

"Holy hell!" Titus yelled. "String Bean! Drop it!" Titus squeezed, and the baby started bawling. But Donkey held onto the writhing, struggling snake, absorbing what remained of the creature's fear and anger.

"What's going on?" Molly yelled from the other side of the bridge. "Hurry up, you two."

"Titus!" Rose Thorn shouted. Standish's arms were extended outward, ready to catch Rosie, and when he thought she was falling, he grabbed her. She pushed him away, and he had barely let go of her before falling from the bridge and splashing everyone in the group with mud.

Donkey felt the Lindworm relax against her, but she still held on.

"Just let it go. Sweet Jesus! Let go of that thing!" Titus commanded in a low voice, as though sharing a terrible secret. He saw the two deep red punctures, an inch and a half apart on the side of her wrist; while he watched, the wound began to bleed. String Bean should have been screaming, but she was humming, purring, handling the creature almost familiarly. If not for the baby in his arms, he would have grabbed it away from her—except that he had kids to raise now, three kids depending on him, and he couldn't risk his life.

After what seemed to Titus an eternity, Donkey loosened her hold on the snake, enough that the creature could slide from her hands. In slow motion, assisted by gravity, the m'sauga traveled down her body and to the surface of the island, and it slunk away like a living length of cow gut to hide under the exposed roots of a hackberry tree. If Titus had been wearing boots, he would have stomped it to death before it could disappear. Or so he told himself.

Donkey felt tears running down her face. In addition to the burning, she felt a shock and a vibration moving through her, something like she'd felt after a wasp sting; then a numbness began to spread out from the bite wound on her wrist.

"I'm not crying," she said. "It's just venom in my eye." She knew the Lindworm hadn't meant to bite her; the bite had been meant for Titus.

"Hold on to me," Titus said. He leaned down and picked up his flannel shirt and held it out. "Put this on. We'll get you across to the hospital, and I'll come back later and kill it."

"We have antivenom," Donkey said, stepping out of range. She would go inside now and reach down in the caboodle for the coppery salve made from Aster's blood.

At the other end of the bridge, Darling and Whitby pulled Standish out of the quickmuck. This time, he was covered in fresh mud from the top of his head to his bare toes.

"They got what you need at the hospital," Titus said. "No more screwing around. Right now, String Bean."

Donkey stepped farther away from him. She needed the extra space to think clearly.

"We've got to get all three of you to the hospital," Titus insisted. "Can you walk okay?" When she nodded, he said, "Put on the shirt so you don't go into shock."

"I'll wake Herself up. She can help me." Nobody in Whiteheart had cured more snakebites.

"Not this time," Titus said. "You don't have to be loyal this time."

It wasn't loyalty that made her want to use her granny's antivenom. It was the medicine itself, as elegant and simple as a mathematical proof. An island cure could work exactly right for the person taking it, unlike the crude hospital medicine that didn't know who or what a person was. And even when Hermine's remedies didn't work, the way they didn't work was better than how the hospital medicine didn't work. Hospital medicine was like a hammer blow to the head to kill a mosquito, a blow you hoped didn't kill you too. Even for Primrose, even for men as misguided as Reverend Roy, Hermine's medicine had been better. Even Donkey's own crude fixes were better than the medicine of Nowhere, for they were delivered without shackles, without needles, without the chemical stink. Plus hospital drugs cost money—money you might need for the power bill. The medicine from the Waters was more logical. But it worked in a way the people of Whiteheart didn't understand. If Donkey stayed there on the island, she would heal, wholly or partially, from the bite without their witnessing, and it would seem like magic. Or witchcraft.

"Come on, kid," Titus said. "Let's go now."

But none of this was easy enough. If the choice were just about the cure for her snakebite, Donkey would have run into the cottage for the salve; she would have awakened Herself, who would cut into the skin around the wound with Wild Will's sharp paring knife, and the medicine would surge through her. But Donkey wanted Rose Thorn to go to the hospital, where they could treat her cancer. And she wanted Rose Moon to get weighed and measured and tested and vaccinated.

If Donkey avoided the hospital and chose the island's cure, Rose Thorn might do the same—she might change her mind and carry herself and the baby back to the island to heal with Donkey, and the whole cycle would begin again.

If the Zook women continued living mysterious lives separate from the town, men would resume watching them like prey from Boneset and making up stories about them, good and bad, calling them witches or angels. Burning fires and pissing *Rosie* into the snow. Standish might not shoot at them again, but somebody else would; there was no end of men with guns. Men's dogs could lope across to attack them anytime they left the bridge down. Men and dogs could even swim across, right through the quickmuck.

"Your arm is swelling. Look at it!" Titus demanded. "Please come with me now."

For more than a year—371 days—the cottage had been warmed by Donkey's own fire, one she'd had to keep going. Without realizing it, she had become the biggest of the nested dolls, the doll that contained the other dolls, and now what she did would determine the future for her mother and sister and grandmother, all of whom, in this moment, she carried inside her. She wasn't sure she was making the right decision as she slipped Titus's flannel shirt over her shoulders and grabbed hold of his T-shirt. She left the wholesome and elegant medicine behind, left paradise and followed the procession into Nowhere, compounding the duplicity Herself had always known was coming by letting her sleep through the birth of her new grandchild. But Donkey had to go with Rose Moon into this strange new territory. She had never felt as steady and heavy on the bridge as she did with the venom coursing through her. The voices of the men across the river, their growls and buzzes, had become as strange and alluring as the language of the birds and the snakes.

She couldn't leave the bridge open while Herself was asleep and vulnerable. There was no way to work the contraption to lift the bridge boards from the Boneset side, so once they reached the Boneset landing, she let go of Titus's shirt, kicked at the last set of boards—above where the troll was, if you believed in it—with her bare feet and wrenched them free with her good hand. When Titus saw what she was doing, he shouted at her to stop, but she finished the job, leaving all three boards off, their ends floating in the muck out of reach. Titus, or someone else, would have to bring new boards for them to return to the island, but Herself would rest unmolested in the meanwhile. Donkey ran to catch up, only then noticing her right foot was red and swollen from kicking the planks. In doing what she did, while her arm burned like hellfire, she considered Herself and her strange behavior over the last year: Merely losing her hand should not have incapacitated Hermine as much as it had. There must be something else wrong with her, something that was making her sleep so much. Sleep was medicine, but for what illness or injury? Donkey was not enough of a healer to know.

"Hurry," Titus said to Donkey. And then to Molly, who was coming back down the stairs. "String Bean just got bit by a muck rattler."

"Oh, she's telling you a story. Aren't you, Dorothy?"

But Molly saw in the girl's drained face, without even looking at her arm, that it was true. She wrapped the flannel shirt around Donkey more tightly, pulled her gently to her side, and hurried her up the steps toward the car. With Rose Thorn and all the men watching, Molly helped Donkey into the front passenger seat, which was covered with cat hair and smelled slightly of pee and french fry grease.

As she tucked her legs into the car, she felt something even worse, a glimmer of Hermine's dream from Rose Cottage: A baby in white wool drifting across the Waters toward the Old Woman River. She felt her granny's alarm, powerful enough to wake her up at last. Herself would be distraught at the loss of this baby. Or furious. Or both.

"Where's my pistol? Did one of you take it?" Dickmon asked the assembled men, loudly enough that Donkey could hear. "It was with my shoes."

The burning in Donkey's arm intensified, shutting out Hermine's dream.

Rose Thorn stood at the back of the Buick, but the men supporting her were blocking her view of her daughter. Once Donkey was in the car, Molly began to extract Rosie from the cluster of men and hustle her into the back seat. In the pasture across Lovers Road, Triumph and Disaster hee-honked wildly at the goings-on. Aster looked fat enough to burst, though it would be another month before she would give birth. If Rose Moon wouldn't drink mother's milk, the hospital would probably force-feed her rather than aborting another donkey foal. Donkey's heart pounded in fear for the new world she was guiding her family into. She made a wish, that Rose Moon would nurse.

Rose Thorn was trying to climb back out of the car when Molly ushered Titus into the back seat with the baby. "Titus, you're coming with us!" Molly said.

Titus put his free arm around Rose Thorn, cradling her as well as the baby. Rose Thorn seemed to liquefy as she studied the baby between them in stunned amazement. When she spoke to Donkey, she briefly looked up, and her words slurred with exhaustion. "What's wrong, Freckle Face?"

"It was a muck rattler," Titus said. "She was bit. It's my fault."

"What?" Rose Thorn said, trying to rouse herself from her stupor. "Did you get some of your granny's medicine?"

"I'm okay, Mom," Donkey said, but even as she replied, Rose Thorn's gaze was returning to the baby. Donkey felt a pang of jealousy. She wanted the new baby to be hers, or at least all of theirs. And then she felt another more diffuse kind of pain, knowing that her mother had not wanted her in the same way. The venom, her venom, was moving just under her skin, slithering up over her elbow and drawing the swelling with it like a tight blanket.

As Molly was getting in the driver's seat, suddenly Whitby was shoving a hard plastic infant seat through the back window onto Titus. "Had this in my truck," Whitby said. "You got to use it to be safe."

"Oh, Poor Jesus!" Molly said. "Just please hurry." She reached across Donkey's body and held her right arm for a few moments. As she did this, Donkey felt the venom stop at her biceps.

"Wish we had a soft blanket," Titus said as he handed the baby, still nestled in his army jacket, to Rose Thorn.

"Now stay still and don't move a muscle," Molly said as she released Donkey's arm. "Buckle up."

Instead of following Molly's illogical command, Donkey opened the car door, ran out to the Boneset Table, and grabbed the bloodroot-orange blanket from the Babby Basket. Molly shook her head in exasperation as Donkey got back in and passed the blanket into the back seat. Rose Thorn was now watching Titus arrange the baby in the hard plastic seat, which he'd installed between them. He tightened the straps over Rose Moon, who was, by now, shrieking. Rose Thorn laid the orange blanket over the baby, and Titus tucked it around her. Donkey's swollen arm longed to tuck the blanket around her more tightly, and, as though reading her mind, Titus did exactly that, and the baby quieted. Rose Thorn made a shushing sound until she quieted further. Rose Thorn leaned toward Titus but could not get close enough to him with the car seat there; the plastic thing was a wall between them, and the distance from him was terrible for her. Titus stretched his bare tattooed arm across the back of the seat for her to rest against.

"Whitby, go tell Lorena what's going on," Titus said out the window. He wished he were driving the baby and Rose Thorn in his own truck. "Tell her I'll call her from the hospital."

As soon as Donkey got buckled into her seat, Molly turned the key to start the engine. The car heater came on loudly and issued a wave of air carrying the scent of warm cat piss. Molly had to back up a little to pull onto the road, and Donkey felt her world shifting direction. She wanted to look behind them but knew better. Why should she risk being turned to salt, risk seeing Rose Cottage sink into the muck or be overrun by snakes before her eyes? Risk seeing all the grand old willows collapse into the swamp behind her? She was moving forward, into the future. She wasn't supposed to move a muscle, but when she sensed the slapping of the cottage screen door, she rolled down the window by reaching across her body with her left hand. She stuck her head out. What she saw behind them as they maneuvered onto the road was men milling about at Boneset, as though having a party. But what she heard were bare footsteps on the bridge planks and then a terrible splash. It could have been a troll or another monster of the Waters, but Donkey felt in her bones who it was.

"Aunt M, we have to go back!" Donkey said.

"Child, if you want to keep that arm, we have to get you to the hospital. I'll get you a new notebook there."

"Help her, please!" Donkey called out her window to the men. They looked at her, puzzled. If Rose Thorn knew Herself was in trouble, they might never get to the hospital, so she didn't say any more, but Donkey saw with relief that Two-Inch Tony was already heading down the steps.

Molly didn't hear anything, focused as she was on her exodus, with time ticking on Donkey's snakebite. She maneuvered between the trucks parked on both sides of the road. The fresh air felt good on Donkey's face, so she didn't roll the window back up. When they got a mile and a half down the road to the Muck Rattler, Molly pulled into the parking lot and ordered Titus to keep both Donkey and Rosie in the car. She held the screen door of the bar open and used a brick to break one of the glass panes on the front door. She reached through and unlocked it. Once inside, she used the phone to call the hospital.

With his arm stretched across the seat, Titus had a perfect view of his own tattoo. He'd known exactly what he was doing when he was twenty-three, known the river flowing through him, and the tattoo was a reminder now that having married Lorena meant battling his own current for the rest of his life. What people called the foolishness of youth was actually young people's clear view into the truth of the world, something they lost when they grew more practical. By marrying Lorena, Titus had pleased his parents, and he'd chosen what was good and sensible for the farm and the family, but here he was, still all strung up.

"They're ordering the antivenom now," she said when she returned to the car, ignoring the fact that she was bleeding from several cuts on her wrist. She buckled up and pulled back onto Lovers Road.

As Molly accelerated conservatively up School House Road, Donkey felt her lips starting to go numb. Something in her throat choked her. She turned just her head toward the back seat.

"Do you think you just wanted the choice with me too, Mom?" she said with difficulty.

"I did have a choice," Rose Thorn said sleepily. "Ask Prim. Are you going to be okay?"

"Maybe you wouldn't have taken the fix back then even if Herself gave it to you," Donkey suggested. She was glad to be here now, with her mother, with a little sister, but if she weren't here, if she were, instead, a cuntshell or a notion or dead from a snakebite, she wondered if that might be okay too. As something like ∞ rose out of the marrow of her bones, Donkey was having trouble following the logic of her own thoughts. To think of her mother not having given birth to Rose Moon made her cry more, but it really wasn't her choice to make. Rose Moon could always be sure she had been wanted—they would all tell her so. But Donkey felt how complicated it was. The same baby could be both wanted and not wanted. A baby could be negative or positive, or even imaginary, and have great value.

Rose Thorn's eyes opened, and she smiled. "A world without you wouldn't make any sense at all, Freckle Face."

In the back seat, Titus tried to get more of his body closer to Rose Thorn by leaning across the back of the baby seat. Each of them kept one hand on the baby.

"Rosie, oh why wouldn't you marry me?" Titus whispered.

"I thought we were married," Rose Thorn said. "I gave you that ring."

He blanched. "Oh God, Rosie."

Molly nudged Donkey to turn around and sit still, and when she did, her arm began to burn fiercely. She felt the skin stretching so tight at her wrist that she feared it might split. She unfastened her seatbelt, scooted over on the bench seat, and pressed against Molly, who patted her leg and didn't even yell at her. With one hand, Donkey fastened the middle lap belt and stayed right there, trying not to think of what had happened to Herself.

Donkey had always said she would not betray Herself the way everybody else did, but her readiness to do so had lived inside her all along like a trickster animal, something she'd raised from a pup. That shameful willingness to abandon the woman who had wanted her, who had loved her, taught her, raised her must have been gestating since Donkey's first trip across the bridge on her own two feet. She'd been three years old, tied to Herself with a rope, counting her small steps across the bridge: 131 steps—she still remembered the number, though she hadn't known then it was a prime or a palindrome. She remembered that feeling of freedom she'd had about a year later, the first time she'd gone across alone to see her beloved Aster, and she'd marveled at how the world opened up at Boneset. Now the woods and fields of the Michigan landscape opened before her, wide with possibility. Infinite, it seemed.

JUST AS THE SIX MEN GATHERED at Boneset had thought the story was ending, as they were thinking about morning coffee and church and whether their families were worried about them, a whole new chapter opened with a splash. Their attention had been focused on the lives they'd just saved. They had watched Molly start her Buick and maneuver onto the road as though all of them were looking through the scope of the same rifle. But the tip of the barrel then swung toward the new view, the sight of Herself, mud covered, lying motionless in the skunk cabbages below. Instantly, they jogged down the wooden steps to the landing, brimming with a renewed communal sense of duty. Two-Inch Tony was the first to jump into the cabbage flowers to pull Hermine's face out of the mud.

Once the six men got her up the stairs—though she did not struggle, lifting her was like lifting the weight of the earth—they emptied out the back of Standish's truck, parked closest to the Boneset Table, tossing lumber and pop bottles, extension cords and a chainsaw on the mosaic of precious objects, and they hoisted Hermine up onto the sheet of plywood covering the rusted truck bed. Standish drove away from Boneset barefoot and clad only in underwear, with Two-Inch Tony and Smiley beside him on the bench seat, none of them buckled in. Darling, Dickmon, and Whitby rode in the back, their heads bowed over Hermine's body, their hair whipped by the wind. Whenever Standish flew around a corner, the men in the back were thrown toward one side of the truck bed or the other, but they held Herself steady as best they could with their bodies.

When Molly slowed at the intersection right before the highway, Standish finally caught up and pulled his Ford truck close behind her Buick. The two vehicles stayed together for the rest of the journey and pulled into the emergency lot in tandem.

Molly told Donkey to stay put and hurried into the hospital through the emergency double doors. Donkey watched Standish park nearby, watched the men emerge and open the tailgate. Only then did she know for sure what was in the back of the truck. Three emergency room staff burst out through the doors, and Donkey remembered a promise she'd made, one that was more important than any other. She opened the door of the Buick, jumped across the divider of poor shrubs mulched with coffin-nail butts, and scrambled over Whitby and into the back of the truck, pushing Dickmon and Darling aside. Holding her swollen arm against her chest, she managed to reach under her granny's muddy braids and pull the cuntshell necklace off over her head. She heard Molly yell to the men, "Grab that child and bring her back here, for the love of God!"

Donkey pulled the mud-covered shells over her own head and tucked them inside her T-shirt. She put her face close to her granny's, where she saw no movement but sensed life, somewhere deep down.

"I'll keep them safe for you, ma'am, don't worry," she said.

The men, who had meant to follow Molly's orders, stood back in awe of the tall girl's swollen arm, her long thickened fingers.

As Donkey walked into the emergency room beside Molly, her right arm felt as big as Wild Will's, and she had begun to sweat and drool a little. A few minutes later, she was in a wheelchair, but she refused to take off the necklace until the nurse agreed that she could keep it and her T-shirt in a plastic bag on the seat beside her. A nurse inserted a needle into a vein on the back of her left forearm and hooked her up to a bag of IV solution while they waited for the snakebite medicine to be driven in from Lansing. The doctor listened to her heart and lungs, asked if she was nauseated. She was, but she said she was fine. Maybe her nausea was from the smell in the room of antiseptics and harsh cleaners, not the snakebite. She could have yanked free of the IV and run down the hallway, but she was here by her own design. She was the snake who'd eaten all the other snakes, and now she had to sit still and digest what she'd swallowed. Seventy-three minutes after her arrival, the nurse inserted another needle with tubing and a bag attached, this one into the jugular vein in Donkey's neck, and began administering the hospital antivenom. The fluid slipped cold as reptile blood through her veins, and she didn't fight it. Antivipmyn, it was called, and when the nurse said it was made with horse blood, Donkey thought of Aster.

An hour later, they moved her into a surgical room, where they numbed her arm with more needles as Donkey leaned her head on Molly's shoulder. One balding male doctor and one younger woman doctor, a specialist from Lansing, who had arrived with the antivenom, worked together on her arm, where the skin had swollen so severely that it had split, and the two doctors decided they could relieve the pressure by cutting a snaking line through her skin from inside her elbow to her wrist, where they were forced to cut away a triangular patch of dead skin they called necrotic tissue. Donkey wondered if the doctors would take out the pencil lead tip in the heel of her hand, but they left it there, poking inward like one tooth.

It would take weeks for the skin on her arm to heal, and the incision and debridement left a scar as indelible as a tattoo of a rosy-dark river running up the inside of her forearm. The swelling and bruising around the wound lasted almost a month, and some of the numbness in Donkey's hand and arm would be permanent. She tried to be as strong as Herself during these procedures and refused the pain medicine, as Herself had refused it after losing her hand. With so much m'sauga in her, Donkey felt she had every right to lie about the level of the pain. She was ashamed when she gave herself away by crying in the face of the nurses' kind inquiries. She'd cried so much already that she didn't know what was in her eyes anymore.

Rose Thorn developed a fever that first evening in the hospital, and everybody was scared about the possibility of infection, but after treatment for exhaustion and dehydration, the fever subsided. Prim arrived at ten p.m. and brought Donkey the book on calculus by the female professor A. Schweiss, and sat erect in her chair beside Donkey until the girl finally fell asleep. The following day, Molly was able to arrange for Donkey to stay in the same room as Rose Thorn, a room filled with exotic bouquets of flowers. Over the next few days, between her antivenom treatments, Donkey read the new math book a little at a time, the way she used to read the Bible, finding its contents as hard to swallow as those holy words. A. Schweiss claimed, for example, that there could be a narrow vase of infinite height that could be filled entirely by a finite amount of water.

"My poor girl," Prim kept saying. "I should have protected you."

When Donkey allowed this terrible aunt to hug her, she felt the soothing power of Prim's body and realized that they all had the healing touch, every woman in their family. Maybe everybody in the world had it if you could accept it from them.

Each day in the hospital, Donkey asked Molly, "When are we going back to the island?"

"Nobody's going back to that island," Molly said each time. "Don't start with that."

Donkey let herself drift and separate from the island life. She took deep breaths of the chemical hospital air and let it come into her cells. She let herself begin to change, to transform into whatever she would become as a girl who was no longer precious, no longer in paradise. Anyway, her arm was weaker than it had been, and she couldn't have milked a cow or hung laundry in her condition, but she was capable of many things, including doing math in her notebook, even calculus, if she took it slowly.

She would remain in the hospital for four days, as vial after vial of Antivipmyn fluid dripped into her through the needle in her neck, but she could move around, dragging her IV stand along with her like a pet on a rope. She visited Herself, who was unresponsive in her hospital bed, sweating under a sheet, hooked to a 0.9 percent saline drip. Donkey was relieved to see that she was not shackled. She learned that Hermine had suffered a heart attack, either before or after stepping off the bridge into the quickmuck. As a result of the accident, she had cracked several ribs and her pelvis. Donkey suspected there was more to the story, that Herself had thrown her body onto the Lindworm or done battle with the bridge troll, but Herself wasn't talking. Or maybe Herself had gone into the Waters to drown her love for Donkey so she could love the new babby instead. Every time Donkey saw Herself lying in the hospital bed, her own mouth filled with a bitterness that was older than she was, a bile known by any snake that had bitten down hard and settled in to swallow its prey only to discover it had sunk its angled teeth into its own body. She didn't know how she'd live without her granny's attention, but she would find a way, just as her mother had. Just as Prim and Molly had.

The hospital water didn't smell right, and so Donkey didn't dare wet her granny's brow as she would have at home on the island, but she held her hand for a long time every day, and after a while, she always felt the hand squeeze hers in return. Donkey suspected Herself was not going to die. Why would she die now that she had someone new to live for? Now that she was needed to raise a new babbling babby who might succeed where Donkey had failed, a babby to replace three difficult daughters who had abandoned her. Only a dim witch from a corner of an imaginary land like Oz could be vanquished by merely dropping a house on her or by drowning her or by shooting off her hand with a rifle. In the real tales, the old stories that stayed true, the queen or sultan or witch was pure spirit, and, when mortally wounded, she simply got her old bones boiled and reassembled or cut herself out of the wolf's belly to live anew. Lived for a while in a fire or in the body of a viper or a fluttering insect or a crow.

The doctors said Hermine's vital signs indicated that she was not in a coma, and they did not know why she was unresponsive, but meanwhile they'd discovered a severe blockage of two coronary arteries, which had caused the heart attack. Since Herself was mysteriously incapacitated, Prim, Molly, and Rose Thorn gave permission for angioplasty.

"She's got to live forever," Rosie said. "I'll take care of her."

This garnered a raised eyebrow from Molly.

The nurses allowed Donkey to sit in a rocking chair and hold Rose Moon, helped her prop the baby's downy head on her good arm. Rose Moon sent out tendrils that latched onto everybody who touched her, and Donkey saw that she would be one of many resting places for her sister. Donkey objected whenever they came to take Rose Moon away for a test or an inoculation, and sometimes Molly had to hold her to prevent her from following the nurses. It became a hospital joke that this tall girl was in love with her tiny sister.

Molly contrived—by overheating Rose Thorn to induce a fever and by falsifying some numbers—to keep her sister in the hospital for two extra days, during which she brought the oncologist from Grand Rapids to her bedside. She convinced him to hurry the surgery—luckily there had been a cancellation—so it could take place on the day of Hermine's angioplasty. Rose Thorn opted for a mastectomy and declined to have reconstructive surgery. Donkey was grateful for her decision, relieved that the cancer would be banished so resolutely. Molly and Prim, on the other hand, were furious that she had chosen such a radical option and that she refused even to consider a cosmetic breast implant. But Rose Thorn wanted the scar.

She signed the consent for treatment with *Rose Z*, and the tail of that Z was the same as it was in Hermine's and Wild Will's signatures, but Rosie's ran right off the edge of the page, so nobody saw the rattle at the end. Her hospital gown wouldn't stay on her slender frame, no matter how the nurses tied it. Everyone commented on her glowing skin, even as they goggled at the tiny snake head pressing out of her right breast, that knot of anguish she'd begun to unravel in the Fox Den, with help from the quiet companionship of her father and the gestating Rose Moon. She nursed her baby until the surgery, and her milk came in as it had not the first time, even in the cancerous breast. Each evening, Titus visited, but he stayed only a few minutes and then hurried home. Together, the new parents negotiated a plan whereby on the day of Rose Thorn's surgery in Grand Rapids, Rose Moon would go home with Titus, and that baby would nurse at Lorena's flowing breasts, rather than letting her get used to a bottle. Lorena prayed to St. Giles for sanity while she made milk enough to nourish all of her husband's creations.

The greatest of Lorena's personal trials and tests of faith was to continue to believe that the girl who looked so much like her husband, who moved like her husband, was not his child. It baffled her that everyone in Whiteheart acted as though these similarities did not exist or did not matter. After learning the girl was distraught at being separated from her baby sister, Lorena reluctantly suggested that they bring Donkey to stay a few nights with them too.

Molly had been concerned when Donkey refused to eat almost anything at the hospital, and when she took her home to Whiteheart Village, it was the same, and so she agreed to allow Donkey to stay with Titus and Lorena. In a rare afternoon hour when all the babies slept, Lorena made a rhubarb and peach pie while Donkey sat beside her, on the kitchen stool where Titus usually sat. The canned peaches Lorena used still contained the taste of summer. She asked Donkey to make the pastry with the cutter, and Donkey had to use her left hand, which made her feel as lazy as Rose Thorn, but she still worked the dough a little too much. Then she watched Lorena weave a lattice-top pie crust, with its elegant mathematics, something they never did on the island. That evening, she learned that Lorena did not use magic to divide a pie into seven equal pieces; she had a special frame she put over the pie that showed her exactly where to cut.

Donkey ate three-sevenths of this pie in one sitting, and she ate one-seventh of it with Titus the following morning and two-sevenths more for lunch with ice cream. She watched in awe in those days as Lorena soothed Rose Moon and the twin boys, and as she braided her own waist-length hair, starting behind her and pulling that thick dark snake up in front of her partway through the process, rather than hanging her head upside down the way Donkey did hers. Lorena smiled at how intently Donkey watched this process, and then she braided Donkey's hair too, in a French braid. For the next few days, whenever Rose Moon was with Titus and Lorena, so was Donkey. She'd thought that, in knowing the women of her family, she knew all about women, that only men were a mystery, but Lorena was a new fascination, especially when she spoke in Spanish. For her part, Lorena appreciated Donkey's assistance with many household tasks. When Titus wasn't otherwise busy, he and Whitby and Standish were preparing the Boneset House for occupation, mostly by replacing windows. And Molly spent her free time scrubbing.

The dream that woke Donkey more nights than not in those ensuing weeks after the snakebite was the dream of taking her other sister, her blood sister, the Lindworm, into her arms. Of cooing at that snake and luring her forward, directing her to slide down Donkey's own throat, rattling tail first. In the dream she studied the snake's face as though looking into a mirror, until the cat eyes finally disappeared inside her. And when she woke up at Titus's or in Molly's tin can full of purring cats, she rolled over and felt that snake lodged solidly inside her, curled around the cuntshell she'd swallowed, a ferocious protector and prison guard.

She wore Hermine's necklace under her shirt every night while she slept, and it soothed her to listen to the whispers of those souls not born, souls who Herself had said were preparing to travel on in their own time. She'd expected to feel weighed down by the burden of keeping the necklace safe, but most of what she heard from the string of clinking bodies was laughter, and what she felt was a tickling energy and a sweet pure light rising from someplace without fear or desire, a place of healing kindness without this life's uncertainties. Some of the energy and light she sensed might have come from the relieved and renewed souls of the women who had been freed from burdens they could not endure; this energy of having a second chance permeated Donkey's body when she wore the necklace. When Donkey visited Herself, still stubbornly sleeping to spite the doctors—to spite all of them, probably—she pressed close, held the shells against the old woman's skin and promised to get her home. She didn't say *one way or another*, but that was what she meant.

CHAPTER ∞ — EPILOGUE

Fathers keep showing up.

THE EXPLOITS OF Wild Will Zook are still a topic of conversation at the Muck Rattler, where his youthful photos hang. In his new incarnation, the old man has settled quietly into the Waters, where he gardens lettuce and celery, collects wild rice and honey, and fishes, figuring he is old enough that he need not worry about the toxicity of the occasional smallmouth bass or snapping turtle. He is adept by now at trapping and skinning swamp critters, though he keeps a healthy distance from the massasauga, which is under state protection anyhow. For now, his health remains vigorous, though he does occasionally pick up a tea for his arthritis from the Boneset Table. Since Rose Thorn left the Fox Den, the little nanny goat seems a suitable companion, and he continues to milk her using just two fingers of each hand, a humbling task. Before sunrise most days, he delivers a jar of fresh milk to the Boneset House, where he leaves it on the doorstep. He takes great satisfaction in knowing that the Zook women now live in the house that he built, but unless he is invited in, he will remain hidden like any other good ghost.

It is nothing new that the greatness of great men often leads to their downfall and that their downfall often pulls the women around them down too. What is new is that Wild Will's doggedly sober solitude, as well as his experience taking care of his daughter, has finally made a woman out of him, which is to say it has made him a better man.

His only visitor is Primrose, who dons tall rubber riding boots and treks out to the Fox Den before visiting anybody else when she comes to town. She has moved her law practice to Detroit to be closer—but not too close—to her family. The view from her office is of the Detroit River and Canada beyond.

What happened on the night of Rose Moon's birth is a favorite topic of conversation at the Muck Rattler, as wonderous a story as any that gets told, of how Rose Thorn needed the men of Whiteheart and they were there for her, of how they brought her daughter into the world.

Titus can only wish he had carried Rose Thorn across the Waters himself, can only wish he'd brought Rose Moon into the world without all the noise and sensuality of these men who indulge in the details of the telling: the haunting of the hot wind that had drawn them from their beds; the vision of Rosie, swollen, materializing out of the Waters; the silken texture of the swamp muck, how cool it felt deep down, how it was almost luxurious squeezing between their toes. Titus could have been magnificent under those circumstances, he still believes, and even two years later, he doesn't yet appreciate how these men, his friends and cousins, saved him from the terrible fate of being that kind of a savior. Everybody expected Titus to live up to Wild Will's example of strength, but the town performed this miracle collectively, democratically, and mostly without his help. Because men's hearts fill naturally with longing and love for a strong leader, ordinary men often do not see their own strength. That is why a half dozen ordinary men of Whiteheart—even violent and foolish men, men who fumble in their uncertainty—can often do the right thing when a great man cannot. The six men, a perfect number of men, and the whole town by extension (for any of dozens of local men could have been there that night) can hold their heads up now, because they have a story that proves them worthy.

Those men tell how they held Rose Thorn above the quickmuck, how she was as light as an angel despite her burden (which is not true), and how she made it to the island without a splash of muck on her (also not true, for she went in up to her shins, and, anyway, she was covered with their muddy handprints and splatters until Dickmon cleaned her up, and Smiley had to rinse her overalls). There was a moment when Two-Inch Tony, the shortest man, had gone under (not true, he initially protested, but he has given up his insistence under the weight of the many retellings). By the time they delivered Rosie to the island, the rest of them were coated with slime. And Dickmon birthed that baby as handily as any maternity nurse before collapsing in ecstatic exhaustion. ("I didn't know what I was doing," he protests proudly. "I just prayed!")

And when the half dozen men thought nothing more could possibly happen, twelve-year-old Dorothy rescued Titus Clay from a rattlesnake and took the bite herself. What a brave child! A true child of Whiteheart and a mathematical genius besides! Long live that brilliant girl! And it's too bad about that long curving snake of a scar on her arm, elbow to wrist. (The men say this, but every one of them is jealous of that mark.) And finally, the men were called again to save another life, this time that of Hermine Zook, Herself, whose body was so heavy it must have been waterlogged. That old woman would surely have died had they not hauled her from the quickmuck and loaded her into the back of Standish's truck. Standish smiles here and doesn't offer any elaboration; he strives now to preserve life without judgment, and he argues in a different, better way with his wife and daughter and mother and sister, or he's trying to anyhow. Together these men saved the Zook women, and it is precisely the act of saving a thing that makes it precious to the saviors.

The men struggle to find the words to describe the softness and the tenderness these acts released in them, how precious Rose Thorn was in their hands, how they felt kindly toward one another, how their limbs and torsos brushed, and how they felt other fluid creatures touch them under the mud. (And how, deep down, the swift flowing stream took their boots and their guns and Standish's pants. Standish always says, "I didn't like them pants anyway," to get a laugh.) The swell of these feelings is too intense for such men to hold in their hearts without an object to attach it to, so each man has turned the sensation into love and affection for Rose Thorn and both her daughters, and even Hermine Zook, who people say is still alive. This allows them to maintain the love as a living thing, creating more space for teaching their daughters and sons, more tolerance for their spouses, even sometimes a forgiveness for themselves. They feel that love most purely and powerfully, though, when they are near the Waters.

Their adventure does not exactly discredit Titus, but it has changed slightly the town's story about him. Titus can't talk about his feelings of impotence with the other men these days, nor with Lorena or Reverend Roy, who has given up his efforts to buy the island, since Rose Thorn will not budge.

"Maybe she'll drink herself to death, and I can talk sense to the child one day," Roy once said in the presence of several of the men who had been there that day. They forgave him, of course, because everybody knows the reverend is in pain and can only sleep when Molly or Titus brings him merry poppins tea. Molly continues to call on Roy and somehow loves him even more than before. She wants to alleviate his pain, but she also hopes his pain will overwhelm and change him. If only he would break down entirely, he could be cobbled back together better, with more humility. The whole congregation gives him special consideration, forgives his occasional lapses into vitriol, but they do remark on his vitriol to one another. Some say that Titus would make a better reverend than Roy, but Titus is too busy with his family and farming.

ONE VERY EARLY MORNING IN JUNE—about an hour before sunrise—two years and one month after the birth of Rose Moon, Titus sits in his truck at Boneset with his lights off. Across Lovers Road, Wild Will's high-ceilinged house is as dark as the island, but he feels Rose Thorn inside, senses her sleeping body. Titus is afraid to go into that house of women, for fear he will be overcome by Rose Thorn's longing, and his own. And nobody has ever invited him in.

Back at home, Titus's two-year-old brown-eyed boys are asleep in their room, and his wife is asleep in Aunt Ada's bed. They replaced the old mattress but kept the dark-stained white-pine bedframe his great-uncle made. Sometimes he can convince himself that the family house—smelling of clean laundry and Lorena's almond shampoo and hot cocoa and homemade bread and simmering meat stew and, every Sunday, a sweet pie of some kind—is the only place he wants to be. But here he is in the dark, parked near the Boneset Table. He listens into the distance and hears no other human sounds, though a thousand swamp creatures respond to his presence, sharing with one another things about him he doesn't even know himself. He takes a long pull of ginger brandy and returns the bottle to the glove compartment. He takes his pistol out. He wishes he could share what he feels, wishes he had a new holy language, wishes he could be involved in a common project or a secret society, wishes he could even just sidle up to the other men at the Farm Bureau to talk about fertilizer without his reptile soul slipping around and through his ribs to remind him how lost and primitive he is.

He opens the door of his truck only enough to slip out, because he doesn't want it to creak. The Ford is only two years old, but the door sounds just like his old truck's door. The faded photograph of Rose Thorn is not under the new floor mat, because Lorena discovered it when she cleaned out his old truck. She burned it in front of him without a word; she speaks two languages but prefers not to use words at all when she argues. She might dig in the ground in silence while he watches her, or she might water the garden and sigh. Instead of that photo, Titus carries two holy trading cards of Catholic saints he's taken from a collection of dozens Lorena keeps in a box in a drawer beside the bed. Though she says her rosary privately, she attends the Church of New Directions (Titus still hears Rose Thorn's voice saying *Nude Erections*) and never mentions what she misses about Catholicism. It is Titus who has become intrigued with her old church and its saints. Sometimes he holds her rosary and traces the beads and follows the cord to the rattle at the tail end, before letting himself touch the cross.

From the back of his truck, Titus takes a two-by-ten plank and carries it down the steps. He gets on his hands and knees to set the board over the missing expanse. Twice, the far end of the plank drops into the fog-covered mud, but he gets it lined up correctly the third time. The contraption Wild Will made still works but only from the island side. Titus checks on the island every day—makes sure that no roofs are leaking and that critters haven't come into the cottage. He usually goes to the circle of stones where he and Rose Thorn made love so many times, gets a whiff of the sulfur pool. String Bean tells him to be careful, because the big m'sauga that bit her lives under Rose Cottage. He can't be sure the girl really knows which snake bit her, but last week he found a rattlesnake shed under the porch with two wounds in its middle, like she described, so he set a minnow trap. Yesterday afternoon, he discovered a m'sauga coiled inside, a big one.

Titus's week has not gone well. It was not going well even before
Whitby's confession last night, Whitby's claim about what he had seen
Titus Sr. do to Rose Thorn all those years ago. Whitby was drunk when
he spewed his story, too drunk to be believed, and that was why Titus
said, "Get the hell out of here, Whitby. I don't need to hear shit like that."

Titus has filled in more of his aunt Ada's bog over the last two years,
with the intention of growing celery there. He's always dreamed of
growing celery like his grandfather, and he has been dreaming lately
of showing his sons, in a few years, how to plant the celery with measuring sticks and cupped hands, the way Ada described. Then, four
days ago, when he drove his old 8N tractor with the dirt blade onto
the field to smooth out some topsoil, the machine began to sink. The
new land had appeared stable all winter, had seemed solid under his
feet this spring, so he thought nothing of driving the tractor out a little farther than before. But then it stalled out, and by the time he got
done messing with the carburetor, his rear wheels had gone ten inches
deep in sandy muck. When it finally started, he goosed the gas to
turn the big gripping tires, half full of calcium carbonate for traction,
and they only dug deeper. What had he been thinking, driving the 8N
down there with those heavy tires?

He ran back to the house to tell Lorena, and she called Don York to
come with the big wrecker. By then the tractor, left idling because he
was afraid it wouldn't start again, had run out of gas and was eighteen
inches in the muck. York was there in forty-five minutes, hooking up
the tow chains, but then York's wrecker started to sink as well. Whitby
showed up with more chains, and they tried a dozen times in a half
dozen configurations to pull it out, but there were no trees nearby for
winching, and by then the machine was too far gone. Once they all
gave up, it was a hell of a sight. Titus was glad his father couldn't see
the muck swallowing the front wheels of what had been his favorite
old tractor, then the seat and big back tires, and, finally, the engine
block. On that mournful day, the many assembled men who had been
watching—how had those sons of bitches heard the news and gotten there so fast?—took out their rifles and pistols and shot the tractor, and somebody shouted that it was a mercy killing, and they shot
again. Though Dickmon warned everybody about the ricochet, he
took two shots himself. For a full minute, the air was filled with the

scent of gunpowder and the sound of gunfire and bullets pinging off steel and cast iron. Finally, the steering wheel and top of the fenders went under, and the tractor was gone. That day, two other men who were filling in their own swamp fields called Marshall Wallace to suspend their gravel deliveries.

Before retrieving the minnow trap from under the porch at Rose Cottage, Titus takes the two holy cards out of his pocket and studies them in the dark. One card features the emaciated St. Eulalia he'd first seen in the church basement, hung upside down by her medieval torturers, her breast cut off, leaving a bloody void. The other shows a voluptuous version of Mother Mary with the golden Christ child on her lap. He can only say that he finds himself compelled to look at both these images and that beholding either image makes him desire the other.

Because Titus wears only a sleeveless undershirt, his tattoos are visible to any creature that can see in the dark. Even the island crows who sleep with one eye open see clearly enough the thorny rose with a rattlesnake and crescent moon. In particular, the crow perched just above the tin roof of the cottage sees it now. She sees also the tattoo on his right biceps, which he has amended for Lorena's sake. What used to be a crude indigo cross now has a pretty red border, and below it in cursive is her name, and there is a double sun in the sky above it for the boys. Parts of the tattoo are smeared where he bled excessively after the procedure, but Lorena appreciated the effort and the risk. He doesn't mention that Dorothy now provides him with the old thinblood medicine, but Lorena has no doubt seen the bottle in the bathroom cupboard.

As he carries the mesh cage out onto the grass where Rosie gave birth, mosquitoes try to feed on him, but they are repelled by the catnip dope he smeared on.

Titus came here intending to kill the m'sauga, but now, in the predawn light, he studies the captive creature's dark coils. He has his family's old blue jar of snakebite medicine in his pocket, but he wonders sometimes if the venom itself might be the cure for thinblood. His father taught him to kill a muck rattler with whatever he had handy, a shovel or hoe or splitting maul, or to run over it. Or shoot it, if he could. His father had not been one of the snake handlers, would never have imagined Titus would want to do anything other than kill a m'sauga. But Titus can't shake what Whitby said. Yes, his father was disrespectful of women in a way that made Titus uneasy, even as a kid. Yes, his father drank and became mean—everybody in the family knew that. But such an important, hardworking man had to blow off steam. That's how they'd all seen it. And there is no denying that one time his mother had called out for help from the bedroom, and when he, then a teenager, knocked on the master bedroom door, she told him, through her sobs, to go back to his room.

Instead of taking the gun from his pocket, Titus finds a sturdy forked stick and breaks the forked part off short. He opens the lid of the minnow trap, uses the fork end to pin the snake's head. He takes a deep breath and reaches in, grasps the snake's neck with his left hand and its tail with his right, and lifts it from its chain-mail cage. This snake is almost as long as his arm and more muscular. And so alive and angry! What steels his nerves as he holds it isn't the vision of St. Paul from the church basement mosaic, it is remembering how Dorothy, a living child, took hold of that big muck rattler to save his life. If he could be half as brave for one moment, he might deserve to be her father.

After Titus sent Whitby away last night, he had a dream of Wild Will holding out a m'sauga to him, its tail rattling, its mouth open to reveal its fangs, and he woke up sweating. He now moves this serpent carefully, almost lovingly, positioning it with his left hand until most of its body rests on his right arm. When he feels it relax slightly, then he lets go of its tail, which wraps around his right wrist for balance. A thrill travels up from his hand to his heart, and he stands up straighter. In the pinkish predawn light, Titus studies the triangular head, the unblinking cat eye. He takes a slow breath, and as he exhales, he releases his hold on the snake's head until he lets go entirely. Now he is at the serpent's mercy. But instead of attacking, the m'sauga retracts her neck and surveys the lay of the land that is Titus's big left arm, smells his body and the catnip.

He has never been more afraid. Or more confused. Or more alive.

Titus loves Lorena more every day—he can't stop watching her. He loves her facial expressions—which are easy to read—her glossy dark hair, and her strong hands. He loves her especially when she is working or mothering. His gratitude toward her is crippling, and he some-times gets down on his knees and begs her forgiveness, usually, but not always, while she's sleeping. His life with her and their beautiful boys is, moment by moment, as rich as the pies she bakes. He is the luckiest man in Whiteheart to have her for his wife, and yet that rich-ness makes him crave the other richness he knows so well he can taste it always, that which he has given up for her.

At two years old, his twin sons are fearless, as fearless as Titus and his cousin Alan, Roger's father, were as kids. For now, Titus has to hold his sons' fear for them, until they come to understand they're in danger from any fall, any wound.

But what about Rosie and her daughters? He wants to call out for Rosie now but doesn't, for fear his tongue will relearn the habit of saying her name and then release it in his sleep or during lovemaking. Snakes are sensitive to vibrations, and calling out any woman's name now might get him bitten. He briefly longs for his father's decisive-ness, his unwavering dominion over the land and over women. And yet, for all that man's godlike certainty, he's now blind and weak, child-like. And whenever Titus Sr. calls now, he only wants to talk about old times and especially about Wild Will.

The longer Titus sits with Whitby's words, the more he's starting to understand them. Evidence of the crime has always been there, shim-mering all around him. Why the hell else does String Bean look so much like him? He'd told himself Rosie had been with his cousin Alan, but she'd never been close with Alan, who didn't look like any of the rest of the Clays anyhow. But if it was true, why the hell hadn't Whitby told him sooner? If it is true, Titus doesn't know how he'll wear his skin now. Everybody has said his whole life how much he favors his dad.

Titus slowly moves his arm toward his chest, as though inviting the snake to dance, and the m'sauga grips him more tightly, afraid and angry but also becoming curious about this new way of mov-ing through space. For a moment, Titus thinks of nothing—his heart is pounding too wildly to allow thoughts—and he slowly unwraps the m'sauga from his arm, more slowly than he has ever done any-thing. He wishes he had slowed his lovemaking with Rosie this way, so it would have lasted all through the night and into the next day, through spring, summer, and fall, and into winter, and then she never would have gone away. But even in those ecstatic moments, their romance was being undermined by the twin seeds sprouting in Lorena's womb and Titus's involuntary commitment to them and to saving his farm.

The sun is beginning to wash pink light over him as he slowly lifts and drapes the m'sauga over his right shoulder. The snake passes behind his neck and stretches down his arm on the left side, pausing at the top of one of the suns on his Lorena tattoo. Because of his own stubbornness, he missed the birth of his daughter. After String Bean had run down the road to get him, he'd called Molly. He'd lain awake on the couch congratulating himself on his restraint, his decisiveness, before giving up and going to the island. He hadn't gone into the bedroom to get his boots for fear of waking Lorena.

God, have mercy on me, he thinks. A shiver passes through him— God's grace or something equally mysterious that is peculiar to the Waters. His body goes to gooseflesh across his back and arms. Gently, he guides the snake's head off his left arm, onto his chest, to show God or whoever's watching how he isn't afraid, though he is, in truth, terrified. His body softens, becomes serpentine and spiralized. The snake recognizes him as a fellow creature again instead of a landscape.

Rose Moon is his child as clearly as Donkey is not, and Lorena accepts this now too, though she says he's a fool for assuming Rose Thorn wasn't with somebody else. He knows better, knows Rose Thorn was true to him in every way that mattered. Rose Thorn might be his very soul, asleep in the Boneset house. With her, Titus has been his worst and his best. For almost twelve years, Rosie had offered him the chance to be a father, to String Bean, and it was a test he failed. Why had he insisted so strenuously to the whole town that the girl was not his? He could have embraced her resemblance to him as a miracle: she offered herself to him as a worthy daughter, imitated his walk and his hand gestures, grew tall like him—at fourteen, she's his height now, six foot two! Rosie could have helped him with this, could have led him through the labyrinth instead of letting him wander in confusion. Now he sees the girl every day, works with her in the garden, the barn, and the field, and hungers for the innocent affection and adoring gaze he once dismissed. But these days she is practical and calculating, looks out for her family as well as attending school and astounding her math teacher. She has asked Lorena to teach her Spanish. That simple father-daughter love could have been Titus's larger story, a noble story to sit alongside his passion for Rose Thorn. Why had he never considered that the girl's love could save him? He can barely think of that day when he broke her heart, when she asked him to be her father, and he, point-blank, refused.

Could it be true that she is his half sister? For Christ's sake, what a mess! His new daughter is his half sister's half sister! The snake freezes, alarmed by his accelerating heartbeat.

Rose Thorn has never in these two years denied him access to his little one. The Moon, as they call her, gets carried around on her tall sister's hip for all the world to observe. The Moon, his curly-headed girl, is fresh and wild and beloved by everyone. Beloved especially by some who were long suspicious of Herself. Titus brings Roger over to work with them sometimes, still offers him to Dorothy as a kind of brother but doesn't let the two disappear from his sight for even a moment after once catching these cousins lying side by side in the hayloft.

Rose Thorn has not left town since the surgery, which took her right breast. He imagines her body as St. Eulalia's martyred one, emaciated and burned, torn limb from limb, dangling upside down. Eulalia suffered thirteen tortures, a prime number, Dorothy would say. According to Dorothy, Rosie has been sober since the surgery and is still nursing the baby from her left breast. This news is scandalous to the other women of Whiteheart, who believe in breast-feeding but consider six months more than sufficient, even with two breasts.

Herself is still alive, Dorothy assures him, and he's seen a Hermine-shaped silhouette through a window in the first-floor bedroom. "She's in a chrysalis," Dorothy says. "I don't know when she'll come out." He doesn't know what this means, and Dorothy shrugs when he asks, the same way Rose Thorn always shrugged after quoting from a book, as if the truth needs no elaboration. The story goes that Wild Will built this house to lure Herself off the island, but she'd never gone inside, not until she was put there in a hospital bed, too weak to resist, finally realizing the old mule trader's dream. No wonder she's not coming out of her cocoon. When Titus was a kid, he met Wild Will, even watched him train donkeys to pull a wagon. Now Titus needs nothing more than a heart-to-heart conversation with the man. Maybe his dance with the snake is that talk. He doesn't know yet that Wild Will is alive and nearby.

When the snake slips silkily over Titus's chest, electricity zaps him straight down to his privates. He closes his eyes and wishes for Rose Thorn to be resting against him the way the cool viper rests on him now. The m'sauga is as light as a bird in his hands, and its skin against his is as soft and velvety as a baby's perfect skin. The sun is rising, rose-gold now. He considers letting the snake go, but when it crawls across him, rests its chin on his right arm before heading to the earth, he lifts it again, slowly—so slowly that he knows lovemaking with Rose Thorn could have extended from full moon to full moon. If only those other men were watching him with this serpent now; if only they could be here, afraid for him, afraid with him; if they could see him not giving in to his fear, the men of Whiteheart might respect him the way they used to. Somehow that respect is part of the sacrifice he has unwittingly made to the town; it is a twin to the sacrifice Rose Thorn has made by submitting to her mutilation and to remaining sober. With her parties at Boneset, she held the town together, and now she continues that work simply by staying put.

Titus slowly bends and kneels on the ground. He gathers the snake's coils slowly to his chest, holds the reptile's light body against his heart the way String Bean did. It is like embracing a flowing stream.

The night before Rose Thorn disappeared the last time, Titus tasted Wild Will's whiskey, just a few drops left in the bottle, but it was enough that he's never forgotten the heat in it. Rose Thorn is the fire in his belly, the knife in his heart, while Lorena is the cool water that soothes him. He committed to Lorena in the eyes of the law, and he does not regret it. A sane man can't rationally choose a woman like Rose Thorn, who points out every lie he utters. A man can't choose a woman who makes him question himself at every turn, a woman who would read a book while bales of hay lie in the field with rain clouds approaching from the west. A man would have to be a saint to tolerate her laziness, her self-destructiveness. Who could tolerate a woman who celebrates her ruin by refusing reconstructive surgery? What kind of woman burns herself with a coffin nail because a man loves her? Rose Thorn would string him up every day of his life, while

Lorena will work beside him and then mop his brow, massage his muscles, and tell him how fine a man he is.

Titus slowly lifts his left arm above his head, feeling like Moses bringing the Israelites to triumph in battle. The m'sauga slips a little but catches herself, is growing accustomed to this ride, these new views. God said Eve would suffer for her sin, and part of her suffering was bearing Adam's children. Rose Thorn carried her children alone, without Titus to massage her, as he had massaged Lorena as her delivery approached. He gently takes hold of the snake's neck and pushes the triangular head into his biceps, inviting the snake to sink her fangs into his rose tattoo, inviting God to smite him through the snake— that is why he's come out here, he realizes, to have it out with God— but the fangs remain folded inside the snake's mouth. Titus lets go, lets his heart slow.

The snake moves down his body again, seeking the earth, the way Titus keeps seeking Rose Thorn in every wild place: in the swamp, at the wind blocks and edges of fields, at the tops of trees. The snake has removed everything hard or angular from him— even his bones feel soft. He imagines himself standing before a heavenly throne to say, *I'm cleansed, I'm whole, I'm as good a man as you made me, and I beg forgiveness. Kill me if you want.* To say, *If you want me better, God, please make me better.* He thinks this so powerfully that he hears his own voice above the humming and buzzing insects, over the gu-gunging frogs, but nobody in the Waters responds in a language he understands. He will have to take responsibility for himself.

Why didn't Rose Thorn ever say a word about the rape to anyone? How can a woman expect justice if she won't talk about the crime? Or if she doesn't want justice, what does she want? Who did she think she was protecting? In response to his angry questions, the m'sauga freezes, sensing danger. But Titus suspects he wouldn't have believed her—only one of the good reasons she had not to tell him.

His hunger for Rosie grows monstrous inside him, and he fears it will eat him alive. Should he go see her now? Beg forgiveness for what his father did? For his own cruelty? Yell at her for not telling him what had happened? Rose Thorn would probably invite him in; maybe she'd even invite him into her bed. She's never refused him in the past. Not once. But he can't do that. All he can do is farm the fields around her family's house and bring in excellent and occasionally profitable yields of corn and soybeans and some alfalfa; it's too late for celery in those fields.

Clearly God isn't going to help him with Rose Thorn, so he's stuck where the two paths of his desires cross, stretched out between two lives, one a horizontal life that contains the whole community, the other a passionate life burning as vertical as a flame, burning up rules and laws in the name of love. He holds both lives the way he holds this snake, which somehow reminds him of how Aunt Ada held the big celery head on that postcard from way back when.

In her years on the island, the old mama crow has fledged five broods and has seen Titus Clay Jr. come and go. Now she watches him with one eye, looks down on the whole ridiculous business of Titus fucking around with a rattlesnake. To that crow, his actions look about as foolish as a woman burning her own arm with a coffin nail. The crow hears a slight rumbling and opens her other eye to see better what comes next.

When God speaks, finally, it's a whisper in a ripple of this m'sauga's semispinalis muscles, and simultaneously, it's a wave moving across the Waters, and the message is clear and simple: *Take care of your kids.*

When Titus can breathe again, he sighs, is disappointed by this answer. He always prays for his children, promises to care for his beautiful, vulnerable sons and his outrageous daughter. But is he nothing but a father now? Maybe this is God's own anguish: God is the father and the son; as the ghost, God is even the good neighbor; but He is never the lover. Titus's desire for Rosie, his love for her, is a wall he's erected between himself and God. And he's not ready to topple it. He will apologize to Whitby. He's got a lot of work to do today—the sun is about to rise—and he needs his cousin for troubleshooting the irrigation equipment in the old Darling field. His father never apologized for anything, as far as Titus can recall, but Titus will listen to Whitby's terrible story and apologize. And he'll have to tell Lorena, who will close her eyes and say nothing.

But what has shaken him, more than the message, is the voice. Not a low rumble like his father's. God's voice was not a man's voice at all. He lowers his arms and plants his open hands on the island, lets the rattlesnake reacquaint herself with the earth. She propels herself quickly away from him, underneath Rose Cottage through an opening in the foundation.

He sets the trap again and heads home.

ACKNOWLEDGMENTS

Bill Clegg and Jill Bialosky, thank you for creating a place in the world for this book and making the long winding journey of writing and revising possible. Thanks to the Clegg Agency for their support and expertise and to W. W. Norton, the world's finest publisher, for all they do for readers and writers.

As I wrote my way through the swamp, friend and editor Heidi Bell was there with love, camaraderie, and wisdom from beginning to end. Thank you to Diane Seuss, for meeting me at the crossroads and guiding me back onto my snaking path. Thank you, Jaimy Gordon, for putting your dazzling gaze on this, so at last I could see it clearly; also for (way back when) cajoling me away from the bright sunshine of mathematics and into this moony landscape.

Thank you, Andy Mozina, for generously, doggedly reading drafts and noting the many devils in the details. Thank you to the uncommonly wise writer Mimi Lipson—cousin, you understand the lay of this land as nobody else could. Poet Susan Blackwell Ramsey—a mind like yours is indispensable. Thank you, Lisa DuRose, Chris Fink, and Don De Grazia for all your help—your students are very lucky! Big thanks to Katie Edkins Milligan for meaning-clarifying edits. Thank you, Don Troyer, for your soulful perspective. Sass Havilar, for your knowledge of healing herbs. Dr. Art White, thank you for the math. Shirley Clay Scott and Heather Sappenfield for graciously, handily proofreading. Juliet Bradley for advising on the birthing scene. Debra Gwartney, Jaimee Wriston Colbert, Margaret DeRitter, Kathleen McGookey for reading early versions before I found my swamp legs.

This novel could only have been conceived and written in my river shack, which was twice saved from destruction by philosopher-builders Steve Barrett and Mike Plosick.

Thank you to publicist extraordinaire Erin Sinesky Lovett. Glass of wine raised to the magnificent Sheryl Johnston, who spreads the word with so much grace. Clink-clink to Audrey Seilheimer. Thank you for moral support from baker Judy Sarkozy, Katherine Joslin of Comstock, Ombudsman Thomas Bailey, bookseller Dean Hauck, Dawgs Poetry Group of Kalamazoo, magnificent sister Sheila, hardworking Brian Stephenson, surgeon Nancy Kalinowski, oncologist Sunil Nagpal, Dr. James Hunt, radiation team at WMCC, Mary Szpur, Sonia Lipson, Sam Lipson, Gina Betcher, Becky Cooper, Lori Moore, Janie Boer R.I.P., and many more folks who support, inspire, educate, and humor me!

Thank you, Susanna, for being the spirited mother a writer needs, for continuing to guide me even now that you are transformed entirely into spirit. Thank you Granny Betty of the island for directing my gaze to nature; thank you Grandpa Frank for Little Lulu. Love you, Uncle Terry!

Thank you, most of all, Christopher Magson, for four decades of companionship and dedicated adventures in love and real estate. Thank you for fixing everything. Be assured I'm always listening, even while I'm arguing with you.

Shelley Washburn convinced me to leave the shack on occasion to become part of the Pacific University Low-Residency MFA program, where the faculty and students have taught me so much. Thank you, DePauw University, for inviting me to teach as the Mary Rogers Field and Marion Field-McKenna Distinguished University Professor in Greencastle, Indiana. Thank you, Beloit College, for hosting me as Lois and Willard Mackey Chair in Creative Writing. Thank you, Blue Flower Arts Literary Speakers Agency, also Edinburgh International Book Festival and novelist Jenni Fagan for taking me on the road.

So many writers have helped me through their words and stories:

Carolyn Chute, Toni Morrison, Marilynne Robinson, Carson McCullers, Tove Jansson, Charles Portis, Andrew Lang, Lewis Carroll, Astrid Lindgren, and Virginia Woolf, among others.

Thanks to Diane Seuss and Graywolf Press for allowing me to excerpt the poem "Bowl," which appeared originally in *Michigan Quarterly Review* and then in her 2018 collection *Still Life with Two Dead Peacocks and a Girl*. Thank you, Monica Friedman, for the wonderful and true map of fictional Whiteheart that appears in this book!

A bit about the massasauga rattlesnake, *Sistrurus catenatus*, a species of special concern in Michigan and Ontario, an endangered species everywhere else: *massasauga* is an Ojibwe term meaning "great river mouth," and some people call them muck rattlers, swamp rattlers, black rattlers, or prairie rattlesnakes. Most people will never see one of these reclusive, timid creatures, but they are an important inhabitant of our wetlands. Though there have been many fanciful claims and depictions (including the ones in this book), bites from this snake are extremely rare. It is illegal to attempt to handle or capture one, but please do report any sightings to your local nature center or to the department of natural resources. You can see them in captivity at the Detroit Zoo; the John Ball Zoo in Grand Rapids, Michigan; and several other zoos in the US and Canada.